JARALII CHRONICLES

Gilraën and the Prophecy

Book One: I Came

by J. R. Reid

ISBN: 978-1-7344680-1-4

Cover by 100 Covers

Table of Contents

Dedicated to Denise Trask

It was your idea and your character.
I built the story,
But it was your inspiration.
I miss you

Prologue

I Came, I Saw, I Conquered

Julius Caesar, 47 BCE
Report to the Roman Senate
regarding victory over Pharnaces II of Pontus at the Battleof Zela

"A High One among High Ones shall come from Beyond.

She shall wear an old face of the Verdant Hills

She shall befriend the Mighty and the Weak.

She shall unite the High, the Deep, the Many, the Few

The Usurper shall fall before her; all will rejoice.

Unite and be Free."

Thane Cadrazhulea, Seer of Clan Camazhule

Special Offer to readers of Jaralii Chronicles:

Get your map of Jaralii

See where it's at!

Email your request to jaraliichronicles@gmail.com

A High One among High Ones shall come from Beyond.

She shall wear an old face of the Verdant Hills

Chapter 1 – The Game Begins

Panic!

I thrashed wildly trying desperately not to drown, geysering stinking, muddy water into the air. Clambering to my feet, I shivered. The water was damned cold, as though it had just come off a snow pack. Half drowned, I gasped, "Damn. What the hell...?"

It was all I got out before I clamped my mouth shut.

'Okay, let's try this again,' I thought.

"Hello? Testing, one, two, three."

'Okay, this is a little on the far side. My voice sounds like it's a girl's voi... Uh. Okay; Uhm. I guess my avatar is a girl. So why the culvert, the mud, or the sewage?'

I scrambled to my feet, but everything was wrong. A bright, whitish sun was high overhead. A forest grew closely on the other side of the culvert with plowed ground on my side. Okay, so I wasn't in Kansas anymore.

My arms and legs were puny–like a girl's. I was wearing leather armor that had some metal circles all over it and was very curvy like it was something a female would likely wear. I had bracers on my forearms and greaves on my shins, so my character could be an archer, but if that was true, why not my male character? The only female character I had played was my sorceress, and she didn't dress like this even on a bad day. I stood gingerly, fighting the flow of the water, the stream deep enough to submerge me above my knees.

Struggling to the edge of the culvert, I grabbed a thick tree root sticking out of the wall. Scrambling up the slippery slope, I reached the muddy ground next to the culvert just as a wave of sludge and roots ripped past me. The edge of the mucky embankment gave way, treacherously, as though intent on hurling me back into the sewage. I clambered over the edge to lie on the flat land above the flood and looked back down into the culvert. I was lucky this river hadn't been in full flow. My character... whoever I was... would probably have drowned, been washed out to sea, wherever that might be, and my chances of any rewards would have been washed out with it.

When I finally reached dry ground, the light wind chilled me to the bone. I considered jumping back into the culvert, but, looking at the surging flood, I gave up on that alternative. Instead, I hunkered down into the lee of a tree and shivered.

'Where the hell am I?' I wondered. *'Does anyone know I'm here? What do I do now?'*

With nothing to do but wait for someone to rescue me, my mind wandered back over the events of the last few years. It was all Rueben's fault.

* * *

"Where are they?" I'd shouted at the ceiling, pacing the length of my living room, glaring out the windows at the empty street. "They said 6:00, and it's 6:30 already!"

I had checked the pile of stuff I had set aside for the trip. The guys in the robes had told me that the location of the game world was 'rather primitive.' My pack contained the usual – trousers, shirts, socks, shoes, extra money, even my old S&W with a box of ammo. And six rolls of TP. I'd been in the Army far too long to go anywhere without a reasonable supply.

"Rue! It's all your fault!" I'd fumed. "Rueben and Greg... and Linda, too."

Rue was the one who'd involved us in the world championships. I called him Rue just to pull his chain. His name was actually Reuben Frederick Mayhugh the Third. He was our manager – the one that had found our gigs, arranged transport and lodging, and made sure we got home when it was all over. Greg, who'd played the giant monster in our games, was Rue's best friend. His humungous tarantula always gave me the willies. Linda, who generally played a Valkyrie or something like that, had been my lieutenant and best field commander.

Anyway, the three of us were skeptical at first, but Rue's enthusiasm had convinced us. Ninecents, the big Chinese gaming site, had offering a huge prize in a team knock out event with a million dollar prize for each winning player. It'd taken us a year to get to the finals.

The finals were between us and Sam Talbert's team. Sam, better known by his moniker, Neutron, was a big blow-hard, convinced he knew more than everyone. He always fought to win ... to conquer and damn the consequences.

I, on the other hand, had spent nearly twenty years in Army intelligence, and then taught strategy and tactics at the Army War College for eighteen more. As the General of our forces, and the one who made all the strategic decisions, I fought my opponents to an impasse, offering generous terms in return for an alliance. If they refused, I crushed them; if not I had an ally eager to work with me

So, in the final battle, I'd held back my allies, simulated weakness. As I had hoped, Sam came at us with everything he had, leaving little in reserve. Rue, Greg, and Linda had feigned weakness, giving ground reluctantly. Sensing victory, Neutron had committed his reserves. Then I released our allies. Enveloped from both flanks, Sam's army fell apart. The game was over.

We had won! We'd won! Even I got slightly plastered, even though I was too old to do so and survive the next morning. I don't know about the rest of the team, but I had invested my winnings in Blue Chips and T-notes. A bit conservative, I know, but that's me.

Then, there was the four-week world tour. Ninecents had sent us to twenty cities in thirty days, advertising each event heavily, and simulcasting it across their worldwide Internet sites. We had staged 'combat' with local teams, 'proving' our championship play. Of course, the games were fixed. We knew the terrain, the best avenues of attack, and the best defensive positions. Our opponents didn't stand a chance, but that was the whole point. We were the world's champs, after all.

When we finally arrived home, we sorta went our own ways. Frankly, we were tired of each other. We'd been together for more than a year. I had returned to my job as a project manager installing, modifying and training users on high-end management programs in medium-to-large businesses. I had kept my hand in, playing a variety of on-line games, mostly on Ninecents' site.

A few weeks later, I had just got back to the office, when, out of the blue, Rue called me all excited. "Tony! Get over here right now!"

Then he'd hung up!

"What now?" I'd muttered, closing up my system and preparing to drive all the way across town to his house. Although I was reluctant, Rue had made me a millionaire, so I sorta owed it to him.

It turned out Greg had found an advertisement in a gamers' blog and had called Rue. So, they had called me, demanding I get to Rue's house as fast as I could. The advertisement had offered big rewards for players to test of a new "fully immersive, reality experience." However, to qualify a player had to exceed the master's level in an on-line game before they could even apply. It was a really great game, and I'd played it often. My Archer avatar had already exceeded their minimum requirement, and both my Sorceress and Druid Priest were close.

Of course, the whole idea of a new, fully immersive VR game was intriguing, I must admit. Then, Rue, Greg and Linda had begged me to help them bring up their scores so they could enter. It was a good thing I was on the last leg of my most recent project; otherwise, I wouldn't have had the time to coach them.

The four of us had gone online at the same time to enter. There was a short test, followed by a message telling us that someone would contact us.

About a week later, I got a call from Rue. "I'm in!" he'd yelled, almost taking my ear off. "They want me to come down to interview." Greg, Linda and I got ours just minutes later.

We'd met downtown and trooped up to the office where they interviewed us. The whole thing was odd. First, the guys who interviewed us wore long black robes with cowls hanging down their backs. They also spoke in an odd accent and talked about revolutions rather than days and orbits rather than years.

They had really grilled me about my avatars. Typically, I'd played three: the Sorceress, the Druid and the Archer. My favorite had been my Archer. He was tall and lithe, armed with the Singing Bow and Golden Arrows that never missed and always returned undamaged. Although not magical, he could slip behind enemy lines, scout their numbers and dispositions, and return without being seen. My second character was a Druid priest. He was a mighty magician with the Circlet of Wisdom on his brow, the Staff of Power in his hand, the Signet of Adamantine on his finger, and the Scarab of Isis around his neck. The Druid was our in-game strategist, tactician and field general. My third avatar was the Sorceress. Beautiful and magically powerful, she wore the Helm of Moregan and was armed with the Sword of Destiny and the Shield of Invincibility. She was always at the point of the attack—our forlorn hope who never failed us.

At first, it had surprised them that one of my avatars was a 'womban,' as they called her. I'd explained that my opponents never expected that a beautiful woman could be a threat, giving me all the advantages. When they'd asked if they could combine the different attributes of my characters into one, I had agreed, advising them the Archer was the one I preferred. They'd said it was up to the Adjudicars, whoever they were. Anyway, they wouldn't guarantee anything. Obviously, they were just the sales agents; I'd probably meet the software developers later.

I thought back to my second interview with the guys in the black robes. They'd plopped a lengthy contract in front of me and told me to sign it.

"No way!" I'd told them, "Not until I've read it all."

For the most part, it was OK—standard hero stuff. However, I'd insisted on a few changes. I wanted guarantees of payment after the game. These gaming companies blind you with promises of big money rewards at the end of the game, only to nickel and dime you

I Came

to death within the game. When they subtract the money you'd spent within the game from your promised reward, you often end up in debt to them. No way!

I had also driven a hard bargain about arms and armor. There was no way I would pay for either. They had to be furnished and to my specs at a minimum.

The robed guys had hemmed and hawed about repairs and replacements, especially arrows, and I had been forced to give on a few items.

Finally, I'd demanded that when the game was over, and I'd completed my contract, they would return me to my home with all my winnings. I'd been stuck in the boondocks before and wouldn't stand for it again. I reasoned, I am a World Champion, and they were paying for my services.

They'd given me 'six rotations' to wrap up my affairs. My boss had told me I could take eight weeks, but I had to be back to manage the new installation we'd just contracted. I promised I'd be back and ready. It was the largest contract we'd ever signed, and it was my responsibility to make sure everything went in on time and at cost.

A car had driving slowly past my window, breaking my reveries. I thought I might have seen it before and resolved I'd run out to stop them if it showed up again

'Tickets?' I'd asked myself.

I'd just remembered they'd given me a 'token' that I was to wear around my neck. I had raced upstairs to grab it off the bureau. When I bounded down to look out the window, that same car drove up again.

It had slowed just outside…

* * *

Master Talbot, first among the Sorcerers of Shesol Vys, raced into the throne room to report the bad news. "My Prince, we have a problem."

Prince William smiled, "That would be something approaching the twentieth of the day, Talbot."

"This one is of a… more delicate nature, my Prince."

"Ah, so we have a political situation, I take it."

"Uhm, a little worse than that, I believe."

"You haven't begun some war without consulting me have you?"

"I hope not, my Prince."

"Then out with it, man. What is the problem?"

"We have... lost a rather special person, my Prince."

"Lost a person? Perhaps if you begin at the beginning and explain this to me slowly, I might understand more fully."

"Yes, my Prince. As you know, we have had some difficulty in training Sorcerers for the transport rooms. Master Farmount is rather hard on his apprentices, and many of them cannot abide the smell of the torches."

"Yes, I know. He is also quite particular concerning the use of transport energies, and the talismen used as anchors."

"Yes, that is true," Talbot mused for a few moments.

"So, what does this have to do with losing this 'special' person?" the prince asked.

"Ah, Master Farmount had his apprentice bringing some new recruits to the castle, and he lost one of them, my Prince."

"So you've told me. Is anyone trying to find this 'lost' recruit?"

"Yes. Masters Thackery, Johnsstone and Simmons are attempting to research the recent path to find this missing person."

"How did this happen?"

I Came

"Apparently, the recruit in question was not wearing the talisman but was holding it. The talisman arrived, but the recruit did not. It would seem recruit the accidentally dropped it while in transit."

"Surely, losing one recruit won't severely affect our war effort."

"It is a little more complicated than that. This particular recruit was hand selected by the Council of the Adjudicars and is so marked in the lists they provided."

"What? Other than providing the additional energies to ease transportation from the other world, why would they be involved?"

"We believe the recruit to be a womban, my Prince, despite the lists the Adjudicars provided declaring her to be a male."

"If the lists proclaim him to be male, why do you believe she is a womban?"

"The... flavor of the person who was holding the talisman is female, my Prince."

"Perhaps she was arriving from some other departure location and was not one of our recruits. Or, mayhaps, they collided en route. That has been known to happen, though rarely, and not usually to the betterment of either."

"That is possible, I suppose, my Prince. However, there are no indications of a second individual. If the person is female, then she is a bit of an anomaly. The lists declare her to be an archer..."

"We have scores of archers. What makes her special?"

"She is also a Sorceress, my Prince."

"Ah, now I begin to see. The Adjudicars are playing games with me again, are they not?"

"It would seem to be so, my Prince."

William waved his hand, and turned to walk away, declaring, "Very well, find her, and if she is injured, heal her. Bring her to the transport chambers as though nothing has happened. Then show her to the barracks, give her clothing and prepare her for tonight's supper."

* * *

I had no idea of where I was, or what to do. I tried to think of my Boy Scout training. I figured that I should just stay where I was, looking for any signs of a search party. I thought about a fire, but I'd given up smoking years ago and had nothing to light one.

Rather than just sitting there and ruminating, I began cleaning as much mud off me as possible. I took my boots off and dumped out the water. They were probably ruined, which was a shame, because even though they were wet, they were comfortable and were keeping my feet warm. I took off my soaked socks, wrung them out as best I could, and then hung them on a branch so the light wind would dry them out.

After ten or fifteen minutes, my feet were getting cold… well, colder than the rest of me… so, I put the socks back on. They weren't much drier and were still squishy. I pulled the boots on, knowing that wet leather contracts, and that these might conform to my feet, becoming less comfortable. Kneading them for a minute, I hoped to soften them enough that they might do the job for which they were intended. I hoped my armor wouldn't shrink, since it was already form fitting and accentuated the fact my character was indubitably female.

My stomach growled, reminding me I hadn't eaten since lunch. I was getting tired of waiting and was just about to search for some kind of civilization, when a tall, gaunt fellow stood at my feet, staring down at me. I hadn't heard him approach… so much for being alert to the world around me. One moment, the sun was shining down on me, and the next I was in his shadow.

The guy was wearing a black robe, girdled with a wide, brown leather belt, which matched his hair color. He didn't appear to be a threat, but you can never tell in a game. I was careful not to turn my back, and kept my hand on the dried branch I had collected earlier, just in case I needed to defend myself from something or someone while I waited.

"It's about time someone found me," I spouted. "Look at me! I'm wet, I'm cold, I'm bruised, and I stink."

I Came

He seemed taken aback. He thought for a moment before he answered me.

At first, I couldn't understand him. He was speaking gobbledygook.

He blinked and muttered something. Then, he said, "Ah, lady, might you be our wayward recruit? If you would be so kind as to come with me, I shall deliver you to the collection rooms, at which you should have appeared had all gone as planned. Master MacGregor will see to it that you are housed and clothed following your arrival."

"Thank you." I replied, as he nodded again.

The black-robed man uttered what sounded like a short chant, and then grasped my hand, before chanting yet another.

The world shifted in strange ways.

We were in a large, dimly lit room, which had rock walls and several metal reinforced, wooden doors of various sizes. Smoky torches provided a flickering light, and it stank! I didn't think I could smell anything after being doused in that culvert but this...? Mostly, it was the smoky torches hanging in brackets on the wall, but there were underlying smells of men, sweat, and various animals. My head began spinning, just as it had when I landed in that culvert. Then I sneezed. It didn't help.

As my head spun, and I fought the bile rising in my throat, the walls blurred for an instant, shimmering for a moment or two as they wobbled out and back almost like someone breathing. I dropped, landing on my knees and hands, desperately trying not to be sick. Twice in one day seemed a bit much as far as I was concerned.

As my vertigo passed, the walls solidified, and my savior vanished much as he had appeared. *'Ah, great, another glitch in the software. Okay, so they don't have all the kinks ironed out yet. No wonder they wanted gamers to beta test this.'* I made a mental note to let the developers of this VR know about the blurring, nausea, the glitch of dumping me into a culvert, as well as the flexing of the walls and disappearing people, as soon as we had our first debrief. Even with those problems, this VR experience was terrific!

10

As my eyes became accustomed to the darkness and the smoke hanging in the air from the torches, I found I was on all fours at the center of a pentagram drawn on the stone floor. I glimpsed movement out of the corner of my eye. "Uh, hello? Anyone there?" I called. "What happened to the man in black that brought me here?"

A harried fellow, dressed in a long, black cloak with hair as white as it could get, rushed up to me and helped me to my feet. Then he gently pushed me aside. "Please move from the arrival pentagram. I have four more collections still to do, and you are disrupting the progression," he said, pointing to a door.

Gathering myself, I clambered to my feet. With his assistance, I stumbled towards the door. I had to lean on the nearby wall just to keep my balance.

The white-haired man studied the drawing of the pentagram for a moment before he grumbled, "Did you have to smudge it?" He knelt down first to erase and then to redraw it where I had smudged part of it.

"Oh, Sorry."

He complained lightly, "Why does everyone need to scuff their feet and disturb the drawings? Don't they teach you youngsters anything?"

"Uh. We don't have magic where I come from."

He looked at me in open-mouthed amazement for a few seconds, before he continued to erase and redraw the damaged parts of the pentagram.

As I watched him carefully make the corrections, rubbing out one set of lines he had just added, then redrawing them a second time, I reconsidered the sound of my voice. I wondered how they did that. I could feel it resonating in my throat, but what I heard was a woman's voice. I was glad this was a game, because, if these changes had been real, it would mean I had gone through some extensive changes. Now that I thought about it, there were a lot of things that felt different, not just my voice, or my arms and legs. My avatar was decidedly female even under all the dried mud, which reminded me ... I wanted a shower. Dirt, especially mud caked on a body, has this unappealing characteristic of making one both smell and itch.

I wondered if they had merged more than two of my game characters, as they said they might. I was dressed something like I would expect if I were an archer, but I was female, which meant I might also be the sorceress. I tried to extinguish a torch, using 'magic.' The torch sputtered and flickered as if a moderate wind was buffeting it, while the others remained more or less steady. However, it didn't go out.

"Okay," I muttered, "so I have some magical talent, but it needs further training."

The old man barked, "What? Womban, why are you still here?"

"Nothing, nothing. Just thinking out loud."

"Please, leave the room, womban. This next collection could be dangerous, and, for your own safety, I advise you to be elsewhere when it arrives." He pointed toward the small door just ahead of me. "Those who have been waiting for you are through that door. I've had enough delays. I have others whom I must collect before I'm to send a shipment of supplies to the Phaedham guard and send healers to Higgleston to handle the injured troops at that location.

"That reminds me, Gendar... Gendar! Where has that boy gotten to? Ah, there he is. Gendar, go find out what has happened to the healers we were to send to Higgleston. They and their supplies should have been here by now. That's a good boy...

"Womban, you're still here? I don't have time to chat nor to be civil at the moment. Go through that smaller door. Go!" He pushed me, somewhat less gently than he had previously, toward the door he mentioned, then turned his back and began to rummage through a pile of small parchments.

I stumbled and glared at him. Then, I raised my chin and sauntered toward the door in question, my boots making squelching noises and leaving wet footprints despite roughly two hours drying in the wind. I paused long enough to remove them before continuing toward the doorway. "Urk!" I exclaimed.

"What? You're STILL here? Just go through the door, womban. They will answer any questions you might have. Be careful, transport travel can be extremely disorienting."

"Yeah? You think so?" I was considering sitting down before I fell down.

He frowned, as though thinking about what I had just said, then added, "Yes, usually, unless you have had a great deal of experience with it. Through that door, please, and hurry. Now... where was I?"

"You were reading that little piece of paper?" I ventured.

"Ah, yes. My thanks." He began to puzzle over the piece of parchment he had pulled out of a pile, and then began to mumble. Moments later, he stood before his freshly restored pentagram and began to chant. As his chant progressed, a slight haze collected over the center of the area above the pentagram slowly forming into the outline of a large shape, which occupied much of the transfer platform.

Seeing a huge miasma forming, I decided I didn't want to meet whatever it was, at least not until I knew it was housebroken and that it had already had supper. I opted for discretion, hurrying as best as I could through the indicated door.

I stumbled into an empty room, my wet boots slipping on the smooth stone floor. I shut the door behind me just as a roar and several loud thuds resounded on the other side. There were several benches in this chamber, so I sat on the nearest one, took off my boots, and wrung out my socks.

I considered my initial opinions about this game. First, the game was entirely too real not to be taken seriously. They had a funny way of starting it out, but one thing was sure... this VR experience was world-class. Obviously, the developers had spent a lot of time and money working out most of the kinks from the VR system. However, they were accomplishing all of this, it was one hell of a realistic experience.

I reached up to feel for a headset, but all I touched was my hair and face, or rather, the muddy hair and face of my character. I thought, *'Well, it's not 3D VR. How the hell are they doing this?*

I Came

These people had come up with something that everyone else could only dream about. Whoever these guys are, they will make a mint from this game once the word gets out about their ability to create a game reality that feels, well - real.'

Now their call for so many gamers to beta the game made sense. Once we all returned to our homes here and there around the world, and then began to tout the game on Facebook and other social sites, people would line up at the stores weeks before they released it.

Several men arrived, and I snapped out of my reverie. Among them was one of the guys with whom I had spoken during my negotiation of the contract. He was still wearing those funky robes, which made him appear to be a Sorcerer like those from many of the RPGs I had played.

"Ah, good," he said. "You have finally arrived. Brahms will show you to your barracks. We have a room, a bath, and suitable clothing prepared. You will be given time to refresh yourself before we direct you to the great hall. We shall partake of the supper meal, where further explanations shall be provided by Prince William."

I nodded. "Okay. Thank you. I've got to tell you guys, so far this is one hell of a great VR experience, other than the headache and nausea. How do you do it? Man, I've got to buy a copy of this. All the other games are lacking in fine detail, but this... this beats them all, hands down. Great job. Man, I can even smell the torches."

He looked a little puzzled at my comments, as though he didn't understand. "Thank you, young womban. If you would just go with Brahms, he will guide you to your quarters." He glanced at the others as if to determine if my observation had confused them as much as it had confused him.

"If you would follow me," said a young man in a black robe, whom I assumed to be Brahms.

As I followed Brahms out a door on the opposite side of the reception room, I noticed someone in livery hurry over to another person who was also wearing funky robes... another Sorcerer, I supposed. He accepted something, read it, and then studied me as I slipped and slid across the stone floor trying to follow Brahms. I don't know what the message was, but suddenly that other fellow seemed very interested in me.

I hoped Beethoven, Bach, Tchaikovsky, or Stravinsky weren't around, or this could deteriorate into a Monty Python sketch. This Brahms guy was probably an NPC, or non-player character, generated by the software, and whatever computer was running it. I wondered what level processor would be necessary to run the gaming environment while maintaining this level of detail in VR. My God! I could even see the color of the various characters' eyes!

This could be a bitch if the game required a highly advanced computer to run it. That could adversely affect sales. Maybe the game was layered, so the better computers could give an improved experience, while those of lower capacity and less memory would give a slightly lesser experience. With a VR like this, I couldn't imagine the processor or the amount of high-speed memory that would be required. It obviously wouldn't be very low, or slow for that matter. Maybe the VR was a plug-in card with its own processors. Hopefully, they would have a USB3 version for those of us who used notebooks.

Geez, my notebook was a top-of-the-line, quad-core, 64-bit, high end of the high-end computer with the best and most powerful graphics card I could find, and here I was, wondering if I would need to upgrade that to run this game. In admiration, I looked around at the graphical detail, which was something marvelous to behold. The flames on the torches looked real, and I could see every hair on the head of the NPC who was guiding me to my rooms.

This game had already locked in my positive vote, dizziness or not. If they could accomplish this on a computer like mine, I'd give them a solid six stars out of a possible five. Boy, I couldn't wait to get into the nitty gritty of the game. If I am an archer-mage, as I thought I might be, I'd love to see my bow or to try out some spells. With any kind of luck, they'd be awesome! I was beginning to think I should have spent more time with my Sorceress character. My archer had been male, as was the Druid priest. So, being a female was a bit of a surprise, since I had selected my archer as my primary avatar.

I Came

It might have been nice if my Sorceress stats had been a little higher before I submitted the characters to these guys for consideration. As it was, I had played my archer character while Reu and Greg were busy working at raising their stats as high as they could before we had to submit our scores. My archer made it up two more levels before I submitted my data, but I only played an hour or so each evening, well - except on the weekends, so sue me. I had to protect my well-earned reputation from everyone on my gaming team since they were submitting theirs, and we would all see who had what in the process of preparation. Nearly all of them had been cramming as hard as they could to build their numbers prior to the submission deadline.

As I followed Brahms through the corridors, I hoped we would pass a mirror somewhere so I could get the full experience. I was dying to see what they had put together for my avatar. Her fingers were long and elegant… probably more suited for playing a harp than stringing a bow. That reinforced my feeling that I was playing the Sorceress character… not my first choice, but they had reserved the right to make the final decision regarding which character I was to play. I guess it wouldn't do to have every character be an archer. Then again, this leather over mail armor seemed to indicate I was playing the archer or some other character that was possibly military-oriented.

In the meantime, I needed a shower!

* * *

Master Talbot approached the throne. "My Prince!"

"What is it, Talbot?"

"We found the missing person, but there is another problem."

"Yes, Talbot… another?"

"Yes, My Prince, she is an Elf!"

"What?" Prince William leapt to his feet, his face red with anger. "They sent an Elf and didn't tell us beforehand?"

"Indeed, My Prince, but in the meantime, what do we do with her? We had intended on berthing her with the other Amazons. Worse, Farmount reports she has tricorn ears!"

"She is high born? Curse their hides! This is intolerable!"

"Indeed, My Prince, but what do we do about it? We can't treat her as an Amazon, and I don't recognize her tribe or know of her ruler. We dare not affront any of the Elvin folk. We have long hoped they would join in this war as our allies."

Prince William thought for a moment. "Cassandra! She will know. She dealt with my wife and the local tribes for many years. Come!"

The two men sped through the corridors, arriving momentarily at a lightly colored, wooden door inlaid in gold, silver and ivory. The door opened as though they were expected. A tall woman, whose blond hair hung in curls around her shoulders, greeted them. "Brother, Master Talbot, welcome. You have come in haste. Why?"

"Cassie," Prince William said, entering her rooms, "We have a problem with a new arrival. He was to have been a mage-archer. However, SHE is an Elf ... a high Elf at that. We were going to house her with the Amazons, but now we don't know what to do. So, I've come to ask your advice."

"A High Elf?"

"My lady," Talbot inserted, "A High Elf of unknown talents from an unidentified tribe."

"Oh!" Cassandra exclaimed, "I see the problem. The Adjudicars are playing with us once again." She thought for a moment. "Ah! I have it. The Northerly Apartment! It's perfect. It is empty, and we have no one expected for which we would have need. Let me alert Dame Eleanor. I'm sure I can convince her to serve as Matron d'Chamber. And, between us, we can make up a staff of four maids. Gentlemen, leave it to me. Take her by an indirect route. Show her some sights. Give Eleanor and myself one-fourth of a glass, and we'll be ready for a queen!" With that, Cassandra sped away, muttering as she disappeared around the corner of the hall.

I Came

William and Talbot looked to each other, smiling. Both knew that everything was in good hands. Moreover, they knew to stay out of the way when Cassandra began to act like this.

* * *

"Lady?" my escort inquired.

This 'Lady' business would take me a bit to accept. Even in gaming groups, we always just used first or last names, so there was none of this 'My Lady' and 'My Lord' stuff used, except by the NPCs. I figured while playing the game there would be some adjustment necessary, but calling me 'Lady' every ten seconds while we were playing was something that was proving to be driving me a little crazy, and my character had just started out.

Brahms hadn't waited to see if I was following. He'd marched halfway down the corridor before he discovered I wasn't following him. When I hurried to catch up, the room spun, and I pitched forward, falling into a heap on the floor, nearly landing on my face.

Brahms hurried back to help me up. He held out his arm, steadying me as we walked to my room.

"You know? They are carrying this virtual reality shit just a few steps too far." I made a mental note to bring that up as well at the first debrief.

"I apologize, my Lady. The effects of transporter travel can be disorienting. I should have known."

"So can sudden gender changes and the VR interface," I mumbled.

"What was that?"

"Nothing. Nothing important." '*No, not much.*' I reached my free hand up to move my hair that was tickling one of my ears and felt... ears! "No shit! I'm an Elf?"

"Pardon, Lady?" This time, he halted abruptly and turned to stare at me.

I took several quick breaths before I answered, "Uh, nothing, nothing. I was just startled. Uh, we may continue. Lead on."

He looked at me strangely, nodded, and turned back, heading to wherever we were going. We turned right at another corridor and then left again just before we nearly walked into yet another of those black-robed men. The new guy pulled Brahms aside and whispered in his ear. Brahms eyes opened wide as he glanced my way, acknowledging whatever the new guy had whispered to him.

When Brahms returned to me, we continued but more slowly, as he pointing out various things I should likely know for future excursions within the castle halls. Some ten minutes later, we walked up a flight of stairs, down another couple of hallways, and then down yet another flight into one more hallway. Eventually, we arrived at a door that, apparently, led to my barracks.

'Where the hell could I find a mirror? Did they even have mirrors in this game?'

Brahms opened the door a crack, just enough that anyone inside could hear him as he addressed me, "Your Matron d'Chambers and maids are expecting you. They will help you with your bath and prepare you for supper.

"Tomorrow, you will begin the training trials, which will continue all week. They tell me you shall also spend time with the Sorcerers following the more physical training. That will be most welcome. We have not had an Elf in this castle in some many years. Good day, Lady." He marched off, leaving me standing alone in the corridor before the door.

I pushed the door, entering one of the most beautiful, but girly, rooms I'd ever seen. The room was huge—probably as large as my entire ground floor back home. Immediately to my right was an alcove with a sitting area with a small fireplace covered by a marble mantle. Just to its right was a golden velvet, three-person sofa dressed in lace. Two golden chairs faced it with a small glass-topped table between them.

The length of the room was to my left. A long, reddish 'oriental' rug ran almost to the doors opening onto a balcony. Various chairs and settees sat along the walls clustered into small groupings, ideal

I Came

for small, intimate discussions. Three large candelabras hung from the ceiling, their glass globes illuminating the room. Smaller, silver candelabras with teardrop-shaped globes graced the tables.

Several identically dressed women, who had been sitting near the door, rose as one. They stood staring at me for several seconds, no doubt shocked at my appearance. Then they dropped into a curtsey.

One woman remained standing. She was dressed richly in a long silver and blue gown. A silver circlet offset her dark hair. A necklace with large blue stones sparkled at her neck. She stood, staring haughtily at me, studying me as though I were some strange lab specimen.

As she was studying me, I was studying her. She was tall… at least my height, if not taller. She was shapely. Her bearing and attitude exuded wealth, power and authority. And she was beautiful. Were I still in my male body, I might have been incapable of rational, non-carnal thoughts.

The richly dressed woman approached me, her right arm across her body, with her hand above her breast. "Welcome, Lady. I am Viscountess Eleanor of Grampus. Prince William and Princess Cassandra have asked me to fulfill the role of your Matron d'Chamber. I am honored to do so.

"We were not informed of your arrival, and I understand that mishap accompanied your voyage. I must apologize for both.

"Please, let me introduce your maids. Rosie is your chambermaid. She will attend to your person and your attire."

A young, buxom, dark-haired woman rose. She had a charming face with the hint of a smile on her lips.

"Beryl is your parlor maid. She will attend to the appearance of your apartments."

Beryl's hair was a dark red, almost auburn. Her eyes were green, and she was blessed with freckles. She smiled and giggled.

"Daisy is your assistant maid. She assists your other maids, performing lesser duties as needed. She is of good family and is seeking a position within the household of a noble family."

A tall, thin, almost angular teenager rose and curtsied. Her figure was just erupting, and her mousy brown hair was in a bun high on her head. She seemed overwhelmed and blushed becomingly.

"Dorothea is your cook. Although you will often eat in the main hall, you will want to entertain, eat at times other than those of the hall, or simply wish to be alone. The food in the main hall is mostly meats, which provide great energy for our men-at-arms and other soldiers. Since you are an Elf, you will want meals with more fruits and vegetables and fewer meats. Dorothea will make sure you are properly fed. You will need the energy, both for your training and for your other duties."

Dorothea was the archetype of the cook. She was short and round. She had a round face, a sweet but knowing smile, and laughing eyes.

"Lady," Eleanor continued, "in the rush, we were not only not informed of your arrival, but not informed of your name or tribe. How should we address you?"

For a moment, I was at a loss. '*Who am I? I have no idea. Don't they know?*'
Then, out of the blue, it came to me, as though someone was whispering in my ear. "I am Gilraën Gulámae of the Elves of the Green Mountain-Maidstone Forest."

Almost instantly, a group of clucking hens surrounded me, each picking at my clothes, chattering quietly to each other. After a few moments, my matron asked, "A bath has been prepared, Lady. Do you wish help in preparing for it?"

'*Oh? A bath would be great, but did I want company in the tub? That was the sixty-four dollar question.*' Summoning all my mental faculties, I blurted, "No. Er, I don't know. Perhaps."

They looked at each other, probably questioning either my intelligence or my sanity. The matron issued rapid-fire instructions to the others, who began to peel my clothing from me, leaving me as naked as the day I was born.

Well, I wasn't born this way!

For just a second, I wondered whether the matron was a gamer or an NPC. Regardless, here I was, playing the all too real character of

I Came

a female Elf, and at the mercy of who knows whatever or whoever my supposed ladies-in-waiting really happened to be.

Hey, I may have played this character or a similar one in some other games, but I'd never had any ladies-in-waiting in any of them, nor had I ever been as immersed in a role as deeply as in this particular game. I mean, this game was so well planned out that it could have been some sort of weird reality. I'll bet they spent millions setting all this up and developing the VR interface, which I had yet to figure out. Now that I had the time, I'd give it some thought.

* * *

Talbot sought Prince William. "My Prince, a word if I may?"

"Talbot, you should know I shall never gainsay you. You are free to voice your thoughts in my presence."

"Thank you, my Prince. If you have a moment, I should wish to speak of a delicate subject, privately."

"Privately? I may spare but a short time, since I have several tasks I must yet complete before preparing for the supper meal."

"It shall not require much time, my Prince, but it is something of which I think you should be aware prior to the supper meet and meal."

Resigned, William agreed, "Very well, Talbot."

He turned to the men with whom he was speaking, "If you would pardon me for a few moments, I shall return shortly."

"Will the hall do, Talbot?"

"Yes, my Prince."

They walked out of the room into the hallway. Talbot cast a spell, muting their conversation to prevent eavesdropping and fogging their appearance to prevent lip-reading.

"Now, what is it you would have me know?"

"I followed Cassandra to observe the arrival of the Elf at her chambers. She is the archer-mage of interest to the council, as I informed you previously. What the Adjudicars failed to mention and Farmount did not report is that her appearance is that of your deceased wife, my Prince."

"It is WHAT? My wife? How dare they?"

"I don't know, my Prince. Should I have her returned to her own world?"

"Yes. No. Perhaps this might be something we can exploit. The Adjudicars meddle in our affairs often enough. Perhaps now we can make some advantage from their interference. Leave her for now, but learn all you can about her. If they want to play their games in this realm, they'd best be prepared for the consequences. You say she looks like my wife?"

"Very greatly. Even were they to be standing together, it would be difficult to determine who was who."

Prince William began to smile. "Then, perhaps, we might send the Adjudicars on a false trail should they expect me to react in ways certain to old memories. Learn all you can about her and tell me what you learn each day."

"As you wish, my Prince."

Talbot paused, as William stood there, obviously considering the situation. Several seconds went by, as he remained deep in thought. Eventually he asked, "Do you think the Adjudicars deliberately seek to mock me?"

"I don't know, my Prince. It is an interesting departure from their usual fare."

"Oh, I do wish you would cease saying 'my Prince' every ten seconds. As I have told you countless times, you are one of my oldest friends and most trusted advisors. Surely, we might have a simple conversation without all that taking up so much time?"

"Very well…. my Prince."

"Very well," he laughed and shook his head. "Talbot, tell me your thoughts."

I Came

"From our initial investigation of the lists, the recruit is a highly accomplished archer and more a Sorceress than a Mage. Without seeing her on the training fields, I am, as yet, unable to say with accuracy. Her talents in our lists show she is quite high in both abilities. At a guess, I would place her perhaps at, or above, the highest of your archer guards, worthy of the top five of my inner circle as a Sorceress... certainly capable of placing a shot into a ripe eidi at one hundred paces even with both herself and the fruit in rapid movement; or a spell upon something larger at even greater distance.

"The lists indicate the male was to be equal to Harding or Cooke in his ability to cast spells, but we both know that continual practice is the proof in such matters. Elves are thought to be more powerful, but, for the moment, she has had little training, both physically and magically. She might be of lesser status for now, but once she gains experience and her magic becomes intuitive, she could readily be a worthy opponent for any who cross her. For now, knowing spells and using them are two very different things. What the morrow may bring, I cannot say."

"Should I ask you to predict her ability at magical wordplay once she gains training? Would you place her at the level of Dom... Dom... I still cannot speak her name, but for the feelings I had."

"Yes, my Prince. I believe she could be as powerful as was your wife before the treachery occurred."

"Think you that this one might be susceptible as well?"

"I don't know, my Prince. I will cast some spells to limit and define, searching for answers. When she begins her training in the magical arts, I will observe and learn what she might feel. There is one silver lining: she has no local affiliations to clutter her sensibilities, and her tribal markings are none of which I am aware."

"But, she is of some tribe, and not simply one who has been cast out?"

"I believe this to be so, perhaps a minor one."

William nodded his head, "I will think on this. Meet me in my rooms half a glass prior to supper. We shall discuss this more as I prepare."

"Yes, my Prince."

* * *

So here I was, partially immersed in a wooden tub shaped more like a gigantic gravy boat than the tubs of the real world. Unlike regular tubs, there were no faucets. Instead, one of my maids was waiting with a bucket of hot water and a pitcher of cool water. I had a washcloth and a brush along with a bar of smelly soap.

I took a long time 'washing' the VR avatar into which I had been ensconced. It was amazing! As I moved the soapy cloth over the breasts, I felt a sexy tingle race through my entire body. When I reached down to wash the VR vulva, I felt an unmistakable sexual urge. In fact, I felt the washcloth on my skin, no matter where I placed it.

This was mind-blowing! How could they do this? This was total physical immersion into a virtual world. Such a system was almost impossible, technologically, and extremely expensive... far beyond my budget. It'd take the resources of a major industry or a small country to afford such an elaborate system. Then again, if it were just a new technology, it'd change the world. It would be worth billions.

I stood, and Rose draped a towel around me, patting me dry from head to toe.

"My lady, I regret to inform you that your baggage has not yet been found. We have selected several gowns and undergarments from other ladies of the court, so we will dress you appropriately for supper this evening."

At that, Rose and Daisy lifted a slip over my head and pulled it down over my hips. Then they approached me with some pieces of cloth held together with strings. Little did I know that this was really one of the most diabolical of torture machines. Within seconds, they had it wrapped around me and began to pull on the strings. OMG! I couldn't breathe! I tried to fend them off, but failed miserably.

"Stop fighting us, Lady!" Eleanor pleaded. "You must be properly dressed for supper with Prince William."

"Supper?" I gasped. "I'm just trying to breathe!"

"Nonsense," she replied, "This isn't even tight, yet."

She was right! Minutes later, I fainted. When I came to, a multitude of faces were staring down at me.

Eleanor glared at me with a caustic look in her eyes. "Have you never worn a corset before?"

"No!" I gasped. "I haven't. Even our women don't wear them."

She nodded emphatically and stomped her foot. "Well, now you do." She turned to the others. "Help her up and get her dressed. Prince William is waiting."

For the next twenty minutes, I was pushed and prodded. My breasts were positioned and entrapped… and partially exposed. (*My breasts? What the hell? What kind of mess have I got myself into? No, not me. It's the avatar. This is a computer simulacrum, not me. Just go along with it, at least for now.*)

They rolled lightweight stockings up my legs and fastened with ribbons. Then they encased my feet in light, low-heeled shoes. Working as a team, they pulled a dress over my head and laced up my back.

They stopped fussing, stood back and eyed me, appraising me as a lion might a tasty-looking zebra. I turned to Eleanor. "You're absolutely certain this is what I'm supposed to wear to dinner this evening?"

She sputtered, "Dinner? No, this is for supper."

For the next several minutes, she corrected my use of the terms 'supper' and 'dinner.' Evidently, 'dinner' was a meal taken around three to four o'clock. 'Supper', on the other hand, did not occur until around seven. It was that which we were attending. She also instructed me about three other meals: first meal, mid-morning, and mid-day.

I asked her how she, or anyone for that matter, could keep their figure if they were eating nearly all the time. She explained it was up to each person to select the meals they would attend, each according to their duties. For instance, many people would have only breakfast and either dinner or supper each day.

I looked down at the deep blue, floor-length gown I was now wearing. I wasn't sure whether I should be repulsed or pleased. Wearing a dress was something I'd never even considered. I'd look ridiculous—a fat, old man in a gown. Furthermore, I was not like the men who did wear dresses.

Yet, I wasn't me wearing the frock. It was my avatar. Well, not mine, but a combination of my avatars. This one was more like my Sorceress—beautiful, but all female. As an avatar, I was indeed beautiful. My slightest movement made the silk and satin gown shimmer and rustle. It reminded me of sunlight reflecting off a swiftly flowing stream filled with small rocks over which the water flipped and splashed, refracting sunlight all about like multicolored confetti.

"When in Rome…," I muttered.

I glanced at Eleanor to see a look of disgust cross her face, as she turned her attention to my hair. "Tend to her makeup, while I decide about her hair."

Moments later, she threw up her hands in disgust. She told the ladies to just try to put it up mostly on top of my head, where it would be out of the way, while they put makeup on my face. "Perhaps we should leave it there for the meal. No braids."

Then they were upset to discover that my ears weren't pierced. One of them came up with a needle and fixed that little problem.

"Ow! Hey, I thought that wasn't supposed to hurt."

"It didn't. You are simply being overly dramatic."

I Came

However, when they came at me with the needle, preparing to give my ears a second set of holes, I managed to fight them off. After two of them found the floor, the game wasn't quite as interesting to them.

As it was, my ears wouldn't quit bleeding. Okay, so it was only a drop or two, but still any loss of blood on my part was to be avoided at all costs. And yeah, Elves bleed red blood, just like anyone else, at least this Elf does.

'Gee, even bleeding is realistic here.'

Come to think of it, I think everyone bleeds red blood in the games. I'd seen 'blood' in RPGs before, but it was this undefined semi-red, third person stuff, which suddenly showed up as a blob of color to indicate bleeding. This game had the pain of the piercing and the bleeding down to something a lot like what I had experienced myself… not the piercing, but the pain. The small droplets of blood were like that time I accidentally cut myself with that carving knife. Now, *that* was bleeding. As I noted before, these people would make a mint with this game and their virtual reality mechanism, however the hell it worked.

Oh, and did they have a good patent attorney? They'd need one, unless I could somehow divine their secrets. Then, hopefully, he was a bad one.

"If you would cease pulling on your ears, they would halt their bleeding much more rapidly, Lady," Eleanor admonished me.

I gave her a dirty look. Unconsciously, I rubbed at my poor abused ears. She swatted my hands for what was probably the umpteenth time. Isn't there some kind of law that says ladies-in-waiting can't abuse their lady? If not, then they need to write one. And my ears were testimony as to the overuse of the virtual reality.

Eventually, I was wearing a pair of earrings, which matched the necklace I was also wearing. I don't know what the stones were, but they were pretty and probably expensive. They glowed with an internal light in a blue sort of way and were a bit like that mystery fog movie producers liked to throw into scenes where they didn't want the viewers to see all the details that didn't quite fit with the mood of the scene. As the swirls and shifts moved around in the stones, it was all kind of special. I didn't remember seeing the swirls and glow moving around in the stones when the maid was holding them.

Ah! A mirror! A real, full-length, narrow mirror with no distortion. My first chance to see my character.

I was young. My character was barely into her twenties at first impression. The hair piled on top of my head was long and red with orange and yellow highlights. My eyes were green and almond-shaped. My skin was a light, pinkish with orange, yellow and brown freckles in mass profusion. My avatar's figure could grace the cover of Sports Illustrated ®. I was a real beauty... one who would instill lust in any man.

As I took stock of my new appearance, I wondered, *'Why do gaming companies always make the characters youthful and beautiful? It's like they don't believe anyone over the age of twenty-five will play these games.'*

Then again, their advance team had met me, and, although they didn't ask, I was obviously well into the mid-portion of my life. If they could tailor a character to this extent, you would think they could also have made my age more apparent. Then again, now that I think about it, Elves don't really show their age, do they? My character might be two, three, or even four centuries old, and still look like she was barely out of high school. Well, if nothing else, I'll ask about it. Geez, I've barely started and already have quite a few discrepancies and questions to ask about or point out.

Being coiffed and wearing scents of powder and perfume plus the glowing, shimmering color from the jewelry might get me killed if my adversary had a good nose, eyes, or ears. The light tinkle of these things hanging from my ears could probably be heard for a hundred feet, if not more.

Now that I thought about it, that was weird, too. When the earrings were down in their velvet-lined case with no light moving through them, they still tinkled, like soft little chimes. They reminded me of small music boxes, but one that could play their music in synchronization or sometimes back and forth like they were having a conversation. Some of the stuff programmers came up with for their game was really off-the-wall, but still it was kind of neat. At least

I Came

the game wasn't filled with background music. I guess not having that pervading the entire game helped to make it all seem more real.

My ears bugged me again. I rubbed at the pointed lobes, only to have Eleanor smack my hands. It was a vicious circle. I remembered hearing women say something about the holes in someone's ears closing up if the earrings were removed for any length of time. I shuddered at the thought of these women piercing my character's ears again, especially since this damn VR made certain I could feel it. Maybe I could ask for some kind of studs that wouldn't tinkle when worn by my character. That would limit notice by an adversary, and I wouldn't need to go through getting them pierced again.

That thought made me rub my poor abused ear lobes once more, which resulted in... you guessed it... she slapped once again. *'When will I learn?'*

"Ow. Stop that," I complained.

"Then stop pulling at your ears, my Lady."

How could they program for all the eventualities that might occur? How could they know someone might rub their ears just when I happened to do it, or that they might need to pierce someone's ears? The interactive features found in this gaming software were unbelievable and probably had driven some poor software writer or writers to the edge of commitment. Then again, all the software writers I knew were absolutely nuts, but in a good sort of way.

After satisfying herself that I was ready, Eleanor grabbed my arm and rushed me into the hallway. Things were continuing to move along so rapidly that I didn't have much time to fret about appearing to have become my character. I was too busy worrying about my character bleeding to death or falling flat on her face, because this body didn't move the way I was used to walking much less nearly running. That meant I didn't have time to worry about walking down the hallway dressed like a girl. Hell, I was too busy to even worry about being female. I needed to make a mental note to recommend to them during the after game debriefing that they might dial back the pain level a bit though. After all, they wouldn't want their game to cause a heart attack in someone who was coming up for one.

I stumbled along down the hallway, much to Eleanor's chagrin. I couldn't blame wearing heels, because I was wearing slippers or soft shoes that probably didn't have more than a one-inch heel. No, the problem was nothing moved the way I thought it should. Everything I was wearing was flaring out at least a full body width beyond myself and was trying to interact with everything it could. I was afraid that if I leaned too far, I'd topple over and be unable to get up again.

Actually, being my game character had taken a distant second in the list of items to worry about. I was too busy just trying to get from point A to point B without causing major harm to either myself, or others. I grimaced as a suit of armor crashed to the floor behind me, having been caught by my gown as I passed. When I peeked over my shoulder at the squeal I heard behind me, I noticed one girl helping the other one up from the tangle of armor.

Eleanor heaved a big sigh, shook her head, and was probably wondering how she could gracefully back out of the position of Matron d'Chambers to someone who was obviously a klutz. Did I mention that she was easily navigating the hallway in a gown wider and more stiffly constructed than my own without so much as moving a speck from a small pile of dirt someone had hidden behind a pillar that once held the bust of someone probably important? I say 'once', because when I followed her, I brought it all down, and only the pillar remained intact. The noise of it echoed down the hall, and I thought for a moment that Eleanor was contemplating running off and leaving me behind to fend for myself. There has to be some sort of secret to navigating the halls in this clothing.

"I'm sorry…" for the umpteenth time. "This gown just reaches out so far…. I'm not used to wearing something like this."

She halted before yet another door, and then quietly admonished me, "Please! Do nothing to embarrass either me or yourself. We are about to enter the great hall. Do try to avoid entangling your gown in anything. We shall go directly to the table and sit, so there will be some chance of success. Remember to sweep your gown from under you as you sit."

I Came

"Hey. It's not like I'm doing this on purpose. I've never worn anything like this before."

She glared at me, her eyes again considering the possibility of releasing herself from my service even, as she stated, "Next, I suppose you shall tell me you wore trousers, like a man, all your life."

"Well, yeah."

She looked at me curiously, "Yeah? Means this, yes?"

"Yea... er, yes."

She rolled her eyes toward the ceiling, sniffed in that disgusted way only a noble woman can do, and muttered quietly under her breath, "Elves are a very strange race."

The girls didn't seem to hear her. Finally, she took a deep breath before slowly letting it out, her eyes remaining closed. She gently shook her head back and forth, before opening her eyes to look straight into my own, "Please, pretend you know how to be a lady, even if you don't. By the stars! You do know which fork and spoon to use, don't you?"

Obviously, she was less than enamored with my efforts so far. She guided me into the banquet hall, and the ladies of the court followed.

As we entered, I noticed this end of the room was rather cool despite a fire roaring away in an overly large fireplace at the other end of the hall. I expected some of that heat would radiate to this end of the hall, but, evidently, the room was too long for comfort... long but narrow. It was also really tall. The roof was at least three stories high with V-crossbeams, strategically placed to support the massive structure.

I began a hasty count of the number of people now seated. There were four rows each of eight tables. Four men sat on benches at each side of a table with one man at the head and another at the foot. There were benches along each wall, where another twelve to fifteen sat. Then, there was a head table that seated about a dozen. I guessed there were about three hundred seventy-five people seated for supper.

Then, I noticed that they had moved the head table about a third of the way from the fireplace at the far end of the room closer to the two entrances to the huge room. '*Aha!*' I thought to myself. *'They've deliberately moved the head table forward to make the room seem more crowded. Psychologically, everyone here should feel a greater kinship, a shared experience. Quite a clever device. I must remember to compliment the developers when I'm debriefed.'*

The people sitting at the tables in the main area appeared to be regular soldiers for the most part. There were groups that appeared to be men-at-arms. There were other groups that appeared to be archers; others were slingers; others were non-descript warriors whose function I could not determine.

The people at the raised tables along the two sides were much better dressed. Many wore ceremonial armor. About half were well-dressed women, often haughty in their mien. I assumed that they were all nobles or high-ranking military.

Eleanor led me to the left side of the long table at the head of the room. She greeted a tall, muscular and very handsome man (*Handsome? Where did that come from?*) dressed in highly polished, blued steel armor. She turned to me. "Geoffrey, let me introduce you to our guest, Lady Gulámae of Green Mountain-Maidstone Forest. Gilraën let me introduce my husband, Sir Geoffrey, Viscount Grampus.

"Please, Lady, sit with us. I shall ask Prince William to allow you to sit with us in the future so Geoffrey and I can explain the comings and goings, the people, ceremonies, and the affairs of state as they happen. In that way, you will become more familiar with our ways."

Their reception heartened me, and I was awed to be sitting with the Prince, his family and high retainers. Even I, an ordinary American, understood that this was an honor seldom bestowed.

"Thank you, Dame Eleanor, I would be most pleased to sit with you and Sir Geoffrey. I have much to learn before I make a fool of myself in front of everyone. Ooh, what's happening?"

Eleanor, Geoffrey and everyone else suddenly rose to their feet. I looked about, seeing that I was the only one still sitting and leapt to my feet. Suddenly, I felt faint. I couldn't breathe! I grabbed the table and felt strong hands grab my arms.

My head cleared. Geoffrey held me firmly, but gently. "Are you all right, Lady Gilraën?"

"Yes, thank you," I whispered. I tried to suck in a lungful of air, but failed. *'Damn corset!'* I complained to myself. *'Never again,'* I swore. Gasping for air, I asked, "Who is that man … those men?"

Several men had entered the hall. The first was a tall, broad-shouldered and handsome man (*Again? Handsome?*). He had fair features, blondish hair, and light eyes. He wore burnished steel armor with a sword at his left hip and a long knife at his right. As he walked toward the head table, he glanced around at the assembled men, smiling heartily, nodding at many, and exchanging words and jests with a few.

Immediately behind him was a large, dark warrior. Behind him was a tall, thin man in a long black robe, followed by a dozen others. It took a moment before I realized that I knew some of them from the interviews. I'd also noticed a couple from the arrival room just after I'd gotten here. As the line of black-robed men walked, I saw flashes of red from the insides of their robes. Those nearest the head of the line wore bright scarlet. Towards the rear, the red color faded, becoming orange and white.

'Aha!' I thought. *'An old ploy. The redder the robes, the higher ranked, but always hidden from the uninitiated.'*

Eleanor leaned towards me to whisper, "The man in the lead is Prince William of Umbeqjaralii. He walks with General Abuahad, who leads our armies. Behind him is Talbot, Chief Sorcerer and Prince William's most trusted advisor. He leads our Sorcerers: Baron Richmond and Masters Norton, Falsworth, Thackery, Johnsstone, Simmons, MacGregor, Jacques and Transport Sorcerer Farmount. After them are Sorcerers of lower rank.

"You are being honored. We seldom have all the Sorcerers at any single meal. They are generally working or teaching, so they are seldom all here at the same time."

William led the procession to the far end of the table, turning to walk to the middle of the table before stopping at a high-backed chair slightly elevated on the dais. He stood there for a moment, first looking to his right towards us, and then to his left, acknowledging everyone. He hesitated for just a moment and then looked back directly at me. He nodded in acknowledgment and then seated himself.

Immediately, scores of men and women hurried into the hall, bearing platters, bowls and tureens. They swooped towards the tables and deposited their burdens. A wonderful aroma of cooked foods filled the room, and my stomach growled, much to my embarrassment.

I reached for the nearest platter, but Eleanor touched my wrist. She shook her head, and I dropped my hand.

Prince William leaned to the large platter containing a massive roasted beast. He slipped his knife from his hip and sliced off a large hunk. He sniffed it and then bit off a large mouthful. He chewed it with evident enjoyment. Swallowing it, he grinned and said, "It is good! Let us eat!"

Suddenly, the room, which had been almost deathly quiet, erupted as men seized spoons and ladles, knives and forks, and began to pile quantities of food onto their plates. Within a few minutes, the hubbub subsided to a mere drone, as men were suddenly too busy eating to talk.

I looked at the assortment of foods laid out on the table before me, wondering what was what. A large roasted beast lay on a platter in front of Sir Geoffrey. A pile of green, mushy looking stuff was in front of me. A tureen of orange soupy stuff was in front of Eleanor. Other platters of white pancake-like things were just to my right, and slices of brownish stuff sat the other side of Geoffrey.

"Here, try this," said Eleanor, sliding a large slab of beast onto my plate. "And, you'll like these," she said, spooning a glob of green mush and one of the pancakes onto my plate. "Don't try the orange soup, yet. It is an acquired taste. My husband loves it…" She turned up her nose.

I Came

I laughed out loud. Several heads turned in my direction. I was aware of several of the men's expressions. Some seemed to be angry or upset. One seemed to be curious. None appeared to be friendly.

"Don't let them bother you, my dear," Eleanor said, patting my arm. "They are afraid of Elves."

"Why?"

"Ah!" Sir Geoffrey interrupted, "Elves are faster and stronger than Humans, you see. They view that as a personal disadvantage. They are jealous and fearful of someone who could kill them before they could raise a hand to protect themselves.

"At the same time, if Elves, such as yourself, were to ally with us in our war against Unterjaralii, we might gain the upper hand against the traitor, Lord Beckworth, and reunite the kingdom."

I pondered his words for a moment. I had volunteered to fight, not caring particularly about who I would be fighting or why. This was a game after all. However, it appeared that the game makers really wanted to engender loyalty to the Prince and the Kingdom. Why? What purpose would it serve? It'd be a waste of code, resulting in a concomitant decrease in performance. Yet, up 'til this time, the game has been nothing but sophisticated. It just didn't make sense.

And what should I do? How should I react? Was this a test built in by the game developers? What would happen if I passed or failed? What would constitute either? I concluded, '*I guess I'll just go along with it. What else can I do?*' "Lord Beckworth? Tell me more about him."

"Beckworth!" He almost spat the name, "He is a traitor! He has torn our beloved kingdom in half. He destroyed the beauty that was Umbeqjaralii."

"But who is he?"

"Prince William is King Richard's younger brother, and Cassandra is their younger sister. Beckworth is their half-brother. Their mother, Anne of Coephalli, died of a fever a few years after Cassandra was born. King Patrick then married Agnes of Beckworth, Baron Richmond's aunt. Their son is George, who now styles himself as Lord Beckworth. Georgie was always a troublemaker even as a child. We were all playmates, you see: me, Richie, Billie, Cassie, Freddy and Georgie. But, Georgie always cheated and tried to hurt everyone he could. He was just mean.

"You see, he blamed King Patrick for his mother's death. She died in childbirth. Georgie believed the King's Sorcerers could have saved her, but didn't. So, when he came of age, he murdered King Patrick and seized the ancient fortress of Shalal'm Caer, the first capital of the Humans of Jaralii.

"Richard gathered the forces available to him and marched on Beckworth, but we were repulsed. Somehow, George had gathered a force of men and Sorcerers who where faithful to him. Since that time, we have been building an army capable of defeating Beckworth. There has been war between us for over five years, with but little prospect of success in the near future. Still, we live in hope of our ultimate victory."

'*Aha!*' I thought, '*the noble quest in a good cause. It's a classic game scenario. And I'm the hero, marching to my doom.*' That was an unpleasant thought.

The room, which had been almost silent while the men ate their fill, had become a cacophony of noise and shouts of men. Suddenly, it hushed. Prince William had risen from his throne. He spoke in a melodious baritone voice, which carried to the far corners of the hall. "Viscount Geoffrey, Dame Eleanor, Lady Gilraën, and all of you gathered here tonight, welcome."

My first thought was, '*How does he know me? We haven't been introduced. And he has named only the Viscount, his wife and me. She is a very important person to be noted, which means that I am, too. Why am I so important? Is that why he is seeking my support?*'

"I am Prince William. I am your host this evening. I would like to take this opportunity to welcome Lady Gilraën, who is new to this realm, as are most of you. Those of you who have been selected to attend to our needs, and given contracts of service to our King, are now present. Each of you has special talents, and, in some cases, attributes that are not apparent upon first glance."

One man shouted, "The Elf can offer her talents to me, any night." A light roll of snide laughter passed around the room.

I Came

"I would not be so cavalier as to risk her ire, gentlemen. I, for one, would not care to meet with her upon the battlefield or during some dark night, lest I was absolutely certain she was fighting for the King's forces, and possibly not even then." He turned to me and bowed his head.

He then looked out over the throng. "When those of you read of our request for champions, it said that you would be in a 'fully immersive experience'. That was not worded as I would have had it. You have been transported into this reality, which is greatly different from your own."

"You can say that again," one man chortled. Several others laughed wryly, as did I.

"Tomorrow, each of you will begin training for your new roles in my service. Over the next four to five weeks, you will become more proficient at your chosen skills than you have ever been. And, you will become highly skilled in other areas, in which you are less skilled at present. I warn you now; your instructors are excellent. They will test you to your limits.

"Do not be discouraged if you do not measure up to your own high standards. It is our goal to teach you new measures and techniques, enhancing your present skills. You will become the most capable fighters this world has ever seen. Only then, will you be ready to meet the forces of Lord Beckworth.

"So, warriors, I bid you good night. Retire to your barracks and prepare yourselves for a strenuous day tomorrow. First meal is at first light. Your instructors will be here, ready to lead you to your training grounds." He reseated himself and began conversing with a General Abuahad.

I looked towards Eleanor, wondering what we were to do. She whispered, "Not yet. We wait for them." She nodded at the men shuffling out. "The real business of the night begins when they are gone."

As the last of the men exited, the pairs of great doors closed, and a robed man took up his position guarding each. William stood, and we followed suit. He moved further into the room, nearer to the fireplace. Stewards arranged chairs in a semi-circle with William at the apex of the arc. A beautiful and statuesque blond woman sat immediately to his right in a chair similar to William's. The large warrior sat to his left. Three couples, including Geoffrey and Eleanor, sat to William's right. Several men and women sat to his left. Master Talbot stood behind him, peering into the flames.

Eleanor whispered to me, "The lady to William's right is his sister, Cassandra." She was about to add further comments, but William spoke.

"Master Richmond!" William said in a commanding voice.

Almost instantly, a man dressed in a black robe appeared just behind the throne. He was tall, with dark hair and flashing eyes. A hint of the darkest red lined his robes. "My Prince," he said in a quiet tenor voice.

"Richmond, would you *Summon* those weapons which we discussed earlier?"

"Of course, my Prince," he replied quietly. The air seemed to swirl, and Richmond was suddenly standing with a bow, quiver, and an assortment of knives in his hands.

"Thank you, Frederick. Would you present them to Lady Gilraën?"

Richmond glided to my side almost instantly. "My Lady," he said, presenting them to me.

I examined the bow closely. It was thick and heavy looking, as though meant for a man. Yet, it wasn't wood, or at least not any wood with which I was familiar. Whatever it was, it was smooth and warm. And it was light… perhaps too light?

The arrows were heavy - about three-eighths of an inch in diameter - with an arrowhead shaped in a very wicked looking bulbous cone. I noted the fletching was attached in a slight spiral, needed to supply spin to the long shaft as it flew. The arrow was light, save for the head, and seemed to be made from the same kind of wood as the bow. Out of curiosity, I touched the arrowhead. It tingled!

I Came

'Oh. Duh! I'm an Elf now. Be careful of iron. Okay, Tony? Still, the attention to detail in this game is unbelievable.'

I turned my attention to the five knives. Their scabbards were long and slim, designed for very pointed blades. There was a small gap between one of the blade's guard and its scabbard. The blade sparkled brightly, illuminated from within rather than from the flickering torch or firelight. Drawing it slightly from its sheath, I noted it had two sharpened edges rather than just one. When I touched the blade gingerly, I expected another burn. Instead, a slight glow radiated at my touch. As I reseated the blade within its scabbard, it hummed eerily. A shiver flowed down my spine, as I deferentially patted the hasp of the sheathed blade on the table before me. As if in answer, a bright but brief series of glowing pulses radiated from within its enclosure. I patted each of the five and received much the same from each.

William spoke almost somberly. "These are the weapons of an Elfin Queen. The bow is formed from a wood known only to the Elves. The arrows are of our own manufacture. That is, we can replace any arrows you destroy or lose, but the bow is beyond our skills. The knives are Soul Blades, attuned to an Elf's touch."

I considered what I knew about 'Soul Blades.' The blade was imbued with the soul of a warrior who was dying in battle. Such a blade would seek and kill on its own, requiring only a throw, or, in some cases, only a slight motion to set it on its course. After killing, it tapped the life energy of the one whom it had killed, strengthening itself. A Soul Blade could not be damaged, lose its edge, or its ability to kill, as long as it had any life energy remaining. After it killed, it would return, blood free, to its scabbard, ready for its next use. But it only answered to its soul-mate; no others could use them. Such a weapon could be a very terrible thing if they had modeled this game blade after those in the stories I had read.

I replied, "Prince William, these are weapons beyond price."

"Yes, they are. Such weapons cannot be owned. They chose whom they will obey, and once that decision is made, they will perform any task that their possessor assigns. When that person dies, the weapons become useless and impossible to employ until they deign to accept a new owner.

"The fact that the blades accept you is important. It tells us more about you. We now know that you are indeed a High Elf with noble purpose. However, we do not yet know about the bow. Please string it." He leaned forward to watch with great interest.

I knew this was a test of my position within this game. The bow was unstrung, so I stepped through it, bracing the lower half against my leg. I bent the upper half, easily stringing it. I nocked an arrow to the string and drew it, easing off several times to get a feel for the pull of the bow. It was not as heavy a pull as were some bows I had used during my college archery classes.

William sighed audibly and bowed his head into his hand. After a few seconds, he looked up at me, a melancholy look on his face. "Use them well, Gilraën Gulámae. May they protect you better than she whom they once obeyed."

Talbot leaned down to whisper in William's ear. William nodded and then looked at each of us. He sighed again, straightened his shoulders and addressed us. "It would appear that your presence here, Lady Gilraën, is a manipulation by the Adjudicars. We had expected you to be an archer-mage, but a male. Obviously, we were mistaken. Further, we expected you to be an Earthman. Instead, you are an Elf. Moreover, you are a High Elf, which complicates our governance, our alliances, and our relations with other kingdoms in our land. I cannot begin to fathom the consequences.

"Regardless, it is my opinion that we should continue along our present course of action. Lady Gilraën, I feel that you should proceed in your training as though you were nothing other than an Elf. Only the Weapons Masters will recognize your weapons, and I will forewarn them not to say or to do anything that will disclose their powers or origins. Master Talbot will attend to that.

"We will do nothing that will disclose our knowledge or our suspicions. We will meet like this after supper to discuss anything we may have seen or anything that aroused our suspicions.

"Cassandra, you and Eleanor will introduce Gilraën to female society. You three will use this opportunity to learn as much as you can. The fact that Gilraën is new to our society and does not know our customs will be your entrée. Essentially, you can pry without arousing suspicion. Do so.

"Is everyone clear? Remember that you may always contact me through Talbot. Is there anything else? No? Then, sleep well."

Eleanor and Geoffrey stood, and I followed them. Cassandra wrapped her arm with mine. "Let us go to your apartment. We have much to discuss." Eleanor nodded, and Geoffrey harrumphed his agreement.

When we arrived, Rose was awaiting us. She dipped a curtsy and led us into the small sitting area to the right. A warm fire greeted us. Dorothea swooped in with a tray of hot beverages and what looked like toast. She poured four cups of the beverage and handed one to each of us.

"Oh, thrak!" Cassandra enthused, sipping eagerly.

Thinking it was some kind of coffee, I took a sip. It was good!–a little like mocha, but sweeter. And it had an almost instantaneous buzz that was most delightful. "OOH!" I exclaimed, "This is good! What is it?"

"Thrak," Eleanor replied. "It is an infusion from jut-joo berries that grow in shady spots near the mountains. It's quite refreshing, isn't it?"

I nodded and took another sip. I had finally put my thoughts together well enough to formulate a question. "I don't understand what's happening. When I interviewed, I had several talents. I was an archer, and I was also a female Sorceress. They asked if they could combine my talents into a single player. However, none of my avatars was an Elf. I'd sure like to know how I got here, especially as a female Elf. William seems to think this is important. How? Why? What's going on?"

Geoffrey cleared his throat, but Cassandra interrupted. "We are at war, and, frankly, we're losing. We don't know why or how. Umbeqjaralii is large in area and in numbers, but ours is largely forested and agricultural land. We have mines or other natural resources in the Jaralii Hills, but few beyond. We are rich in food, forests and water, but our greatest resource is our people.

"Richard is a fair and just king, but he can be cold and haughty. William is beloved by all. He has befriended refugees, Dwarves and even Orcs. He listens to counsel, gives advice seldom, except when it is warranted, and gives of his time as he can.

"Beckworth seems to know what we are going to do before we do. He defeats our forces; he invades where we are weakest. He gains allies, while we lose ours. He is relentless in his attacks upon us, and we seem powerless to defeat him. Our people are beginning to grumble. They see what is happening, and, despite their fondness for William, they are becoming disaffected.

"Then, the Adjudicars sought us out. They said they would help us reinforce by finding volunteers from other worlds to help our cause.

"Of course, we were elated to receive their help. We listed our requirements, and they set out to fulfill them. It was they who created the concept of the game, administered the interviews, and provided lists of the people and their talents to us.

"We now receive some fifty to sixty volunteers each month. They are skilled warriors who have aided our war efforts. Yet, we still are losing, and we don't understand how or why. What we do know is that Beckworth is overpowering us with forces beyond our ability to defend ourselves.

"In that regard, Lady Gilraën, you are our one bright hope. William has high hopes for you. He thinks you are the one who will turn the tide. He doesn't know how, and, frankly, neither do we. Regardless, we follow him, and we hope that you are the person he believes you to be."

* * *

I lay in my bed that night, my brain in a tizzy. This was not a game! This was real… perhaps too real. Magic existed. Magic existed in this world. As an Elf, I was a magical being, but of what

I Came

sort? War existed: good vs. evil, and evil was winning, which it usually does. And, somehow, I was the keystone that would hold the arch of state together or, by failing, would be responsible for its fall.

I laughed at the irony. Who said this wasn't a game?

* * * * *

Chapter 2—Training Begins

It was morning. Rosie was kneeling by my bedside. "My lady, it is time to arise. You need to dress, eat your first meal, and prepare for your first day of training."

I groaned, but slid out from under the covers. It was cold out there, and when my feet touched the icy floor, I jumped back into bed.

Rosie laughed, "I thought Elves were made of sterner stuff!"

She handed me slippers and a warm bathrobe made of some shimmery material. Wrapping up and donning the slippers, I followed her to the lavatory. Then, I thought about shaving, which was a part of my normal morning ritual for the past thirty-odd years. Giggling to myself, I quickly dismissed the thought. I poured some warmed water from the ewer into a basin, washed, and returned to my bedroom.

Eleanor had laid out my clothes. To begin, there was a soft bodice, providing firm support for my breasts. (*I still can't believe it. My breasts?*) There were also soft, long-legged panties somewhat like old-fashioned knickers. I pulled a largish undershirt, made of the same soft fabric over my head. Then, I stepped into brown leather breeches and slid into a leather pullover shirt. After I stepped into my soft leather boots, I wrapped my hair in a band, and donned light, leather gloves.

Eleanor had also laid out a sturdy belt. She had draped my armor over a wooden stand in the corner, a long dirk and the five, sheathed Soul Blades over the torso. She had slung my quiver of arrows over a stand with my new bow rested against it.

Five minutes later, Eleanor joined me. She was dressed similarly, except in cloth, not leather. She looked quite fetching in an athletic sort of way. At her hip was a short sword. Looking at it, I raised an eyebrow.

She smiled. "We are at war, Gilraën. We are prepared to repel an attack at all times… womben as well as men."

I shrugged. It sounded right to me.

I Came

She led me from my rooms to the great hall. Large groups of men had assembled, eating, shouting to each other, generally acting like a bunch of high school boys. The moment we entered, the hall went silent. It was as though someone had thrown a switch. Every eye turned to us. Some men who were staring at us still had half-chewed food hanging from their lips.

Talbot suddenly appeared at our side. He scared the crap out of me! "Damn! Where did you come from? My heart is almost in my throat!"

Talbot smiled. "My Lady, I apologize, but your appearance here was unexpected. Prince William has requested that you await him. He will arrive shortly."

He had hardly finished when Prince William and Cassandra strode into the hall. Spotting us, a huge smile split his face as he approached us. "You have arrived early, my ladies. It is a good omen that you are eager to begin your first day of training. Come, let us eat. You will need your energy today." So saying, he led us to the head table and held our chairs for us. He sat next to me and then clapped his hands.

Almost immediately, servants arrived bearing platters and bowls of delicious smelling food. Others placed dishes and tableware before us, while still others laid pitchers of different kinds alongside.

Back home, my breakfast was a piece of toast and a traveler mug of coffee on the way to my office. I was completely unprepared for such a repast. I glanced to Eleanor, with one eyebrow raised, asking a silent question.

Eleanor smiled. "Yes, all meals are large, because each of us has different schedules and duties. You, however, should eat a small meal rich in meats or oyes, along with shaer and brew. You should not eat a large meal, since you will be training, and a large meal would slow you and might even lead to cramps. However, you will expend much energy, so you must prepare for an active morning."

"Ah, I see, but which is which?"

She leaned towards a bowl of green lumps and spooned two of them onto my plate. She ladled some brown gooey stuff over them.

Then, she cut a slice from a loaf and poured pint or so of amber liquid into a cup. "Try that. I think you will like it, and it will give you enough energy to keep you going until the mid-day meal."

I tried the green lumps with the brown goo. It was sorta like eggs and gravy, but not quite. The slice was definitely bread. And the liquid was a light ale that tasted really good. It was a damned fine breakfast, even if it was huge by my standards.

"Good, My Lady," the Prince exclaimed, "I see you are eating heartily before today's efforts. I am looking forward to hearing from the Training Masters about your progress."

"Prince William, at what will I be training? No one has explained anything. Is there some kind of schedule? Where will I be going? What will I be doing?"

"Ah, that is easy. Today, the Training Masters will assess your skills. We must understand your skills and abilities before we can develop your training course. Once we know your competencies, we can develop a training program to improve your skills, and teach you new ones.

"You, however, are unique. You are an Elf. You are faster, stronger and quicker than almost all Humans, Orcs, Trolls and the other sentient beings of this world. Only Krells could challenge you successfully, or, of course, either Dragons or Gaunts.

"Regardless, we need you to mix with the recruits. So, you will receive two different training sessions. In the first, specialists will work with you in hand-to-hand, blades, bows, and other weapons. In the second, you will train with the volunteers. I expect you will exceed their skills easily. Do so, and as you do, assess them carefully. We need to know if they are who they say they are, and if they are loyal or traitors. We must identify the sociopaths, who are here to kill or to be killed.

"Just remember, they won't like you from the start. You will give them plenty of reason to despise you. They will try to take their revenge. So, I am assigning you special protection. Brahms will lead you to and from your training sessions, and Talbot will watch discretely.

I Came

"When the Training Masters judge you are ready, you will begin training in sorcery. Again, Brahms will accompany you, but he is only a Junior Sorcerer. Your trainers shall be Senior Sorcerers or Master Sorcerers, capable of deceiving a Sorcerer of Brahms rank. Therefore, Talbot will monitor your training from afar. He is an extraordinary Master Sorcerer, even more capable and powerful than other Masters.

"Your job is not just to learn the skills of a Sorcerer, but to monitor your trainers. To do this, you will develop control of your mind to detect other's thoughts and to shield yourself from them. Meet Talbot after supper. He will help you learn those skills. Once you have mastered them, you will proceed with your sorcery training.

"It would be inappropriate for you to seek me out, or to seek Talbot or the other Sorcerers. Instead, report your thoughts to Eleanor or Cassandra. Nobody can suspect a meeting between you and your matron. And, nobody can suspect a meeting between Cassie and Ellie. They've been friends since they were babies. Still, remember to be careful not to let others overhear you. We don't know who to suspect."

"But, why do you trust me?" I asked.

"I didn't; the weapons did." He smiled wryly, hanging his head. "They were my wife's, imbued with her spirit. The Soul Blades see into your soul. They found a kindred person... one they could trust.

"The bow was also hers. It tested your loyalty. If you had harbored ill will towards me, you would not have been able to string it. It would have been an unyielding rock in your hands. Instead, it yielded to you, even making its draw easy in your hand.

"Gilraën Gulámae, I did not test you; my wife, who was also a High Elf, tested you. I trust you as I did her. You and I are linked through my wife's weapons. May they serve you as they did her."

He smiled, and quietly said, "Talbot."

Talbot glided across the hall. "My Prince, did you call my name?"

William turned to his Sorcerer. "Would you assist Lady Gilraën to her training site?"

"Indeed, I have assigned young Brahms to escort Lady Gilraën. He is youthful, but well trained in his duties. I will accompany them this time, but, hereafter, Brahms will have the honors."

"Excellent!" William exclaimed. Turning to me, he said, "I leave you in good hands, My Lady. Will I see you at supper?"

"I'm not sure, but if I can, I will."

He bowed and turned aside to meet with others of his men. Talbot led me to the door where Brahms awaited us. Together, we walked down a long, wide passageway to a huge, iron-bound wooden door. To the side was a smaller door into a tall, round, stone turret. We entered, turned quickly, and arrived in a dark, enclosed space between the two doors leading into the castle. We entered a second turret, turned quickly left, right and left again, before coming to another small but heavy, iron-bound door.

Suddenly, bright sunlight blinded me. I gasped, shading my eyes with my hands.

"You have just died, My Lady," Talbot stated in matter-of-fact voice.

Summoning all my mental faculties, I replied, "Huh?"

"You exited first. Mummia blinded you. You could not see if there were enemies gathered before our gates or an assassin lurking and ready to strike. You just died, because you didn't take the most elementary precautions."

"I did what?"

"Brahms and I are here to protect you. One of us should have preceded you. We were prepared for the transition from dark to light. We had no moment of blindness. Had our enemies been at this door, we would have seen them and taken action. If nothing else, we could have slammed and locked this postern, sealing you in the castle removed from harm.

"Remember, Lady Gilraën, you are an important person. Prince William's future may depend on you. Without you, this kingdom may fall. Please, take precautions and let Brahms and I protect you until you are ready to defend yourself. Even then, you must remember you are not immortal, and that we are pledged to your service."

Brahms quickly led the way down into the village that surrounded the castle. The road turned to the left, going halfway around the castle. Then, it turned back, going all the way around the castle before turning again to a gate in another smaller wall. Again, there was a pair of turrets with sturdy gates. Unlike the castle's gates, these were wide open, and a steady stream of people, animals, carts and wagons were coming and going. A few of the men heading out were obviously warriors. Some were armed; others weren't. All seemed intent on getting to wherever they were going and paid little attention to us.

We turned to the right and walked on for the next ten minutes or so. I began to hear a sound reminiscent of wooden spoons beating on metal pots. I heard men shouting and cursing. Slowly, a large field filled with men appeared.

Talbot led us to a tall man standing alone, shouting loudly at a group of men grappling with each other. "No! By the shoulder! Drammon, show him how it's done."

Talbot cleared his throat, and said, "Master Perseus!"

The tall man turned, revealing a craggy face with a dark scar running from the hairline over his left eye, down his jaw to his throat. His left eye was cloudy, and his left ear was missing. He stepped towards them with a noticeable limp in his left leg. At his waist was a large sword, with a long-bladed knife on his opposite side.

He eyed us all carefully, before speaking with a craggy voice, "Master Talbot, welcome. Who are these lagging behind you?"

Talbot's composure was unaffected by the roughness of Perseus' greeting. "Master Perseus, I introduce Lady Gilraën. She is new to the court, and Prince William has instructed that we train her in combat skills.

"Let me also introduce Junior Sorcerer Brahms, of my house, who will accompany Lady Gilraën."

Perseus studied me carefully. Slowly, and evidently painfully, he staggered around me. Then, he stood before me, looking me directly in the eyes. "Lady Gilraën? I see you are an Elf. Do you have any training in combat?"

I thought for a second, considering my answer. In the gaming world, I had lots of experience. I had achieved level 30 or more in three different characters, and in every one I had been a superlative warrior. But, in reality, good old Tony Richardson had been highly skilled, but that was several decades in the past. "I have some, but not enough. I look forward to your instruction, Master Perseus."

He pursed his deformed lips before croaking, "Better warriors than you have replied similarly. We will see what skills and abilities you have. Then we work to develop yours to the highest level of achievement." He mused as he stared at me, and then turned and shouted, "Vigash! I have a new one for you!"

Less than a minute later, a huge man lumbered up to Perseus. He had to be eight feet tall if he was an inch. His arms were like a wrestler's legs, and his legs were as big as a bear's. Yet, the man moved more like a lion than a bear. "You bellowed, mighty one?" he asked Perseus.

The hint of a smile lurked for just a second at the edges of Perseus' mouth. "Vigash, I have a new trainee for you." He pointed at me. "Prince William wants this one trained. She says she is not unskilled. Test her for me and develop a training program for her."

Vigash stared down his nose at me. All I could see was a pair of holes lined with hairs, a scowl, and two beady eyes.

"Elf, huh? Ain't seen one of your kind here in many years. Well, I'll see what you can do. Come with me." He turned and stalked away.

I had to run just to keep up with him. I took three steps for his two, and he was trotting at high speed. Even then, it took several minutes before he stopped. He pointed to a half-acre, grassy knoll, fairly isolated, and out of view of the rest of the training areas.

He pointed, and said, "We will wrestle here. I will do my best to throw you to the ground. You will do your best to throw me to the ground. As we wrestle, I will judge your skills and abilities. Once I know what you can do, I will train you to be your best. Come."

He led the way into the grassy area and turned to me. "Defend yourself, Elf!" With that, he hurled himself at me, grabbed my shoulder and sent me sprawling.

"Again!"

Again, I hit the ground. He spent the next hour humiliating me. Finally, he stopped and walked from the knoll to a small table. He poured liquid from a ewer into a large brown vessel. "Water?" he asked.

"Indeed, Master Vigash. You have wrung me dry."

He handed me another vessel and poured water into it. I gulped it thirstily. "Tell me, Master Vigash, where did you learn to wrestle like that? You threw me around as though I were a child."

He grunted. "Had I been an ordinary man, I could not have done so. You have some rudimentary skills, which would have been more than enough with most. But, I am not ordinary. I, too, have special gifts, which I use in the service of my King.

"The reason Perseus chose me to train you is that I am one of the few with the strength and speed to fight an Elf. However, when I am finished training you, not even I will withstand you. The day that occurs, we will work together to improve your skills, but I will no longer fight you, for if I do, you might injure me, and then my usefulness will have ended. In the meantime, you will learn, and I will teach."

'Shit!' I thought. 'This guy is going to manhandle me. What the hell? I'm supposed to be an Elf–strong, agile, fast and all that crap. And, I'm sore already.'

Instead of voicing my thoughts, I said, "I am eager to learn everything that you can teach me, Master Vigash. When shall we begin?"

"Hah!" Vigash laughed, his face a mockery of humor. "If you think are ready, then let us begin."

For the next two hours, Vigash showed me what he had done to me, moving slowly and with great precision. Then, he did it to me, but more quickly. At first, it seemed easy to counter his moves. Then, he did the same move at real speed… and set me on the ground… again! By the noon hour, I was sore, tired, and ready to crawl into a soft bed and cry.

As we walked back to the area where the rest of the recruits were training, we talked. Upon reaching the training area, he said earnestly, "Lady Gilraën, you show great promise. However, even an Elf can feel pain. Before you go to bed tonight, ask Lady Cassandra for her help. She understands the healing arts. She will help you recover by tomorrow, when we will begin again. Sleep well, My Lady."

He bowed his head toward me slightly, turned, and studied a pair of wrestlers grappling with each other. He shook his head in disgust then began to bellow at them as he walked away leaving me standing there.

Brahms appeared at my side, a look of awe and wonder on his face. "That was marvelous! Never have I seen such speed and power displayed. I am pleased I am a Sorcerer and not a man of combat."

I laughed ruefully. "Brahms, I was beaten thoroughly for hours. That brute manhandled me and slammed me to the ground repeatedly. I would hardly call that marvelous or a display of speed or power."

"Ah, My Lady," Brahms countered, "that is because you were wrestling, not watching. To me, you two were almost a blur. You tore up the ground, and dirt was flying in all directions. It was as if watching two tornados embattled. Had you been fighting with anyone other than Vigash, you would have won handily. But, you were, so you lost, but that was expected."

"Expected? Why? Who is Vigash exactly?"

"Ah, My Lady, his origins are a mystery. However, he is the strongest man I've ever met. His fame spreads far and wide. None have ever beaten him, and even Sorcerers are afraid to face him in mock combat.

I Came

"Here we are, My Lady. This is the knock that will alert the guards to your presence." He knocked a pattern on the door.

"Who goes there?" a disembodied voice rasped and echoed.

"Brahms of House Talbot."

A port behind an iron grate opened, and an eye appeared for just a second. Sounds of rattling chains and creaking axles resounded. Then, the postern door edged open just enough for the two of us to squeeze through. Several men stood facing them, each with the business end of a pike poking at us.

"You, I recognize," he nodded at Brahms. "But who is the wench?" he asked, leering at me.

Something in me snapped. I was tired, humiliated at having been thrown around like a rag doll, and now this... this, lout, had the audacity to call me a wench as though they had brought in me to service the troops. I knew that my avatar appeared to be a young, beautiful and extremely sexy young woman, but there was no way I would accept this insult after being abused all morning. I stepped forward in a blur, swept all the blades that were threatening us from the grip of the guards who were holding them. The pikes hit the wall some ten feet away before falling to the floor. It happened so quickly, none of them had so much as a chance to blink.

Grabbing the speaker by his neck, I raised him a foot off the ground. I growled, "I am Lady Gilraën. LADY Gilraën! Never. Insult. Me. Again. Do you understand?"

When I released him, he fell to the ground, landing on all fours and gasping for breath. It took several seconds before he could weakly reply, "Aye, Lady. Aye."

Brahms was staring at me, his eyes as large as saucers. "Lady Gilraën," his voice quavered, "please don't harm our gate guards. They are an important part of the Castle's defense. Please, come with me to the great hall where we can find refreshment following your training of this morning."

He grasped my arm and tried to drag me away from the guards who had been slowly moving toward their pikes while I diverted my attention to the one who had insulted me. I turned back toward them and glowered. They drew back once more, unwilling to become further examples similar of that which had befallen their leader. I lifted my chin, assumed a haughty air, and gracefully followed Brahms. Within just a few minutes, we had wended our way through the gates, through the town, and into the castle. From there, I attempted to show that I knew the way to the great hall. I needed only one correction from Brahms to find it.

No sooner had I entered the great hall than Talbot appeared at my side. If he had done so in a puff of smoke it might have been less of a surprise.

"Will you stop doing that? My heart goes into my throat every time you sneak up on me like that."

"Apologies, Lady. Prince William and Lady Cassandra will join you shortly. Your place at the table has been reserved." He glanced toward Brahms. "Was Brahms a satisfactory guide?"

"Oh, yes. Brahms was a perfect guide. He got me there, and back, in an exemplary manner."

Talbot smiled, "Except for a minor discussion at the town gate?"

"Oh, no. I simply found it necessary to remind a gate guard of his manners. And, Brahms was a great help to me."

Talbot looked a bit surprised, but said nothing. Instead, he led me to the table and pulled a chair out for me. As I sat, Cassandra and William entered, deep in conversation. William glanced up, and seeing me, nodded to Cassandra. She too looked in my direction. Both stood more erectly and moved slightly away from each other. Both pasted similar smiles on their faces, before greeting me enthusiastically.

William sat to my right and Cassandra to my left. He asked, "How was your morning?"

"I met Master Vigash. We exercised each other for several hours before he released me until tomorrow. Then he will probably exercise me for several hours, and the next day and the next. It seems I show great promise, according to Master Vigash. I, however, feel more like a rag doll that was badly abused by a rather large bear."

I Came

William guffawed, while Cassandra tittered behind her hands. Both appeared seemed amused at my tale of woe.

When William recovered, he remarked cheerfully, "Indeed, Master Vigash can have that effect on trainees. However, I have received a complete report of this morning's training session, both from Master Perseus and from Master Vigash. According to my esteemed Masters of Combat, you do indeed show great promise. In particular, Master Vigash was most complimentary. So, what do you have to say to that, Lady Gilraën?"

"The man beat me, threw me to the ground, and brutalized me for hours. I hardly find that to be a subject for amusement!" I tried to pout and look hurt. "Master Vigash even suggested that you, Lady Cassandra, are learned in the healing arts, and that I am in need of them."

Again, the two of them laughed merrily. "Oh, dear lady," Cassandra gasped, as she tried to control her laughter, "I would be more than happy to help you recover from Vigash's tender mercies."

William chuckled, "Lady Gilraën, we are delighted that you survived Vigash's training methods. I remember when I was a puffed up lad, full of myself, my father sent me to learn combat skills. I had been training all my youth in such skills and thought I was tough as they came. Then I met Master Vigash. He had no respect for my position, my combat skills, or my youth. Instead, he thoroughly trounced me and beat me into the ground time and time again. I was sore for a week, in spite of my mother's ministrations.

"Ever since then, I have followed in my father's footsteps. Those who come to us full of themselves or too prideful, I send to Master Vigash's tender care. Regardless of who they were before meeting him, they are quite changed afterward. You, My Lady, are the very first to at least hold your own against him, and to merit his approval. You are all I had hoped you would be and far more. For the first time, I think Master Vigash will achieve his goal of training a new recruit up to his standards."

"Gilraën," Cassandra said, "I have the healing skills of which Vigash spoke. I will gladly assist your recovery from Vigash's training. However, this afternoon, you will be with the men you see

56

before you." She nodded towards the mass of men jostling, teasing, and joking with each other. "They will join our army, along with others we are recruiting. They must know you, and you must know them for our army to be effective."

Prince William interjected, "We need them badly. Please, don't break any of them!"

"Now," William continued, "Go to your quarters and return here in your full field armor. Remember, you are an archer, so much of today's sorting will be to determine the limits of your skills. Your armor will distinguish you from that of our men-at-arms, knights, slingers and others. Be prepared for a rough-and-tumble reception."

When Brahms and I returned to the training grounds, Master Perseus led us to a different area. He growled, "Chin! I got another one for you!"

An Oriental man disengaged from the crowd of men. He was old! Even by my middle-aged standards, he was ancient. He was small; less than five feet tall. He was emaciated. He was so skinny a strong breeze might blow him away. And he was homely as the proverbial hedge fence! One eye seemed was looking for the other, and might have found it if his nose weren't in the way. His jaw was crooked, and his left ear was missing its tip. I almost laughed, but decided that if he was like the other Masters, then he was far more than he appeared to be.

He waved his hand. "Over there! Over there!" He indicated a large group of men and women, all in armor. They were a motley mixture of soldiers, as Prince William had said.

Seconds later, several of Master Chin's assistants arrived. They quickly sorted us into groups of five, each with its own trainer. Master Chin stood amid the groups and raised a hand in the air. When everyone was silent, he said in a soft voice that somehow carried to the furthest corners of the grounds "You good!" He nodded, spinning on the spot to view each group. "We make better." He smiled. "You fight. Best fight best. Then Winner! Go, now, you fight."

The trainers explained that we were to pair off. Then, we would fight each other until there was one winner. They handed each of us a long, stout, wooden stick about six feet long and an inch-and-a-half in diameter.

'Quarter staves?' I chuckled to myself, *'how quaint.'*

Regardless, we fought, but it was an unequal match. I was much quicker and stronger than any of the other soldiers. Three matches later, I was the champion of our group. The champions then fought until I was the overall champion.

Master Chin congratulated us all. Then, he took up his own staff, and stood before me. "Fight!" he ordered and attacked me!

A second later, I was flat on my back! I then recognized why he was the Master, and I was the student.

He looked quizzically at me. "You learn?"

I sat there for a second or two. "No," I replied, "I must learn more. Teach me!" I leapt to my feet, poised with my staff in hand.

"Good!" he replied, but the words had not left his mouth before he moved to strike.

I saw both his action and his intent. His initial attack was to my left shoulder and head. However, this was a feint. He was actually going for my ankle, and then my right shoulder. I stepped back, caught his staff and twisted ready to deliver a blow to his left shoulder and head. But he wasn't there! He too had moved and was already striking a blow at my left leg. I leapt and struck his staff to the ground. We struggled with each other's feints and parries for several minutes, before he stepped back, smiled most horribly, and bowed to me. "Good! You learn!" He clapped his hands and bowed to me.

That afternoon, we also fought with magically blunted swords, spears, and javelins. In every joust, I won handily. But then I met Master Chin. He drubbed me with the sword three times! He didn't smile or bow. "Not good," he said, shaking his head. He waved his finger at me, stating, "More work."

He had no such luck with the spear or with the javelin. I could keep him at a distance with the spear, and I nearly threw the javelin outside of the training grounds.

I had a similar 'problem' with the sling. I really didn't know rocks could fly that far! He looked at me, shook his head, and gave me that horrible smile for a brief instant.

Finally, we bent our bows. Most of the others were utterly inexperienced. They could neither string their bows nor fire their arrows. I was a natural archer. I placed arrows in the center of targets at the most extreme distance of the archery range. I had them set up a target at the far edge where it was almost a dot on the horizon. In spite of the distance, my arrows found the mark. I ran, I jumped, I hurdled, firing arrows as quickly as I could. I even fired five arrows in high arcs so they all landed in the bull's eye nearly simultaneously.

Master Chin nodded to me and bowed. "Me learn; you teach. Never any better, but one other. She teach; I learn."

Master Chin and his assistants began dividing us into groups. The largest group was nearly a hundred strong. Smaller groups contained soldiers who were spearmen, javelin throwers, slingers or archers. Obviously, I was with the archers.

Master Perseus met us all just as we were about to leave for our evening meal. "We have tested each of you to determine your greatest skills. You now stand with your compatriots. We will train you together. You will learn to fight together and to defend this realm against our enemies.

"Tonight, you will sit in the Great Hall with your compatriots and your Training Masters. As you learn your skills, your officers will train with you. Then, you will march to your destiny. So, learn well."

I was still with the other archers when we hurried to the castle. Several approached me, but seemed unable to speak. Finally, one, who was more brazen than the others, asked, "How did you learn to shoot like that? I've never seen anyone do anything like what you did out there."

With the ice broken, the others began to ask questions. "What kind of bow is that?" "If I had one like that, could I shoot like you?" "Is it that because you are an Elf, or can anyone shoot like that?"

I Came

Finally, one summoned up the courage to ask, "Who are you, anyway?"

"Whoa!" I shouted. "Too many questions all at once. My bow is Elvish, and I doubt any of you have the strength to pull it. I am Gilraën Gulámae of the Green Mountain-Maidstone Forest. And, I am an archer."

"No shit!" one man jested.

"And, who are you, archer?"

"I am Harold the Archer."

We had arrived at the gate. As we passed through, the men turned aside and went to their barracks. Harold asked, "Will you be sitting with us or with the Prince?"

I thought for a moment, before answering, "I will ask the Prince. This is a matter of protocol, which I don't yet understand. If I can, I will sit with you, even if it is just for a few moments. Farewell, until tonight!"

I managed to find my rooms. I only took one wrong turn, but figured out where I'd gone wrong without asking anyone for help. When I got there, Rosie and Dorothea were waiting: Rosie with a hot bath; Dorothea with a tall glass of cool fruit juice. However, they wanted me to rush to dinner, even though I wanted to luxuriate in the warm water that felt so good after a long day of hard labor.

Eleanor arrived, dressed in a long, flowing, flowered gown. Rosie laid out a similar red and white flowered gown for me. Then they approached me with that horrible instrument of torture–the corset!

"Oh, no! Not again," I said, backing away from them. "I shall not wear that again."

"Now, now, Gilraën," Eleanor warned, "We womben must do these things. It is the fashion of our court."

"But, I am not of *your* court," I replied. "I am an Elf of the Green Mountain-Maidstone Forest. And, I am a warrior, not a simpering Human female. I need to breathe, not faint."

Rosie seemed to be convinced, but Eleanor was unimpressed. "Lady or not, this is necessary," she declared, advancing menacingly.

I knew that in a physical confrontation, I could easily defeat her. However, I had to avoid such a confrontation, if possible. Yet, I had been adamant, and now it was a point of honor.

"What's all this?" Lady Cassandra had appeared in my bedchamber.

Eleanor, her face red in anger, spun to face Cassandra. "Cassie, she is refusing to wear her corset!"

Cassandra doubled over in laughter. It took her a while to recover before she could sputter, "But, Ellie, you've complained about them for years! Why do you now force her?"

"Well!" Eleanor sputtered, "If she won't wear one, neither will I!"

Cassandra burst out laughing. "Then, neither shall I!"

With Rose's help, they quickly disrobed. Moments later, we three stood in our under-garments, looking into the tall mirror. Three comely women stared back at us.

Cassandra stated, "We will start a new fashion, we three. Down with our corsets; up with our hemlines! Tonight, though, we still have to dress in clothes that need a corset. What shall we do?"

"Are you sure?" I asked. "I mean our waists are slim enough. We might just fit. Let's try at least."

"Well said," Cassandra replied. "Come on, Ellie, let's get yours on, and then we'll try mine. Gilraën's so thin, she really doesn't need one, anyway."

It wasn't all that difficult. Zippers had not made their appearance here. Instead, gowns laced up the back. The combination of the weave of the cloth and the tightness of the lacing was more than sufficient to give us the slim-waisted appearance, without causing me to faint. So, arm-in-arm-in-arm we marched off to the great hall like schoolgirls sharing a super secret.

I Came

We met William and Geoffrey at the door. The big man who sat at William's left was also there. Up close, he was even more impressive. He was huge... not as big as Vigash, but at least six-six and a solid 250 pounds or more. His shoulders were broad, waist small, with the bulging muscles of an NFL tackle. His face was smooth shaven, well tanned with large brown eyes beneath heavy brows. His hair was brown with just a touch of gray beginning to form at the temples. Obviously, he was the epitome of a man.

"Ah," William caught me staring at the soldier. "Lady Gilraën, let me introduce General Abuahad, my chief of staff and leader of my armies. General, let me introduce Lady Gilraën of the Elves of Green Mountain-Maidstone Forest. I'm sure the two of you will have much to discuss in our future."

He briefly took us in with a sweeping glance. He grinned, boyishly, "Shall we enter before the starving masses revolt?"

He entered, leading us to the head table. Everyone stood in silent respect until we had taken our seats. Again, the meal was fantastic, both in quantity and in quality. Eleanor introduced me to a new dish. It was gray-white and lumpy. Although it didn't look it, it was good– sorta like parsnip potatoes, but tastier.

As the meal wound down, I took a few moments to look around. The mass of men was in the middle. There was a group of women with them, but at a separate pair of tables. There were a few tables located off to the left, with men I recognized as slingers. Spear throwers gathered more towards the front. The archers were off to my right at a long table. When I looked toward them, Harold waved at me, then stood and pointed to an empty chair next to him.

I looked to Eleanor, saying, "The archers want me to sit with them. Is that permitted?"

"Oh, yes. Soon, Abuahad will drink with the soldiers, trying to get a measure of them. Others of high rank will gather, then wander over to talk with the soldiers to raise their morale. So, if you want to sit with the archers for a few, do so. Just remember to keep a clear head. William might decide that we meet after supper."

I took my chalice, still half-filled with what I assumed to be wine, and wandered over to the archers' table. Harold stood and gallantly helped me to an empty chair. One and all greeted me, and we quickly began to talk shop. Frankly, they were far more familiar with their gear than was I. We all had different equipment, different arrows and different fletching. Yet, the basic fact of aerodynamics resulted in everyone's equipment ending up performing similarly. Only mine were different, it seemed, and all the men and both of the women wanted to know more.

I had hardly begun talking about them, when a burly fellow from the large group of men-at-arms turned and shouted, "Hey, you bloody wood benders, share the wench with us all." He leered at me, shouting, "Come on, deary, I have a knee waiting for you... a man's knee, not some wimpy fletcher's."

Thoroughly pissed, I rose to take the drunken sot to task. However, the Prince's shout interrupted us. "Aha! I see that some among you are not aware of the remarkable skills of Lady Gilraën. It is now the time for you to understand." He nodded to Talbot.

The air where Talbot had stood shimmered. For a second or so, the place where he had stood was empty. Then, he was beside me, holding my bow, quiver and one of my blades, scaring the crap out of me. "Damn, Talbot! Warn me next time!" I exclaimed.

In a bored tone, Talbot replied, "Indeed, my Lady. Your bow and blade."

I took them from him, wondering what was going on. I looked up to William.

"Excellent!" William declared. "Now, Lady Gilraën, would you go to the end of the room? Talbot, a fruit, please." One seemed to appear in his hand. "Excellent. Now, which among you would stand here with this fruit upon their head so that Lady Gilraën can shoot it off?"

The room was suddenly silent. Men grimaced at each other, shaking their heads.

"What? None of you are brave enough to match deeds to your words? Ah, then I shall do it myself."

William marched to the opposite end of the hall before the fire. He stood calmly and placed the fruit on his head. He took a few moments to balance it, then shouted, "Whenever you're ready, Lady Gilraën."

I could barely see him. The fire behind him was a wavering light, dancing about, making it almost impossible even to see him as more than a shadow than anything else. Of the fruit, there was no sign.

Heads turned. Some men stood, crouching to see me, blocking my view of William. I leapt lightly atop a table, scattering drinking cups in spite of my care. Regardless of my vantage point, I still couldn't see William as anything but a flickering shadow. I hesitated, not sure of what to do or how to proceed. Yet William trusted me. If he trusted me, why should I worry?

I stepped through my bow, bent it, and, slipping the loop over the notched end, secured it. Pulling a heavy arrow from my quiver, I laid it on the bow just above my hand and nocked it. Unable to see my target, I concentrated on the fruit. In one sweeping motion, I lifted my bow, and pulled the string to my lip. Loosing the shaft, I directed it to the target with my mind.

A gasp rang out. For just a moment, I thought I'd killed William. But then, I heard him laugh and shout, "She's done it!"

I leapt to the floor, my skirts parachuting out, and tried to walk to the head table calmly and serenely, not disclosing that my heart was beating like a trip hammer.

Evidently, William hadn't completed his little demonstration. He stood against the far wall, behind a table of nobles. He tossed a lop-sided half of the fruit I had shot into the air high above his head. "Lady Gilraën, this piece of fruit is yet too large for me to eat. Do you have a knife that you could use to split this into smaller pieces?"

At first, I wasn't sure what he wanted. Then I realized William wanted me to use a Soul Blade. I wasn't sure that was a good idea. Should I use such an extraordinary weapon for such a mundane purpose? Yet, William had asked.

I watched as William threw the fruit high in the air. He caught and threw it at a steady pace. I pulled the blade from its scabbard, listening to its eerie hum, and watching the blue-black blade flare in the firelight. The knife seemed alive in my hands, ready to fulfill its deadly mission. I flexed my wrist, and the knife flew across the room, cleaving the fruit neatly. As pieces fell into each of William's hands, the knife penetrated the wall, spalling a chunk of stone that flew off, clattering to the floor. Then, the blade disappeared, only to reappear in the scabbard still held in my left hand.

William smiled ear to ear. "Thank you, My Lady." He brought a chunk to his mouth and bit off a piece. "Excellent!"

He walked towards the head table. "Gentlemen, just yesterday, I warned you not to take Lady Gilraën lightly. Today, you have watched her in training. You have seen her skills with stave, sword, spear, javelin and sling. Tonight, I remind you of her skills with the bow. You have also seen just one of her other skills and weapons.

"When you see her on the field of battle, be thankful she is with us, and not against us."

* * * * *

I Came

Chapter 3 - Sorcery

I awoke the next morning feeling battered and bruised, despite the green salve Cassandra and the girls had slathered all over my body. It had felt good, especially when applied by five such lovely women. I groaned as I rolled onto my side, preparing to put my nice warm feet on that, oh so cold, floor.

Evidently, my groan was louder than I had intended. Rosie, my maid, was instantly at my side. "Are you in pain, My Lady? Is there anything I can do?" she asked, as she retrieved my robe and placed my slippers on the floor before me.

"Thank you," I replied, struggling to get my arms behind me far enough to slip them into the armholes, but my muscles cramped. "Argh!" I complained, as Rosie sprang into action, aligning the arms of the robe with mine. I stumbled into the lavatory, my legs cramping. Moments later, I tried to stand with similar painful results.

Eleanor rushed to my aid, bearing a pot of green goop. She helped me to the bed and slathered more of it over my arms, legs and back.

I felt better almost immediately. "Oh, that's wonderful! What is it?"

"The extract of a bean that grows in the deep forest. It relieves pain and prevents further injury to your muscles."

She helped me to get dressed in similar garments as yesterday. Then, we went down to breakfast, where Talbot greeted us.

"Good morning, Lady Gilraën, Dame Eleanor. I see that you, Lady Gilraën, are prepared to meet with Master Vigash for further instruction.

"I must also inform you that Prince William will not be joining you this morning. He is meeting with his lords, but extends his greetings to both of you. He wishes that you, Lady Gilraën, should have a good morning of training. Further, because of the excellent progress you made yesterday, he has rescheduled this afternoon's training. You and I will work together to discover the potential of your mind. Later, you will meet with Lady Cassandra, who will teach you about other important subjects.

"Viscountess Eleanor, Princess Cassandra, and Prince William request your presence at Council as soon as you have broken your fast."

Eleanor led me to the table, exuding a sense of purpose. Lady Cassandra was already at table, awaiting us. As we sat, platters were set before us, and I dug in with gusto. As I wolfed down my food, I asked, "I understand you will be my instructors later this afternoon. About what?"

Cassandra and Eleanor exchanged glances, as though deciding just how much they could tell me. Eleanor bowed her head and took another bite, leaving the decision to Cassandra.

Cassandra took a deep breath. "I told you women were powerful amongst our people, and that women sat upon our councils. I, as King Richard's heir apparent, must participate fully in the event I must assume the throne of this principality." She gulped another bite of food and rose to leave. "I will see you again at mid-afternoon. Do your best and relay my greetings to Master Vigash." With that, she raced from the hall, skirts flying.

Brahms appeared at my side, scaring the crap out of me. "Lady, Master Vigash awaits you. Please, follow me."

"Thank you, Brahms, but I have not eaten, yet. I need some food, right now. Master Vigash will have to wait to slam me repeatedly into the ground."

Regardless, I ate a light meal, quickly. Brahms led me through the gatehouses and to the field where Master Vigash glowered at me.

"You took your time, Elf!"

"Elf?" I answered, haughtily. "Elf, you call me? Master Vigash, I respect your position, your skills, and the fact that you are my teacher. However, I demand that you respect me. I am *Lady* Gilraën. And, yes, I am an Elf, with all that implies. Do we now understand each other?"

I Came

"Demand? You *demand* respect from me?" he sneered. "Elf or not, you are still a trainee. And, as for you being a lady, that's for grand balls and displays of finery. Here and now, you are a warrior in training, and I am the master. My word is law, and yours is insignificant until you prove otherwise. Now, prepare yourself!"

With those words, he attacked me with fury. I had no option but to escape, and I did so by leaping straight upward. He swept beneath me as I hung in the air. He stumbled, tearing up the ground for ten feet, before turning back to face me. I landed, smiling. "Master Vigash, you have acted foolishly. I had not expected such rashness from one who claims to be my master. Shall we now resume our training, or must we both resort to our natures?"

Vigash stared at me, a smile playing at the corners of his mouth. "Ha! You remind me of another I once trained. She too had the ability to both anger me and appease me at the same time. And, she too understood her position, even as I taught her to become a warrior." He shrugged, "Let us begin."

Today, I was more prepared for Vigash's size, strength and speed. I had experienced his moves, and I remembered his instructions. My mind had been replaying our exercises of the day before, and I seemed to sense what he was about to do just before he did it. I could see the interplay of his eyes, his muscles, his balance, and found I could deduce his plan of attack.

Figuring out what he was going to do was entirely different from knowing what to do about it. At first, I just used my speed and flexibility to avoid him. Unfortunately, that didn't always work out. More than once, Vigash grappled with me and, with utter disregard of my status, threw me on my Elvin ass.

As mid-day approached, I was beginning to figure out how this new body in which I had found myself moved. I found the limits of my speed, my agility and my strength. My knowledge of what I could do and how to do it increased geometrically. Then, it happened - I saw Vigash preparing to strike toward my left shoulder. As I began to move to avoid him, his left leg whipped towards mine, intent upon sweeping my legs from under me. I twisted to the left and leapt over his leg. His momentum carried him beyond me just far enough that I could strike his left shoulder blade. My jab increased his momentum, causing him to move his left leg further than he had intended to maintain his balance. In doing so, he presented his entire back to me. I landed on one foot, and leapt again, striking him in the back with my foot.

Vigash fell heavily, but rolled, and in one motion rose and faced me. "Hah!" he shouted in triumph. "You are learning! Well done! Tomorrow, you will learn more, but now, you need food. Go with Brahms, and I will see you first thing tomorrow. First thing, Lady!"

As we strode towards the great hall, I could feel Brahm's barely contained excitement. "Out with it, man!" I demanded.

Brahms blushed and stammered. "My Lady, I have never seen such fighting! You and Vigash were blurs. Then, suddenly, one of you would lie on the ground for the merest moment. Then, you were at it again. And think, you threw Vigash! None have ever done this that I know. I am just amazed that I have seen such mighty warriors training. You are beyond anyone I have ever known."

Now, it was my turn to blush. "Master Vigash brings out my best. He is a wonderful instructor, and I can see why Prince William and Perseus value him so highly. He would be an inexorable force in battle."

When we arrived at the great hall, Talbot was awaiting us. "Greetings, Lady Gilraën. Please, sit with me and let us discuss how we will proceed after we have eaten." He nodded towards Brahms, who bowed and departed.

Instead of proceeding into the great hall, Talbot led me into a smaller room just off to the side. There were three smaller tables with chairs for six at each. There was a large, deep fireplace they used for cooking. Several large pots hung on iron hooks just within the mouth. Two large iron doors were to each side. Several women scurried about tending to the pots. One very large table stood across the fireplace with one smaller one at each end. As Talbot led me to the table closer to the fire, a woman opened one of the large iron doors to extract three large loaves of bread. A wonderful aroma filled the room. My stomach growled, and my mouth watered in anticipation.

I Came

"Master Talbot!" the round, red-faced woman exclaimed. "To what do we owe this honor? And who is this Elvin maid?"

He bowed, gallantly. "I thank you for your welcome, Bethea. This is Lady Gilraën, recently arrived here. Now, let me introduce Lady Gilraën to you." He turned to me. "Lady Gilraën, let me introduce you to the finest cook in all the lands of Jaralii: Bethea, maestra of the hearth." He spread his arms wide. "This is her realm, and we are here only because she permits it."

I stood and curtseyed. "Bethea, I ask if I may enter your realm."

Bethea laughed, shaking her finger at him. "Don't listen to this glib-tongued Sorcerer, My Lady. You are welcome at any time; it is he who must ask my permission!" She laughed again, "Bread? I have just taken a loaf from the oven. With butter, cheese and ale, it is a meal worthy of Prince William himself!"

She hurried off, and Talbot led me to a back table. Within moments, she set a freshly baked loaf, green cheese and amber ale before us. I reached for the loaf, but Talbot stopped me.

"Before you touch it, Lady, tell me about the loaf. Close your eyes, and search into the loaf with your mind. Tell me what you see."

I didn't know what he meant, but I still closed my eyes and concentrated on the bread. At first, all I could 'see' in my mind was the image of the bread lying on a board in front of me. But, as I considered it more closely, I began to sense something more. There was structure – bubbles! Even closer, the chemistry was different between the brown crust and the light center. I couldn't tell what the differences were, but they were obviously different. Even deeper, there were bodies… jillions of the tiniest cells… mostly within the bubbles. Weird!

"Ah!" Talbot interrupted me, disturbing my investigations and bringing my mind back to 'normal.' "You see? The world is not what it seems. There is much more to it, and you have just begun a journey into the depths of reality, natural forces, and so-called magic.

"I am pleased that you could see so deeply into the reality of the world about you," he continued. "Most Sensitives can't, at least at first. It usually takes time and training to achieve what you have done in just moments. But, then again, you are an Elf, and could progress to a far greater understanding of the forces of this world than can I.

"I am a Human, you see. I can shape the forces to my will, but it requires words of power and enervates me according to the power required to perform the task. Unlike Humans, you will be capable of perceiving the forces that exist and align your power with it. Therefore, you could become more powerful than any Sorcerer, myself included.

"Regardless, you must start somewhere in your quest for understanding. And, this is where I will begin. Let us eat of the loaf, and, while we do, consider the processes of eating. I want you to perceive the very essence of eating and digesting. I want you to see the breakdown of structure, both mechanical, and in the very constituents of the food that nourishes our bodies."

He tore off a chunk of the loaf and handed it to me. "Take a small bite. Chew it thoroughly while studying what is happening to it. Consider well your own processes as you eat, not just the chewing or the bread, but the processes of digestion occurring in your mouth."

I knew enough of biology to understand the enzymatic processes involved with the chemical breakdown of starch by the sputum generated by my cheeks, tongue and soft tissues of my mouth. Yet, until this time, I had never studied it as it occurred in my mouth. It was fascinating! I'd never 'seen' chemistry at work before, but there it was happening before my inner eye. My teeth mashed the spongy bread, mixing it thoroughly with my own spit. Long chains of starch split into tiny bits. Then, with a swallow, they were gone.

"WOW!" I exclaimed.

We ate mostly in silence, as I considered each bite. Somehow, this insight made the food taste even better as I watched and felt the food interacting with my taste buds. And, the differences between the soft solid of the bread, the creamy smoothness of the cheese and the aerated liquid of the ale were almost overwhelming. Then, when I combined two or all three ingredients in a single mouthful, it was almost ecstasy. I was overwhelmed by the wonderful intermix of flavors, tastes, textures and aromas. Never had I enjoyed food as much as I was at this moment.

When we finished, Talbot thanked Bethea, and we left. Instead, of heading back to the training fields, he brought me to a smallish room I could best describe as a chapel. I wondered about their religion. Did they have churches, and worship, and stuff like that?

Talbot led me to a small table. He sat on one side, facing me. "Now, before I send you to the Sorcerers for training, I must instruct you how to defend your own mind. All Sorcerers can perceive your bodily actions and reactions to interpret your mental state and your intentions. Most humans can also do this, but not to the degree Sorcerers can.

"The most adept among us can penetrate your active mind to detect your thoughts. Some of these thoughts are your preparation for mental or physical activity. Others of these thoughts are the detection of other's thoughts and actions, including the interpretation and conclusions upon which future actions depend. Essentially, they can picture what is uppermost in your mind at any moment. This gives the Sorcerer enormous advantages in any interaction with you.

"There is only one defense. You must learn to block such images and thoughts so that no Sorcerer, no matter what the circumstances, can perceive your mind. Before I loose you to your training, you must master these skills to protect your mind whether you are awake or asleep. Do you understand the need to acquire this skill?"

"Indeed, it is obvious. Back home, most of us have a basic, almost instinctual, understanding of other people's intentions. We use what are called mirror neurons to understand vicariously, explain and predict what others are about to do or doing. In reality, none of us can perceive other people's thoughts. If we could, it might lead to greater understanding or greater disputes, I'm not sure which. Regardless, it would change my world at a fundamental level. So, I can appreciate the problem, and I look forward to learning how to defend my mind from invasion."

"Good, let us begin. I will probe your mind, gently. I want you to find my probe and try to block it. Are you ready?"

After I had nodded, he stared at me, his eyes seeing far into the distance. I felt funny. There was an itch somewhere inside my head, almost like when my ears ring, but deeper. I searched for it, starting with my ears. But it wasn't there. It was deeper, so I followed it, finding a disturbance almost like an eddy. I homed in on it, considering it more closely. I compared it to the chaos of my mind, seeing it was different and foreign. I moved to block it, but found I didn't know how.

I struggled to determine how to block the eddy. My first thought was a shield. So, I pictured a shield and placed it between 'me' and the probe.

"Very good!" Talbot breathed.

I concentrated on the shield, making it larger, stronger and brighter to not only stop his probe, but reflect it on itself.

"Excellent!" he whispered. "Now, try this."

A second and then a third eddy appeared. I blocked them by expanding my shield.

"Excellent, try this."

A huge eddy swept into my mind. It encompassed my entire mind, pressing in upon me. I created a mental helmet surrounding and containing my entire consciousness. Then, I turned it into a burnished mirror with the power to reflect and deter the alien invasion.

"Superb!" Talbot exclaimed, withdrawing his probes.

I relaxed, my mind tired from its exertions. Then, WHAM! A huge force assaulted my mind. I collapsed onto the table, trying to muster the strength to recreate my helmet. But, the probes were relentless, torturing me, driving spikes into pain centers of my brain, further distracting me.

I screamed in pain. Yet, it was this release of my emotions that gave me just enough relief I was able to grasp the image of the helmet. With it came a modicum of relief, which I turned into a greater conviction in the strength and invulnerability of my protection. As my helmet grew in strength, the intrusion and its concomitant pain, weakened, and my resolve grew. I rebuilt the entire helmet and then, for the first time, intensified the reflection. I incorporated my resolve into the reflective energy, building a brightness that emanated from me. I threw my entire strength into the attack, finding the source and crushing it!

"Gilraën! Stop! You're killing me!"

Talbot's words penetrated my ears, despite my concentration. I looked up to see him sliding to the floor, blue in the face, gasping for air. I ceased my power output, relaxing my mind, while maintaining my defensive helmet.

Talbot lay on the floor, gasping for air. As the color returned to his face, he panted, "Enough!" He struggled back into his chair, leaning heavily on the table with his head in his hands. "Never has anyone abused me so thoroughly, especially a novice. I have always known that Elves had a superior grasp of magic, but I had never experienced one's power. Now, I understand."

He gathered his strength and sat upright. "Lady Gilraën, you have mastered me, and I am the strongest in Prince William's retinue. Guard your mind as you are now, but do it at all times.

"Tomorrow, you will begin training in more mundane, but nonetheless useful skills. You will need these skills to survive and to carry out your assignments on behalf of your prince.

"Now, I release you to Princess Cassandra's and Dame Eleanor's tender mercies. I warn you, theirs will be the harder lessons to learn. Come, let me guide you to your rooms."

When we arrived at my rooms, both Lady Cassandra and Lady Eleanor were awaiting me.

Rosie intervened before either could say a word. "Come now, it's time for you to get cleaned up, and then we'll get you dressed."

I was still mentally exhausted from my wrestling match with Talbot, so I didn't resist. Rosie led me to my gravy boat, and I just fell into the nice, hot water. After a vigorous scrubbing, I began to feel mostly Human… or Elf, or whatever. By that time, both Cassie and Ellie had joined me.

"So, how was your day?" Eleanor asked.

I started by describing my morning with Master Vigash. I built up the story slowly, describing each time the giant had thrown me. Then, I strung out the story of my awakening, my observation of his movements, and my prescience of his attack. I culminated the story with my one and only victory over the Master.

"You threw Vigash?" Cassandra exclaimed.

"Nobody's done that," Eleanor agreed.

"I know. That's when he dismissed me. But, he did say we'd start early tomorrow. So, I will need more of that green goop." I gave Cassandra my most appealing hang-dog look of sympathy, cracking her up.

"I see you've achieved the 'Pity' look. Now, tell us about Master Talbot."

"Ah," I stammered. "I still haven't figured it out."

"Oh?" Cassandra asked. "What has you puzzled?"

"He tested me, preparing for my instruction sessions with the Sorcerers. The first thing was looking at bread. He made me see into it, its structure and even its composition – down to and including the yeast."

"Ooh, I remember that," Eleanor replied. Cassandra nodded in agreement.

I found it hard to believe that they had undergone a similar experience, but this wasn't my world, and I really didn't know who or what these people were.

I continued, "Then, he attacked my mind."

Both women winced and glanced at each other as though sharing an unpleasant memory. "Go on," Cassandra said grimly.

"He started slowly, helping me to figure out what he was doing and helping me figure out how to protect myself. He built up in stages, making me build stronger defenses. Then, he attacked me with everything he had."

Both women were holding their breaths. They looked to each other empathetically. They nodded, and Eleanor nodded, saying, "Did he hurt you?"

"At first, but then I fought him off. I didn't know what I was doing, and if I hadn't heard him, I would have killed him. But, I heard him, and turned it off. He's OK now, but he's said I can go on with my training, as long as I protect my mind from them."

They both looked at her in awe and amazement. Cassandra exploded, "What? You almost killed him? What did you do?"

Eleanor sputtered, "First, you defeat Vigash, and then Talbot all in the same morning? Nobody's ever done either before you. It's no wonder you are exhausted.

"I remember when Talbot's predecessor trained us. It took me a half a moon before I could close my mind, but I could never beat them off. Finally, I just curled up like a prickleball. They couldn't penetrate beyond my spines, but I could do nothing other than defend myself."

"Me, too," Cassandra responded. "I could only hold out for a while, before they got in. It took me five or six rotations to build up the strength to defend my mind. I took a similar approach to Ellie, but I was a spiner. No matter how they attacked, I presented long, sharp spines. After a while, they gave up. I guess the spines were too much for them. But, throwing them off and attacking them was far beyond anything I could even imagine. So, what did you do?"

I shrugged. "I was a helmet, warding off the attacks. Then, I polished the helmet to reflect all the energy he was throwing at me. Then, once I had neutralized his attack, I added my own energy to the reflection. After that, I kept turning up the brightness until I heard him cry out that I was killing him.

"Really, I still don't know how I did it. At first, he almost crushed me. He stabbed me and hurt me. But, then, I blunted his attack. The more I blunted his, the more energy I had to defend myself. Finally, when I had overcome his attack, I just turned my energy on him, and it was all over. I just don't understand it or what I did."

Cassandra shook her head, as though trying to clear it. She and Eleanor exchanged glances and then sighed, as though they were reading each other's mind. Finally, as though coming to a hard-fought decision, Cassandra announced, "We're getting you dressed, and then we will introduce you to society. You will host a party here, tonight, for twenty of the most important women in Umbeqjaralii.

"Ellie and I have known these women all our lives. Some were like aunts to us; others were cousins; still more were nieces, but, you will see them with fresh eyes. You can ask them questions that we can't, because you're new. You don't know our customs, so they will forgive you for any errors of protocol. Just remember everything and don't let them into your mind. Remember who tries to probe you, and how they do it."

Eleanor added, "Let us each explore each other's mind. We will have to know each other's mind sense to distinguish it from other people's mind. Cassie and I know each other, but you know neither of us, nor we you."

Surprised at her revelations, I asked, "You mean you can perceive other people's minds? I didn't know you had any magic."

"We really don't. However, all our family is sensitive to magic. For instance, we know when someone is penetrating our consciousness, and we can counter it, although we're limited. We can also perceive other people's moods. We can't figure out what they're thinking, but we can feel their emotions. When coupled with our training in body language, we can usually understand what they're thinking and what they're planning, even if we're not sure why. Let me show you."

I retained my helmet, but reduced its reflectance to a dull matte. As Eleanor gazed into the distance, I felt the gentle touch of her magical mind.

"Good, I think I'll know you," I announced. "Now, let me touch yours." I reached out mentally, trying to locate her. Suddenly, there she was – a soft, gentle facade over an iron core. I reached, finding a ball covered with short, sharp spikes. Then I withdrew.

I Came

Eleanor blushed, "Oh, you're nice, but powerful. I'll recognize you."

"My turn," Cassie announced.

Almost instantly, I felt her. Unlike Eleanor, Cassandra was a needle, stabbing none too gently. I'd recognize her anywhere.

"You really do have a helmet!" she exclaimed. "I bounced off it like a ball of yarn off an iron plate."

"My turn!" I probed Cassandra, finding a dark maze. Within seconds, I was lost, but I learned her aura. I withdrew, announcing, "Got it."

Cassandra led the way to my wardrobe and began selecting clothes. As we assembled my garments, we discussed who would be there, their relationships, their likes and dislikes and everything they thought was relevant. And we discussed our plan of attack. If there was a traitor amongst them, we were sure we could find her.

Two hours later, we three were dressed to the nines. Looking in the mirror, I still couldn't believe it. The pudgy, gray-haired, middle-aged man that was me had disappeared. In my place was a woman of extraordinary beauty. If I hadn't known that this was just the image of an avatar, confined to this game and ending when it was over, I'm not sure how I'd handle it. As it was, it was still disturbing. The sooner I got home and returned to my life, the happier I would be.

So there I was, dressed in a long, silver gown that lifted my bosom indecently, hugged my waist and hips, and then flowed down about my ankles. I wore a sparkling white diamond necklace and earrings. My hair was up, exposing my diamond-shaped ears, long throat, and green eyes.

Cassandra was dressed similarly, but her gown was many shades of blue, fading in and out as she walked or moved. She wore the blue shimmering necklace and matching earrings. She too wore her hair up.

Eleanor wore a full gown that was pink and lavender. Unlike us, she wore her long hair down, but held back with silver barrettes above her ears. Her necklace and earrings were pink diamonds that sparkled brightly.

We also agreed as to our titles. Cassandra was a Princess, so needed no further title. Similarly, Eleanor was a Viscountess. But, what was I? My diamond-shaped ears declared I was a High Elf, but was I regal as well? We decided that the more snob appeal, the better, so I became 'Princess' Gilraën Gulámae of the Green Mountain-Maidstone Forest Elves, new allies with the kingdom. My title was more than a mouthful, but that was part of its cachet.

I ensconced myself in before a window on a two-person settee with Cassandra seated similarly to my left. A small table was behind us, decorated with a small lamp with an inverted glass bowl that reminded me of a Tiffany shade. There was no other furniture in the bay, forcing anyone introduced to us to stand somewhat awkwardly, the light shining in their faces, while our features were a cameo to them.

Beryl stood by the door, greeting the women as they arrived. Eleanor escorted them the length of the large room to bring them before us. Since this was a formal introduction of visiting royalty, they curtseyed deeply. Cassandra, as the mistress of the castle, held them in that subservient mode for just a heartbeat longer than demanded by protocol. She then addressed them informally, bidding them to rise, before introducing them to me.

I, of course, greeted them warmly, making suitable comments about them, their gowns or families, as I remembered snippets of what Cassandra and Eleanor had told me. Dorothea entered pushing a cart piled high with dishes of appetizers. Daisy followed close behind with another cart of glasses and bottles of vin, brews and distilled spirits. Rosie assisted the ladies, while Beryl arranged chairs and tables for our twenty guests.

After a suitable time, I began to circulate counterclockwise around the room, while Cassandra went the opposite direction. Eleanor buzzed back and forth, ensuring that everyone was both well fed and that their glasses were never empty. The girls were immensely busy, moving quickly, but not hastily, to ensure the comfort of our guests.

As I circulated, I asked about their positions, their homes and families. I asked about their friends and relations. I also inquired about their cares and difficulties, their problems and the joys they faced in this war. As they talked, I listened intently, as though each of them was the most important person in the world. I dragged the other women into the discussions, to compare and contrast the life situations they were experiencing and their hopes for the future.

As they talked, I could glimpse their minds. Most, it seemed, were just as they appeared. Universally, they embellished their experiences and their positions. Yet all were suffering. Many had lost family members; some their sons, and a few, a daughter. They cloaked their sadness behind facades of joy, yet each felt hopelessness creeping into their hearts, a weakening of their resolve, even though they were sternly and resolutely devoted to Prince William and King Richard.

One mind seemed different. Her mind was well guarded. She sought out other minds, trying not to touch them, while learning everything she could. I felt her try to touch mine. It was as delicate as a feather floating on a zephyr. Regardless, I felt it, and I knew who was trying to touch my mind.

In spite of my sure knowledge of her mental invasion, I resisted the temptation to confront her. Instead, I continued to chatter and gossip with the noble ladies of the court, discussing both the important and the trivial, laughing and sharing, eating and drinking.

I felt Cassandra's mind touch mine, but I didn't dare to weaken my helmet, lest that woman touch my mind. Instead, I wandered towards Rosie to whisper, "Ask Eleanor to join me at her leisure." Rosie meandered through the throng, carrying dishes to the cart. As she passed Eleanor, she stopped, whispered in the Viscountess' ear, and proceeded in her duties.

Eleanor wandered in my direction and then followed me towards the woman who was searching minds. As we approached, Eleanor introduced us. "Princess Gilraën, let me introduce you to Baroness Isadora Phaed. Her husband is Master Richmond, with whom you will train in the next few days. Baroness Phaed, let me reintroduce Princess Gilraën Gulámae. Princess Gilraën is training with us to learn our ways before her Tribe arrives."

I could feel the Baroness gulp and felt her twinge in alarm. As she curtseyed, I nodded my head, and then asked her about her children, even though I knew she had none. I committed one or two other minor faux pas before moving on to talk with the next group. Before we arrived, I whispered, "She's a spy. She's very good, but I felt her."

Eleanor looked querulously at me. "You sure?" she whispered.

I nodded and then approached the next group.

Several hours later, the ladies began to depart. They as tired of this forced protocol as was I. Only when Beryl had closed the door behind the last of them did I finally relax, flopping down into a large chair in the alcove next to the fireplace. "I'm bushed," I declared.

"Bushed?" Cassandra asked.

I smiled, and explained, "Tired. But we did learn something."

Cassandra looked up, her head slightly askew.

"Yes, Cassie," Eleanor gushed, "Gilraën felt Isadora prying into minds." She nodded emphatically.

"Freddie Richmond's wife? How interesting. I wonder if they are both Sorcerers, or if she's a Truth Seeker?" Cassandra continued, "Regardless, we have to tell William. We can't let either Richmond or Isadora know what we know. That means we must be prepared. I will tell William and Talbot. They will determine our response."

That night, my mind was awhirl. I tossed and turned, certain that I'd never get to sleep. Of course, I was wrong. Rosie awoke me early and helped me dress for another vigorous day. Brahms met me at the door and escorted me to the great hall. Although there were places for them at the head table, I didn't see Cassandra or Eleanor.

"Gilraën!" Harold called. "Come sit with the archers." Several others grinned and waved to me.

It was an invitation I couldn't ignore. Within moments, we were enjoying our morning meal, talking about important things. We talked about the different materials used for bows. All of us had started with wood, and I was still using it, although I didn't know what kind of tree it was. Many had opted for horn. There was much to say in its favor. Such bows were stronger, more durable and with a powerful pull that could send an arrow a long distance. However, they could not withstand immersion in water. Others preferred a compound bow, primarily made from spring steel, and strung through pulleys. They were very powerful, but complicated, with very long bowstrings that were more prone to wear. Still others preferred crossbows. They were also powerful, but slow to load and shoot.

Of course, a bow is worthless without arrows. Such shafts had to be light but strong. Fletching was critical for the proper flight. Long arrows with multiple fletchings flew very far, but tended to float, making accuracy at range nearly impossible. Crossbows had a reputation for their accuracy and impact over short distances, but their bolts were notoriously inaccurate at long ranges. Straight bows and recurves, such a mine, required a strong archer. They also had a high initial impulse that bent the shaft of the arrow, causing it to wobble in flight, again, reducing accuracy. Compound bows had a smoother action, but their slower speed of firing made them less suitable in battle, where quantity of arrows in a volley was often more important than quality of individual shots.

We were deep in technical discussion, when Talbot and Brahms appeared at my side. Talbot said, "It is time for you to attend Master Vigash. You know how he hates to be kept waiting."

I thanked my newfound friends and asked, "This afternoon then?"

They all smiled and waved, excited about our training session.

"My Lady," Talbot whispered. "We have considered your discovery. When you attend the Sorcerers this afternoon, be wary. Protect your mind, but do not attack with it. You must not make anyone aware of your power. You should only show that you are protecting you mind, as one would expect of an Elf."

"Ah, yes, about that," I replied, "I must also attend archery practice this afternoon. I am thinking I might have a loyal following, which I may be able to rely upon in the future. I think it will be important to encourage this relationship."

"If that is your desire, My Lady, then I will arrange for archery training later this morning. However, your training with the Sorcerers will take all afternoon. So, enjoy your time with Master Vigash, but don't tire yourself."

I laughed. "I am training with Master Vigash. How can I not tire myself?"

* * *

"Ah! You have arrived, Lady." Vigash's voice rang out. "Take a few moments to prepare yourself before we begin." With that, he led me through five minutes of intense warm-ups.

"Now, let us begin," he announced.

I thought I was prepared. Once again, I was wrong. He had changed his style and was using techniques more akin to judo or karate. When combined with his great power and speed, I found myself flat on my back, time and time again. When he was finished with me, I was thoroughly exhausted.

Harold and the rest of the archers were sitting, watching Vigash annihilate me. As I limped off, he shouted, "That's why we use bows, Gilraën!" They all had a really good laugh.

In spite of myself, I grinned. "Indeed, and well said, Harold. My friends, let us let fly!"

For the next hour, we enjoyed firing at a variety of targets. Since we had already shown that we could hit stationary targets, our training involved movement. We fired at moving targets and learned the processes of leading our mark. Then we were moving while firing at stationary targets. Finally, we were moving, and the targets were moving, albeit in straight lines. This exercise even taxed me. Finally, we ran an obstacle course, firing at moving targets that popped up for brief intervals, as though firing at us. When we finished this obstacle course, we were tired and hungry.

I accompanied 'my' archers to the great hall for our mid-day meal. Along the way, a huge mass of men-at-arms, also heading for their meal, joined us. They looked tired and bruised. Although most of them paid us but a glance, several fellows began to berate us. At first, I thought it was good-natured rivalry between infantry and light artillery branches. However, it rapidly devolved into outright hostility. One particularly large and ugly brute became more obdurate and abusive. As we arrived at the gates, he and a few equally large fellows muscled us aside, forcing my archers to the side so that they could pass into the hall before us. One of them back-handed Harold, knocking him to the ground and bloodying his mouth.

In a flash, I was beside their leader. I struck him once in the ribs and then kicked the next man in his chest. Before the next two could react, I dropped them with sharp blows to their ribs, being careful not to kill them, but to make sure they would be in pain for the next few days. Then, before anyone else could intervene, I pushed several of the soldiers aside and held the doors for my archers to enter. It had all happened in just a matter of seconds, and few saw what had happened.

Several of us helped Harold to his feet and guided him to our table. The huge mass of foot soldiers followed us. As they found their seats, the rumor of what had happened spread amongst them. Several of the men growled angry threats, leading to ever more provocative pronouncements regarding how they would take their revenge on the archers once I had gone.

I was determined not to let my archers suffer on my account. As William and Talbot entered the hall, I hurried to meet them, determined to head off any trouble. But William had already learned of the harassment we had suffered.

"Lady Gilraën, please join us. I fear that some of my men-at-arms have not learned to work and play well with others." He laughed, saying, "Others from your world have explained to me the kindergarten. I think such an analogy applies."

When we arrived at the head table, William remained standing, forcing everyone else in the hall to remain on their feet. He looked out over the throng, a fatherly expression of disapproval on his face. "We are facing an implacable enemy who is intent on our destruction. You have volunteered to defend our kingdom from this enemy. Each of you has passed the test provided for you, and each of you has agreed to the contract between you and this kingdom. Each of you is being paid for your services according to that contract.

And, each of you will face the enemy, hoping to achieve honors and distinction, as well as the prospects of great wealth. I encourage you in achieving these goals.

"However, the enemy is not in this hall. You are MY army, each and every one of you. MY generals will lead you. MY captains will command you. MY Sorcerers will defend you.

"I will not have any more displays such as happened earlier. You," he pointed at the mass of men in the middle of the hall, "are men-at-arms. It is your task to engage the enemy, in force, and, by so doing, defeat them."

He pointed to the archers' table. "They are MY archers." He pointed again. "They are MY slingers." He pointed again and again. "They are MY spearmen, and they are MY javeliners. Each of you has an important part to play in the battles ahead.

"I will not have you fighting among yourselves. I will not have you act on the behalf of our enemies, by attacking and destroying the other disciplines of my army. Any man found to be in violation of this simple directive will be punished. I hope I have made myself understood. If I haven't, please speak to your captain, who will help you understand more clearly."

Harold looked at me and barely stifled a grin. All the archers were staring into their plates, trying desperately not to laugh out loud. Their inadequate attempts at solemnity were almost too much for me, and I could barely contain myself. Suddenly, Talbot appeared at my side, scaring the crap out of me once again. "Shit! Will you stop sneaking up on me?"

"Sorry, My Lady."

He didn't look sorry. "This afternoon, your instructor will be Master Richmond. Go with Brahms and remember to defend yourself at all times."

Harold was about to ask about me protecting myself, but Brahms interrupted. "Lady, we must leave now if we are to arrive on time."

I looked at the food, which was just arriving at the tables. I grabbed a mug of ale and two of what looked like some kind of

I Came

vegetable plus a slice of bread. I gulped the last of my meal, drank the last quarter of my ale, and then handed the mug to Brahms.

We hurried to a stretch of forest northwest of the castle. Two robed and hooded men stood before seven warriors. As I joined the others, the taller of the two men removed his hood. "This afternoon, you will begin your training in various elements of extra-normal activities, often called magic by the unversed. As you will discover, you are simply channeling elemental forces to perform work that would otherwise be arduous, causing you to expend more time or energy than is desirable.

"These forces do not exist in all times or places. Therefore, you must learn to sense these forces to utilize them when you are in need. Then, by using words of power, you can focus your mind on bending these forces to your will to accomplish your goals.

"We will begin by developing your ability to sense the forces around you. You will sit quietly concentrating on nothing. You will attempt to observe everything around you. Now, sit quietly, open your mind, and stretch your mind outward to sense everything around you."

We sat quietly on the forest floor. I relaxed and began to open my mind, but the moment I did, I felt the others touching my consciousness. Instantly, I projected my helmet, but made it matte black to absorb rather than reflect their minds, simultaneously reaching out, listening with my mind to the emptiness around me.

But then, it wasn't empty. Huge, massive objects were all about me. The noise of their existence obliterated any consideration of the world outside our circle. I felt like an astronomer on Earth when the brilliant background of light pollution obliterates his sight of the stars.

I had to move away from the others, if I was to perceive the tiny specs of life nearby. I walked deeper into the wood until I had could barely feel the others. There, I sat, contemplating the world around me. Tiny creatures lived in the soil, in the air, on the ground, on the trees… everywhere! I'm not sure if there were ants on this planet, but there were critters in the dirt. There were flying insect-like things. There was a huge monster leaping from bough to bough above me. Even the long, slow lives of the trees seeped into my consciousness.

A huge presence entered my sphere. I tried to determine who it was only by his chi. He was not one a novice... nor was he Richmond. Therefore, he had to be the other robed man. I pondered whether he was a Sorcerer or just an observer. Then I felt his mental probe. It was just a waft, barely detectable, but it was there. I opened my eyes.

He was a man about middling height, with heavy jowls, a massive nose, and drooping lids. His voice was sonorous. "It is not wise to wander the wood alone. There are beings who might do you harm. Even Elves are not impervious to the vicissitudes of life."

"Advice, or a warning?" I asked.

He shrugged. (I wondered if the shrug was universal among humanoids.) "The meaning is yours to derive, My Lady. I merely inform." He stood aside, beckoning with his arms toward the others.

I submitted, ambling towards the others at my own pace. As I approached the others, I could feel the novices, but both the robed men were gray ghosts against a murky background. Yet, I had felt the probes from both Sorcerers and would recognize them in the future.

The taller one whispered, "I see you found her, MacGregor."

"Indeed, Richmond, she was not far."

"May I have your attention!" Baron Richmond announced. "You have been contemplating your surroundings for half the afternoon. What have you discovered?"

The first man described very little. In fact, of them all, only one seemed to have experienced the world around them. He talked about the birds, and the squirrels, and even some insects.

"Excellent, Rodriguez." He turned to me. "And you?"

I described everything I had experienced from the smallest crawling thing in the soil to the larger animals and birds. I described the life of the trees, the grass, and the even the moss growing on the rocks. I described the very air and its currents. I did *not* describe the weft and warp of the forces of the world, or of its interactions with the beings that inhabited it. To me, it was an emulation of Einstein's space-time hypothesis.

"Well done, Lady Gilraën," Master Richmond extolled, "but, of course, you are an Elf. No doubt, you have greater insights into the magic of this world. Master Talbot had informed me that you might, so we prepared to accelerate your training program."

He looked toward MacGregor. "I will work with Lady Gilraën to advance her skills. You will work with the others."

MacGregor nodded, replying curtly, "It will be my pleasure."

Richmond turned to me and asked, "Lady Gilraën, if you would accompany me?"

He led me some distance away, to a small clearing. "Walk to the copse and back, Lady Gilraën."

I thought his request was inane, but strode quickly to the grove of trees. As I was about to arrive, Richmond stepped out, and said, "Please, walk back."

I turned, only to see him standing where I had started. It took me but a few moments to return, but by that time, Richmond had disappeared.

"Here!" Richmond cried out.

I turned to the sound of his voice. He had returned to the copse.

I was stunned. How had he done it? I lifted my voice to call to him, but he was gone…then, he was standing at my side.

"It is a simple matter, called the 'long stride' or 'Sorcerer's Walk.'

"Consider how you walk… or, more importantly, how you run. You step off with one foot. Then, for some few moments, you float through the air. Then, you alight on the other foot to spring ahead, repeating your action, as you float to the other foot.

"The 'long stride' simply increases the distance between footsteps. You can cover much more ground with the same effort. It's done in multiples. You think of your normal stride length and then double it… or treble it. Obviously, the greater the multiple, the faster you can move.

"The process is simple to explain, but requires concentration and directed energy. You call upon the energy with the word, *fugitos*. *Fugitos* simply gathers the energy. You must focus your mind to direct your energy into increasing the duration between your steps. That is, you wish to float over the land, alighting only to renew your speed.

"Concentrate on increasing your stride. Speak *fugitos* and run, trying to increase the distance between footsteps. Proceed to the copse and return."

I looked towards the trees. They were a good hundred yards away. Normally, it'd take me fifteen seconds or longer to get there. Of course, that estimate was as an overweight, middle-aged man. As an Elf, it might take me seven or eight seconds, and perhaps fifty paces.

I concentrated on my feet, uttered *fugitos*, and leapt ahead. I thought about lengthening my stride, leaping and bounding over the uneven ground. Then I felt my mind being invaded. It was gentle, and had I been concentrating harder and had not felt it before, I would have missed it. But it was unmistakable.

Richmond was contacting my mind!

For the briefest of moments, I lost concentration. Before I could do anything, I fell head over heels, bouncing along like tumbleweed in a gale. Battered and bruised, I looked up to see that I had arrived at the copse.

Richmond was staring down at me. "I tried to warn you, Gilraën, but you were concentrating, and you didn't hear me. Are you all right?"

My brain was scrambled. My back ached. My ankle hurt. And someone was probing my mind. I erected my helmet, but something was buzzing in my brain.

'*Concentrate*!' I shouted at myself. Slowly, my consciousness responded, and my mental helmet strengthened. The buzzing decreased. I opened my eyes to see Richmond scowling in concentration. '*What is he doing?*' I wondered.

I Came

Talbot suddenly appeared beside Richmond. They stared at each other for just a moment, before Talbot stepped to my side. "Lady Gilraën, are you all right?" He knelt beside me, a look of concern on his face.

"I think so. I was running and fell. I was a bit woozy, but doing better, thank you. How did you get here so quickly?"

"Richmond called me when you fell. A fall from *fugitos* can be dangerous. Even experienced speed walkers are afraid of falling. Now, let me examine you."

I lowered the strength of my helmet, permitting Talbot to examine me. At his very first touch, I knew it had not been him that had been scanning me. I relaxed just a tad to let him examine me. Then, having given him just a moment, I increased my defenses, shutting him out.

He turned to Richmond, "You were correct to call me. She is an Elf, so scanning her mind is difficult at all times. I agree with you that she may have suffered a concussion, so we should discontinue any more training today." He turned to me. "Come with me, Lady. It is important that you relax and to ensure that you are not injured." We walked away, cutting through a wood and across the edge of a field.

"Hey! Gilraën! Join us."

I looked around to see Harold and the rest of the archers firing at a maze of moving targets.

"Come on; see if you can hit them!"

I glanced at Talbot, who nodded. He joined me as I walked over to the firing line. They quickly surrounded me and introduced me to the problem. Seven targets were weaving between each other. As they weaved, they also bobbed up and down. Not only were the targets fast, but they were small. It was hard to see them, never mind follow their intricate dance.

"We're supposed to hit their bulls-eyes," Harold informed me. "So far, Yashi is the best, and he's only hit two."

The large, oriental archer smiled. "Ai! But, I await your attempt, Lady Gilraën."

I reached for my bow and strung it, while I watched the movement of the targets. After a few moments, it seemed to make sense. There was a pattern…a complex one to be sure, but a pattern. I removed six arrows stabbing each into the ground in front of me. Taking up my stance, I nocked a seventh arrow and pulled the string until my thumb touched my ear and the string touched my lip. Sighting the first target, I loosed the arrow. As quickly as I could, I nocked the second, and the third. Within four seconds, I had fired them all.

Harold whooped, Yashi groaned, and the other ten archers fell to the ground laughing. There were general choruses of congratulations as coins changed hands. Harold crowed, "I told you not to bet against her!"

I looked toward the targets. One arrow stuck in the center of all seven of them. Even I was amazed.

"We have to celebrate," Harold declared. "We need wine! Come on, Gilraën! Time's a wasting."

Even Talbot smiled. Again, I glanced at him, and he nodded. "Go ahead. I hear that vin is good for concussions, but not too much vin. If you are meeting Vigash tomorrow morning, you must be physically prepared, not impaired. I will leave you in good hands."

We did. And I did. However, everyone joined in with us, and it ended up being one huge party, regardless of whether it was archer, slinger, man-at-arms, or whatever. What a party!

I retired to my rooms, feeling no pain. That was to come in the morning. However, as I drifted towards sleep, I felt another mind probing me. I struggled against the effects of alcohol, winning the battle of wills. Yet, I almost recognized the feeling. Instead, I fell into a troubled sleep.

* * * * *

I Came

Chapter 4 – Sorcerer's Walk

My stomach was rejecting my entire body. My brain tried to function, but my stomach took precedence. Between the dry heaves and the headaches, I was just plain miserable. Even the thought of wine made my stomach lurch.

Rosie was no help. She just laughed, and said, "Serves you right." She offered me a cup of hot thrak.

I sipped it hesitantly at first, uncertain how my stomach would react. Then, I took a larger gulp, as my stomach seemed to settle, and my head began to clear. "Hmmm!' I hummed. "That's great. I could be a billionaire if I could import this back home."

Rosie laid out my clothes, preparing to help me don my armor. I gulped down another cup of thrak and readied myself for the day. The prospect of food turned my stomach, but another sip of thrak calmed it. By the time I got to the great hall, I was almost feeling Human. Oops… feeling Elvish, if this is what Elves feel like.

Harold looked terrible as he waved to me. His eyes were bloodshot, and he looked as though he were ill. I glanced at the other archers. They looked no better. I joined them for just a moment, and whispered, "Thrak! Hot thrak!"

I went on to the head table to join Eleanor and Cassandra, who were deep in conversation. As I sat down, Eleanor asked, "Are you sure about Isadora?"

I wasn't ready for this. My body had recovered, but my mind was still a spongy mass worthless for anything other than keeping my ears from collapsing inward on each other. I reached for the green oyes and purple bhar. I chuckled to myself as I thought, *Green eggs and ham.*

"Isadora?" I asked.

"Yes," Cassandra emphasized. "You felt her trying to enter your mind? And then you felt Richmond doing the same thing. Could they be spies?"

"How should I know?" I replied. "I felt both of them touch my mind, but they could easily explain it. Richmond was trying to warn me I was speed walking into a tree. He might have even saved my life. As for his wife, it was just a touch. It didn't feel malicious or anything like that. It may not have been deliberate. Remember, I'm new at this, so I could be mistaken. I can say that neither of them felt malevolent."

Eleanor reiterated, "But, they both tried to enter your mind."

I had to admit they were right, but I couldn't go much further. I was just too new at this. I didn't have the experience or knowledge, and I knew I had no control of my own abilities, other than prevent someone from entering my mind. I really needed to know more about my abilities to understand what I was feeling, how this whole thing worked, and how to figure out what was what.

"I think I'd like to talk with Talbot," I replied. "He might be able to help me learn how to use this ability, how to control it, and how to understand what I am experiencing. Do you think he'd help me?"

Cassandra nodded her head. "I'm not sure. He's devoted himself to William's protection, so seldom leaves his side. I'll have to ask."

"OK. I've got to get to training. Master Vigash hasn't had the pleasure of pummeling me in a whole rotation. I'm sure he's missed me and is eager to try out some new form of hand-to-hand combat. So, if you will excuse me, I'm off to be tortured by an expert." I smiled ruefully, rose, and left the hall.

I was a bit on the late side, so I used the long stride of the Sorcerer's Walk. Remembering to attend to the road ahead of me, I concentrated on lengthening my stride as I concentrated on the command *fugitos*. The world flashed by in my peripheral vision, while my sight seemed to extend into the far distance. I could readily perceive objects, but my speed blurred them. Within seconds, I saw Vigash' training grounds, stopped thinking '*fugitos*,' and deliberately slowed to a walk.

"Holy shit!" a man shouted, as I appeared at his side.

Vigash looked up, appearing to be sanguine at my sudden appearance. "'Bout time," he mumbled. "Come. Today, you will learn the most advanced techniques I know. If you can master these skills, you will be a match for any man, Dwarf, Orc, or Elf. You might even hold your own against a Krell, at least for a few moments. However, a Troll will still overpower you, a Krell will wear you down, and either a dragon or a Gaunt will eat you first and worry about your fighting skills later.

"Today, I will use three different fighting techniques: Dwarf, Orc and Elf. Each has great strengths and few weaknesses. I will also attempt to instruct you regarding Krells. So, let us begin."

With that, he led me to a more secluded glen, roughly a half-mile on each side. For the first hour, he fought me using the Dwarf fighting style. It was very different. Somehow, Vigash seemed to become a mere four feet tall. He wasn't really, but it was a mystifying visualization.

I thought that against a Dwarf, I might have an advantage of height. It was, but it wasn't. As a Dwarf, he could attack my legs, while I could only strike down at his massive head and neck. At first, Vigash threw me easily, demonstrating their 'kill' blows.

Then, while still maintaining his diminutive aspect, he switched his style to that of the Orcs. Although there were similarities to that of the Dwarves, it was sufficiently different to be distinct.

Finally, Vigash assumed a thinner and more agile aspect, and fought as an Elf. These techniques were totally different. Instead of taking advantage of their lower center of gravity, and great strength versus weight, the Elfish techniques used quickness and agility.

Regardless of the technique, Vigash dropped me to the ground with ridiculous ease. However, with his patient instruction, I gradually learned the disparate techniques and how to overcome them.

"Now, Gilraën, let us combine all these different techniques – Human, Dwarf, Orc and Elf – into a single fighting system that you will use both to defend yourself and to inflict great harm on others, regardless of race. Let us begin."

For the next hour, Vigash humiliated me repeatedly. His ability to change his apparent size and his distribution of weight combined with his array of fighting skills was devastating. I hardly knew when or how he was attacking me, or how to defend myself, never mind how to overcome him.

Finally, Vigash stopped and raised his hand, palm to me. "Enough for today. You have done well. Consider what I have taught you. Learn in your sleep, tonight. Tomorrow, you will do better. Go, now, and eat. You will have a very full training session later today."

I was exhausted. I wasn't sure whether I was still suffering from last night's debauchery, or whether it was the effects of the fighting just to stay alive, but whichever, I was too pooped to pop.

"Hey! Gilraën!"

I looked up to see Harold, Yashi and the other archers making their way towards the road. I waved, wearily, in welcome.

"You look tired, Gilraën," Harold continued. "I didn't know Elves got tired. What have you been doing?"

I chuckled at Harold's cheery repartee. "I have been Master Vigash's plaything. He enjoys finding novel ways to smash me into the ground. Then, he carefully instructs me on how to avoid and counter him. But, does he let me? No! Instead, he formulates ever new and different ways to batter the defenseless dirt with my body."

"Ah, we have heard of him. Mostly, we've been told to avoid him. Master Drammon and his acolytes are more than any of us can handle. They are so good that we picture them upon our targets. That's why we are so good at hitting them." He laughed uproariously at his own joke, which also tickled the funny bones of the rest of the archers.

By the time we'd arrived at our table, I had recovered somewhat, but was more than ready for food. I had begun to appreciate the quality and quantity of the food served to us. Not only did it appeal to my taste buds, but it seemed to supply far more energy than did food back home. I mentioned it to the archers, who agreed with me. We began to discuss exactly what kinds of meats, vegetables or baked products they were. Like them, I knew only a few names, and none of their origins. I thought I'd ask Dorothea what they were.

I Came

As we were about to leave, Talbot appeared at my side. "A word, My Lady?"

When I removed my heart from my throat and put it back where it belonged, I said, "Sure. What's up?"

Talbot's face assumed a question. "I am uncertain. The roof? The sky? The stars? I suppose it would depend upon one's point of view."

I laughed, replying, "Sorry, Talbot, it's an expression we use. It's a general reply, asking for the reason we should speak."

He nodded his understanding. "Princess Cassandra suggested you wished to speak with me regarding additional training. Prince William has agreed that this would be desirable. I ask when you will be available. I do suggest that it not be on the same day that you train with Master Vigash." He smiled wryly.

I laughed. "I would if I could. However, Master Vigash enjoys pummeling me so much that I will be training with him for the foreseeable future. Therefore, I suggest that we find a break in my training schedule. Perhaps, in the evenings, if that is suitable?"

"Tonight, then. Let us meet at Bethea's kitchen for supper. After we have eaten, we will attend to my study."

"Good! A short afternoon. After today's workout with Master Vigash, I could stand a break. See you then, and thank you."

Talbot bowed. "It will be my pleasure," he replied and left.

Again, I speed walked to the training area. I was getting much better at this. It was wearying, and required concentration, but it was fast.

Master Richmond greeted me upon my arrival. "Well done, Lady. I see you are becoming more accomplished. I do hope you've learned to avoid solid objects." His eyes twinkled.

"Yes, at least so far. Seeing ahead is both better and worse. I can see further, but everything is a blur. Is that how it works?"

"Yes, and no," he nodded. "It would seem to be a property of seeing. The faster one walks, the further ahead one sees, but it blurs the details. However, with practice, one can see moderately well. And, for Elves, that is typically better than normal Human eyesight."

Light dawned on marble head! Of course! It was an application of Doppler Effect. If I was going faster, the light would appear to shift toward the blue end of the spectrum.

But that wasn't right, either. Such red/blue shifts only occurred at high relativistic speeds. Even at a ten-fold speed walk, I only ran at about 200 miles per hour. Pilots routinely fly at several thousand miles per hour without impairing their vision.

Richmond continued. "Since you need to practice the Sorcerer's Walk, I will arrange for you to work with Master Norton. His specialty is the speed walk. He can instruct you in its intricacies far better than can I. Instead, we will try this."

As I stood there, watching him, he simply faded from sight. I was astounded. "Where are you, Master Richmond? What are you doing?"

Just as he had disappeared, he gradually reappeared exactly where he had been standing. "Again, this is an application of a command that distorts and controls energy to accomplish your goal. Your goal is to bend the light around you. In that way, anyone trying to see you will only see the light emanating from behind you. It's not that you are invisible, or that light does not reflect from you, but is a case in which you are in a bubble. The bubble reflects within it, while it refracts the light from behind you around you.

"The command is '*Divergio lepto.*' While you command, you concentrate on bending the light around you. Remember the exemplar of the bubble while you are doing this. Create a prism in your mind to bend the light. Now, do not be concerned if you don't succeed at first. This is very difficult. At first, until you have learned to channel the energy, it will also be very tiring.

"Are you ready? Then let us begin. *Divergio lepto.* Think prism, bending the light from behind you to before you."

I stood for several minutes simply trying to sense the lines of force Talbot had discussed in Bethea's kitchen. I seemed to understand that if I could align myself with them, *Divergio lepto-ing* would be easier. However, I couldn't quite feel them. They were at the edge of my consciousness, but just out of reach.

I was concerned about the effects of my 'helmet.' Was it interfering with my ability to sense the energy fields enwrapping the planet? I reduced the strength of my helmet, feeling the planet's energy increase. I eased off again, and again, until I could perceive the Doppler Effect.

'*Gotcha!*' I thought. Slowly, I stretched the lines of energy around me. I could sense the photons following the force lines as though they were pipes.

But then, I felt a consciousness impinging upon my own. Instantly, I raised my defenses.

"Well done, Lady Gilraën," Richmond exclaimed. "You had faded completely. That is great! I've never seen anyone do it so completely at the first attempt. How do you feel? Such an effort can be enervating, almost debilitating. You must learn how to use the energy to your advantage, so it doesn't exhaust you. Ultimately, you will need to disappear while speed walking, detecting others around you to either defend yourself or destroy your enemies. But, that will take a lot of time and practice. Now, can you fade again? Let's give it another try."

Oddly, I felt surprise and concern in Richmond's aura. I had presumed that I'd feel something more malevolent. The fact that I didn't raised more questions than answers. In fact, those emotions seemed to reflect his expressed feelings. I was confused.

Putting that aside, I tried to concentrate on the lines of force. It was a lot easier this time, since I knew what I was seeking. I reached out to them and bent them around me. I could sense the flow of the photons, to adjust the refractive index of the space about me and correlate the effects. It was just that I couldn't determine if I had 'faded' from sight or not.

Trying to hold my concentration, I looked toward Richmond. He was staring at me. So, I moved at an angle from him. His eyes didn't move. He couldn't see me. But then, his head turned towards me.

"Can you see me?" I asked.

"Gilraën, I can sense you, but I can't see you. I can hear you, but not clearly. If you want to be heard, you must speak more clearly. Try to concentrate on your words."

I did. "How is this?"

"That's better. Very good. Now, move about a bit, and try to see what's going on around you. Generally, it's hard to see properly when you are bending light. Concentrate very hard to detect what's going on around you."

He hesitated as I moved further around him and farther away. I could only see a blurry image of him, somewhat like looking through the bottom of a bottle. I could see a something, but not what it was.

"Good! Great! Well done. Now, I'm sure you are having difficulties seeing objects. They are all blurred and distorted. You need to reach out with your mind to sense what it is and to obtain a mental image of the things around you.

"Remember your training. Reach out and sense the world around you. Feel the things around you. Sense what they are and try to picture it in your mind."

I tried to sense the world around me, but it was still a blur. I did feel him standing off at an angle from me, but I couldn't see his features. There was a tall thing somewhat behind him, but it was muted against the background. There was a live something in the distance, but it was too far to recognize what it was.

He moved off to my right. "Can you see me?"

I nodded, trying not to lose my concentration.

"Gilraën, are you all right? Talk to me!"

I felt deep concern emanating from his direction. It didn't feel like him, but I was in a Bernoulli warp, and I couldn't be sure of my senses.

"Yes, I'm well. I'm trying to figure out what's around here. I can see a shape I think is you. Is there a tree behind your right shoulder?" I could see the blob I assumed was him turn.

"Yes," he replied. "Does this mean you can see the area?"

I Came

"No. I see blobs and sense feelings. I can see a blob that is where I perceive a consciousness. I assume that's you. I see a tall, thin thing that has no sensation other than life. So, I figure it's a tree. And, there is a something way off over there." I pointed and then realized he couldn't see me. "Ah, it's way off behind you over your right shoulder."

The blob moved. "Yes, MacGregor is over there teaching a class, but he's a distance away. Can you really sense him?

"MacGregor!" he yelled. "Wave your hand."

I considered the distant blob. It moved and wobbled a bit. "It moved," I said.

"Well done, Lady Gilraën. MacGregor is fifty paces away. That's a very long distance to see a blob. Now, tell me if you are getting tired."

I considered myself for a moment. I was tired. I released the energy, and... fainted!

* * *

"Gilraën! Awaken!"

I heard the voice in my mind rather than my ears. It was a familiar voice, but I had trouble placing it. I began to raise my mental defenses, but stopped when I realized it was Talbot.

I fought my way to consciousness. Opening my eyes, I saw both Talbot and Richmond standing over me. I felt their concern – genuine worry.... and not a whit of malice.

I decided a bit of subterfuge was in order. I groaned, "My head! It's exploding!" With that I loosed my control and invaded both Talbot's and Richmond's minds. I felt them react to block my unexpected probe, but, in that instant, I knew that neither of them were my enemies. Of course, that didn't rule out Isadora, but it seemed less likely since she was married to Richmond.

I cleared my mind, restoring my 'helmet,' which also blocked my mental probe. "Ah, that is better." I looked back and forth to them, asking, "What happened?"

"My Lady," Richmond replied, "you fainted. You are not used to such challenges. Once you released the command, your mind relaxed and returned to the real world. Without the power of the energy to support you, you collapsed."

"Just relax here for a moment," Talbot advised. "Then, we will return to the hall and seek sustenance. Such endeavors drain your bodily energy. You need to eat. It is a condition of magic.

"Magic, as it exists in this world, consumes energy. You must work to command the energy needed to perform an action. The energy resists your attempts to change it. The energy needed to change it comes from the magician, namely you. Thus, even though you are an Elf with greater reserves than most, you will drain your bodily energy. It is only a matter of time. The good part is that as you become more accustomed to performing a command, the less energy it will take, and the longer you can go before you need food.

"But, that is not the case at this time. Right now, you need to eat. Let me help you to rise." He extended his hand, which I grasped. "Now let me lead you to the hall."

Within the blink of an eye, we were standing at the door of the great hall. "How did you do that?" I asked.

He smiled. "It is just another skill. It requires the same energy it would take for me to carry you here, but is much faster. However, it is exhausting. So, I will leave you here with Prince William, while I visit with Bethea."

I walked into the hall to see William beckon to me, pointing to the chair beside him. When I sat, he asked, "How was your day, Lady? I understand that it was eventful."

I was hesitant to talk about something as mundane as training or as embarrassing as wrestling with Vigash. Nonetheless, I did, much to the joy of William. He laughed as I told about Vigash's multiple techniques of depositing me upon my royal ass. We swapped stories of trying to fight the Master, and of how many times humiliated us.

I Came

He was amazed at my mastery of fading. "I've never heard of it," he said. "Even Elves have difficulties in mastering disappearing. And, you did it the first time? No wonder you were exhausted."

"Here," he cut a slab of a reddish beast and slid it onto my plate. He ladled bluish lumps from one bowl and thin, greenish beanlike things from a different bowl, and spread a yellow sauce over one of them. "These are foods for energy. They may not be to an Elf's taste buds, but right now I'm interested only in restoring your bodily energy. So, eat up!"

I tried the meat. It was gamy and tougher than I had expected. The yellow sauce hid tasty lumps. The bluish lumps were tart, but seemed heartier than I had expected. The beany things were ok, but hardly memorable. Finally, a servant delivered a pot of hot thrak, which I drank eagerly.

When I was sated, we sat back and talked more about the political situation. William asked if I had learned anything more about Isadora, Richmond and others.

I told him about my encounters with Richmond, especially my probe of him when I was recovering. "He was deeply concerned and worried for my health. I sensed no animosity of any kind. He appears devoted to his teaching, to Talbot, and to you.

"As far as his wife is concerned, I don't know. Neither Cassandra nor Eleanor believes it of her. And, remember, I am new at this. I really don't know what I'm doing. I could easily be completely mistaken. That's why I sought help from Talbot, so I could understand what I'm feeling and sensing. Until I do, I am, at best, a poor witness."

"Yes, I think I agree. Although Talbot is my close friend, advisor and chief of my Sorcerers, Richmond is his second. I have known him since I was a child and have never had a concern for his loyalty.

"I do not know Isadora. He married her a few orbits ago. I attended the wedding along with Richard and Cassandra. She seemed to be a quiet and reserved womban, with excellent insight into character. Richmond often says she is a better judge of character than he is. Perhaps, that is true, especially if she is a Truth Seeker.

"I have asked Talbot to test her, without her knowledge. Depending upon his findings, we will discuss her with Richmond and supply her with training. If she is a truth seeker, her services will be most valuable.

"Now, after the dinner meal, the council will meet. You will attend, and I will expect your presence in the future. However, I understand your training could be arduous. I will ask Talbot to monitor your condition and to alert me if you are too tired to attend. Otherwise, I look forward to your council.

"Next, I will arrange for Richmond to seek the assistance of other Sorcerers to assist you in your training. I do not have that many, but each has an area in which he is better. I will couch your training in those terms, seeking the most talented in each area to teach you.

"You will discover what you can about them as discreetly as possible. We do not want any of them to know of your abilities to perceive their minds. In fact, it might be worthwhile to mislead them regarding your actual skill level. Do you understand my meaning?"

"Indeed, I do. If any of them were to find out my cover would be blown."

"Cover?" he asked.

"Oh yes, it's just a figure of speech. If they knew of my abilities, they would take extra precautions, and I would learn nothing."

"Too true." He glanced up and saw that the hall was emptying. "It's probably time to for you to return to the training area. I believe this will be your first experience in a large armed force. Enjoy the experience, even though it will not be your fate. I look forward to seeing you at supper."

I used a Wizard's Walk to arrive at the training grounds in just moments. It was getting a lot easier to do. I just sorta fell into it. I didn't push it, either. I was only walking at about 4-to-1. I knew I could go much faster, but it'd also take me longer to stop. Since the training grounds weren't that far outside the castle walls, I'd probably overshoot and then have to walk back if I went any faster. Besides, this was fast enough for me.

I Came

General Abuahad greeted me, "Welcome, Lady Gilraën. This should be a novel experience for you this afternoon. You and the other archers will serve with Grampus Battalion in mock battle with Richmond's. This will be a simulated battle, in which you will all use real weapons, but ones deliberately modified not to cause lasting harm.

"Further, we will be testing our wards to determine how effective they are against different weapons. We are hoping that some new wards recently devised by our Sorcerers will be more effective.

"You will serve two roles, today. You will lead your archers, as you might in a real battle. You will also use your magic both to communicate and to protect your troop."

He looked up. "Ah! Here is the battalion commander."

I turned to see Sir Geoffrey approaching.

"Lady Gilraën," he greeted me somewhat brusquely, "Gather your archers and follow me. I will show you your positions and explain your duties. Hurry! I have five hundred men waiting." He turned on his heel and strode away.

I glanced around in a panic. I had no idea of where Harold and the other archers were. I lengthened my stride, doubling my normal running pace heading in the same direction as Geoffrey. I quickly passed him, finding my archers sitting under a tree enjoying a post-meal siesta.

"Harold! Archers! Get to your feet. Sir Geoffrey is here, and we have a battle to win."

We quickly assembled and followed him. He smiled, and said, "You're over here." He pointed to the large field where we had first tested our bows.

He quickly issued orders to several important looking soldiers, who rushed off yelling at the tops of their lungs. Hundreds of men leapt to their feet and assembled in long lines facing away from us. They formed into two rows, with long spear-axes pointed to their front. Each man had a tall, curved shield, which they held before them, and each hoisted their halberds to their right shoulder. They each wore a wide-brim helmet on their head, greaves on their shins and a vambrace on their right forearms. They also wore a short sword on their left hip. To me, they were a formidable force.

Sir Geoffrey led us to a large mixed group of archers, spearmen, slingers and others. A second and then a third group of archers joined us. Squads of slingers formed to our left. Another large group of javeliners formed before us.

Geoffrey turned to the javeliners, each of whom held half a dozen long tapered spears. "Take up position behind the main line."

A man, obviously their leader, shouted, "Follow me!"

Geoffrey then turned to all of us. "Slingers, over there!" He pointed to my right. "Archers, over there!" He pointed to our left, where three men armed with bows stood.

When we approached, the man in the middle addressed us. "Archers! I am Captain Gerard, chief of Viscount Grampus' archers. We divided you deliberately, into two troops of twelve archers throughout your training. Each troop has developed cohesion and an internal leadership. I will abide by your choice of leader.

"However, we are an army. To win in battle requires each troop to obey the orders of your commanding officers. In this mock battle, I am your commander. These are my troop leaders: Bobolati and Ngu." A tall, thin black man nodded first, and then a smaller oriental. "Each will lead a Company comprising several troops to the wings of the line of battle. Your objective will be to fire diagonally across the enemy's line of battle to kill as many of them as you can before they engage our men-at-arms.

"Secondarily, you will seek out and destroy any enemy archers, slingers or spearmen you see on our flanks.

"Now, you," he pointed at a group, "go with Bobolati. You," he pointed to the second group. "go with Ngu. Gilraën, follow me."

My archers and I moved nearer to Gerard. He raised his hand for silence. "We will be on the left flank." He pointed beyond the long line of halberds before he jogged off. The rest of us glanced at each other, then trotted off behind him.

I Came

I looked around. There were about three dozen of us, with a similar number behind us. At first, I thought they were missing their bows, but then I saw they were slingers. I should have realized that immediately since they each had some four or five satchels of rocks, in easy reach, belted around their waists. I quickly calculated that we could deliver about 288 arrows and perhaps two or three times as many stones onto an advancing force. But what then? Hopefully, someone would resupply us.

When we finally got to where Gerard wanted us, he raised his hand, and we stopped. He aligned Bobolati's and Ngu's troops on a diagonal to the infantry line. He placed the rest of us to their left, facing mostly in the same direction as the infantry. The slingers were behind our diagonals.

"Now," Gerard bellowed, "We have two duties. You," he pointed to the archers on the diagonal and the slingers. "Your job is to attack the enemy line of battle. On offense, we advance to the left and before our men-at-arms. You fire along the enemy line of battle to give you a larger target. If you overshoot the first line, you may hit the man to the right or left or a soldier behind them. You simply maximize your chances of diminishing the enemy's forces.

"When our lines of battle approach close enough, you slingers will attack to multiply our advantage.

"Now, you," he pointed to me, "You are not a regular part of Viscount Grampus' Battalion. So, you are also responsible for protecting our flank. The enemy will have archers on their flanks. They will try to kill our infantry. It is your job to kill them before they kill our men. Also, if they attempt to turn our flank, you are our first line of defense.

"If they force you back, the rest of the archers and the slingers will fall back with you, fighting to buy time, either for the battalion to reinforce you or to retreat. If they force us to retreat, then you will protect our rear.

"Do you understand your responsibilities?" He looked around. "Good. I will now come about you so I can learn which of you leads your troop. Lady Gilraën, you will lead your troop. I will observe you other leaders and your troop's cohesion with an eye towards ensuring victory. If needed, I will reorganize your troop, but I will only do so to improve our chance of victory. Understood?"

When no one replied, he said, "Stand easy. The time for battle is soon."

I stood amidst my archers looking around. I wandered over to introduce myself to the groups of archers. Each of the other troops were older than ours, formed from previous rounds of recruiting. Slowly, the three groups melded together, finding out we all had much in common.

"To your positions!" Gerard bellowed.

We quickly realigned into our previous positions. I looked down the length of the field to see a dark mass moving toward us. I squinted, trying to magnify my vision. It worked!

A long line of men marched onto the field. A picket of pointed poles extruded from a wall of shields. Archers and slingers advanced on the flanks, mirroring our dispositions. It was easily the most frightening spectacle I'd ever seen.

I looked around. Gerard was staring into the distance, observing the enemy battalion. However, everyone else was nervously looking at his or her neighbors. Fear was seizing the men, and nobody was doing anything to diminish it.

"What's for dinner?" I asked rather loudly. "I really like that purple meat. What's it called?"

Harold looked up at me, a questioning look on his face. "What? The breakfast stuff?"

"Yeah," I replied. "I had that this morning along with green lumpy things with yellow, runny insides. After last night, I needed it, whatever it was."

"I think it's barf!" a woman from the next troop shouted.

Yashi laughed, "Barf!"

"No," someone else yelled, "its bar, like a bar of soap."

Harold commented, "It tastes like ham, though."

Someone else laughed, "Green eggs and ham? It's real?"

I Came

Quickly, everyone was commenting on the food, making comparisons with food we knew. That's when we all began to figure out we were a huge variety of people from Earth who had volunteered to fight for Prince William. There were people from all over the Americas, Australasia, the Far East, and Europe. There were fewer from Africa, and even fewer from the Middle East. But all of us were from Earth.

"Eyes front!" Gerard shouted.

Sure enough, the enemy line was much closer... almost within bow range. They were well within the range of my bow, but, like the other archers, I only had two dozen arrows. I had replaced my regular arrows had with practice arrows, as had everyone else, but mine were much larger and heavier. I wondered if they might still do damage, but that was up to the Sorcerers, not me.

A cloud of arrows arose from the flanks of the advancing army. I looked to Gerard, who stood with his hand raised.

"Wait for it! They are just wasting their arrows. Look at our men. See how the second line uses their shields to protect the first line? They are like a shellback, protected by an impenetrable shell.

"When they get closer, their arrows will penetrate the shields of the first rank. When a man in the first rank falls, a man behind him steps up into his place.

"We will wait. We will hit them on the diagonal and at closer range. Our shafts will be more likely to pass between shields or to penetrate them. Remember that a shield need not be completely penetrated to make its use as a shield ineffectual. A shield with arrows in it is awkward, imbalanced and ungainly, making that soldier more vulnerable. It is the infantry's job to find and exploit such weaknesses to penetrate their line and disrupt their defense."

As he spoke, the archers to our right loosed a volley of arrows. Moments later, a second volley and then a third fell among the front line of the enemy. Then a cloud of rocks filled the air. Quickly, masses of missiles struck down advancing infantry, tearing gaps that quickly filled by the second line of men-at-arms.

The slaughter filled my vision and my mind. I couldn't take my eyes from it, despite the horrors unfolding in front of me.

"Gilraën! Eyes left!" Gerard shouted, pointing.

I followed his finger to see a skirmish line of archers supported by infantry advancing on our left.

"Spread out!" I shouted. "Archers on our left. Fire individually. Take your best shot, but don't hesitate."

I sprinted off to my left, uttering *fugitos* to cover the ground as quickly as I could. I quickly found the limits of their attack and began working my way down their lines. Within minutes, I had 'shot' twenty-three 'enemy' archers, reducing their numbers by half.

I was about to return to my troop, mostly to get more arrows, when I noticed movement far to my left. Curious, I muttered *fugitos* and double-stepped beyond the edge of the field and into the wood where I would be hidden. Moments later, fifty war chariots appeared, moving quickly towards our battalion's rear. I didn't need anything further to understand what I had to do.

I muttered *fugitos* again and took a 3-fold Sorcerer's Walk to find Sir Geoffrey. Moment's later, I saw Geoffrey amidst a group of other officers. They were looking out to their front, pointing first at the oncoming enemy, and then referring to objects arrayed on a table.

I almost crashed into them before I could slow to a walk. Somewhat breathless, I accosted him, gasping, "Geoffrey, they've got chariots coming around your left. Must be about fifty.

"They had a couple of dozen archers and a lot of infantry covering them. I finished off half their archers, but didn't make a dent in their infantry. I gotta get back to tell Gerard. I'd guess you've got half an hour at most. Catch you at supper."

I turned, uttered *fugitos* and raced back to my troop. I saw Gerard and stopped not a two feet from him. "Gerard!" I shouted.

"Garg!" he screamed. "Where did you come from?"

I ignored his question. "There are fifty chariots on our left, coming fast. I've already informed Geoffrey. He's sending support, but I don't know what or when. They also have archers and infantry closer on our left. We'd engaged them, but I infiltrated them and killed half their archers. I'm going back to my troop, if that's ok with you?"

I started towards my troop, but Gerard yelled, "Stop! You did what?"

I glanced at him. "I don't have time to say things twice. They're on our flank, and I've got to save my friends." I loped away, quickly finding Harold and the rest of my friends.

"Oh, there you are." Harold laughed. "We've been busy here. What have you been doing?"

"Be prepared to retreat. I've got to get us turned to the left to face fifty chariots. So, work with me. You're the rear guard. Cover everyone's ass while they retreat."

Gerard appeared, yelling in a voice that carried over the surrounding bedlam, "Form line to the left. Hold fire. Prepare for close combat. When we retreat, you will protect the army's flank. Gilraën, you're in command here. I'll be with the rest of the archers and slingers. They'll be moving to your left: archers in front; slingers in back. We'll move back one step at a time."

Harold shouted, "What are we supposed to do, bite them? We're out of arrows! At least slingers can find rocks."

"Send one man from each troop. There's a cart filled with arrows one hundred paces behind us. Also, each troop of slingers, send two men to collect river rocks from the cart. Keep sending men to the cart to resupply your troop," Gerard then hurried away, leaving us to face perhaps three times our numbers.

Harold pointed at two of the men in our troop. Quickly, a dozen men were scampering to the cart well behind us.

As they were rearming, I studied the land, trying to find some advantage. Perhaps twenty yards ahead of us was a depression. Other than that, the land was flat as a pancake. If I were in a game, at this point I'd have my tanks racing behind the enemy's lines and into their rear.

"OK!" I yelled, "Into the ditch! Archers, kneel. Slingers, lie flat behind us. When they come into view, I'll yell, 'Archers,' to signal the archers to rise and fire. Then they'll duck back into the ditch. When they do, I'll yell, 'Slingers!' you slingers, rise and loose your stones. When you have slung your stones, fall face down and prepare your next one. Meantime, keep up the relay to the cart to re-supply our arrows and stones.

"If we have to retreat, we'll do it in stages. The two end troops drop back first. I'll guide you to the next line. Then, the two middle troops will retreat beyond the outside troops. We'll stagger troops backwards until Geoffrey's reinforcements arrive."

I looked to the edge of the wood. The chariots were racing towards us. The runners arrived with fresh supplies of arrows and sling stones. "Go!" I yelled, grabbing two quivers of arrows.

Three dozen archers knelt in the ditch. Thirty or more slingers lay in the grass. I knelt, judging distances. "Ready your arrows! Ready your stones."

The chariots raced towards us.

"Archers!"

Twenty-seven men, nine women and one Elf rose as one.

"Fire!" I yelled, and thirty-seven arrows arced towards the onrushing chariots.

Thirty-seven archers kneeled in the ditch.

"Slingers!"

Thirty round river rocks flew towards the advancing line of chariots.

"Archers!"

"Slingers!"

"Gilraën!"

I looked up. It was Gerard. Behind him was a troop of soldiers. Quickly, they formed a shield wall five yards short of the ditch. "Align your command behind the soldiers. Support them with your arrows and slings. Well done! You won the mock battle with your quick thinking."

* * *

I resisted the temptation to sit with my archers. I knew what Prince William's wine could do to me. I left after sharing a cup with the troop. Damn! We were good!

Brahms escorted me to a chair between Cassandra and Geoffrey. Eleanor was to Geoffrey's right, William to Cassandra's left, and Abuahad to William's left. It seemed I was in the midst of the Princedom's brain trust.

"So," Geoffrey began the inquisition, "How did you know about the carts?"

"You mean the chariots?" I asked, not fully understanding him.

"Yes!" he sputtered. "That's our new secret weapon. How did you find out about them?"

"Oh, I didn't. I was clearing out a nest of archers supported by infantry who were trying to flank us. I shot a couple of dozen archers and then was heading back to get more arrows when I spotted them. I knew what they were immediately, and their intention – classic cavalry tactics.

"Fortunately, I knew how to Speed Walk. I just had to decide who needed to know what was happening first, and who I could tell later. I decided that you," I looked Geoffrey in the eye, "needed to know first. After I told you, I returned to Gerard to realign the archers and slingers.

"He put me in charge of the immediate defense, while he went off to realign the entire left flank.

"I saw the ditch and realized it was the only defensible terrain feature. So, I used it. Then, I remembered the movie, 'Zulu!' So, I set up an alternate firing routine between the archers and the slingers. It was the best I could do. I just hoped that someone would rescue us. When Gerard showed up, I knew we were reinforced.

"The only problem was that the extra arrows and stones were too far behind us to be effective. Perhaps we should think about a small cart or small detachment with expendables that we'll need in battle. I also think we all need small shields and swords for when the enemy closes us."

Prince William asked, "Movie? What is that?"

"Uh, it's a little complicated. Could I explain that later?"

"If it is not so important to our war effort, then yes; but I will hold you to an explanation as this 'movie' had some bearing upon the practice battle."

Geoffrey breathed a deep sigh. "So, you went off on your own, and, by the sheerest of accidents, blundered into discovering our secret weapon, and in so doing save the day? I don't know whether to punish you, or to praise you."

"Punish? Me? No, I don't think so. I'm a free agent, remember?" I was more than hot under the collar. I'd gone above and beyond as far as I was concerned, and all I was getting was a load of crap? No frigging way!

William interrupted my thoughts. "No, no, we'll have no talk like that. Gilraën, you did exactly as you should have. Your units were to protect Geoffrey's flank, which you did. You took full advantage of your skills as a Sorcerer to achieve the stated goal. You protected your units, you scouted the territory, you observed a threat, assessed it properly, reported it, following the chain of command, and you commanded a spirited defense which led to the defeat of the counterattack."

He looked beyond me to Geoffrey. "Not bad for the first time in battle, right, Geoff?

"Yes, sire, that's true." He looked to me. "I apologize, Lady Gilraën, for my outburst. The idea of chariots is a new one to us. We learned from other recruits about fast moving cavalry.

I Came

"Although we have zhaks, we have none of the size and strength I've heard inhabits your world. Ours stand barely four feet at the shoulder and weigh about 500 pounds. They are sturdy animals, built more for endurance than speed. Because of their stature, we cannot ride upon their backs. That's why we came up with the cart.

"It took some time to design a cart that could be pulled by zhaks. We needed it to be large enough that one or two men could ride within it. And, it had to be light enough that a pair of zhaks could pull it for a distance and over rugged terrain.

"However, zhaks are willful and resistant to domestication. They don't like humans. They run away from us, and they will bite and kick if we approach them. The entire herd will turn on us and will attack if we try to trap them, or attempt to remove one or more of them from the herd. That's our biggest problem.

"Oddly enough, a second difficulty was developing a system that wouldn't strangle the zhaks, while providing efficient power and speed to be of use. Taking the advice from a man from your world, we developed a collar that affixes around their shoulders rather than their necks. After that, it was just creating a T-bar to the cart.

"So far, our experiments have been moderately successful. We find that the zhaks can pull their carts for roughly a half of a day at a walk. However, if we run them, they last for less than an hour. Over rough terrain, they stop after a few hours. However, they recover quickly and can walk again after just half an hour or so.

"We have adjusted our tactics accordingly. The carts advance at a walk until they are close to the opposition's line of battle. Then, they can advance at a brisk pace until they are in position to attack. When they are close, they can race ahead for several minutes.

"We're still trying to determine the best deployments, armaments and number of cart riders. Typically, a pair of zhaks can pull a cart with two men aboard. Three men are too much. The zhaks tire quickly. With one driver, the zhaks are capable and strong. But, it looks like the best combination is a driver to command the beasts, and a second man armed with spears, javelins and bow for offense.

"This was our first use of them. We were testing the technique, trying to pass along the flank and return before they detected us. If we could do that, we would know what we can do, and it would still be a secret. Now, half the army knows. Within a day or two, the whole army will know. Within days, Beckworth will know. And, there goes our tactical advantage."

I asked, "But how would Beckworth find out? Isn't Beckworth a long way from here? How would anyone get that kind of information to him?"

"That's what we don't know." William ground his hand into the table. "We had hoped that you had found the culprit, but, evidently, neither Richmond nor his wife is spies. It's possible that Isadora is a Truth Seeker, after all. However, our hunt goes on.

"Now, what do you think of our new carts?"

"I really didn't see them fight. However, the idea is eminently practical. We have used them on Earth for millennia. The early Egyptians had small horses, the largest not much larger than your zhaks. They used them in pairs to pull carts called chariots. Later, they or some other early civilization cross-bred them with Asian horses. Most of the time, such hybrids are sterile, but in this case, we got the modern horse. Since then, we've bred them into sizes from quite small to very large. So, you may be on the right track."

When I retired, I lay in bed thinking about chariots. They'd be perfect for missions deep into enemy-held territory. Geoffrey's chariot could hold one or two people. If I could mount my archers, we could have a formidable deep raiding force that could penetrate deep into Beckworth's territories. Then…

* * * * *

I Came

Chapter 5 - Fade

The next morning, my bout with Vigash was far more successful. Evidently, his advice about sleeping on it was worthwhile. I actually threw him once! Of course, he thrashed me... as usual, but the one time I threw him, he deigned to smile at me.

At lunch, Talbot took me to Bethea's kitchen. Afterwards, he continued his instruction in mental combat. My job was to consider every person in the kitchen at the same time. I was to learn as much about them as I could, all while telling Talbot about everything that had happened at the soiree I had hosted.

Bethea seemed to be easy. She was worried about ingredients, temperatures, times, schedules and such.

The only man was clearing tables, washing floors, and such, all while thinking about how to seduce a young woman who lived in the house next to his own... a classic tale of the little head controlling the big one.

The woman who appeared to be Bethea's most important aide was very jealous of her. She was sure she could do a better job than Bethea, had a better menu of foods, and could control costs better.

The second woman could only think about a man who had been raping her. Somehow, the womban's father had fallen in debt to a man, who had demanded sex with the daughter as repayment.

The youngest woman was trying desperately to learn what to do in the kitchen. She was an only child and had never had contact with large numbers of people until arriving in Bethea's kitchen. She wanted to learn everything, but was afraid to ask what to do, while also afraid of making a mistake.

Worse, Talbot was distracting me by injecting mental chaff into our conversation. He'd ask about the material in a dress, or the style of shoes. If I didn't remember, he had me mentally review the party until I had pictured the scene and could answer his questions correctly.

I'm not sure which was worse, fighting Vigash or Talbot. By the time I scheduled to begin my lessons with Master Norton, I was exhausted.

Master Norton was not pleased when I was late arriving. "*Lady* Gilraën," he said derisively. "Too important to arrive in a timely manner, *Lady*? Your time is valuable, while mine, that of a mere Master of Sorcery and Arms to the court of Prince William, is insignificant. Hopefully, you will attend to my instruction more attentively than you have attended to your tardiness. Shall we begin?"

Yes, I had been late. My instruction with Talbot had taken longer than expected. However, I was only moments late and well within the bounds of propriety. Further, I was now a princess on this world... a royal personage deserving of at least a modicum of respect. Yet, he was a Master and my teacher. He, too, deserved respect, and because of my tardiness, we'd started off on the wrong foot.

"My apologies, Master Norton. I was with Master Talbot. He only just released me from my lesson with him. How shall we proceed?"

Norton glared at me and then shrugged. "Master Talbot? I shall speak with him.

"How shall we proceed, indeed? Master Talbot has informed me you need advanced instruction involving *Sorcerer's Walk* and perception. Is that correct?"

"Yes, Master. I can increase my stride tenfold, but I cannot see when I do. The world is a blur. Also, I can fade, but then the world is an even worse blur. When I try to do both, the world is impossible to perceive.

"Master Talbot has been working with me to improve my mental perception. We have made improvements, but Master Talbot has told me you are most expert in these matters, and has assigned me to you for advanced training."

"Yes, seeing is, at best, a difficulty in either case. It is true that the difficulty increases dramatically when engaged in both.

I Came

"The problem is associated with the spells themselves. Both distort the lines of energy. When these lines of force are distorted, light itself is equally distorted. A consequence is that when you *fade* and *Speed Walk*, you experience a double distortion. These deformations of energy make normal vision impossible.

"Master Talbot is correct in suggesting that you must develop your mental acuity to augment or replace your physical eyesight. We will begin with a walk along a path. Thereafter, the path will become more rugged. Ultimately, we will include reconnaissance, use of weapons, and endurance. Let us begin. Follow me." He pointed to a path entering a wood.

At first, he progressed at a moderate double speed. The path became narrower and winding. Tree roots arose, and the land rose and fell. We entered a boggy area, and had to leap from the bank, across a series of rocks to slippery mattocks before finally finding the other bank.

We began climbing a hill, and Norton increased the stride length. The path rose more steeply, but Norton never faltered.

BAM!

I felt myself tumbling head over heels down the hillside. Reaching out with both hands, I tried to find something … anything to grab that I could break my fall. I failed utterly, finally crashing into a large rock. Dazed, I looked around, trying desperately to clear my head.

Norton appeared at my side, looking mockingly at me.

I used the same ploy I had with Richmond. I dissolved my mental helmet and lashed out at the nearest mental energy I could locate. Norton reeled backwards, fighting my mental probe. But, just before the door slammed shut, I sensed malice!

I mumbled incoherently and then looked up at him. "What happened?" I stammered.

"You fell," he replied flatly. "Why did you attempt to probe me?"

I held my head in my hands, crying, "Oh, damn, I hurt. Give me a minute, will ya?" I deliberately tried to appear woozier than I was. I

118

blinked a few times and then looked up at him with a grin on my face. "And, I was doing so well!"

"Yes, you were, but then you ran into a tree," Norton replied.

"So, that's what it was," I replied slowly. "I didn't see it."

"Evidently," Norton sneered. "In the future, you must avoid such things if you are to move quickly over anything but the finest roadways. Now, let us begin, again."

Without waiting for me, he turned and headed down the slope we had just ascended. Running downhill is far more difficult than up. It's easier on the one hand because gravity is assisting the descent. It's far more difficult because one's feet are angled downwards, providing less friction against the slope. When combined with higher speeds, it's very easy to lose control and to slam into rocks, trees, or just slip and fall head over teakettle all the way to the bottom. So, by the time I got to the bottom, Norton was waiting impatiently with another scornful look on his face.

"Now, *fade* and follow me back up this hill," he demanded.

I'd barely got my breath back, and he was off and running, *fading* away as he ran. I heard his footsteps and sensed his aura, but they gradually diminished as the distance between us increased. '*Fugitos*" was the easier spell for me. *Divergio lepto* was not only harder, but turned the entire world into something resembling looking through the bottom of a glass bottle.

I headed towards the slope, but it wasn't there. Nothing was. I reduced my *fade* until I could make out something that appeared to be more open than anything else. However, my *Sorcerer's Walk* was barely 1:1. Maybe it was even less. I picked my way, sometimes moving only one step at a time. I seemed to edge my way for hours… maybe days.

"GILRAËN!" a voice shouted in my ear.

I almost fainted! Instead, I dropped my nonexistent *long stride* and released my fade to find out who had succeeded, not only in finding me, but surprising the hell out of me. I looked around to see Norton leaning over my shoulder, his lips almost kissing my ear.

I Came

"Crap!" I exclaimed, "You scared me half to death."

"Only half? Were I your enemy, you would be entirely dead."

Feeling rather foolish, I asked, "What am I not doing? What can I do? You seem to do this with no effort, while I struggle, bump into trees, fall down mountains, and permit a potential enemy to sneak up on me within knife range.

Norton smirked, saying, "What? The royal Elf needs help? Can't do it? Needs the help of a lowly Human?"

His chicken shit attitude was angering me. However, he was my mentor, and I had to trust him to teach me how to accomplish this. I answered, humbly, "Indeed, Master Norton, I do need your skills as a Sorcerer and teacher, to help me acquire these skills. Nor do I denigrate, disparage or defame humans, especially mighty Sorcerers, such as yourself." Hopefully, flattery would be beneficial.

"Trying to flatter me, Elf?" he snickered. "Well, at least you are humble enough to admit your failings.

"You must project yourself into the distance beyond where you are. Consider time and space. You know you will move at a higher rate of speed. You must intercept photons reflecting from surfaces where you will be, not where you are. Therefore, you must project your consciousness into the future both in time and in space, thus space time.

"It is easiest to consider space, before time, remembering that both are the same thing. So, remove your perception from this location to the peak of this hill.

"Move your perception slowly from here to the next step. Consider the step after that, and then the one after that. Concentrate on this, until you have reached the peak."

My mind failed to grasp such a perception. I was stuck in the here and now. Reading the future was an impossibility, but that was exactly what he was telling me to do.

He wrapped a scarf around my head, covering my eyes. "Picture it in your mind," Norton coached. "Reach out to it."

I pictured myself taking the next step. I felt the ground beneath my foot. The trees came one step closer, and the slope increased. I took the next mental step… and then a third. Yet, that was about as far as I could go. It was now the world of imagination, rather than a real step in space and time.

"Now," he said, "take that first step. And, as you do, imagine taking the same step from where you perceive you are in your imagination. Take the same step physically and psychically. Expand your prescience. See beyond yourself."

I stepped forward, rather tentatively, not quite sure of what I was stepping upon. As I did so, I stepped forward in my perceived world. At that moment, my perceived world was advancing at the same rate and time as was I, except it was three steps ahead of me.

"You hesitate. You are not sure of where you will step. You must remember that you have already taken that step. It hasn't changed between the first time you stepped there and this time. Now take your next step, while still looking ahead in time."

I hesitated.

"Go ahead. Step!"

I did, and nothing happened. I performed my mental step while perceiving a small rock on the right and a stick on the left. But that was two steps ahead of me. So, I took another step… and then another. I deftly avoided the perceived obstacles, but saw a tree root crossing the path. I moved ahead… and again, then extended my leg a bit more to step over the root I thought I had seen.

"Excellent! You avoided the rock, the twig and the root without seeing them.

"Now, increase your speed just a little. See ahead of you as far as you can. Experience both time and space as you walk. Reach out! The entire universe is spread before you, awaiting your discovery of it."

He seemed to enjoy my success even more than I was. I moved slightly faster, still maintaining my prescience three steps ahead of me. The path began sloping upward, passing between a y-shaped tree and a largish boulder. Immediately after I passed between them, the path turned left behind the rock, then right, up a steep slope of about two feet.

"Careful now. Examine carefully before you leap."

Gaining confidence, I moved around the rock, left, right and then I leapt upward and beyond the small slope. I was now standing atop what had appeared as a small mountain. There I was – Sir Edmund Hillary atop Everest.

"Well done, Gilraën!" Norton crowed. "You see? You can perceive, even when you can't see. Now take off your blindfold and use your eyes to see what you have overcome."

I did and looked back. I had come some twenty feet. The world I saw corresponded to the world I had perceived in my mind. "Wow!" I exclaimed, "That's impossible, but I just did it."

Norton smiled for the first time that afternoon. "Yes, you did. You did well… far better than any Sorcerer I've worked with in the past." He shook a finger at me, warning, "Now don't let this go to your head. You are better, but then you are an Elf. Most Elves are better at magic than are Humans, and Elvish magi are generally better than Human Sorcerers. Yet that *is* a generalization. My congratulations, Lady Gilraën, you are learning.

"You must be careful with this skill, Elf. It is dangerous to extend prescience to its limits. The mind does strange things; the Elvish mind is far worse. Be careful as you advance in the world of magic. It is dangerous to practice skills before you understand both your own limitations and their demands."

I wasn't 100% sure of what he was saying. I knew that magic depleted my energy in relation to the difficulty of the task. I concluded that if I tried to expend too much energy, it might be lethal. But what other dangers might I encounter?

"Master, obviously I'm new at this. I realize I could exhaust my life energy if I try to do something too difficult, but what other dangers might I encounter?"

Norton stared at me for several seconds. I tried to 'read' his thoughts, attempting to determine why he was so hesitant. I ran into a maze of gibberish.

He laughed, "Do you think I would leave my mind open to you, Elf?"

I blushed, stammering, "Sorry, it's just something I do. It beats waiting for a partial answer, when I can learn the whole argument, and why something should or should not be so."

"Hmm," he replied, stabbing a powerful mental probe at me.

He almost penetrated my helmet, but I reinforced it just enough to defend my mind, but not more. I didn't want him to know of what I was capable, and surely not to know I had nearly killed Talbot.

"I see you can shield your mind, Elf. It is an elementary precaution, which we all practice. Prying into other people's minds is offensive and should not be attempted without informing the person and asking their permission. Otherwise, it is an attack upon that person and could result in their attack upon you. That is a lesson I would have assumed Master Talbot should have taught you. If not, Elf, be forewarned."

"Oh, I didn't know," I replied, feigning ignorance. "I just sorta do it without thinking. I'll try not to do so in the future. But, you had said that my ignorance might be dangerous. In what way?"

Again, he glared at me. I felt the touch of his mind and displayed curiosity. He paused a moment as though thinking, "Let me ask you this: What would happen if you cast a spell, and you didn't have the strength to complete it?"

I was at a loss. I didn't know, and I wasn't sure if an extrapolation would be accurate. So, I took a stab. "I guess that it'd exhaust me until I collapsed."

"No! Not even close. It would kill you!" he declared most emphatically.

I reconsidered my line of reasoning. I had assumed that a magical command would cease with unconsciousness. But Norton seemed to be saying that it would continue even after I had blacked out. "Do you mean that such a command would continue even if I became unconscious… that it's not a matter of my will, but a process with a life of its own?"

I Came

"A peculiar way of describing it, but in a word, 'Yes.' That's exactly how it works. Once you have created a magical process and put it in motion, it will continue until your magical goal is achieved, or it drains you entirely of all your energy. Those are the only outcomes – success or death."

I was flabbergasted. I'd been doing this stuff and nobody had warned me. "But," I stammered, "how shall I know that a task is too great before I actually attempt it?"

"That, my dear Elf, is the most important question in all our attempts at sorcery. And, the answer is, you don't, nor will you, until the moment you draw your last breath."

"But, how then can I use magic if I don't know whether I will commit suicide?"

He laughed. "Elf, ask your mentor, Master Talbot." He drew himself up. "Are you ready to try again? Good. I will lead, and you will follow. I will *fade* and *speed walk* ahead of you. Let us finally go to the summit of this hill. I will await you." With that, he disappeared.

I mumbled, "*Divergio lepto*," and the world blurred around me. I then uttered, "*Fugitos*," and the world became an indistinct mist. I panicked, utterly incapable of proceeding.

Then, I reconsidered my previous lesson, in which I had projected my mind to the place where I would be. I looked one step and then two steps ahead. I began to take my first step, as I projected a third step ahead.

I perceived a tree ahead, but looked beyond it to see the path veering to the right. I stepped where I knew the path was clear, as I projected another step ahead. Gradually, I increased my stride, bounding, twisting, leaping and jumping up a long, narrow and steep path. Seconds and then minutes slipped by and then … I was at the crest.

I terminated my spells, dug in both heels and slid to a stop. Looking around, I saw a broad vista, but no other person. Yet someone was there. I could feel a presence.

Sensing danger, I *faded* and jumped aside. I projected my perception beyond me. Someone else was nearby, and whoever it was intended to harm me. I retreated where a cliff defended my back, while edging closer to a small stand of trees.

Something lunged at me. I leapt backwards off the cliff, grasping with my fingers and toes to find tiny edges of rock to grab and slow my fall. I scrabbled and grabbed, finally finding a ledge. I stood for a moment and looked down the face. Long cracks extended to my left about 100 feet where it leveled off into a heavy wood. As quickly as I could, I scrambled down and into the trees. I stood gasping for breath, trying to sense the presence, but detected none.

'Where is Norton?' I asked myself. 'Why is he not here as he said he would be? Why did he not defend me?'

Still invisible, I descended the hill, returning to our starting place. Norton wasn't there. *'Shit! What do I do now?'*

I took Norton's advice and sought Talbot. Taking advantage of my new-found skills, I *faded*, extended my perception ahead and speed walked back to the castle. Within seconds, I had found Talbot, but I dared not reveal myself to those around him. I projected my thoughts towards him, hoping that he would understand my needs.

His nod was almost imperceptible, as he turned towards our personal classroom. I entered behind him and he closed and bolted the door. "Gilraën? What is the matter?"

I released the spell. Exhausted from my efforts, I sunk into a chair. "Do you have any food? I'm starving."

He looked into the distance for just a moment. "In just a minute; now, what is your problem? Why are you here?"

The words tumbled out of my mouth. I described Norton's attitude. I described his instruction leading to my perceiving the world while *faded* and *speed walking*. Then, I described the encounter on the hilltop, my perception of imminent danger, my escape and return to the castle.

"And, where was Norton while this was happening?"

I Came

"That's what frightened me. He *faded* and went before me, saying he'd meet me at the top. But, when I got there, he wasn't visible, but I felt a presence... a threatening presence. I knew someone or something was there to kill me. I escaped as quickly as I could. Something was terribly wrong."

"And, where is Norton now?"

"I don't know, but I am concerned. Either it was him at the top of the hill and he intended me harm, or some other being was there intending harm to both Norton and me."

Talbot stared at me as though trying to decide. "I need to make a request of you. Let me into your mind to experience your experience. Please, relax and let me enter your mind."

Talk about uncomfortable! He wanted to bang around inside my head, poking and prodding wherever he wanted. Should I let him? Answering my own question, I dissolved my helmet and nodded assent.

I felt Talbot within me. He was gentle, but thorough. When he sat back, I recreated my helmet. Even though I had been without it for just a few seconds, I felt naked without it.

Someone knocked on the door. Talbot rose, opened the door and returned with a large tray of food. As I dug in like the starving person I was, Talbot seemed to chew his cud.

Moments later, Talbot announced, "I am troubled. Your mastery of prescience is commendable. Norton's explanation of magic is correct, and his advice to talk with me about it is correct. His disappearance is most disturbing. Worse is your awareness of danger, especially when combined with Norton's absence.

"If you have finished your repast, we will investigate. I will summon assistance. We will accompany you to your quarters, where you will arm yourself as for battle. Then, we will investigate."

Just minutes later, Talbot, myself and Masters MacGregor, Johnsstone, Simmons, and Jacques the Truth Seeker were fully armed and speed walking to the hill where I had trained with Norton. As the others spread out, Talbot and I remained at the foot of the hill, maintaining mental contact with all of them. For several minutes, the only things I felt were concern and worry.

"Found him!"

Talbot acknowledged, turned to me, and said, "Johnsstone has found him. *Fade* and follow me."

He disappeared, and I tried to following him. It was difficult, but I managed slowly but surely. At last, I stumbled over a root, and fell to my hands and knees. Everyone heard me stumble, and looked in my direction, but since I was invisible, they didn't see that I'd made a fool of myself, again.

I stood and reappeared. Talbot was standing looking down at something on the ground. I edged towards him to see Norton lying in the grass, blood clotting around his ear and down his neck onto the ground.

"What happened," I asked, as I probed into his unconscious mind. For a moment, his emotions, thoughts and plans overcame me. It was a jumble that I couldn't understand.

Talbot moved his hand back and forth over Norton's body. "He was attacked."

Norton groaned, "What has happened to me?"

At that instant, a curtain fell, and he locked me out of his mind.

Talbot shrugged. "We don't know. We might ask you the same question. What happened to you?"

"I was running to the top, and something hit me from behind. I fell."

Something was wrong, but I couldn't quite figure it out.

Talbot stooped and helped Norton to his feet. "Come, let us help you to the healers."

Minutes later, Norton was in the hands of the healers. Talbot seemed to relax and dismissed the other Sorcerers to their duties. We retired to my rooms, where Dorothea served a delicious meal, mostly fruits, vegetables, with some fish.

"Tell me, Gilraën, what did you learn from Norton's mind?"

I Came

"I'm not sure. It was all mixed up and jumbled." Then it dawned on me. "How did you know?"

He gave me a weary look. "Lady Gilraën, who is the Master here?"

I chuckled. "Ah, my secret is out?"

"Indeed. You were clumsy. I will have to teach you to be more cautious. Now, what do you know, what do you suspect?"

"I think someone surprised and overcome him. I don't think he knows who or what did it."

"There are very few things that could sneak up on a Sorcerer undetected. All of them are extraordinarily deadly. Yet, he is alive. That is inconsistent.

"What else?"

"I'm not sure. The one thing I detected was his hostility toward Prince William. He also has a brother with whom he communicated recently. He has a plan. I don't know what it is, but it's not good."

"I, too, felt his animosity, but I was trying to determine his injuries. Keep me informed, Lady. Our Prince's life may hang in the balance.

"In the meantime, Viscount Geoffrey and General Abuahad are expecting you at the paddocks."

"Paddocks?"

"Yes, they are seeking your advice regarding the zhaks. I had told them that Elves often have a unique insight into animals. They are eager for your opinion. Brahms will guide you."

Fifteen minutes later, we arrived at the paddocks. Four large buildings stood at the corners of a quadrangle. Tall fences connected the buildings creating an open, fenced area of about twenty acres.

General Abuahad greeted me. "Welcome, Lady Gilraën. Viscount Geoffrey has related to me that Elves have a gift with animals. We have a problem with our zhaks. We cannot seem to domesticate them. They are stubborn, and willful, and often will not take to harness or bridle.

"We don't understand. We want to understand, and to have them work for us consistently. However, they remain as wild as their parents."

"How many generations of domestication?" I asked.

"Three or four, depending on the individual. Zhaks live about fifteen years. They reach puberty in their third year. They remain fertile for 10 to12 years. A stallion will attract a herd, which lasts for a season. Mares might stay with the stallion for years or just a season. Colts stay with their mothers for two years, before they depart. They'll form a loose herd for a year or two, mostly for protection against candimaers."

"Fine, let me see a herd."

We went into the large building to the right. The interior was divided into four large, fenced areas. Each housed some ten to fifteen zhaks. As we approached the first paddock, a large zhak advanced part way to the wire fence.

I sat at the fence, watching and studying. Three females stood attentively with youngsters at their side. Two other females and an adolescent male stood slightly to the side.

I extended my mind to the stallion, projecting an aura of friendliness and curiosity, mixed with respect. I could feel the stallion's confusion. His ears were forward, and his eyes fixed on me, but he remained determined and watchful.

I turned to Abuahad. "Open the gate and let me enter."

He looked aghast at me "He'll bite and kick. Be careful."

"No, I don't think so. Open the door. I will stay nearby, where you can rescue me if you need to do so."

He nodded to a subordinate who unlocked the gate and swung it aside just enough for me to enter.

The herd rose as one. The stallion neighed, and all the mares and colts gathered into a tight group, ready to flee. He bared his teeth and danced sideways, kicking his hooves threateningly.

I Came

I tried to ignore his threat display and crouched with my elbows on my knees and my chin in my hands. I re-established my mental link with the stallion. Then I projected my respect and admiration. I also tried to project curiosity without fear.

Again, the stallion stood alertly, watching me. The rest of the herd relaxed slightly, but the colts remained behind the mares, hiding. Their ears remained forward, and they studied me with their keen eyes.

I projected a desire for friendship, then looked away and studied their paddock. It was large and clean. At the same time, I felt a yearning to roam and graze on the wide plains. I tried to express an equivalent satisfaction, hoping they would empathize with a kindred spirit. I pictured running across an open field, the wind in my face. I expressed the joy of running and sharing with my family.

I then projected the herd being hunted. I showed them a pursuit by fast and agile hunters. Then, I projected the predators overtaking the herd, killing them one at a time and eating them while still alive. I could feel the stallion's fear. He was frantic, unable to protect his mind from the pictures, the fear and the pain.

Then, I projected a Human racing onto the field between the zhaks and the hunters. He was armed with a bow. He nocked an arrow and shot the leading predator. With the threat eliminated, the Human then calmed the herd and led them to a protected area. He brought them a bail of hay, which he distributed to the stallion first, and then the mares and colts.

I projected predators gathering around the paddock, growling and snarling. When the stallion reacted with fear, I projected the Human yelling and shooting arrows to drive off the predators. Then, I pictured the Human approaching the stallion, stroking it pleasurably on the face. He then fed the stallion from his own hands. I empathized a sense of well-being in both the stallion and the Human.

I reached into the feed bag and grabbed a handful of grain. Extending my grain-filled hand toward the stallion, I projected a sense of hunger and trust. I showed the stallion a picture of him eating feeling of happiness, trust and food.

130

Ever so cautiously, he lowered his head and slurped the grain from my palm.

* * *

Abuahad and Geoffrey joined me, closing the door firmly behind me. "Well?" Geoffrey asked, "What did you learn?"

I considered the last few hours. "They are wild, more interested only in grazing in the wide open spaces with their herd... their family. I instilled fear into the stallion, simulating a successful hunt in which he and others were killed and eaten. I then showed him a scenario in which a Human intervened, killed the predator, guided them to a safe place, fed them and drove off more predators. I then projected him eating out of the Human's hand, feeling safe, secure and cared for.

"That is, I showed him the dangers of his routine way of life. I showed him the protection available with Human intervention. I'll let him decide. Hopefully, he will see the necessity of partnering with Humans.

"The only problem I can see is will he trust Humans enough to confront danger when it appears. Only time will tell."

* * *

I lay in bed, my mind in a whirl. I had discussed my feelings with Eleanor and Cassandra. Between us, we came up with loads of ideas, but nothing conclusive.

I fell into a troubled sleep.

* * * * *

Chapter 6 - Traitor

For the third time in a row, I was flat on my back, with Master Vigash looming over me. "Concentrate, Gilraën, or I shall be forced to gain your attention."

He was right. I'd been wrestling with him physically, but with zhaks and Sorcerers foremost in my mind. I wasn't sure what Vigash was contemplating, but I knew that it'd be unpleasant. I concentrated on his moves, instantly perceiving his combination of Human, Dwarfish and Elvish moves all wrapped up in a single hulking presence. I ducked, swerved, leapt, fell backwards and rolled to my feet. I delivered a blow with my fist, ducked again, kicked into a leap and struck with my heel. I heard an "oof" and looked over my shoulder, as I spun into a combination defense/offense.

There, flat on his face was Vigash. I thought for just a second that I had hurt him, but discovered he was laughing. He was just lying there, laughing! He rolled to his feet, still chortling. "Well done, Lady Gilraën. You are now a Master of Martial Arts, ready to teach the next class as my assistant. In the future, we will fight only to maintain our skills, and to learn more as we fight an equal in strength, speed and ability. Only one other has ever achieved this, and she, too, was an Elf."

He bowed. "Please, seek Master Talbot for your next assignment."

I bowed lower than had he. "Thank you, Master Vigash. I would be pleased to teach as your assistant and to learn more at your side." I bowed again, and *Sorcerer Walked* to the castle.

Talbot greeted me as I arrived. "I have learned from Master Vigash that you are now a Master. Well done, Lady Gilraën. I now ask you to come with me to meet with Prince William and the senior staff. Please, accompany me."

He led me along passages, up flights of stairs and along corridors finally ending at a small iron-bound door tucked beneath a stairway. Talbot waved his hand, and the door opened.

We entered a larger room than was evident from its position under the stairs. It was long but narrow, dominated by a long, narrow table, which filled the center of the room allowing room all around for two to walk abreast while others were seated. A fireplace filled the far end. A multitude of chairs were scattered around haphazardly. A big map hung off the long edge of the table, a knife holding down one corner and weights the others.

General Abuahad leaned on his fists, staring at the map. William stood opposite, also staring at the map. Their heads were almost touching. Sir Geoffrey, Baron Richmond, and Sir Deplos leaned in from the end of the table. All five of them wore serious… almost worried looks on their faces.

"How many?" William asked.

Richmond answered, "A whole Company; one hundred men, plus archers, slingers, and a commissary…perhaps 150 men. Captain Feldersink and his staff were also killed."

William pounded the table with his fist. "Bash! How did they do it? How did they know where they were? How did they trap and annihilate them? How does he do it?"

Talbot cleared his throat. "My Prince, Lady Gilraën has joined us."

William looked up, and, seeing me, beamed. "My lady, welcome." He waved me to his side. "I need your advice. We just lost an entire Company." He pointed to a spot on the map.

I studied it. The continent looked somewhat like South America. The area towards the north was greenish, representing woodlands. Coastal plains surrounded the woods towards the north, west and east. To the south along the waist of the lands were mountains. Bluish lines demarked two other kingdoms: Farrowspike to the southwest and Narwortland at the southeast.

William pointed to the large area in the north. "This is Umbeqjaralii. We are here." He pointed to a spot near the southern border of the woodlands.

"This is Unterjaralii, which the traitor Lord Beckworth controls." He pointed to the narrow area south of the woods and north of the mountains and eastward out onto a large plain. "This morning, Beckworth attacked a Company here." He pointed to a wooded area to the southeast of the castle, which seemed under contention.

"We had just advanced into this area, intent on controlling the territory and protecting it from Beckworth's forces. Our information was that he had only a few soldiers in the area, because he was intent upon his own attack, here." He pointed to an intersection between a North-South and an East-West road to the east of the castle.

"We had reinforced this area to prepare for this attack. We had advanced our newest Company to attack what we had thought to be relatively undefended lands."

Abuahad shook his head. "A whole Company! Destroyed in one swift battle. How does he do it?"

Knowing nothing, I asked, "Did they have cavalry?"

Geoffrey replied, "No, and those which you saw during the exercises were strictly experimental."

"So, what kind of reconnaissance did our forces have?"

"The usual. They had a screen of scouts a day ahead. They reported nothing."

"Where are they now?"

"They were also destroyed."

"Or, were they killed first?"

Geoffrey gasped, his mouth gaping like a fish out of water. "What are you suggesting, Gilraën?"

"If someone killed them, they couldn't have reported anything. If so, then the Company blundered into a trap."

"But, how could they have killed them all?"

I shrugged my shoulders, "Luck? Some warning? Magic?"

"Magic?" Geoffrey gaped at me.

"I'm guessing, here, but aren't there energies of some kind that can Sorcerers use to kill?"

Everyone looked to Talbot. He shrugged, answering, "Yes, why do you ask?"

"If magic could kill the scouts and the troops, couldn't a Sorcerer hide somewhere nearby then kill them all without them even realizing an attack was imminent? A troop of archers or of infantry could provide the Sorcerer with protection if discovered until he could unleash the killing spells."

Talbot shook his head vigorously. "No, that's not how we do things. Sorcerers fight enemy Sorcerers; armies fight armies. No Sorcerer would march with or fight with mere soldiers. I would be like Viscount Geoffrey sharing a tent with a common soldier, or General Abuahad changing places with a common slinger. It's just not done."

His reasoning was so ludicrous I couldn't help but laugh. When I finally regained control, I asked, "Are you kidding? You mean Sorcerers don't accompany the troops?"

"Absolutely not. We have few enough skilled mages. We will not risk them in combat situations."

Prince William added, "Talbot is right. Nobody would endanger their Sorcerers. It would be the height of foolhardiness."

"Why?"

"Let me explain," Talbot told me. "When a Sorcerer broadens his mental horizon, other Sorcerers can sense his presence. When we sense another Sorcerer, we attack... instantly. Therefore, Sorcerers hide their presence, while they try to learn whatever they can about a suspected enemy. Then, once they have deduced weaknesses, they attack.

"If a Sorcerer is with troops, he must protect them. To do this, he must expose his existence. That will allow other Sorcerers to sense his presence and attack him. That is why Sorcerers do not accompany troops."

"But," Gilraën argued, "Knowing you don't defend your troops, couldn't they reinforce their troops with Sorcerers and use them to destroy our troops?"

I Came

William shrugged. "Although what you say is unlikely, it is possible. However, I have no intention of endangering my Sorcerers by thrusting them into the melee of war without evidence that Beckworth is using his Sorcerers in a similar manner. It is unbelievably foolhardy and a violation of all accepted conventions."

"How could you learn if he is using his Sorcerers in that manner?" I asked.

Talbot answered in his stead, "We intend to send you to our southern borders to scout for us. As an Elf, you will have unique advantages in speed, stealth, endurance and magical ability."

"Me?" I squeaked in astonishment.

"Yes, you, Gilraën," Prince William declared. "Talbot has a most interesting group of acquaintances distributed throughout not just this kingdom but that of this entire continent. It is they who can provide the support you will need for operations in the field. Talbot will lay the groundwork, while you continue your training by my Sorcerers in the skills and techniques you will need to be successful. Then you shall report back to me through Talbot's agents."

"But…," I sputtered, "I'm not ready for something like that."

William smiled bitterly, "Yes, I know. You have one week to learn. You will study with Talbot, Norton and Farmount to learn everything you must know in terms of magic. You will also work with my sister and Lady Eleanor to learn other skills you will need.

"I don't know when you will be ready, but certainly within one week." He hesitated, "If you are willing, that is…."

In fact, I was. I had signed on for adventure, and all I'd had so far was food and archery practice… oh, and being Vigash's throw toy. In our games, my Archer had often scouted behind enemy lines, fighting anything from one-vs-one to one-vs-many. I did it for the excitement, for the adventure, for the glory of the highest score, the next level. Yes, I had been a team player in many games, but most of that was advising the others in the tactics they would employ to win the game. Then I would wander off to create my own individual hit-and-run mayhem against the enemy. That was what I had signed on to do.

Reid

"Sure!" I could hardly contain myself. "When do I start?"

Talbot answered, "Immediately. You will work with Master Norton to perfect your prescience and perception. You will work with me to learn mental control and skills. You will work with Princess Cassandra and Viscountess Eleanor to learn the subtle skills of body language, observation and other so-called womban's skills. You will work with Master Farmount to learn 'transporting.' And, finally, I will teach you fundamentals of healing."

A quarter of an hour later, I was meeting with Master Norton. I asked him how he was and if he was recovering.

"What is it to you, Elf? Trying to endear yourself to me? No, I teach you, because Prince William demands my services. I obey. But, Elf, I have no regard for you or your kind. So, let us be on with this.

"I lead; you follow. Let us begin." He vanished.

Knowing what he wanted, I, too, vanished and felt for his presence. He was moving behind me and to my left. I turned to follow, engaging my prescience to perceiving the ground before me. I ran, breaking into a long stride in my attempt to catch him. It required so much of my concentration to chase him I didn't see what was going on around me.

Suddenly, I was airborne. My hands and knees ploughed into the dirt, shredding skin. Before I could move, something smashed into my back, knocking out my breath.

"You see, Elf? You're not that smart, that able, or that strong. I, a mere mortal, have just killed you. Let's do it again. I lead, you follow." And he was gone.

Once again, I *faded* and raced after him. He knew these lands, where he was going, and where the obstacles were. I was at every disadvantage, except one – I was determined.

Again, I pursued his mental presence. However, I now knew that Norton was planning to ambush me. Since my prescience was limited in its scope, I had to slow down enough to broaden my peripheral vision while also attentively watching the ground before me. I glanced to one side and then the other, hoping to see him

I Came

before he could attack me. The more I looked to the side, the slower I walked, until I was loping at a speed only slightly greater than were I running. If he simply ran, he would be gone, and I would have no chance of finding him. Yet, I believed that Norton was far more interested in humiliating me than he was in teaching me.

Then, I felt a presence somewhat to my right, and moving in the opposite direction. I wasn't sure it was him, but I was taking no chances. I turned to my left, and put on a huge burst of speed, hoping I'd put a big distance between us. I slowed and then circled back toward my starting position.

Almost immediately, I felt a presence ahead of me. I put a greater effort into determining who or what it was I was pursuing. I believed I sensed Norton, but I couldn't be sure. Regardless, it was moving really fast, and I couldn't see anything where my mind said it should be.

I slowed, trying to pursue without being detected. I widened my vision, while extending it forward. I adjusted my speed to match his, using his movement to help me perceive the terrain.

Then he veered off to the left. I slowed, suspecting a trap. I moved to the right, running parallel to him, but not overtaking him.

He veered to the right, and I crossed behind him. He veered again, coming back towards me. I put on a burst and turned to circle behind him. But he turned again, turning towards me.

Suddenly, I heard the line from a movie in my mind. "Crazy Ivan!" Jonesy yelled. Scott Glenn ordered, "All stop! All quiet on the boat!"

I stopped as quickly as I could and stood stock-still. I cloaked my mind, making a hole in the energy well where I stood. I tried to see, but dared not use magic. I was blind and immobile, awaiting an enemy intent on hurting me.

Then, there it was. The presence was close enough I could determine that it was Norton. I knew that, if I wanted to escape, I had to be optically invisible, while also hiding my energy signature. I concentrated on non-being – just letting myself become one with the world.

Suddenly, the universe revealed itself to me. I could envision the energy spectrum from a purple deeper than deep to a red beyond red. I could see the weft and warp of energy not just surrounding the planet but actually part of the air, the land, and all the life forms around me. I saw the world as it really is, almost to the molecular level. I saw all the plants and animals simultaneously standing out from the darker, low energy rocks and dirt.

And there was Norton, his face screwed up in concentration, wrapping the energy of his spells around him. Yet, his spells were tangled and knotted, like ropes tossed carelessly into a pile. I could feel his mind working furiously, reiterating, *'Where is she?*

'Aha!' I thought, *'It's working.'*

Maintaining my serenity, I considered my own energy envelopes. Mine were also tangled, but not as badly as were Norton's. I untangled one of mine, aligning it with the fields, 'ironing' the fabric of energies. As I did so, I felt more at ease, and it wasn't as hard to maintain my invisibility. In addition, my sight was much improved; although my peripheral vision was still blurred.

Norton walked right past me.

'Whew!' I thought.

As he continued on, I felt the wisp of a second thought. He seemed both angry and disappointed. He kept thinking, *'Where?'* And the image of a knife in a woman's back underlay the question.

My curiosity piqued, I turned to follow him, rapidly breaking into a *Sorcerer's Walk* some fifty feet behind him. Again, in my newfound serenity, I saw the knots, tangles and inconsistencies of the *fugitos* spell. As I followed Norton, I untangled more strands and loosed knots that had entangled me. Every step was easier, my forward vision improved, and even my peripheral vision was better. I found it easy to look left to right and back as though driving in heavy traffic. I could readily see the path before me and did not need to use my perception to see ahead and remember the way. Best of all, Norton was unaware of me following him.

Unseen and undetected, I studied Norton more intently. His mind was a roiling whirlwind of spells, commands, ideas, thoughts and desires, all clouded by his mental barriers and the combined effects of the *Sorcerer's Walk* and *fade*. Yet, some thoughts were uppermost in his mind. Paramount was his need to find me. Second to that, though, was his desire to kill me!

'*Kill me?*' I almost lost it. My serenity slipped, if only for a second.

Norton seemed to sense me and veered sharply to the left.

I let him go, determined to reacquire him when his fears had subsided. I raced ahead, getting perhaps a mile away, before turning. I slowed to a stop and spun in a circle, 'clearing my six' before returning to where I'd lost Norton.

Neither seeing nor sensing anything unusual, I broke into a long stride, weaving back and forth in a search pattern. After many minutes, I was afraid I'd lost him. Then, I felt him far off to my right. I slowed to find him without being found.

There he was! But something was amiss. I sensed he had given up... quit. He felt despondent and hopeless. Then I felt him overcome with resolve. William. The castle. Utter destruction. Death to them all - especially that strutting princeling. Sacrifice - noble sacrifice! The way open to invasion. Victory! Glory! My glory!

And then he was gone. He was fast, knew the land and his destination, but his course was evident. He was heading for the castle.

I followed, trying to figure out the jumble of thoughts in Norton's mind. 'What was he going to do? Prince William was the key. Something about the castle. William was in the castle, and we were racing there at high speed. Utter destruction? Death? William?

'Is he going to kill Prince William by somehow destroying the castle? How?' I asked myself. "Sacrifice... himself? For Glory? And to open the way for invasion? By whom? For whom? Beckworth?'

The castle loomed. Norton slowed to a stop and entered. I slowed, but ran inside, in spite of the protestations of the gate warden. I focused on Talbot, demanding that he meet me immediately.

Seconds later, he accosted me just outside the great hall.

"Norton's going to kill William and blow up the castle. Protect the Prince." I sped off in one direction, while he headed in the other. I could feel him summoning the rest of the Sorcerers, but knew it'd be too late.

I raced up flights of stairs to the chamber beneath the stairs. It was the only place I could think of. Abuahad and several of his captains sat around the mapping table.

I shouted, "Prince William's life is in danger," and ran off.

I ran up two flights of stairs, turned the corner then up two more. I emerged onto a high balcony far above the great hall. I strung my Elvin bow and nocked an arrow. It was pitifully little, but the best I could do at the spur of the moment.

Evidently, my mind was still working on the conundrum posed by Norton's thoughts. I remembered Norton's mind's eye as he considered 'utter destruction.' He had pictured a white light emanating from his chest. He pictured the ceiling, walls collapsing, and a hole left where the castle had been.

'A bomb?' I thought. 'They don't have explosives or even chemistry. They have elementary extraction, smelting, and foundry skills, but their understanding of the processes themselves or the crystallography of the annealing process is minimal… artisans, but neither metallurgists nor chemists.'

Still, the picture of a terrorist exploding himself in the midst of a crowd was all too familiar. Regardless of their state of chemical knowledge, Norton had envisioned an explosion. But how?

That brought up a second thought: How could I stop it? If it's a terrorist thing, then Norton could set it off regardless of what I did. What I needed was a containment vessel. It didn't have to be permanent, just strong enough to hold the explosion until I could get it away from the castle… sort of a big balloon?

Suddenly, he was there below me. His hatred filled the room. His intent to kill… to explode was his only desire.

I Came

Talbot stepped forward. "Norton, you shall not pass. William is under my protection." A bluish-gray wall erupted around him, expanding from floor to ceiling and wall-to-wall.

"Protection? Ha!" Norton sneered. "I have suffered under your childish reign long enough. It's time for you to learn who is really the Master." He raised his hands and pushed his palms toward the miasma, deforming it like a fist into a pillow.

Talbot scowled, and the cloud grew both in depth and in intensity.

Norton seemed to puff up, becoming both taller and stouter. His hands glowed, and a reddish beam impinged on the cloud. Blue-white sparks sputtered and died, as the crimson beams slowly penetrated the magical wall.

Talbot frowned, and the wall became a whitish-gray solid that reflected and deflected the beams.

Again, Norton seemed to grow both physically and in ascendancy. He took on a glow, which emanated from deep within him. I saw a field of lines appear around him, building in power. Energy surged from him and back into him as though he were a magnet. As the energy increased, a low tone rumbled through the hall. The energy grew, and the tone became higher, stronger, and louder.

Finally, I could see what he was doing. I understood. He was the bomb! He was working himself into a nuclear explosion! The thought was completely beyond anything I could have expected. He wasn't made of fissionable elements, but he was, somehow, intending to convert his mass to energy. It was beyond all chemistry or physics.

I had no idea of what to do. Instead, I did the only thing I could. I pulled my bow, aiming just to the right of his spinal column. As I was about to loose the arrow, I concentrated on containing the impending explosion.

My arrow flew straight and true. Norton collapsed, but his body continued to grow. It grew ever brighter, and the noise became a shriek.

Talbot was already there.

"He's going to explode!" I yelled. "Get him as far from here as we can. Get everyone far away from him!"

Talbot turned, shouting to Fairmount, "Send him as far as you can beyond the furthest practice field."

Fairmount muttered… and muttered… and muttered. Norton's body was the size of a dinosaur, filling half the hall. The sound was beyond loud… it was painful. Paid wracked my entire body. '*What is he waiting for?*' I asked, looking to Fairmount.

He raised his arms and seemed to push the air. With that, the sound ceased. The body disappeared, but the danger wasn't.

"Get out of here!" I yelled. "If the walls come down, we'll all be killed. Get everyone out… and as far away from the castle as we can get."

I raced Talbot to William's side. Each of us grabbed an arm, lifted him up, and sped from the hall, zig-zagged through the village and beyond the gate. We turned left and broke into a ten-fold *Sorcerer's Walk*. Other Sorcerers assisted members of the family, the staff, and the military into the relative safety of the far wood where they joined us.

A bright light flared on the horizon beyond the castle. A huge menacing cloud rose ever higher beyond the clouds. A hurricane swept toward us, bending, breaking and flattening trees, houses and buildings. Then, it was upon us, knocking everyone down who was still standing.

As a dark cloud spread over us, and soot and ash sprinkled down, Talbot sprang into action. "Help me, everyone!" he shouted. Every Sorcerer rushed to his side. They joined hands, acting together to raise a shield

"Gilraën! Join us. We need your strength."

I rushed to his side and joined the rest. As I relaxed into my serenity, I experienced the entire world. I felt the others, and understood Talbot's intent, but he wasn't doing it right. He was doing it the hard way. His method was all knots and tangles, ruining the effect and expending far too much energy. Were this wasted energy redirected properly, we could protect the entire castle, and even cause a lifting that would blow the soot beyond inhabited areas. As it lifted and spread across a larger area, the effects would be diluted.

"Focus through me, Talbot!" I commanded.

Without hesitation, he focused his power through me. Suddenly, I felt the full power of ten masters and about twenty novitiates flowing through me. I disentangled the knots and restored the web of energy. As I did, the size of the shield doubled, and the shape became more lofted. The wind lifted the clouds and spread them wider and higher.

As we dissolved our shield and drew our collective breaths, Prince William and the court rushed up to us. William asked, "What was that?"

"Indeed, Gilraën, what was that? Never have I seen or heard of such a thing."

I thought for a few moments. "I'm not sure, but it appeared to be a nuclear bomb. Essentially, Norton turned his mass into energy. As far as I know, what he did was impossible, but he did it."

"But why?" Cassandra asked.

Isadora stated, "I never trusted that man." She looked to Richmond. "I told you."

Richmond nodded, "That you did. I trusted you, but I had no way to test your observations. Perhaps we should test your perceptions, dearest. You may be a truth seeker, you know."

Cassandra interrupted, "Again, why?"

Richmond answered, "He comes from the border region. I know he has a brother who still lives down there."

Prince William stepped forward. "These are all questions that can wait. Right now, I want to know who was injured, what was damaged, and how quickly we can repair it. Once we have assessed the damage and healed the injured, then we can answer these questions.

"Cassandra, take charge of these efforts. Do what you must. Support our subjects in any way you feel necessary. Richmond, Isadora go with Cassandra.

"Talbot, Gilraën, generals and captains, join me in the war room.

"Throckmorton, Fairmount, we need replacements."

He turned and marched towards the castle, with us trailing behind like puppies behind their mother. As we returned through the outskirts of the village, concerned citizens ran out to greet their prince. With almost infinite patience, he wended his way through the throng, answering questions, and referring problems to Cassandra and her companions.

As we entered the castle, each of us looked up to the ceiling, wondering if it was still safe. Talbot and I attempted to assess the structure, finding nothing unusual. William seemed unconcerned. He led us rapidly to the war room and stood at the head of the table.

"I don't know what happened, but I do know that our realm, our subjects, and our very existence are endangered. I suspect Beckworth, through his agent, Norton. I know of Norton's family. He has a brother, Rodger. They lived in an estate that is now in the contested area in the southeast.

"William Norton arrived in my court some ten years ago. He claimed that he was attacked by his brother and had barely escaped with his life. He further claimed that his brother, Rodger, had become a follower of Lord Beckworth.

"Talbot, Richmond and Falsworth each interviewed him, and found his story to be ingenuous. However, our good Baroness Phaed warned me not to trust him. It turns out she was correct, and my finest Sorcerers were wrong.

"We now know that Beckworth or the Nortons know how to dissemble before the best of Sorcerers. Who knows who else they have taught, or what havoc they intend? Without a doubt, had it not been for Princess Gilraën, we might all be dead, and Beckworth would have won a great victory.

I Came

"As it is, he has exposed his game to us. We know he will expend his Sorcerers, and that he is playing a 'long' game. He is twenty moves ahead of us, and we are vulnerable.

"We need to find what Beckworth intends, what means he will use, and when he plans to execute them. Suggestions?"

Abuahad said, "We do not have the forces to defend every measure of the contested area. Even if we did, we'd be uniformly weak everywhere, in violation of the most basic military principles."

William harrumphed, "So, you took all those words to say nothing?"

Talbot said, "I have been working with Lady Gilraën to reconnoiter the areas to the southeast where our Company was annihilated. She was working with Norton to advance her skills." He turned to me. "My Lady?"

"Yes, I was training with him." I explained what I had experienced on the hill, the unexplained presence, and my escape. Then, I told of today's experience, and how I had learned Norton's thoughts. I did not explain my awareness of the universe, its forces, or its warp and woof. I wasn't sure why, but I felt that my prescience of the world was a thing better kept to myself.

When I had finished, Geoffrey asked, "And what of your studies of the zhaks?"

I explained how I had introduced myself to the zhaks, and how I had befriended them. I described their families, their social interactions, and their attitudes. I also explained my thoughts on how a charioteer could befriend a family of zhaks, and how they might respond. I concluded, "I would suggest we start with my archers. They and I could work together as a reconnaissance team."

The sound of silence filled the room.

"What?" I asked. "Did I say something?"

Abuahad finally found his voice. "It's just not done, Lady. You are a princess, an Elf, and a magus. They are common archers. They are not charioteers or scouts."

I was irritated. This kind of attitude is not only prejudicial, but also incompatible with rational military operations. "Whoa there, General. They are great archers and good people. They are my friends, and they could be an elite military force, and an example of a whole new way to perform deep reconnaissance. My present aspect as an Elf has nothing to do with it."

Prince William intervened. "Abuahad, Gilraën, let us discuss this for a moment. Gilraën, Abuahad is correct. We do not mix classes of people, types of weapons, or order of arms.

"However, Abuahad, Gilraën might have an excellent idea. Her background provides a wealth of knowledge in military matters on other worlds. Perhaps we should study these formations.

"If you are comfortable, and the archers are equally comfortable and can develop as charioteers, then, perhaps, we should try the experiment. If it is successful, we might have an excellent reconnaissance troop."

Regardless of the merits of my argument, Abuahad was unconvinced. Yet, he could not countermand Prince William's suggestion. Instead, he sniffed and returned to the map.

William shrugged and smiled at me. "You've stuck your head out, Princess. I hope you are successful, otherwise Abuahad will mention this incident every time you make a suggestion."

"I don't know that it will work. I do know that such tactics have been inordinately successful in wars on my world. We had Rangers, and Commandos, and Seals, and Delta Force and all sorts of names. They are deep penetration, highly trained, and highly motivated elite troops. If my archers agree, and if they can befriend the zhaks, then there is a chance that we could create such a force. I know that's a lot of ifs, but should it be correct, you will have a whole new type of military force and a new way of fighting Beckworth."

"What other ideas do you have, Gilraën? Obviously, Beckworth is preparing to escalate to a level of warfare beyond imagination. What I had envisioned as a war between armies had become a war of terror and destruction of all that I know. Whatever help, ideas, stratagems or tactics you can suggest, I need to know. Whatever changes we need to make to survive and overcome this pestilence, we must make if we are to be victorious."

"Actually, My Prince, this is my second or third suggestion. I suggested incorporating Sorcerers into Battalions. I suggested trying to understand zhaks. And, now I suggest cavalry reconnaissance.

"You are right when you say that you are engaged in a new form of warfare. I lived in that world all my life until coming here. It is frightening, but all too real. You must adapt or die. If I can, I will try to advise you when I can."

"Good. Could you join me after dinner in my chambers? I'm sure we have much to discuss. Can I entice you with thrak?" He smiled most becomingly.

I laughed. I couldn't help it. "Of course, my Prince, I would be delighted. However, if I do, then you must accept my invitation to my quarters."

He bowed his head, and nodded, "Your wish is my command." He took my arm by the elbow and led me back to the map table.

Talbot looked up, and pointed to the lower right of the map. "In view of Norton's treachery, I suggest we advance the day of Gilraën's departure." He looked meaningfully to me and to Prince William.

William sighed, but nodded his assent.

What choice did I have? If they could nuke us, I had to do everything I could to defeat Beckworth, or I had to leave this world. I had come here for adventure. So far, with the exception of this afternoon's madness, I had done almost nothing, other than be Vigash's play toy. And, if I left Trahe, what would happen to William, Cassandra and all the other people I had met and those with whom I now shared a bond? Without me, their chances of survival were slim. With me, they were still slim, but a lot better.

I nodded my agreement.

Talbot pointed to the south-central part of the wooded area of the northern bulge of the continent of Jaralii. "This is where we are in the castle of Shesol Vys, which means 'burning rock' or coal." He pointed further to the southeast just beyond the forests. "This is the area where our Company was attacked and destroyed. It's sparsely populated with no real roads but many paths and trails. There are five larger villages and around twenty centers of population. There are scattered farms, ranches and orchards.

"Nine of the twelve clans of Dwarves and one tribe of Elves live in the great mountains to our south. However, I must warn you of Krells, Trolls and Gaunts.

"Krell are huge, hairy, and extremely dangerous. They are very fast, often in groups, and we believe they can negate magical spells such as *Sorcerer's Walk*, night vision, and even *Divergio lepto*. It is said that you will sense them before they are so close that you will be in danger, but there are few who can attest to this. They are smart, highly capable, and can be highly sociable. They love to drink and laugh and eat. Should you meet one, make friends quickly, or race away as fast as you can until you are so far away that you can long walk."

"Yes," I interjected. "Vigash has told me about them. He's even thrown me to the ground several times, when he demonstrated their fighting techniques. I must say, they're not all that sophisticated. Then again, they need little technique when they're that big."

Talbot laughed, "Yes, I have to agree, they don't. That's why you must be doubly careful.

"Now, about Trolls. They are also huge with a genetic memory. They are reluctant to speak, but when they have something to say, listen carefully. They have no magical abilities, but are impervious to most magical attack. Befriend them if you can; otherwise, run.

"Gaunts are gigantic, blue, feline creatures. They are lone carnivores. They are incredibly fast and hunt anything they desire – Krell, Trolls, anything… except dragons, of course. Your only defense is to *Sorcerer's Walk* at a high multiple. Fortunately, they tire quickly.

"I will teach you the sigils and recognition signs, including passwords for the Guild of Assassins, the Guild of Thieves, the Guild of Witches and others. They will be your points of contact. They will provide you with food, a place to rest, weapons and refuge. Nobody will interfere with any of these powerful guilds, and you, being one of them, will be doubly protected.

"Beginning tomorrow, you and I will work together to prepare you for an extended journey into the disputed territories and beyond. I will disburse gold for you to buy food, shelter and any equipment you need. I will also teach you the language and customs of the people you will meet, and a name and personal history by which they will know you."

I nodded, and asked, "When should I be ready to leave?"

"On the third day. You have until then to prepare yourself, My Lady."

"When do we start?"

"Tomorrow morning. In the meantime, I believe you have several tasks to complete before supper with the Prince."

A short time later, I found my archers lazing on the side of a hill, watching men-at-arms beating on each other with halberd, pike and sword on armor and shield. Captains were shouting and commanders storming about. It was great theater, and my archers had found a perfect vantage point.

"Gilraën!" Harold shouted with joy. "Come, join us!"

I could hardly refuse. It was indeed a wonderful show of military pomp, glory and arms. However, I had to interrupt their simple pleasure. "Men, I have a bit of an adventure for you, unless you prefer lazing around,"

Suddenly, everyone gathered around, eager for a change of pace.

"You saw the chariots, remember? They were handled poorly and were unprepared for battle. I have met with a family of the beasts that were pulling the cart.'

"What?" Yashi exclaimed. "You spoke with the beasts?

"Indeed," I answered. Then, I told them of my vision of a chariot cavalry reconnoitering deep behind enemy lines. And they would be the charioteers. The prospect excited all twelve of them, but they were anxious about how they would get on with the zhaks.

"Come with me, and I'll introduce you."

After I had informed the Captain of my need train my archers, I led them to the paddocks. We entered, and I went straight to the herd with which I had communicated, opened the door, and edged my way in.

The herd looked up, and the stallion edge closer to me. I was prepared and had my bag filled with fruits. I offered one to the stallion, who accepted it eagerly. Moments later, the whole herd surrounded me, nosing and sniffing my bag. I handed each of them a fruit, being careful how I presented it from my palm rather than from my fingers.

I glanced up to see a dozen archers leaning on the fence. I glanced to the other paddocks to see other families of zhaks with their heads extended over the hip high walls.

I picked my way through the herd and out of the paddock. I walked over to a box I had sent over earlier. "Here," I instructed. "Take a bag of fruits and walk among the paddocks. Reach out with your minds, your hearts, and your senses. Look at them carefully and deeply into their eyes. Befriend them and seek the ones who will befriend you. Then, enter among them and offer the gift of food. Pat them. Touch them. Speak to them. Let them get used to your voice, your smell, and your visage. Let them come to know you as a friend and provider."

"Harold," I said to him, "come with me."

I led him to 'my' zhak family and 'introduced' him to the herd. I patted them and encouraged him to sit with them and feed them. I sat with the stallion, and 'talked' with him. I tried to explain that Harold would be their family's friend, while I was the overall herd leader with all men and zhaks under my authority.

The guys wandered around shyly looking into the paddocks and the big beasts. Each herd of zhaks was interested in one or, perhaps, two of the archers. Slowly, over the course of half an hour or so, eleven archers were sitting at the wire fencing of zhak families.

I Came

I stepped into the area between the paddocks, shouting, "Everyone, gather around." I pictured a scene with pairs of zhaks and archers in a semi-circle before me.

Sure enough, they did!

"You are Gilraën's Ghillies. a zhak family adopted each of you archers. You will honor, support, and defend them." I made sure that I projected the image of a zhak family and an archer together as a family.

"Archers, you have two weeks to become charioteers. Zhaks," Again, I used mental images. "You have two weeks to learn how to pull a chariot."

"In two weeks, I will lead you into the lands of our enemies. Zhaks and their humans must work together. All the zhaks and humans must work together.

"I will lead." Men and zhaks looked at each other, exchanging meaningful glances. "Tomorrow, you will learn how to work together." I went from family to family interrogating both the humans and the zhaks. They all were ready and eager to begin. I crossed my fingers. There was so much that could easily go wrong.

I returned to my quarters, where Cassandra, Eleanor and my household met me. They were dressed for supper and insisted that I do so as well. It was something that I had become used to doing, even if I wasn't comfortable with all the girly stuff. Looking in the mirror, I had to admit, I looked good when all dolled up.

'Whoa, big guy!' I reminded myself. 'This was my avatar, not me.'

My self-admiration was confirmed minutes later when we entered the great hall. Prince William was busy talking with General Abuahad and Sir Geoffrey. They were all quite serious with scowl lines in their foreheads.

William glanced up and stopped. His face hung loose, and his jaw slacked open. His eyes were as wide as saucers, and his attention was riveted on me, so much so that both Geoffrey and Abuahad turned and stared at me.

Cassandra giggled and whispered through the side of her mouth, "Well, you've got my brother's attention. I guess the girly stuff works!"

I couldn't help myself. I blushed from ears to toes. I giggled! I actually giggled! It was the girliest thing I'd ever done, and I was mortified. My VR games had never prepared me for this.

Prince William leapt to his feet, pulled a chair around Geoffrey, and sat it next to him. "Gilraën, sit here," he said, gallantly.

I did as he asked, leaving Cassandra to fend for herself.

"We are discussing our next move. I understand that you have introduced your archers… and we might as well admit they are yours, and not mine… to the zhaks. Do you think this pairing will work?"

I thought about what I had seen and felt as 'my' archers and 'my' zhaks were introduced to each other. I explained that the archers seemed to be accepted by the zhak families. The zhaks, however, were not fully accepting of the archers. Only time would resolve their relationship. If the archers performed well, then they might be accepted. If not, they likely wouldn't.

Prince William nodded in understanding. However, Abuahad was unconvinced. "Lady Gilraën, of what use will they be, even if your experiment is successful?"

I answered, "I think there are several uses for such a force. First, and this is the one I am aiming at right now, is reconnaissance. They can travel deeply into enemy-held territory, explore it, and escape before the enemy can react or trap them.

"A second employment would be rapid attack. Using speed, chariots can swing into range of an enemy force, fire volleys of arrows, and retreat before they can organize a resistance. By repeatedly attacking, they can disrupt an enemy force, potentially splitting small units off the main force and annihilating them.

"Third, they would be ideal in harassing either an advancing or retreating enemy force.

I Came

"Finally, they could be an excellent vanguard or rear guard. So they could serve a variety of functions supporting an advancing or retreating army and also during battle."

I waited for Abuahad to digest my ideas. Sir Geoffrey was much quicker to reply. "Are you sure this will work?"

"No, not at all. We did this stuff with horses. Our horses are much larger than your zhaks are. Still, they are herbivores. Their first instinct is to run away from danger. Much depends on trust.

"Horses are swift and powerful. They are used to being in a herd, next to others of their kind. Horses object to being forced into a team, but they accept being together.

"That's why I wanted the archers and the zhaks to have two weeks to get to know each other. They have to live together and develop trust. They have to work together. They have to trust each other implicitly enough so that the archers can convince the zhaks to go into battle alongside other chariots, driven by archers, pulled by a team of zhaks. I have no idea if it will work. Only time will tell."

* * *

Later that night, I stood with William on my balcony, three-quarters of the way up the tallest tower of the castle. The night was cool and cloudless. A silvery half-moon was high in the sky. A broad swath of light behind my left shoulder moved up and to the right behind the moon, and into the darkness beyond my sight.

He handed me a crystal vessel about a quarter filled with brownish liquid. I started to laugh, exclaiming, "The chalice from the palace is the brew that is true!"

William looked at me as though I were drunk. "What?"

"It's an old movie… The Court Jester. He is a jester that ends up in armor jousting with a real knight. The princess tries to poison the knight so the jester will win. Before the match, each drinks to the health of the king. So, the jester is told which has the poison. The chalice from the palace is the one that's ok, while the vessel with the pestle has the pellet that is poison. It's a really funny story."

A silvery orb appeared in the East, climbing quickly into the ebon sky.

"What's that?"

"That is our other moon, Chrybda. It crosses our skies three times per day. It is relatively close by, perhaps only 50,000 miles above us. We have been measuring its orbit carefully, fearing that it might plunge onto our planet. However, we find that it is moving away from us very slowly. It has taken many years of observations to confirm that, but we have been calculating the angles for almost a century, and can confirm those findings.

"Llombda, the great moon in the sky, is much further away... perhaps, 250,000 miles. We rotate beneath it. It is almost in the same plane as our orbit around our star, but not quite. We see our shadow on Llombda." He pointed at the half moon.

"Depending on our positions relative to our star, which we call Mummia, or Mother of All, sometimes Llombda appears pure silver, sometimes it is a dark on dark ball, but most times it is partially visible, as it is tonight. For some reason, these phases of Llombda are aligned with our orbit around Mummia, so there are twelve full cycles each year. That is how we keep track of longer periods of time, such as moons and orbits.

"Then, there are the stars. We used to think they were fires in the sky. However, since we learned to polish glass, we can magnify them to see them more clearly. We find that they are stars like Mummia. We have counted many thousands of them and find there are always more to be counted.

"We have never determined where they end, or even if they end. Some among us believe they have seen masses of stars so far away that they appear to be fuzzy stars. But, the clear-sighted among us are convinced they are collections of stars, and that there are many such collections. If so, the number of stars is beyond counting.

"Both the Elves and the Dwarves have told us there are other worlds inhabited by civilized beings circling those distant stars. We understand that we are just one of many inhabited worlds. We know we were not alone. This is a comfort to me knowing that others exist. I yearn to meet them, to talk with them, and to learn from them. It was my hope that civilized beings would be friendly with other civilizations.

"I was naïve. When the Adjudicars arrived, I had to abandon the idea that other civilizations were good, kind or tolerant. I now take comfort in the thought that most of them would be our friends, even though some few of them might be our enemies."

He turned to me, looking deeply into my eyes. "Am I so naïve, Gilraën? Or is there love between civilized people?"

I shivered. I wasn't sure if I was cold, or if one of my emotion's strings had been plucked. Was he aware of the double meaning? Was it his intention?

"Oh!" he exclaimed, "Are you chilled? Wait here. I will get something." He was gone before I could object.

Moments later, he returned carrying a blue-white stole. He draped it around my shoulders, his hand falling to my waist. "This was my wife's. I have thrown nothing of hers away, hoping that one day I could summon the courage to visit upon them and the memories they hold before returning them for reuse by the wardrobe. I'm pleased I did not. It suits you. Is this better?"

It was.

He was.

* * * * *

Chapter 7 - Vengeance

The day had lost its light long before I approached the little village. I had wished to enter the village without being noticed, which wasn't all that easy, but the night made it more difficult rather than easier. Fewer people were out and about, so no individual passing through the gates was scrutinized closely. Granted, I could disappear almost instantly, but I was tired and hungry; my energy reserves were low. I needed a place to rest, recuperate, and from which I could establish a base of operations... a temporary refuge from which I could reconnoiter the area. I was still a hundred miles or more from the edge of the disputed territories, but Talbot and I had agreed that this would be a good place to start my mission.

I really needed to rest. The past few days had been exhausting. Richmond had been merciless. His crash course in magic had been brutal. My brain still hurt. Worse, he was doing it all wrong. Human magic was effective, but not elegant. It was all force with no empathy for the forces engulfing, surrounding, and penetrating Trahe. I tried to explain it to him, but he just nodded, saying things like, "You're an Elf," and stuff like that, which didn't help me figure out this whole magic thing. I could have used more training from him, since his methods were forcing me to consider the differences between his magic and mine, allowing me to gain insights into both.

Cassandra and Eleanor helped me learn about clothes I should and shouldn't wear, including caps, hats and wraps that I could use to hide my ears. They taught me the local dialects and customs. They taught me about local food, drinks and social mores. And, they taught me the geography and topology, mapping the lands of Umbeqjaralii, including those usurped by Beckworth.

Baron Richmond of Phaed worked with me to learn about poisons, their antidotes, and how to avoid them. Fairmount taught me about transporting myself or others through space. Thackery specialized in killing curses, while Falsworth emphasized defensive magic.

Best of all, I spent those evenings with Prince William. He was a fascinating man. He was knowledgeable in the ways of magic, even

I Came

though he had no proficiency. His greatest skill was an almost perfect appraisal of people. He seemed to understand the Human animal and could place people into niches where they could apply their greatest strengths amongst people who would appreciate them and work with them. It was uncanny how he manipulated people, getting them to do what they were best at doing, while improving the overall position of the principality.

We spent just two evenings together, looking at the moons, the stars and quietly conversing about ourselves, our lives, and our wishes for the future. On our last evening, he asked, "So, Gilraën, when all of this is behind you, and you have collected your mountain of gold, what will you do? Will you stay here or return to your own world?"

I was honest with him. "I'll go home. I've always said that I was here for an extended vacation. I'm looking forward to a profitable adventure. Then, I'll go home, go back to my profession, and, as they say in the stories, live happily ever after."

He sat for several minutes, before asking, "Is there nothing that would keep you here?"

I knew what he wanted me to say, but I couldn't offer him hope. Yet, I didn't have to be brutal about it. "I really can't say. I've only been here a few weeks. I've hardly had a chance to know this planet, this continent, or any of its people, other than you and your court. I'd prefer to wait on that answer until I've been here long enough to answer knowledgeably."

* * *

I had to retrace my steps through the village before I found the sigil for the Guild of Thieves. After providing the proper passwords and responses, the Warden showed me to a small, but neat, room. A servant brought a substantial meal and a jar of the local brew. I didn't know what it was, but it looked and smelled delicious. I was about to chow down, when I remembered to check for poisons.

"Holy Shit!" I exclaimed. There were three poisons, each of which would have killed me in just minutes.

I bounded down the stairs, four Soul Blades still hidden, and the fifth in my hand ready for use. With lightning quickness, I grabbed the Warden, pinned him to the floor then stuck the point of my blade to his throat. "Poison?" I spat at him.

"My Lady!" a familiar voice called to me.

I turned just enough to see Talbot standing there, a shrewd smile on his face.

"Well done," he declared. "If you hadn't arrived in another few moments, I'd have been in your room administering the antidotes. Please, let our host rise before you do him an injustice. He was operating under my orders. Just a little test, you understand?"

I nicked the man's neck, drawing a drop of blood. The blade shimmered with a blue light, before returning to its normal blue-gray steel. I sheathed the blade, stood, and helped the man to his feet, as i threw a vicious glance at Talbot.

"Food!" I ordered, then turned on my heel and leapt upstairs to my room.

Talbot followed within seconds. "I have ensured that there will be enough for two. This will give us a time to talk about this area, and what you might find.

"This is the village of Willicamp. The Willis family founded it several centuries ago. This was their encampment, thus Willicamp.

"This is the central locale of this region. Five hamlets surround it, each named for one of Willis' sons. Alghelcamp is to the east about 10 miles. Vixhallcamp is north about 7 miles. Esselcamp is southeast about 15 miles. Methiacamp is south about 12 miles, and Porticamp is southwest roughly 18 miles.

"The three southern hamlets are the most direct routes to the border between Umbeqjaralii and Unterjaralii, Beckworth's territory. Were you to go 50 miles or so beyond Esselcamp, you would arrive in the village of Easbister. We lost Captain Feldersink's battalion in the area between Easbister and the Phaed River."

I Came

A knock on the door interrupted us. The landlord himself entered. After the most profound apologies, he beckoned two men into the room, bearing trays littered with covered bowls. How they managed to fit into the tiny room, I'll never know. The men placed new bowls and retrieved those that were poisoned. Moments later, the landlord was bowing out, leaving a table filled with bowls, jars and cups each filled with foods emitting overwhelming aromas promising a delicious meal.

Cautiously, I tested each of the assorted foods, and then looked to Talbot, who took the hint and confirmed my diagnosis. With that, I dug in as though I'd never seen food before. I ate steadily for half an hour, before coming up for a breath.

"Yes," Talbot commented, "You exerted yourself today and delved deeply into your reserves of energy. I must remind you that should you continue to do that, you can become vulnerable. Remember, you can drain energy from living things. Were you to just touch trees as you travel, you could retain your energy. There are many of them. Just touch them as you pass, stealing just a tiny mote of energy from each. There are so many of them, and you will take so little from each, that they will feed you, while suffering no more loss than if a cloud had passed overhead.

"Further, by doing so, you will easily absorb their energy as a small continuous flow, unlike this meal. You will need all night to digest this meal, to store it, and then to convert it to usable energy. With a steady trickle of energy derived from living things, you can sustain yourself for many days."

"You're right, I had forgotten that lesson. I've tried to absorb so much in such a short time, I've still not sorted it all out."

He asked, "Where do you travel next?"

"I talked to Princess Cassandra, Lady Eleanor and Prince William about this. We concluded that Beckworth might be consolidating his holdings, knowing he'd defeated the largest contingent of our forces in the area. It's likely he'll attack other villages nearby, using whatever techniques he used to annihilate Captain Feldersink's forces.

160

"I intend to travel the area, looking for anything unusual. I'll start in the east, and move south and west. I will disguise myself as much as possible, but I will need gold to pay for my needs. And, I'll need to find armorers, fletchers, or whatever artisans I might need to resupply me, as needed."

"Correct. I have thirty Golds for you. Have you discussed the value of money in these areas with Princess Cassandra or Viscountess Eleanor?"

"Yes, I did. Even more so, I talked with Rosie, Beryl and Dorothea. Lords and ladies understand one set of values, but see the world from their perspective. Rosie, Beryl and Dorothea see the world from the perspective of a common person, and especially that of a woman. Women are the backbone of any economy. They are the ones who demand products, determine quality, and define value. They are the ones who save, spend and invest. They know the value of the coin of the realm. And, it was they warned me about Golds. So, I asked you for small coins – Silvers, Coppers and Zincs. They are the real coins of commerce."

Talbot chuckled, "Yes, anyone who proffers Golds will be suspected immediately, will be cheated whenever possible, and will be overcharged for everything. It is far better to appear to be poor than to be wealthy.

"You can exchange Golds for lesser coins at any guild. Do you understand the official and unofficial exchange rates?"

I hadn't, so Talbot explained, "Officially, one Ingot of gold is divided into 10 parts called pounds. Ten Royals is a pound. A Royal is worth ten Golds. A Gold is ten Silvers. A Silver is ten Coppers, each of which is worth ten Zincs.

"However, reality is different. Each Guild will demand one Copper for every Gold in payment for the act of exchange. Often, they will try to extort more, but I'm sure that you can dissuade them. I warn you not to attempt cheating them, or the Guild will disbar you, which would be disastrous.

"Also, be aware that all coinage in the realm is protected by magic. This magic is evident to any person handling the coins. Here, feel one of these." He opened the bag of gold.

I Came

I reached in and picked out a Gold. The instant I touched it, I felt a warmth that I didn't expect. "It's warm," I said.

"Yes, and everyone can feel it. It's part of the minting process to deter counterfeiting. Counterfeiting is a serious crime in the kingdom. The penalty is death, so it's seldom attempted. Be sure that all money is real, lest you be accused." With that, he dumped the bag of coins into my hands. I felt each one before replacing it in the leather purse. Then, one of them felt odd. It was warm to the touch, as it might were it held closely in the hand. However, it didn't feel like the others. The warmth did not come from the metal but from heat it had absorbed from its surroundings. I studied it and compared it with other coins that did feel right. I laid out several coins alongside the odd one and studied them. Not only did the real coins feel warm, but they shimmered ever so slightly, whereas the slug just lay there in my hand like the dead hunk of metal it was.

"Very clever," I said. "I've seen lots of attempts to stop counterfeiting, but this is a first. How long have you been doing this?"

"Yes, it is," he replied, swelling with pride. "I thought of this many years ago. Beckworth was flooding our kingdom with worthless coins. It undermined our king's coinage and brought the realm to the edge of bankruptcy.

"I was just a second level at the time, but I approached Prince William with the idea. He talked with his father, who encouraged me to devise the method to do it. I worked with old Durbin, my master, for several months before we could be sure of how to mint the coins and deter magical interference.

"Thereafter, the problem disappeared. However, it took several months to weed out the bad coins, to determine who was cheated, and who was deliberately undermining the coin of the realm and to eliminate the counterfeiters. We have had no problems for the past ten years, but we are always on guard to detect any counterfeiting."

I filled a small pocket inside my bag with 28 gold pieces and 15 silvers. I tucked the bag into the interior of my pack. I put only 4 silvers, 9 coppers and 10 zincs into my purse. For most, this was a fortune, and I knew it. It would provide me with a measure of respect, without inspiring dreams of avarice. Further, my adopted aspect as a huntress and adventuress would deter any but the most desperate or dangerous from attacking me.

I left Willicamp early in the morning, before sunrise. I was well beyond Esselcamp and approaching the area of the disastrous defeat by sunrise. I literally stumbled upon it, tripping over a pile of burned bodies.

I took my time, studying the scene of carnage. I was seeking evidence of battle: broken helms, notched swords, splintered spears and hewn shields. There were none. In fact, there was a lot of 'none.' That is, there was no detritus, no armor, helmets, greaves, or braces... nothing!

Yet, there were bodies, or, at least, the remains of bodies. The fire had consumed most of the meat, but not all. The smell was terrible. Bones were piled haphazardly, partially burned. Crows and foxes (at least they looked like smallish dogs) dug into the pile, seeking meat and marrow.

I stood near the pyre, drained myself of all emotions to experience the aura of the place. I felt no terror, as I would if men had been embattled, injured, and dying in pain. I felt no blood in the land, as I would if men had been wounded and were dying on this spot. The only emotion I could sense was that of surprise. Although I couldn't confirm my suspicions, I was convinced that something other than physical conflict had destroyed Captain Feldersink's Company.

But what of Feldersink's supply train? Surely, one hundred twenty men would need food, healers, spare arms, and equipment. All of it would travel in carts or wagons. In turn, either men or teams of animals would pull them. I knew that such animals existed. I'd seen deer-like animals in local farms. They were slow but steady, and would probably serve similarly to oxen.

Regardless, where were they? Where were the wagons? Where were the teamsters, or the quartermasters, or other supply personnel?

I began a great circle, seeking roads large enough for wagons. There were none. I found one rutted and somewhat overgrown trail headed due south, the other similar one to the northwest. After a moment's thought, I turned away from the border and headed deeper

I Came

into Umbeqjaralii. An army might have retreated along its line of supply. A group of Sorcerers probably wouldn't. Having won a great victory, they'd head further into King Richard's realm, spreading death, destruction and fear.

I doubted they'd travel quickly. They'd explore, seeking opportunities. They'd investigate, looking to find the optimal locations wherein they could profit, while reducing the people's faith in their king. This would be their equivalent of Sherman's March unless I could prevent it.

I was invisible, flowing over the road at five-fold speed. I extended my perception in a large circle around me, complimenting my vision. Extending my senses to their limits, I attempted to feel for any life within miles of me. At first, all I saw was a hard packed, rutted, overgrown, and dusty dirt road amid lots of trees and little else. I reached out to extract tiny bits of energy from them, compensating for that which I was using. After a while, I became so involved in running, absorbing energy, and perceiving, I almost missed a flicker of sentience. I slowed slightly, allowing my senses to home in on the disturbance of the flow of energy.

It was weak, coming from my left. I had passed a trail that branched off, heading up a slope and into a wood. I returned to it and once again sensed that disturbance. As I closed on it, I slowed to a walk, approaching a farmhouse. A large dray stood before the house. Two smaller wagons were towards the side. A few heavy-legged herbivores grazed nearby.

Feeling several sentient life forms, I stood quietly, watching the fabric of space-time. I dared not reach out for fear that whoever was here might sense me.

Ever so slowly, I moved toward the nearby concentration of sentient life. I crept around the house, only to discover a small pile of bodies, including a few men, several women and many children. At least a dozen recently killed bodies were heaped haphazardly. It took all my self-restraint not to be sick.

Edging further around the house, I found four men sitting in wooden chairs, quietly eating. Each had a metal plate piled with hunks of meat and vegetables. From the smell, I knew the meal was cooked rather than raw, but of what ingredients, I didn't know.

I also knew each of those I saw was a Sorcerer. There was no doubt. They were guarding their presence. I doubted that even experienced Human Sorcerers would have detected their presence.

They were talking mentally, which was the energy I had detected. One, who might have been their leader, was talking about their next objective.

'Our orders are simple enough. We continue to the northwest, destroying every farm we find. Kill the people, slaughter the herds and flocks, burn the buildings and fields. No matter how powerful Richard believes himself to be, his troops can't march on empty stomachs.'

'I agree,' a second Sorcerer thought, *'and a hungry populace is a dissatisfied and rebellious one.'*

I edged back around the house. *'What do I do now?'*

Obviously, these four were Sorcerers. Any attempt to attack them with magic would become a contest of strength vs. strength. There were four of them and one of me. Regardless of my strength, their numbers would be too much to overcome.

'Weapons?' I thought. I hadn't seen any, but that didn't mean they didn't have swords under their traveling cloaks.

A plan slowly evolved in my mind. If I could take out one or two before they could react, it was likely I could avoid the others. My ability to fade was beyond that of William's Sorcerers, so it was likely that it was beyond that of these Humans.

'Likely, but not definitely,' I reminded myself.

I moved away a few hundred yards, and then dug into my pack, removing my quiver. I mounted the quiver in the pack such that the arrows would be readily at hand, yet held firmly so they wouldn't fall out or rattle against each other as I moved about. After stringing Bohesta, I extracted two arrows and glanced toward the farmhouse. I held the bow and the second arrow in my left hand, nocked the other, and then held the bow vertically in front of me, ready to pull. Slowly, I slipped back towards the farmhouse. Staying deep in the woods, I swung in a wide arc.

I Came

Ever so slowly, the group of four came into my sight. They were still sitting quietly, relaxing after their meal, completely unaware of my presence. I lifted my bow, aimed carefully, and loosed the shaft. Before the arrow was more than halfway to its destination, I nocked and fired the second.

Knowing the survivors would trace the source of the arrow almost instantly, I broke into a 3-fold Sorcerer's Walk. By the time the first arrow penetrated the leader's chest, I was ten yards away from my firing location. By the time the second hit home, I was nearly a hundred yards away and beginning to move faster. I dodged between trees, barely touching the ground as I circled beyond the farmhouse.

Both of the remaining Sorcerers acted immediately, disappearing. Their chairs flew backward as they rose and fled. However, they were careless, and I saw them heading in opposite directions as they faded.

I continued to flee as quickly as I could, putting more distance between me and them. No doubt, they had far more experience murdering than had I. Yet, they had made a tactical error by splitting up, rather than staying together.

I was a more capable Sorcerer than either of them. If I could find either of them, I could kill him without interference from the other. Then, I could hunt down the last of them, before seeking any other Sorcerers who had been loosed upon the kingdom.

There was no sign of any pursuit, so I began to work my way back toward the farm. I maintained my serenity, watching the fabric of the world, ensuring that I was not perturbing it, even as I sought out those who were. Human Sorcerers were powerful, but they didn't understand what they were doing. The result was a disturbance in the fabric the universe that reduced their effective use of magic. It was something I could observe and track.

I searched slowly and carefully, working back and forth in ever-widening circles. I had traveled some thirty miles before I felt a tiny twinge in the ether. It was tantalizing. I lost and regained it several times, but it seemed always ahead of me. I lost him again and again. At first, my searches took a long time. But each time, I found him more quickly, so I knew I was traveling in the right direction.

My pursuit lasted through the night, continuing into the following day. I gained on him slowly. By the following midmorning, I was very near him. I could feel his fear. As tired as I was, I knew he was far worse. He was exhausted, and I knew it. Thanks to Talbot's training, I had worn him down.

Suddenly, he slowed, and then stopped. Appearing in the middle of the road, he shouted, 'Come out, damn you! I know you are there; I can feel your damning presence. Come out and fight me, you coward!"

His words stung me. How dare he call me a coward? He had used his magic to kill hundreds of soldiers, giving them no chance to protect themselves. He had murdered an entire family and plotted to murder every other family with whom he came into contact. How dare he?

I reached to my belt, grasping Dashemba. "Die!" I said in a voice like thunder, which reverberated through the heavens and rolled across the land. He raised his hands to ward off my attack, but before he could complete the movement, the Soul Blade appeared in his chest. For just a moment, it remained in his chest as he fell backward. He landed in a heap on the road, then twitched and fell limp. Having drunk its fill, Dashemba returned to its sheath, glowing brightly.

Having killed yet another of Beckworth's Sorcerers, I was suddenly at a loss. I was lost, deep behind enemy lines, but this predicament was my archer's forte. My pursuit of him had been so single minded that I was unaware of time or space. I needed to rest and recuperate, but, more importantly, I needed to contact Talbot to inform him of the dangers moving through the kingdom.

Searching with my mind, I discovered a nucleus of energy just a few miles away. Within minutes, I was in the central square of a prosperous village. My diligent search for the sigils I knew had to be here was nearly fruitless. Finally, I saw one near the bottom of a wall. It was half covered in splattered mud – the Guild of Assassins.

My attention diverted as I thought of the old Groucho Marx one-liner, "I wouldn't belong to a club that would have me."

I Came

Following the sigils down an alley to a blank wall gave me some concern, but I knocked carefully. A voice came out of the wall with a challenge, which I answered in kind. Once inside, we exchanged signs and countersigns, until the Warden accepted me. "Place your weapons here," he said, pointing at a table in the foyer.

I hesitated.

"Do you think anyone would disturb the weapons of an assassin?" he asked, his eyebrow raised in mock astonishment.

I smiled and placed them on the table. He led me to a lovely little room. The bed was soft and comfortable. The window overlooked a lovely atrium. It was cool and inviting in every way. Evidently, assassins traveled and relaxed in style.

After I had arranged my belongings, I separated my dirty clothes. Then I rang the little bell beside the door.

A man appeared at my door. When I asked about laundry service, he looked askance. I explained that my clothes were dirty and smelled. They needed to be cleaned and properly folded before morning. Before he could say more, I asked him when dinner was served.

With that, he smiled, eagerly explaining, "Lady, the tavern is open at all times. If you are hungry, all you need do is ask. I could even bring food to you, if it is more convenient. But I do not know about cleaning clothes. It's just not done."

"Ah, it is now." I stated emphatically. "However, I'm sure that it is unusual, and might require an '*extra service charge.*'" I handed him a copper.

He looked at the coin for a moment, then back at me. I added a second copper to his hand, which was obviously much more than the job was worth.

"The remainder is yours that you might provide me with the knowledge of events concerning me should I be unaware of them."

He smiled, nodded his head, "Aha! I believe I can arrange for this special service. Will you be joining the company at dinner?"

"Yes, I think I shall. Also, I will need to meet with the Guild Master as quickly as possible. I have information critical to the Guild."

The man nodded and left. After I locked the door, I unpacked cleaner clothes and took advantage of the ewer and basin. I carefully arranged a silk around my head and over my ears. Then, I pulled a Silver from the depths of my pack, ensuring I had more than enough money to serve any need I might have. Finally, I dressed in black leather trousers, a brown cotton-like pullover shirt, and a black leather jacket.

Just as I was about to step out, I had an idea. "Come!" I commanded, thinking of my blades. Almost instantly, all five of them appeared at my hands. Satisfied, I stowed them in their usual places: one in each of my boots, one strapped to each forearm, and one tucked behind my neck.

'So much for security,' I thought.

I bounded downstairs, following my nose until I found the bar. Smoke filled the room. It wasn't tobacco, but smelled just as good and bad. As always, the smells of smoke, alcohol, sweat, burning animal fat, and such filled the air. Obviously, this was the place I was seeking.

As expected, it was dark. Even my Elvin eyes took a few seconds to accommodate themselves. A group of five men stood near the wall to the left end of the bar, looking inward at each other, laughing loudly. A table with three men was to my right. The corner booths were empty, as were the ones along the back wall beyond the bar. The other three tables to my right were empty. I approached the near end of the bar, attracting the attention of the barkeep.

He glanced up at me, looked away, and then his head snapped back to me. "We don't allow womban here," he growled.

I glowered at him, quietly warning, "It is a poor idea to make an enemy of an assassin, barman. I'll have a pint of your finest... over there." I pointed to the corner table. "What are you serving for dinner?"

I Came

He gulped, as the five men began to jest with him. One shouted, "Yes, Sheyburn, it's a poor idea to anger an assassin."

A second shouted at me, "If you are an assassin, you are the prettiest I've ever seen. Where are you from, dear womban? And, why is it we have never heard about you before?"

As the barman plunked a tankard of brew on the bar before me, I replied, "I wouldn't be successful were I known to many. It might be best if you forgot you have met me. There are few who yet live, who know of me."

I took my jar to the back table, where I took a seat allowing me to watch the entire room while I remained in the shadows.

After a few moments, the barman delivered a whole pie to the table. It was six inches in diameter and two inches deep. And it smelled wonderful! I hoped it wasn't poisoned.

"Lady, can I get you another one?" he indicated the tankard.

"If it's as good as this one, then yes, thank you," I replied enthusiastically.

The barman beamed. Evidently, he was also the brewer.

I tested the pie for poisons, and, discovering none, dug in. It was as delicious as it appeared. Assassins certainly knew how to live.

Half an hour later, I swallowed the last morsel. Then, I sat back, thoroughly sated. While I slowly finished my tankard, I took the time to study the room and its patrons. I had noticed several others arrive while I had been eating. I had noted the numbers in each party and where they sat. I hadn't studied them when they entered, but now it was my chance.

Three odd-looking fellows sat at a corner table opposite me. They were short, broad and swarthy, with black hair and long beards. They talked quietly among themselves in an odd guttural language.

'Dwarves?' I asked myself. 'Could be.'

The Dwarves live in the mountains to the south and southwest. There were twelve clans, all descended from a single line, supposedly created by a pair of gods. What were they doing so far away from their mountains and mines?

The group of five who had been standing had taken refuge at the large table between my corner and that of the Dwarves. The five were drinking heavily and becoming increasingly boisterous. They glanced surreptitiously towards me, and then away, as though with guilty thoughts.

To my right, two large men sat in a booth. Both leaned in towards each other, as though talking about something both serious and secret.

Beyond them at the other corner of the bar was a small table. One man sat there watching everyone. He was definitely the odd man out. All the men in the tavern had shielded their minds, but his was blank, almost as though he were dead or his mind somewhere else with some unknown entity animating the body.

Although I wanted to explore him further, I knew that if I tried, someone would detect it. At that point, I'd die. After all, these were all assassins.

I rose, and, as I passed the bar, I tossed the keeper a copper. He caught it in one hand and stuffed it into his pocket. "Thank'e, Lady. See the Warden on your way."

The Warden spotted me as I exited the barroom. "Lady! I don't know how to say this, but someone has stolen your weapons. It's never happened before, and I don't know how it has happened now. I have informed the Master, and he is investigating. Can you shed any light on the matter?"

I nodded. "I believe I can, but I can only discuss it with the Master."

The Warden led me to a small door behind the stairs. He knocked a pattern on the door, and after hearing, "Enter," he opened the door to let me pass.

An old man looked up from a table covered with paper. "Ah, Lady, I assume the Warden has spoken to you about your stolen property. It is unheard of, and I can only express my shame. Needless to say…"

I Came

He would have continued had I not interrupted by holding up my hand. "Master, they have not been stolen." I drew a sheathed Soul Blade from my back. "They returned to me, because they cannot long be parted from me. I thank you for your search and for your honesty. Others might have tried to dissemble, but neither you nor your staff did so. I shall inform the Grand Master of my appreciation of your efforts on my behalf."

I continued, "Please pass a message to the Grand Master. Can you arrange that?"

"I'm not sure that I can do that, Lady. I would not want to disturb the ruminations of the Grand Master."

"Nor draw his interest to you, either, I'm sure. Regardless, it is important that he receive my message."

Obviously, the Master wasn't taking the chance, especially on the word of a woman. It was time to drop a bomb.

I uttered one word that Talbot had taught me. I said it quietly so that only the Master could hear it, but with such inflection that it would instill fear in the very heart of the Master.

"Lady!" he recoiled from me, his hands raised in defense. "Only Masters know of this command password. How come you by it?"

"You question my authority?" I loomed over him.

"No, Lady!" His voice quavered. "I can pass a message to the Grand Master."

"What means do you have?" I asked.

"You may speak the words to me, and I will speak them to others, who will travel to the next Guild hall until the Grand Master receives it. He will respond in the same way. I can pass a written message by hand in the same way."

"And, what is the fastest of ways, Guild Master?"

He hesitated. Then, with a deep sigh, he said, "Very well. I will inform him immediately."

"No, Master, I will inform the Grand Master, personally. Not even you can hear my message. Prepare, and I will do the rest."

The Master sighed, stood and went to a bare section of wall. He touched the molding in two spots. The section slid aside, exposing a tiny nook containing a large mirror.

"Lady, if you know the Master's password, then you also know the cipher that will open a communication channel with the Grand Master. If you don't, the only thing you will observe is your own visage. I will leave you now, but I will return shortly."

He left, and I stared at the mirror, unaware of what to do. The Master was quite right. All I could see was me, looking worried.

'Ok, I know the Master's secret password. Would that be the key?'

I looked at my image and then uttered the code word. The mirror shimmered. I concentrated, and commanded, "Talbot, speak to me!"

The mirror turned gray, then blue. It shimmered, and Talbot's face appeared.

"Gilraën? I was not expecting you. You have discovered the secret of the Elvin mirrors. What drives you to this extreme measure?"

I told him everything to this point, including the mystery man in the tavern. "I believe Beckworth is using Sorcerers to kill our troops. He is also using them as marauders to spread death, destruction, and fear among King Richard's subjects.

"It is as I suggested. Richard and William must incorporate Sorcerers into their armies."

"When you return, we will discuss it. I'm sure Prince William and the staff will consider your suggestion most carefully. Now, return to the castle. Your job is done."

"I can't. I don't know where I am. I have no idea how to come home."

"Hah!" he laughed. He lifted a map of southeastern Jaralii to the mirror. "You are here." He pointed at the map.

I was southeast of the castle, deep inside Unterjaralii, almost on the border with the Supreme Guild of Narwortland. I was in the narrows between the Dwarf Mountains to the West and the sea to the East near a tiny village called Wendleford on the Wendle River. I had at least 150 miles of enemy territory to traverse, then another 150 before returning to William's castle. No wonder I'd seen Dwarves.

He shook his head. "How did you get there? Never mind, you were blindly chasing a Sorcerer. Now, how do we get you back?"

He thought for a moment. "What I'll do is to guide you from guild hall to guild hall. You'll travel to the northeast. Due north is Beckworth's Duchy. To your west is Dwarf country. We are friendlier with some than others. Regardless, I don't want you to take a chance.

"He's conquered all the country between his duchy and Eastport. He has invaded the coastal regions northward towards Phaedport and is attempting to cross the Phaed River. You'll be in greatest danger southeast of Beckworth's duchy. Once you've crossed into the disputed lands, you'll find more friends, but there will still be many enemies. Once there, though, you will travel northwestwards into friendly lands.

"Travel quickly to here." His finger pointed to a dot seventy-five miles north on the major road in the area and just south of the area demarked as 'disputed'. "This is the village of Bursk. It's perhaps the largest habitation in the area. Seek the Guild of Assassins. Speak to the Master and then speak with me.

"Proceed north on the Great Eastern Road to Goerskim. Go to the Guild of Thieves, and contact me. Continue north on the Great Eastern Road through Phaedham, Tamvill and Higgleston. At Higgleston, head west to Willicamp.

"Be very careful, Gilraën. These are dangerous lands, filled with enormously powerful enemies. Trolls come down from the mountains to find food. Orc clans raid the area for flocks and herds. Krell are rumored to be in the area. There is even the possibility of Gaunts. I don't wish to frighten you, My Lady, but terrible and powerful beings inhabit these lands – so terrible that even powerful Sorcerers avoid them. Be extremely careful. Remember: Run! Don't fight unless your life depends on it."

Our mirrors went dark, just as the door opened, and the Master entered. "Lady, have you finished?"

"Yes, thank you. The Grand Master sends his regards. I shall stay the night and leave on the morrow. I shall break my fast before dawn and leave immediately after. I expect that you will keep this information secret. I have informed the Grand Master of this, and he will be most upset should he discover that I was betrayed."

He puffed up like an old owl. "Who are you to speak of betrayal? You are a guild assassin. It would be unthinkable to betray one, especially a Master. Were I to do so, my life wouldn't be worth a Zinc!"

He spoke the truth and was deeply offended. I bowed to him. "My apologies, Master. I had to test you to determine if I was in danger. I am not. The Guild protects us all. I shall inform the Grand Master when I next speak with him. Good night, Master, until the morning."

* * *

By the time the sun had risen the next morning, I was miles away. Guided by the stars, whose positions I had learned from Prince William, I headed to the northeast, following a large, well-traveled road. I drew energy from the woodlands as I could, but it was mostly agricultural. Large tracts were grasslands, inhabited by herds of deer-like herbivores with their heads down, or multitudes of cheeners pecking in the dirt. Much of the rest was farmlands, with half-grown crops, or fruit trees with tiny green nubs emerging from the tips of limbs.

I often felt the presence of a sentient being. Only once did I feel the kind of being of which Talbot had warned. It wasn't a magician. Its presence was large, and it felt dangerous, even though I didn't know what it was. I felt it draining at my energy, pulling on me. However, I didn't wait around to find out what it was. Instead, I raced at ten-fold speed and more, determined to avoid it, whatever it was.

Whatever it was, it was fast. Even at 15-fold, I barely drew away from it. I sucked energy from a large herd as I passed, then from a crop field. My energy renewed, I sped even faster, drawing away more quickly, finally leaving my pursuer behind.

Suddenly, a habitation loomed in the distance. I slowed as quickly as I could. *Fading*, I entered the village of Bursk, avoiding people, wagons, animals, and all the other hazards of a town. I took my time, searching for the Guildhall of Assassins. As usual, it was well hidden in an alley off a side road that seemed to go nowhere.

Again, the Warden ensconced my weapons behind a counter before he escorted me to a nice, little room at the end of the corridor on the second floor. The window looked out over a small patch of grass and into a wood. Again, I made the request for clean clothes. He replied with a suspicious look and a denial of such a service. Repeating the pattern, I bribed the Warden, who promised that my clean clothes would be ready by first light.

I retrieved another Silver before heading downstairs to the tavern. This time, the bar was bright and sunlit. Windows lined three walls. They had arranged eight tables with four chairs each in the large space to my right. The bar extended from the wall at my left across the length of the room. More than a dozen stools stood at the bar. A large door behind the bar housed the kitchen, from which the wonderful aroma of baked bread filled the entire downstairs. My mouth watered with thoughts of warm bread, fresh butter and a tangy cheese.

"Lady?" the young barmaid asked. "How can I help you?"

"I'll take a tankard of your finest, and I'll take the table over there," I pointed to the one in the near corner.

"I'm sorry, Lady, but that table is reserved for Lord Beckworth's Sorcerers."

I gulped, but tried to remain calm. "Are other tables reserved?" When she said they weren't, I chose the table nearest to the bar. "And, what is the fare from the kitchen?"

When she replied, I ordered, took my tankard to the table, and then sat with my back to the brightness outside. I concealing my features, remaining as a shadow outlined in a halo.

The tavern filled slowly. All were men, except for the two barmaids. A man arrived to take over behind the bar, relieving the women to attend to the tables. By the time I had finished my meal, the tavern was filled with noise and smoke. Everyone seemed to know everyone else, and they were enjoying each other's company.

Families began arriving. The tone and feeling of the place changed dramatically as women and children began to fill the seats around the tables. Cheery bar maids exchanged greetings with families. Trays of food and beverages appeared as though by long established routine. I began to relax amid the joys of families and friends gathered for an evening meal.

Suddenly, the room was silent. I looked up to see four hooded men stalk to the corner table.

The two barmaids glanced at each other before disappearing into the kitchen. The barman took a deep breath, ducked under the bar, and, summoning his courage, approached the Sorcerers. Moments later, he returned, his face ashen. Families gulped down their meals, paid and left. I joined the evacuation, anxious not to be discovered.

As I reached the door, I felt a mental probe. Someone was trying to penetrate my mind. I knew it was the Sorcerer whose back had been to the corner. I was careful not to let on that I knew the source of the probe. Instead, I leapt up the stairs, entered my room, and closed the door behind me. I placed a command on it, ensuring that no one could open it without my permission. That done, I relaxed to consider the scene I had just witnessed.

This was a Guildhall of Assassins, yet it was also a public inn. Which was the disguise? More importantly: four Sorcerers? Beckworth's Sorcerers had a standing reservation and were well known to the staff. How cozy! Worse, how close was Beckworth or his army? I was deep in enemy territory, with four Sorcerers immediately downstairs. I smoothed my texture, carefully making certain I was aligned with the planet and the universe.

I slept lightly, awakening while it was dark. Removal of the protection from my door allowed me to access the hallway. I looked out. A bundle of clothes was on the floor. I quickly retrieved it and packed. Going downstairs to the tavern, I hoped I was not so early that they had no food prepared. They didn't know the word buffet, but that's what it was. I paid the Warden, leaving just as first light began to make itself known.

Feeling nothing untoward, I headed north. My decision to avoid the larger roads and to stick to the trails and paths seemed only prudent. I wasn't sure if someone was hunting me, but I figured that if they were, they'd be looking for me on the main roads. However, using the winding, twisting roads slowed my journey. Not only that, it was necessary that I avoid every hamlet and settlement, every farmer's cart, and every herd which might be tended. That slowed me even further. Regardless, I felt better using the roads less traveled, to borrow from poetry.

I arrived in Goerskim after sunset. It took some time to find the Guild of Thieves, and even longer to convince the Warden to let me take my weapons to my room. I unpacked and wandered down to the tavern some time later.

This was a small and dingy place, dark, smoky and dirty. I didn't like it. Finding the Warden, I asked if I could have food and drink brought to my room. A few minutes later, there was a knock on the door. The Warden entered and deposited a tray on the table, turned and left all without a word.

The food wasn't poisoned, although it should have been. Had it been so, it might have explained the poor quality. The vegetables were old and overcooked. The meat was fatty, grisly and boiled, without flavor. The brew was warm and vapid. The meal was virtually unpalatable.

Disgusted, I picked up the tray and carried it downstairs. Finding the Warden, I said, "I would speak with the Master."

He replied, "The Master is not here. How may I serve you?"

"You will summon the Master, or I will report these abominable conditions to the Grand Master. Get him, now!"

"I do not take orders from womban. Only the Master can instruct me as to things he might ask of me. Return to your room, womban, or lose the hospitality of the Guild."

178

I was about to challenge this boob, when I remembered where I was. I handed the tray to the Warden and leapt up the stairs. Grabbing my pack and my weapons, I bounded down. "You have insulted a thief in good standing. The Grand Master will hear of this, Warden." I turned on my heel and left.

It took only minutes to find a road heading to the northeast. I settled into a five-fold Sorcerer's walk. Chrybda rose, shedding light on the winding path. I stretched my prescience into the distance, seeking any flaws or discontinuities. Llombda rose, turning night into a pale semblance of day, and still I ran on.

As I entered the outskirts of a large town, I slowed and faded, not knowing exactly where I was. A sign announced its name as Phaedham. *'Phaedham? Why is that name familiar?'* I searched my memory until light dawned on marble head. *'Baron Richmond of Phaed and his wife, Isadora. This must be their fiefdom.'*

Phaedham was much larger than any of the other villages through which I had passed. It was at the crossroad of two major highways, one East-West and one continuing northward across a large, stone bridge. I searched for the Guild of Assassins, finding it eventually. This time, the room was clean, the food was good, and the Master was friendly. My passwords sufficed to obtain access to the mirror. I told Talbot about the deplorable conditions of the Guild at Goerskim.

"Ah, that explains a lot. I had heard from others that there were problems in Goerskim. Now you have confirmed it. Anything else?"

"Yes. I feel that I am pursued."

"Really? By whom?"

"I don't know. That's the point."

"Speed, Gilraën. Speed is your only option. Eat well. I doubt that anyone will try to attack you while you're in Phaedham. However, it is a long road to Tamvill. Once there, you will find a trail heading to the northwest. Take it to the Southeast Highway and then West to Esselcamp. Remember to drain energy from living things as you go. Keep your energy up; you will need it. Travel straight through if you can."

I Came

When the mirror went dark, I sought the Master and asked that traveling rations be delivered to me, along with my cleaned clothing. He was most amenable and agreed that he would have it delivered an hour before dawn. And so, I was underway before Mummia had arisen.

After I crossed the bridge, I resumed a 10-fold Sorcerer's Walk. I felt the hint of pursuit several times, but I put on a burst of speed and felt the danger diminish. Regardless, I was happy when I arrived in Tamvill and veered off on a trail to the northwest. I slowed significantly. The fear was not pursuing me. I slowed my headlong flight to conserve my energy, while sipping from the great forests.

Then I recognized the village of Esselcamp. Minutes later, I arrived in Willicamp, and was soon at the Guild of Thieves. It took some time to arouse the Warden, who recognized me, immediately.

"My Lady, what brings you here at this hour?"

"I have traveled far. I must speak with the Master."

The Warden's face drained, but he answered, "Of course, My Lady. I shall awaken him. Would you wait here? Everyone is asleep."

I smiled, and he rushed off.

Moments later, the Master appeared, still dressed in his nightshirt. "My Lady, what brings you here?"

"I must speak with the Grand Master, right now."

"Ahh," he sighed. "Of course. Please come with me."

We rushed to his office, where he opened the tiny room. "I will leave you. Please call if you need me."

I spoke the password, and then said, "Master Talbot, I must speak with you."

The mirror was unchanged for several moments. Then, it became silvery gray as Talbot appeared. "Lady Gilraën, are you all right?"

"I am, but I have much to report." I reiterated details of my trip to Bursk, and the threat that pursued me. I told him of the four Sorcerers at the Guildhall, and my suspicions. I described my circuitous route to Goerskim, and the horrible conditions in the guildhall. I related the exemplary treatment I had received in Willicamp, and my intention to return to the castle the next day.

"Very well, Gilraën. You have been far more successful than I had hoped. However, your information is disturbing. Bursk has been a public house for many years. Almost none know that it is a front for the Guild of Assassins.

"As for Goerskim, I am surprised, but I've not been there since Beckworth seized the territory. However, for a guildhall to treat a guildsman disrespectfully is unacceptable under any circumstance. Obviously something is terribly wrong.

"Return to the castle, quickly. We have much to do, and little time to do all the things we need to do."

"I shall return tomorrow, but I am concerned that I am being followed. Can Fairmount transport me?"

"I am afraid not. He has several volunteers scheduled and must take precautions to ensure their safe arrival."

"Fortunately, the road is good, I suppose I can travel at very high speed. I shall rest for a few hours and then eat. I will travel during the day, and should arrive before noon."

I ended the communication and called the Master. Moments later, I re-entered the same room I had slept in just days before. Feeling safe, I lay down and slept soundly for the first time in days.

* * * * *

Chapter 8 – A Change of Tactics

"Welcome home, My Lady," Talbot beamed. "Let me escort you to your rooms."

I had hardly opened the door when I was engulfed by a bevy of women, all gabbing giddily. Rosie was in tears, and Daisy had fallen to her knees gently weeping at my ankles. Beryl held me closely, sobbing uncontrollably.

Dorothea attempted to take charge. "Let the Lady in! Let her sit and relax. Remember your places, dear children. Come, My Lady, Rosie has prepared a bath for you. When you have dressed, we will have a table prepared for your guests."

"Guests? What guests?"

"Prince William and Princess Cassandra wish to hear your words. There will also be other important persons who will also hear your adventures. But, I insisted that they put that off until you have bathed and dressed."

"Bless you, Dorothea. I leave the preparations to you and Beryl. Daisy, I'm sure you know your responsibilities. Rosie, lead me to the bath."

An hour later, I was clean. Rosie had dressed me in a long, emerald green, flowing gown. I wore a necklace of emeralds mounted in silver with matching earrings. We piled my hair up on top of my head, exposing my tricorn ears. Rosie had made up my face before showing me the results. Were I a man, I'd have fallen in lust with me.

'But, I am a man,' I reminded myself. 'My avatar is female, and she is beautiful, indeed." I laughed to myself, 'So, I might as well enjoy it!'

Beryl guided me to a large table erected in the near end of my parlor. Prince William, Princess Cassandra, Viscount Geoffrey and Dame Eleanor, Baron Richmond and Lady Isadora, General

Abuahad and Commander Deplos were already seated. Prince William guided me to a seat in the middle of the near side.

Prince William leaned to me, pouring a wine into a goblet. "Welcome home, Princess Gilraën. We have already had some news of your journey, but we yearn for the full story. Let us dine at our ease, while you tell us what you have discovered."

Rosie and Daisy served under Dorothea's watchful eye. Beryl attended to the wine, hovering attentively with her ears flapping, at least metaphorically. I accepted their presence, knowing full well that if one were present, then all would know eventually.

We ate and talked for several hours. William was highly solicitous of me, ensuring that I had enough time to eat properly and slake my thirst. Cassandra took her lead from her brother and asked about the people I'd met. She was most concerned that the people were happy and contented. As expected, General Abuahad insisted that we talk about things military and the threat to the kingdom.

I took my time, but told my entire tale, emphasizing several points. First, I spoke of the three guildhalls. William was pleased that the Guildhall of Thieves in Willicamp and the Guildhalls of Assassins in Wendleford, Bursk and Phaedham were maintaining their standards, as required of all guild establishments. However, he was disturbed at my report of the Guildhall of Thieves in Goerskim. Evidently something untoward was going on, but he suggested that it was evidence of Beckworth's influence.

The mysterious pursuer became a topic of general discussion. Everyone had a pet hypothesis. None of them held up under closer inspection. Finally, William summoned Talbot.

As I explained what had happened, Talbot reached for a chair and grabbed a chalice of wine. Gulping it down, he declared, "A Krell! My Lady, you were most lucky to escape alive. Had it been closer, it might have neutralized your ability to control magic. Krells have the ability to diminish magic, even in the most powerful of Sorcerers. You have greater reserves than do humans, but my understanding is that even Elves fall prey to Krells.

"Beware, My Lady, you have a powerful enemy – one who can summon Krells to do their bidding."

I Came

Everyone gasped, except me. "I know you told me about Krells, Talbot, but could you tell me how you came to this conclusion, and what I can do about it?"

"Yes, Talbot," Prince William interjected, "I, too, am most concerned. A Krell? Are you sure? And, why would one pursue Princess Gilraën across hundreds of miles of from the border of Farrowspike almost to the very walls of my castle?"

Talbot frowned, explaining, "I am no expert on Krells. I know of no one who is. Most who encounter them die long before they know what a Krell is or what motivates them.

"Only Krells, Elves and Gaunts are fast enough to chase you at a ten-fold pace. Your prescience would tell you if it were an Elf. Gaunts are fast, but are stealth hunters that tire easily. None would ever pursue you for mile after mile, day after day. Only a Krell is fast enough to chase you, relentless in its pursuit and weakens your magic.

"Krells are large – up to eighteen feet in height and weigh accordingly. They and Trolls are similar in that regard. Both are also intelligent, but we know little about that. Trolls are just large, whereas Krells are large, fast and neutralize magic. Trolls are thinking beings, capable of complex thought and language. They just don't talk a lot. We think Krells can talk, but, again, we don't know of anyone who has survived an encounter with a Krell, except you.

"Obviously, a Krell is on a mission to kill you. Why? I don't know. I guess that someone convinced it to find and kill you. Who has this power, I don't know, but whoever is dangerous in the extreme."

"We shall have to consider that," I said. "However, I now know that my idea that Beckworth is using Sorcerers is correct. I followed the four Sorcerers from Beckworth's army. They bragged about their victory and declared Beckworth had sent them on a mission of murder and mayhem throughout the kingdom. They were about to disperse, each heading in a different direction. So, regardless of your thoughts on the use of Sorcerers, they are not the same as Beckworth's.

184

"He is using Sorcerers to defend his troops while attacking yours. If you don't change your tactics, Beckworth will utterly defeat you."

General Abuahad chortled, "You may be many things, Gilraën Gulámae, but a military tactician you are not. Sorcerers attract Sorcerers. I don't want them attracting Sorcerers to my soldiers. However, if they do, we will put an arrow through them, and that will end it."

Talbot agreed. "We Sorcerers do not want to be near armies. How could we possibly perform our duties? Should we extend ourselves to detect enemy Sorcerers, the huge mass of thoughts generated by the men, each of whom is fighting for his survival, would overwhelm us.

"Further, how shall we tell the difference between the deaths caused by sword or sling or arrow or that caused by a Sorcerer's spell?"

"Finally, how could we protect ourselves? All Sorcerers are cautious when seeking another's magic. We would be detected instantly, bringing the wrath of the other Sorcerer upon ourselves. No, Lady, such a tactic can not succeed."

I shook my head in disgust and dejection. "First, my dear General, I have been teaching military strategy and tactics at the highest level in my country's army. I am an expert.

"As for you, Prince William, I suggest suicide before Beckworth seizes your realms and tortures you to death.

"Fortunately, I have a way off this planet. I will seek out Master Fairmount in the morning and return to my home." I rose. "I'm sure you can find your way to your own quarters. Good night." I walked toward my bedroom.

"Princess Gilraën!" Prince William commanded, "Return to this table. I have not spoken."

I turned to see him standing, a scowl on his face, and a hand on his dirk.

I Came

He pulled my empty seat from the table and waved his hand toward it. "There is much for us to discuss before I make any decisions. And, as far as you leaving, we will discuss this later.

"Now, how shall we proceed? You suggest that Beckworth is using Sorcerers to defeat my armies. You assert that unless I use Sorcerers in this manner, I will be utterly defeated.

"On the other hand, both my general and my chief advisor tell me it would be disastrous to utilize my Sorcerers as you have suggested.

"Which of you is correct? How am I to know which is the better tactic? How can I prove this one way or the other?"

Both Abuahad and Talbot sat back, crossed their arms over their chests and smirked knowingly. They had the advantage and knew it. How could I persuade them? Then an idea popped into my head.

"Sir Geoffrey, has your battalion departed to Coephalli?"

"No, My Lady. Why do you ask?"

"Then, let us test my hypothesis. I will lead my archers. You will lead your Battalion. We will meet in mock battle. My troop of archers and I will soundly defeat your Battalion under your leadership."

William's palm slapped the table. "Yes! This is what we will do. If, as she claims, Gilraën defeats your battalion, then we will integrate Sorcerers; if not, we will continue as we are now."

* * *

That night, I was too exhausted to do anything other than sleep. However, I was up bright and early the next morning. As I walked into the great hall, an excited bunch of archers greeted warmly me.

"Hey! Gilraën!" Harold yelled so loudly that the entire hall went silent for a few moments. When they figured it out, the noise level built back up to its normal uproar. That didn't stop my friends from mobbing me and pulling me to their table. Yashi and Nasif cheered, stumbling over each other's words, begging me to tell them about my adventures. Erin and Donnachaidh chimed in supporting them.

It was obvious I would not get a word in edgewise unless I acknowledge them and told them everything. I gave them the short, short version, but that was enough to get several dozen oohs and aahs and tons of advice. However, several suggestions were worthwhile.

Bhutta suggested that Vigash might be knowledgeable about Krells. Cheekwahnee suggested that the Guildhall of Thieves in Goerskim had been appropriated by Beckworth's Sorcerers, and that we needed to investigate it. All of them had great ideas about how to destroy Grampus' Battalion.

I asked about their zhaks and chariots. All of them were effusive about their families of ponies and how they were progressing as a military force. After we had eaten, they led me to their training grounds.

It was a huge field, in which all the zhak herds were milling about. I studied them for a few moments, observing that each herd was separate from the others, each grazing in its own area and not trespassing into another herd's territory. Yet, the moment the archers arrived, each herd perked up, and gathered around 'their' charioteer. The archers groomed each of the ponies, fed them, and led them back to 'their' territory.

After they completed their greeting ceremonies, the archers went their separate ways. Shortly, they returned pulling the light chariots. When they approached the herds, a few of the zhaks presented themselves. Each archer went to the stallion, and, while patting it on the head and shoulders, selected two mares. Then the four of them returned to the chariot.

Quickly, the archers harnessed the zhaks to the chariots. I was surprised to see the arrangement. The stallion was in the lead, with the pair of mares behind him in a triangle. I asked why, and they told me that that's how the zhaks wanted it to be. Basically, the stallion was in the lead, with the mares following, but off to the sides so they could see. Further, they explained, it wasn't always the same mares.

I Came

The stallion would nose them until two 'volunteered,' and it was never a nursing mare.

I was amazed. In just a few days, the archers had bonded with their herd of zhaks. Somehow, they'd become a team, liking and trusting in each other's judgment. I wondered how this relationship would be affected by privation, exhaustion and battle.

When all twelve chariots were ready, I investigated them more closely. The chariots were very light. They had a tubular iron framework, a wooden floor, and heavy fabric stretched tautly around the front and sides making a rugged but lightweight body. The wheels were attached to an iron axle. The axle was attached to the body by an inverted leaf spring, which would make the ride far more comfortable. The four-spoke wooden wheels were bound in iron.

Within the body, there was enough room for two moderate-sized people. The archers had inserted their unstrung bows in their quivers along with two dozen arrows. A second quiver situated at the bow of the chariot had thirty or more arrows. Alongside the charioteer was a long, narrow quiver for a sturdy spear.

The archers wore a full breastplate, helmet, greaves and braces. They had small shields at their elbows. The body of the chariot rode high in front offering some protection, but fell off rapidly as it neared the stern.

The zhaks were also protected. Each had a small helmet that extended up their noses, behind their ears and over their jaws and upper necks. Their horse collars had small plates extending down the chests. Iron hoops extended from their traces over their backs. Heavy fabric was drawn over them to provide protection for the zhak's bodies from branches and small weapons.

From what I could see, the chariots and charioteers were well equipped for their function.

I gathered my troop and began walking briskly towards the forest north of the castle. On the way, I explained my plan. We would advance to the northeast, hopefully to the flank of Geoffrey's battalion. I would range ahead of my troop, scouting for the scouts, as it were.

Once I'd discovered his force, I'd call in my troop to reconnoiter the area to find a suitable place to ambush them. We wanted a field that was firm but hilly. We needed to be able to attack from hiding and then disappear. And we needed the freedom to advance or retreat at our convenience.

Once the engagement started, we'd attack from cover. Sweeping in, we'd loose a volley of arrows before retreating. We'd harass and worry the Battalion, forcing them to do as we wished. Then I'd move in and…. Well, I'd move in.

They asked that I explain the plan to their zhaks. I was surprised at their request, but they insisted. So, I laid out my plan, using mental pictures, and working hard to explain that this was what I wanted, not what would be, and that nothing was certain. I hoped I'd gotten my point across, but couldn't be certain.

Each of the charioteers spoke to their charges in a sing-song, whinny, as though they were horses. In their turn, the zhaks whinnied and stomped and shook their heads and tails. After a few minutes, all the archers nodded, patted the stallions and mounted their chariots.

"Ready!" Harold shouted, a huge smile splitting his face.

I asked, "Did you talk with the zhaks?"

"Oh, yes." He laughed. "You're not the only one who can talk with animals. When you 'talked' with them before you left, it did something to them and us. You told us to learn to communicate, and we did. It took a bit of doing, but we stuck at it, and now we're pretty good at it. In the future, you must remember what you did, so you can do it again."

"I'll be back when I've found them!" I waved and raced ahead. After I'd turned a corner and gone over a hill, I *faded*. I reached out as far as I could, trying to sense a presence. A battalion comprised some 700 men. They'd stand out like a sore thumb.

Except they weren't there!

I raced back to my troop and reappeared in their midst. "They're not there! I don't know where Viscount Grampus is hiding, but he's not where he's supposed to be. Spread out and search, but not so far that you are out of communications with your comrades. I'll search ahead. When you've found something, think of me and call out "Gilraën!" I'll return as quickly as I can. If I find them, I'll return, and we can determine our course of action."

The archers nodded and turned their mounts aside. I *faded* and raced ahead, performing a great circle around us before heading further ahead. Performing a box-search, I scouted the lands seeking any semblance of sentience. I searched for more than two hours, covering over 100 miles, mostly along paths and animal trails, finding only deer-like animals, birds, small fox-like creatures and birds.

Then, there was a hint… just a hint of something. I turned left and then right trying to locate the source. I edged closer and closer, sensing an increasingly large number of humans. Then, I passed over a hill and beyond a copse of trees, and… there they were!

Geoffrey had selected his battlefield with great care. He had arrayed his men on a broad hillside. A marsh and lake guarded his right flank. A steep embankment and a stone wall guarded his left. A heavy wood stood behind the hill. A narrow, rock-strewn field extended several hundred yards to his front. A ditch and palisade of sharpened stakes lined their immediate front. It would take an army to assault his position.

I stood studying it for several minutes before deciding it was time to assemble my forces. It took only fifteen minutes to return to my troops. Rather than tell them everything I knew, I told them that I had detected the presence of a large body of men some twenty miles to the northwest. This would be their opportunity to scout the land, to reconnoiter an enemy's position and disposition, and to develop a plan of attack.

All twelve chariots headed off into the northwest, each taking a slightly different route. Trotting along, they covered the ground in slightly more than five hours. Rodriguez was the first to contact me, followed quickly by Faelnirv and Harold.

Harold gathered his companions and began a systematic search and study of Geoffrey's position. As evening darkened to night, the thirteen of us sat around a fire, roasting meat, boiling vegetables, and setting up our encampment. They had fed the zhaks a few handfuls of maidzh and loosed them to roam in a nearby meadow, where they quietly browsed and prepared to bed down for the night.

"Wow!" Harold exclaimed, describing Grampus battalion's position.

Schmidt added, "It's like a badger backed into his hole."

I agreed with them both. "Do any of you have an idea of how to attack them?"

They all shook their heads. Faelnirv added, "We are too few to besiege them."

Yashi reminded us, "But, we are all archers."

"Yes," I agreed, hoping to encourage them.

That was it. We were archers. Our chariots had delivered us quickly to the field of battle. We had plenty of supplies and plenty of weapons. We knew exactly where Viscount Grampus' battalion was and his disposition. We knew everything we needed to know in order to attack him.

As archers, we could attack at great distances without being attacked. We could harass them, driving them crazy, as swarms of biting insects drive caribou crazy on the steppes of Canada and Alaska. Then we could escape; our zhaks racing far faster than Geoffrey's men could run. Even better, we could do it at night.

We gave the zhaks six or seven hours before we woke them. The waning half-moon, Llombda, was high in the sky, illuminating the forest with a wan light. The zhaks had good night vision, so could navigate the trails reasonably well. As Trahean Humans, my Ghillies also had slightly better night vision than when they had lived on Earth. As far as I was concerned, it was as bright as midday.

We approached to within a mile or so, and left the zhaks behind. As stealthily as possible, we crept up on Geoffrey's left flank. We worked around slightly to their front, so we could see the men sitting around their campfires. Two pairs of archers assigned themselves to six campfires. I took two campfires. Among us, we had targeted about one hundred me.

I Came

We each stuck half a dozen arrows into the ground. These were special arrows that Talbot and I had prepared. None was lethal, but they'd temporarily disable anyone struck by one of them. These arrows would have the same effect on the Battalion as would real arrows delivered in the dead of night without warning.

At my signal, we launched thirteen arrows into the darkness. Seconds later, a second barrage, and just seconds later a third and a fourth.

Sentries shouted! Horns blew! Drums rolled!

Men leapt up, seized shields and raised them. Quickly many more joined them, followed by an officer. A line of shields formed. Archers and slingers crept behind the wall and prepared to return fire.

We were long gone by then. Chrybda had edged over the horizon, giving us ever increasing light by which to travel. We rejoined the zhaks who greeted us with soft neighs and stomping feet. Moments later, we were off, racing deeply into the wood and marsh behind the battalion.

An hour later, Chrybda has passed overhead, and Llombda was descending as we approached Geoffrey's right flank. As we slinked forward, we saw that the Battalion had dowsed their fires. No longer were they targets illuminated by their fires. No longer were they blinded by their firelight, and their eyes would have acclimated to the dark. No doubt, they would have sentries posted all around.

Regardless, there was more than enough light for me to see everything. They had gathered together in an ellipse on the face of the hill. A shield wall protected their front and flanks, and they would be prepared to lift a second wall overhead. Their position couldn't have been better for me. They were almost literally shoulder-to-shoulder.

I whispered, "Stand fast! My turn."

I considered my words carefully. I had to envelop all of them at the same time. I had to make it strong enough to send them all to sleep, but light enough not to kill them. I had to word it delicately to achieve the effect I wanted, while ensuring it was within the limits of my strength and endurance. I didn't want to kill myself by creating a spell that I couldn't complete.

Moments later, I *faded*. Then I sped in front of them so I could see them all. Then, I uttered my carefully worded chant, ending with the booming command, *"Mel!"*

Seconds later, the entire Battalion tumbled to the ground in a pile of arms, legs and bodies.

"Come out!" I yelled to my men.

They assembled quickly. "What's up?" Harold asked. The rest nodded, looking around.

"We have won!" I announced.

Their voices rose in a cacophony of protestations as they all talked over each other, denying that anything had happened. Instead of explaining, I led them up the hill, picking our way over and around bodies to Sir Geoffrey's command quarters.

"What did you do?" Harold spoke for the group.

I explained, "I needed them close together so that I could hit them all with a single spell. I figured that sneak attacks by archers would force them into a defensive shell. It worked. I could then temporarily stun them, sending them to sleep. If I'd wanted, I could have killed them just as easily."

The men looked at me in awe. "Really?" Williforte asked.

I nodded, but said, "Let's get the zhaks here and let them graze. I'm sure they're as tired as we are. Then, we can camp out here until morning. That's about when they all should awaken. Then, we'll have the last laugh."

It took a while to recover the zhaks and to loose them from their collars and traces. The men fed them another couple of hands full of maidzh and prepared to set them loose in the meadow. Before they could, I gathered men and zhaks together.

"Let me tell you how proud I am with all of you." I projected feelings of friendship, happiness and togetherness to them all. "You have done well to become as family, learning each other's language, and coming to trust and admire each other. You have succeeded beyond all my expectations.

"You will serve as an example to the many who will come after you. You will teach them and lead them in the future. Well done to you all. Now, go, eat, rest and recover from your day's labors."

I touched each of the zhaks, sharing my admiration for them all. Then, I led the men to Sir Geoffrey's tents, where we drank his wine and ate his supper of broiled cheener and warmed tavor, jhig, and brot.

* * *

"Lady Gilraën!" a man's voice shouted. "What have you done?"

I stirred, rolling onto my back and looking up towards the opened tent flaps. Viscount Sir Geoffrey of Grampus stood there, obviously in high dudgeon. I eased my way to a sitting position, and replied, "Welcome, Sir Geoffrey. Did you sleep well last night?"

"Bah!" he growled. "My back is broken, my neck will never work again, and I have an enormous headache. But other than that, I'm terrible!"

I laughed, "We slept well. Thank you for the use of your beds, your tents, and your fine food. My archers and I spent a pleasant evening relaxing. It is a shame you and your men slept so soundly, otherwise you could have joined us."

"Bah!" he growled again. "Well, you won your bet, didn't you? Now what?"

"I think I've demonstrated that a Sorcerer can overcome a large force. I've demonstrated that a cavalry is an effective scouting, reconnaissance, and harassing military force. And we've demonstrated that zhaks are a fully capable of drawing a chariot for extended periods, performing admirably."

"True, Princess Gilraën, but what do we do now? How shall we implement it? How shall we persuade Prince William, Abuahad and Talbot?"

"That's easy. My archers shall escort you back to the castle as prisoners!"

"What!" he shouted. "You can't! We would be humiliated beyond measure."

"Nonetheless, that is what we will do. Later, we will let Prince William and the court in on our subterfuge. Our goal is to convince, and what better way is there?"

* * *

Some eight hours later, the blare of horns alerted everyone in the castle. As the house guard manned the battlements, a column of men appeared in the distance. As they approached, the guards on the walls saw two columns abreast. The men in those columns were bound hand and foot to those before or behind them. Further, each man in the first column was bound to the man opposite him in the other column. Six chariots rolled on each side. Within each was a warrior armed with a spear pointed at the column. In the lead was a woman, but not a woman. Soon, all recognized her to be Princess Gilraën, the Elf. Behind her was a man with hands bound behind. The Elf held a rope in her hands, with led to a noose around the man's neck. It was only when the column arrived at the gates that the man was seen to be none other than Viscount Geoffrey of Grampus.

Prince William greeted them at the gates. "Princess Gilraën, I see that your mission was successful. You have proven your point. Now, would you release your captives? And, I would ask you to introduce your troop."

If Prince William was surprised when I introduced him not only to my archers but also to each of the zhaks he didn't show it. Instead, he clasped the forearms of the men and patted the foreheads of the zhaks with equal enthusiasm. He talked knowledgeably with the men, surprised that they had a common language with the zhaks.

Yet, as he talked with the men, he scratched the heads of the animals that nosed him. He even ordered a basket of fruit, which he doled out liberally to the charioteers and their teams.

I was even more surprised when he accompanied the chariots back to their paddocks. There, he mixed easily with all the zhaks, bestowing scratches, patting and fruits, while expressing his delight and satisfaction with them all.

Of course, my archers felt highly honored. Not only had they captured a far superior force, but they had earned the high praise of their Elvin leader and their Prince. They were eager to tell him how they had established their rapport, the basis of their language, and the techniques of their tactical mission.

Finally, while absent-mindedly patting a particularly friendly pair of mares, he asked, "Princess Gilraën, Archers, zhaks, how will we teach others what you know? I will need other such scouting troops as you, but I don't know how to accomplish it. How should we proceed?"

The men were eager to launch into a detailed discussion, but I interrupted. "My Prince, I think we should allow both my archers and their steeds the opportunity to relax after their arduous mission. The zhaks need to return to their families, eat, relax and renew their energies. My men need to eat. Then, we need to talk among ourselves, since each of us has a unique perspective. Then, we can consider how we can teach others."

"Very good. Join me at supper." He looked around, encompassing the archers. "… all of you. However, I must ask you to accompany me now, Princess. We have much to do."

As we returned to the castle, he asked. "What prompted you to return with Battalion Grampus as prisoners? Wasn't Sir Geoffrey upset with such humiliation for himself and his men?"

"Oh, yes, he was," I replied. "However, I had won our wager. It was important to show even my greatest critics not just that I was right, but that I could have killed them all just as easily. We have a war to win, and if, as I think I have shown, Beckworth is using Sorcerers to defend his troops while attacking your forces, then we must not only copy him but beat him as his own game."

"Well, you certainly did that!" he chuckled.

We walked up the stairs and turned beneath them into the war room. Abuahad stood at the head of the table, scowling. Geoffrey and the other battalion commanders were arguing among themselves. Talbot, the other master Sorcerers, and several others stood aside, trying to look serious and serene at the same time. Cassandra sat in a high chair overlooking the table, a long pointer in her hand.

The moment we walked in, the room silenced. William led me to Cassandra's side opposite Abuahad. He looked up to Cassandra, asking, "Progress?"

Abuahad started to speak, but Cassandra cleared her throat and raised her index finger. "Thank you, General." She turned to her brother, stating authoritatively, "It is settled that we need to incorporate Sorcerers into our battalions." Abuahad tried to interrupt her, but again she spoke over him. "In spite of suggestions to the contrary, we are now working to determine who and how."

"My Prince!" Abuahad raised his voice, "we have done no such thing. I am not convinced, nor are many of our commanders or captains. Princess Cassandra has taken it upon herself to command, which is not her right."

Cassandra began to answer the general, but William interrupted her. "General, my sister is a royal princess of this realm. She is the heir apparent, following myself. She is highly skilled, and knowledgeable of our brother's strategy. Further, she has our complete confidence. Perhaps you account her to be a weak and feckless womban. If so, you are very much mistaken."

William looked to her, asking, "Sister, what have you decided?"

"Brother, as I said, Princess Gilraën has shown that Sorcerers can, and may have taken control of a battle, killing an entire Company. She and her twelve charioteers have just captured Sir Geoffrey's entire Battalion. Obviously, she could have killed them had she wished.

"You have two Battalions in the field – Richmond's and Deplos'. You have one Company sufficiently trained to reinforce them, and our final Company in training. Viscount Grampus' Battalion is here undergoing training, and I have one more within my Principality of the Blue Vail. I have determined that one of our Master Sorcerers should accompany each Battalion. We are now discussing if other Sorcerers should accompany Companies within each Battalion. We have yet to determine strategy, tactics, communications and other details. Further, I'm sure that Princess Gilraën will have much to add to our discussions."

"But, Your Highness," Abuahad continued in a more apologetic tone, "how will a Sorcerer defend us without other Sorcerers finding him, attacking him, and then attacking the force he is supposed to defend? If he searches, he opens himself to discovery. If he doesn't search, then an enemy Sorcerer might still destroy us and our Sorcerer before we are even aware of his presence. That is, there is no way a Sorcerer can help, many ways he can hinder, and in all of them, every instance, they all die."

"If I may?" I interjected. "You are both right and wrong, General. Let us say a Sorcerer is beside you as your Battalion marches. What shall that Sorcerer do? If he actively seeks out an enemy Sorcerer, he will be detected. The enemy Sorcerer will bide his time, use his prescience to determine the direction and approximate distance to your force, and direct his own forces to intercept you. They will have the advantage.

"But, what if you have no Sorcerer? Then, the enemy Sorcerer will still detect the presence of so many men, will direct his force toward yours, and will have all the advantages.

"Yes!" Abuahad exclaimed. "That is my concern."

"Then, let me pose this scenario," Gilraën continued. "I am with you. I do nothing. I just open myself to all the forces of the universe. I am aware of the insects in the ground, the birds in the air, and the animals in their burrows. I am aware of every breath by everyone in your army and feel their hearts beating. I am aware, but no one is aware of me, because I do not exist, hidden among all your men.

"Now, I feel the presence of a Sorcerer probing, seeking and finding your army. I am aware of him, but he is not aware of me. Now, who has the advantage?

"Then, I feel the Sorcerer prepare to attack. I am aware of his attack, what he plans, what he will do. He is not aware of me. Who has the advantage?

"Then, I feel him about to use magic against us. I know the spell he intends. I know the very words he will say. I know what power he has, how he will use it, and when. Who has the advantage?

"As he is about to utter the spell and invoke the magic, I strike him! He is unaware of me until I strike. He is unaware of my knowledge of him, his power or his intentions. I strike before he even knows I exist. Who has the advantage?

"But, let us say there is no Sorcerer. I am vulnerable. I have extended my presence across the lands, awaiting some sense of magic. But, there is none. I detect a large body of men and alert you to where they are. But, I still extend my mind, seeking an enemy Sorcerer. The armies engage, but I do not. I am seeking the enemy Sorcerer. Can the enemy's arrows or sling stones kill me? Yes. Can an enemy javelin, spear, lance or sword kill me? Yes, I am actively looking beyond them, trying to find the enemy Sorcerer. It will only be until I am sure that none exists that I will direct my mind to the battle at hand. Even then, I will do it slowly, ensuring that if an enemy Sorcerer does exist and has simply withheld his magic, I will still be prepared to counter him. I will I loose some of my magic at the enemy soldiers but hold a reserve for a strike at a Sorcerer.

"Now, do you see how Sorcerers can work with and for your battalions?"

"Yes," he said hesitantly.

"Now, consider this, General. Within each Company, I have a Junior Sorcerer. Their job is to place and maintain wards against enemy missiles, to strengthen the shields of our soldiers, and sharpen the blades of your swords and the points of your spears and arrows. Would not an enemy Sorcerer detect them?

"Yes, indeed they would. And, what will they do? They will attempt to negate these less powerful Sorcerers, killing them if possible. But, then I will know of their presence. I will reach out and destroy them, if necessary combining my power with that of all my other Sorcerers. So, while each Company protects its Sorcerer, and the Sorcerer protects the Company, I will protect my Sorcerers while the Battalion protects me."

Talbot stood forward. "My Lady, all that you have described is possible. However, it would require every Sorcerer and, perhaps, more. With two Battalions we need two Master Sorcerers plus one more to coordinate their activities with each other, the general and captains. Then, we would need four additional lesser Sorcerers, one for each Company. That's thirteen Sorcerers for us, and thirteen more for Princess Cassandra. We do not have that many Sorcerers."

"I'm not sure we'd need that many in a full battle. However, in a smaller one, let's say one Battalion against another, we might need as many as five Junior Sorcerers in addition to a Master. You see, it's a matter of numbers. If all four Battalions were on the same battlefield, then they would be adjacent to each other. It would not be possible to attack one without the adjacent Battalion observing and moving to protect them both. If each Battalion had as few as two Junior Sorcerers with two Senior Sorcerers and one Master Sorcerers plus one Senior Master Sorcerer, there would be some sixteen Sorcerers protecting the three Battalions of the Prince's army.

"However, with only one Battalion, there would be as few as three, with only one Master. As long as it met only one other Battalion, there would be little chance the enemy would have the magical means to destroy them. However, with fewer, such as the situation I found, four of Beckworth's magicians might. They would have to be quick and careful to disable all the defending Sorcerers before the Battalion could close on them and kill them by more normal means."

Talbot volunteered, "Then, I suggest that I learn to be, to use your words, a Senior Master. I would suggest that Falsworth, Thackery, Johnsstone, Simmons, McGregor, Wilam, Janneece work with individual battalions. In turn, each should choose one Senior and two Junior Sorcerers. Perhaps this will provide us with another training opportunity for our apprentices.

"Further, we must scour the lands to find Sensitives to train as Sorcerers. Perhaps, in this regard, we should ask Lord Armjurst to seek out others either in Narwortland or Farrowspike surreptitiously and with the utmost of discretion. Perhaps some Sorcerers in those distant lands might feel moved to help us."

Princess Cassandra added, "Let us not forget that I, too, have Sorcerers in my court. I can contribute at least three Masters and perhaps six or seven lesser Sorcerers.

Prince William nodded, and said, "Then, let us begin. We have much to do."

* * *

Several hours later, I joined my archers at dinner. They were still on an emotional high from their mission and their victory. As I entered, they jumped up as a group, surrounded me, and led me to their table. They had a large flagon of wine, which they dispensed eagerly.

We had just poured each of us a large cup when Prince William joined us. All of us leapt to our feet, greeting him enthusiastically. He joined us for a flagon of wine and congratulated us once again. "Men, please excuse me for taking your leader to the head table. I'm sure you will have plenty of time together in the future."

He took my arm and led me to the seat to his left with Abuahad to my left. Cassandra sat to his right, along with Geoffrey and Eleanor. Talbot stood behind his chair as though he were a statue. "Let us enjoy the meal. However, we must eat more quickly and meet after we dine. We have had news."

He refused to discuss his ominous statement, even though we all prodded him. Instead, he insisted we maintain a bright and happy demeanor, while eating and enjoying a good meal. Now, I understood why he had separated Cassandra and me. We'd have talked about Abuahad and his chauvinism. So, I initiated a discussion with Abuahad, aiming to plumb his depths.

At first, he was reticent to talk with me. However, I pressed him as to his knowledge of the southeast, its towns and villages, its people and their customs and anything else he could tell me. I started by telling him of my adventures in Willicamp, and my pursuit to the borders. I asked him about those lands, through which I had traveled so quickly and so blindly.

Slowly at first, but ever more quickly, he began to talk. He had been born and raised in that area, a little town in the piedmont of the Dwarf Mountains on the border with Farrowspike. As a child, he had climbed the mountains, visited with the Zhaenstain Dwarves and even with the Elves of the White Cliffs. He was naturally intelligent and had excelled at school. He had joined the guard of the local baron and had fled with him to Lord Armjurst's lands. By that time, he had become the captain of the baron's guard. Still later, he sailed to King Richard's lands determined to fight against Lord Beckworth. Because of his intelligence, his skills, and his unswerving devotion to Prince William, he had risen to the rank of General of the Guard.

He laughed. "I have been the unassailable master of the army for many years. No one has attempted to contradict me, for I am always right. But, that also means that I have become set in my ways and do not take other's advice, even when I am wrong.

"Today, I was wrong, twice... no three, maybe four times. I was wrong about using Sorcerers. I was wrong about your ability to capture my Battalion. I was wrong not to listen to you or to Lady Cassandra. And, I was wrong to lose my temper when you both showed me I had made a mistake. I was bitter and resentful.

"Please, accept my apology. And, if you have any other suggestions, please inform me how I can make my armies even more capable."

After that, we had a pleasant meal, conversing with Abuahad, William and Cassandra. We kept it light, with lots of smiles, but there was an underlying tension hidden within the Prince's words.

After the meal, the Prince spent half an hour mingling with his troops, answering questions and joking with the men and the few women who were his army. We, in the meantime, gathered toward the fireplace, where Talbot placed spells of silence and secrecy. At first, we sat around, not knowing what William was planning. We ended up talking about how to deploy Sorcerers, command & control, signals, and other tactical considerations.

When William finally appeared, we all stopped talking, awaiting whatever he had to tell us. It didn't take long. "Guild halls of the Guild of Thieves have been attacked throughout the eastern lands. Moreover, they were not attacked by soldiers or mobs, but by Sorcerers in Beckworth's employ.

"At least five guildhalls were utterly destroyed. Some were simply entered and sacked. In most cases, the staff, wardens and masters were killed. A few escaped and contacted the High Master of the Guild of Thieves, asking for his assistance. The High Guild Masters of several guilds have also been contacted, seeking their assistance. The High Master of the Guild of Assassins, of the Guild of Witches, Truth-Seekers & Wise Women, and of the Guild of Pawnbrokers, Bailsmen and Exchangers, as well as several more reputable guilds have promised every guildsman's assistance.

"However, I want you, Lady Gilraën to undertake a mission to determine who is behind this, to seek them out, and bring them to my justice. If you cannot do this, Princess Gulámae of the Elves of the Green Mountain-Maidstone Forest, then I charge you, as my deputy, to bring them to justice in my name, and that of King Richard.

"I expect you and whoever travels with you to depart by tomorrow morning at the latest. What resources do you need? How would you proceed?"

I sat back, stunned at the news, the sudden turn of events, and the enormous responsibility thrust upon me. What could I do? How should I proceed? What the hell was going on?

I looked into William's eyes. They were so deep, so blue, I lost the train of my thoughts. A sudden feeling of warmth spread all throughout my body.

"Lady? Princess?" he said.

Suddenly, my brain cleared, and I realized that I'd suspended all thought, all actions for moments. Time had passed, but I hadn't been aware of its passing. "Where was I?" I asked. "Ah, yes. I'm not sure how to begin. What advice would you give me?"

I Came

For the next half an hour, they bombarded me with different ideas and strategies. Obviously, Beckworth was involved, but beyond that, there were several lines of inquiry.

Cassandra suggested I interview the surviving staff, wardens and masters. Talbot suggested they investigate the mirrors used for communications and determine who had passwords and commands for them. Eleanor suggested I talk with village women and children, and especially the town fool. Abuahad suggested I talk with local farmers and innkeepers, since they would know about travelers.

"But, what should I do if I find they are Sorcerers? Surely, you do not expect me to overpower them all?"

Prince William replied, "In fact, I do. You overcame three of them just days ago. Talbot tells me that you have extraordinary powers… those of an Elf, and a powerful one at that. I have known such an Elf in my life, and I would have had such confidence in you as I had in her.

"However, if you need help, you may seek Talbot at most guild halls, as you have heard."

* * *

I had gathered my Ghillies around me. "You will need to work with your zhaks. We will be gone for about a week. I don't know how to explain time to them, but I do know their families will miss them and are not prepared for the death of their loved ones. Explain this as well as you can and be prepared to leave at first light."

"Gilraën?" Harold asked, "Will supplies be available or should we carry our own? And, the same for our zhaks."

"Yes," I replied, "Enough for a week. I hope we'll find food and provisions, but I want to be sure we can survive for at least a week.

"One other thing: I am concerned about the zhaks' stamina. Are they capable of many days of dawn-to-dusk travel? If not, do you have additional herd members who could travel with us?"

The archers looked to each other. Yashi answered, "We don't know. Let us talk with our zhaks. If we need to do so, we can probably bring one or two others of their herds, but the stallion is the only lead we have."

* * *

I searched the training grounds. "Master Vigash!"

"Lady Gilraën? Have you come to practice?"

"No, Master, I have come to ask your advice. Master Talbot believes a Krell is pursuing me. I'd like to know what you know about Krells, and what I should do to defend myself."

"Defend?" he laughed. "Defend? You don't. You run until you can't. Then, the Krell kills you. Now, what makes you think a Krell is stalking you?"

I described both occasions in which I had felt the presence, and how I had escaped each time. Then, I told him how Talbot had deduced a Krell that was pursuing me.

Vigash was most impressed that I had outrun a Krell. "Yes, if you can sense their presence, your best option is to flee. Drawing energy from your surroundings was a good idea. Krells are extremely powerful and very fast, and can negate some forms of magic, some say becoming invisible, but I'm not sure if that applies to Elves.

"However, Krells are also intelligent and known for their loyalty on the one hand and their sense of humor in the other. It is said that if you can make a Krell laugh, it will be your friend forever. It is also said that if a Krell accepts your challenge, they will work with you until you succeed. After that, who knows?"

Gilraën paused before asking, "Is there any weapon, tactic or technique I can use against a Krell?"

Vigash shook his head. "Krells are tough. They can be injured by swords, spears or arrows, but their hides are as tough as armor. And they are so huge that it's difficult to penetrate to a vital spot. They are a lot like trolls in that regard.

"They are really fast and strong, so it's extremely hard to stab them or shoot them with an arrow or anything like that. And then, since they negate most magic, it's even hard for Elves to engage them.

"No, Gilraën it is best to race away and keep as far from them as possible."

"My thanks, Master Vigash, I shall try, believe me."

* * *

I sat beside Prince William, looking out from my balcony. Dorothea had cooked a wonderful meal. She had prepared fresh baked bread, with charder and bhar for William's palate, and with extra tavor and jhig with graz for me. She finished it off with large mugs of steaming thrak.

Even though we intended to relax after our meal, I was too tense and wound up, thinking about my mission. Would the zhaks have the stamina? What if it was a Krell? Who was raiding the guildhalls? What if it is a Krell? How many Sorcerers would I face? What if it was a Krell?

"You are very quiet tonight, Lady." William stated. "Tell me what you are thinking."

"Nothing," I replied, not really ready to discuss my worries.

"No, that is not correct, Gilraën. You are concerned about the length of the mission, and its effects on your charioteers and their steeds. You are worried about the enemy forces and their Sorcerers. But, more than anything, you are worried about the possibility of a Krell, aren't you?"

How could I deny it? "Yes, you are quite right. I even talked with Vigash about Krells. He wasn't all that helpful."

'So I understand. As you might expect, there is very little that happens here of which I am unaware." He reached out and gently held my hand. "As you may know, I was married once. She, too, was an Elf. She taught me many things. One of those things is that fear is the real killer. Prepare, Gilraën. Study. Learn. Do everything to ready yourself. Then, once you have done so, put aside your fear. That which will happen, will. You are prepared. You are skilled. You have planned. Needless worrying will not change anything, but it will exhaust you, diminishing all your preparation."

What he said made sense. "Yes, you're right. I am as prepared as I can be. I'm just worried that I forgot something."

He chuckled, "No, you've done everything that anyone could have done and more. What inspired you to talk with Vigash? I'm sure you'll be fine. Believe me, I know these things."

I didn't, but I felt better with him saying so.

"When will you leave?"

"Tomorrow morning. I will check with my archers to find out what they will do. Then, I'll precede them to Willicamp. It'll take them two days to get there. By that time, I'll have scouted the area towards Higgleston, visited several guildhalls, and talked with others. I'll meet my troop at Willicamp and proceed from there."

"Gilraën, you really need to get your sleep." He stood and reached out his hand to help me up. I took his hand and stood. He pulled me to him and hugged me to his chest. He was tall and strong. He smelled good. I rested my head on his chest and relaxed.

It was a while before I stood away and looked up at him. "Thank you, William. Your words were helpful. I think I will get a good night's sleep."

I returned to my rooms and sought my bed. I was no longer worried about the next day. However, I was disturbed. He was warm and nice. He aroused feelings in me that just should not be. This was not a game. I would return to my world, not as an Elf maiden, but as a middle-aged man.

Strange dreams haunted my sleep.

I Came

Chapter 9 – Justice

The Warden of the Guild of Thieves in Willicamp greeted me warmly. "My Lady! The Master is awaiting you. Please, let me prepare your room, while you attend upon the Master."

Moments later, the Master effused, "My Lady, welcome. The Grand Master informed us of your arrival, and we have prepared your room. I was told that you were arriving and seeking to avenge us against the Usurper."

I sensed his fear. He was sure that Beckworth was just around the corner, ready to pounce on this tiny hamlet. I had to reassure him. "Indeed, I have come. I will use this guildhall as my quarters for the next few days. In the meantime, I need your assistance in quartering my troops. I have twelve soldiers in carts along with three score zhaks arriving in two day's time. I do not want them housed here, but I ask that you arrange for an encampment where my men can bivouac, and they can feed their zhaks."

The Master's raised an eyebrow, but his words belied his actions. "Of course, My Lady, anything you need."

"Then I will retire to my room. Please, deliver a meal to my room. I will be gone before morning."

* * *

As the sun began to cast light over the horizon, I was speeding through Alghelcamp into the rising sun. The guildhalls that had been attacked were all along the eastern border of the disputed lands. I intended to visit the one furthest north and work my way south, going from guildhall to guildhall until I found something.

The hamlet of Higgleston was at the crossing of two roads: The north-south Great Eastern Road and the Southeast Highway, extending from King Richards' capital to the Coastal Road. A trail led eastward toward Talishport on the coast. That crossing made

Higgleston an important location. There had been six buildings: one at each of the four corners with more on opposite sides of the Coastal Road.

On the southwestern corner was a barbershop. As in many parts of Jaralii, the barber was also the town's physician, making him an important person in the entire region. The southeastern corner was the school. There were two rooms, one for the younger students and the other for the advanced students. All children attended Lower School. They learned the principles of their language, simple reading, writing and arithmetic. In the High School, students learned scholarly arts and practical studies. Depending on the pupil's desires and that of their families, students were apprenticed to a trade, including farming, husbandry, metalworking, and/or other skills. They also spent half of each day learning advanced skills in reading, writing, math, history, government, law and military service.

On the northeast corner was the general store. This was the regional center for agriculture. Farmers brought their produce to the store, and everyone else went there to purchase produce. The butcher's shop was just north of the store, making this corner the central location for food purchases for miles around.

The northwest corner was a pile of blackened and charred rubble. It had been the local inn and tavern. It was also the Guildhall of Thieves. Just north of this was the magistrate's building, making this tiny town the center of government for the region. The magistrate's building was badly damaged, but still standing.

I stood at the center of the crossroads, looking around as I tried to sense what had happened. Unfortunately, too much time had passed, and too many people with high emotions had been there. It was all too confusing.

A man approached. "What are you doing?" he asked, confrontationally.

I turned to see a short, stocky man, dressed in a blood-spattered apron and wielding a razor. I sensed his anger, but he also very much afraid. I decided that a reasoned combination of authority and sympathy would be the best approach.

I Came

"I am Gilraën," I announced, imperiously. "Prince William sent here me to help in any way I can. What happened here?"

"John Barber," he introduced himself. "If you're here to help, come with me."

He led the way beyond his shop to an outbuilding. He swung the door wide. There on the floor were a dozen injured people, each lying on a blanket. All were suffering from burns… some very severe. The barber had done as well as he could. He had applied a poultice similar to oatmeal wrapped in cloth. The poultice kept the burns wet, reducing pain and scabbing, while also keeping out the air, which helped. Still, they were all in pain and a few in agony.

"Well done, John Barber. You have treated them properly and well. Where is your Healer?"

He pointed at the woman on the floor to the left. "She is our Wise Womban and mine wibe. He," he pointed to the man next to her, "is our magistrate." He pointed to others. "The inn keeper… the barman… the baker… bar maids…"

I placed my pack against the wall, then turned to Barber, replying, "Then, let us attend to them. I will need your skills. Please prepare a fresh poultice and wrappings. I will do what I can to restore them."

I studied the patients, assessing their injuries and considering how to repair, or at least ameliorate the damage. Although the Wise Woman was among the least injured, I began with her. I needed the woman's skills and knowledge of herbs and medicinals to help heal the rest.

By the time John returned with a pot of simmering poultice and strips of bandaging, his wife was feeling better and was preparing to assist her neighbors. The three of us labored well into the afternoon. I healed minor burns, leaving them red enough for John and his wife to reduce swelling and alleviate the irritation.

Several town folk were badly burned, their skin and muscle charred to the bone. I worked slowly, but carefully, using my scrolls of healing as well as my own healing skills to restore bones first, ensuring that their marrow was undamaged. I slowly created and knitted the muscles together, repaired tendons and connective tissue as I went. Finally, I rebuilt skin, ensuring that it wasn't perfect. I had to leave some damage for John and his Wise Woman wife to attend and heal. Each of these victims would have scars. That was deliberate on my part. They had to have them to remind themselves and others of the evils Beckworth had visited upon them, while also informing them of the healing provided by Prince William, through his agents, John the Barber, Maude the Wise Woman, and Princess Gilraën the Elf.

Later, I joined John and his wife, who introduced herself as Maude, in the rooms above the shop. "Thank you, Princess Elf. Without you, we all might have died. We have food; would you join us?"

I sighed, suddenly realizing how tired I was. "I will, and with great pleasure. Please, tell me what happened here?"

Maude provided a cheese, a loaf, and a jug of wine. As we ate, she asked, "Never in all my life have I seen such a deed. Lady, are you a witch, a healer or Sorcerer?"

I smiled. "I am Princess Gilraën Gulámae of the Elves of Green Mountain-Maidstone Forest. I am a friend and ally of Prince William, and it is he who has sent me to bring to justice the villains who did this to you. Will you help me find them and bring them to justice?"

They both nodded. "We will, as will everyone hereabouts. Let us eat, and then we will talk with others who saw it happen."

The bread was stale, the cheese was moldy, and the wine was verging on vinegar, but I ate heartily. The effort of healing all those people was much harder than I had expected. When I had finished, I placed a copper on their table.

"No!" John protested. "You have healed my wife, my sister, and my neighbors. It is I who should pay you."

I smiled and pocketed the coin. He was right, of course. I didn't want to dishonor my host, or antagonize him either. He was grateful and eager to help. I could find another way to help him with his expenses.

I Came

The barber led me from house to house. By the end of the day, I had spoken with all thirty-seven people in and around the village. The composite picture of the attack was frightening. At least fifty soldiers had invaded the town. They set fire to the inn and murdered everyone who tried to escape. When the town folk had grabbed axes, picks and pitchforks to defend the town, the soldiers attacked them, took away their weapons and threw the men into the inferno. At least fifteen men had died that night. However, there was no evidence of a Sorcerer.

Most of the soldiers had marched south, bivouacking some ten miles down the road. They had stolen a porg, butchered and eaten it. On the following morning, they had continued south along the Great Eastern Highway. A second group of twenty or more, accompanied by a Troll, had continued northward.

John and Maude were eager to help. Evidently, they had traveled extensively throughout the area, which I confirmed with a quick survey of their minds. The next important village to the south of Higgleston was Tamvill, roughly 25 miles to the south, which was about the limit of their travels. Both had heard of the village of Goerskim but only knew that it was a long distance to the southeast.

I asked if there was another inn in the area. The Barbers insisted that I stay with them. I could hardly turn them down. However, I did insist that Maude and I shop at the general store for food and medical supplies. When Maude objected, I insisted that it was Prince William's orders that I help the survivors and do whatever was needed to help rebuild the town. Even though the money came from my pack, I figured that William would support me in this. Before I left the next day, I had dispersed a Gold to the innkeeper, a Silver to the Barbers, and Coppers to those who had been injured or whose homes had been destroyed.

I set out early in the morning after a full and hearty breakfast. I *faded* and headed south at a moderate three-fold walk. I'd cover the distance in just an hour, so I was in no rush. However, I was cautious. This was the area where I'd felt the mysterious presence. I prepared to accelerate to my maximum, just in case. Fortunately, I arrived without incident.

Tamvill was a much smaller village than Higgleston. It stood at the intersection of the Great Eastern Road and two side roads. The easterly trail led to the seacoast. The other trail went northwestward to join the Southeast Highway. I was on the edge of contested territory.

I remained invisible while I searched for a guildhall. Most of the guilds were outraged that anyone would dare to assail any guildhall. Such an assault undermined the entire guild system. The guild system had to be defended, regardless of the proclivities of its members.

Then, there at the bottom of a wall in an alley a few buildings from the crossroads, was a sigil of the Witches, Truth-Seekers and Wise Women. '*Perfect*,' I thought.

The Wardress' smile was less than encouraging until I introduced myself with a password identifying me as a Senior Witch. Then, the Wardress' smile broadened, and she greeted me warmly, "You are most welcome, My Lady! How may I help you?"

I felt the Wardress attempt to scan my mind. I smirked at her. "You know better, Wardress. I could freeze your life's blood for such an offense. Bring me to the Mistress of the Hall."

The Wardress blanched, but led me to a small room beneath the stairs. An elderly woman sat at a corner desk. She turned to face me, and then she, too, reached out to scan my mind.

"Don't!" I commanded. The Mistress fell back as though struck. "I am a High Mistress, far beyond your level. Must I speak to the Mistress of all Mistresses?"

The Guild Mistress roused herself, and answered, "No, Revered One. I hear and understand. What is your will?"

"I will stay here this night. I expect your best room. I will eat in the hall with the others. It is my wish to speak to all the Guild women who are here, yourself included. I will use this guildhall as my center of activity while I am here. I also have dirty clothes, which I will need to have cleaned, folded and returned to me before morning. I undertake compensation for this service. I will retire to my room, now. Please instruct the Wardress as to my needs."

I Came

"Of course, Revered One. As is your will!"

Several hours later, I sat opposite the bar at the smallest table. Ten women sat at the other four tables. The Guild Mistress and the Wardress sat at one. The two bar maids and cook sat at another. Two women sat at the third table, and three at the other.

"I am Gilraën Gulámae, a High Mistress of the Guild of Witches, Truth-Seekers and Wise Women. I am seeking your assistance. As you may know, a guildhall in Higgleston was attacked by armed forces. They burned it to the ground. They murdered Guild members when they tried to escape the flames. When town folk intervened to protect innocent lives, they, too, were attacked and thrown into the flames. This very day, I attended to twelve villagers who had tried to intervene, including Maude, a Wise Woman of this Guild.

"The survivors have told me that some of these soldiers fled to the south, towards this village. Unless they turned aside before arriving here, they came through this village within the past two days.

"I have no doubt that one or more of you know of their passage, their destination, and other useful information about them. I require your assistance in this matter."

I sat back, assuming an imperious air. Folded my hands on the table before me, I looked from one to another of the guild women.

"Revered One," the Guild Mistress began, "we have indeed seen them. About a week ago, over one hundred armed troops entered our village from the south. They split into three groups, one each, marching north, northwest and southeast. Two days ago, a group from the north returned and continued to the south."

I waited for the others to speak. When none did, I asked, "And?"

A woman sitting among the three added, "When they went to the north, they were quiet and seemed fearful. When they returned, they were boisterous, bragging and strutting."

Again, I waited before asking, "And?"

One of the pair of women nodded, and replied, "Revered One, I scanned their minds. They were shielded, but I easily penetrated

214

them. They were rejoicing in the killing and mayhem they had caused."

She hesitated, but I leaned toward her, both encouraging and threatening her.

Taking a deep breath, as though about to plunge into deep waters, the woman blurted, "They were joyful that they could inform Beckworth of their victory over the Guild of Thieves."

I nodded in acknowledgement. "We assumed that it was Beckworth. We believe that he is attempting to destroy the entire Guild System throughout all the lands. Such a pogrom would directly affect you. Therefore, I charge you and all guildswomen in good standing to resist him to the best of your abilities. I hold each Guild Mistress directly responsible for communication with the High Mistress about any activities detrimental to our guild or those of other guilds.

"Further, I ask you to seek information from all persons with whom you come in contact. Learn anything you can and relate that to your Mistresses. Do you all understand?"

I touched each of their minds, prompting an immediate and instinctive answer. All the women responded affirmatively. "Good!" I replied, "We are sisters." I felt a warm glow emanating from them all.

"Guild Mistress, please serve our sisters. Place the cost on my receipt. I request a meal and a tankard. Ladies?"

By the end of the evening, we had gathered in a big group, laughing and giggling. Each of us had different missions. Some were on errands of mercy... healing the sick, attending childbirth, tending to the injured. Others were purchasing goods or products needed in their practices. One was preparing to interview another young woman as a possible apprentice. All of them were exactly as they appeared to be.

The following morning, I continued southward on the Great Eastern Road towards Goerskim, more than 80 miles away. Assured that there were villages between here and there, I proceeded at a reasonable pace of three-fold speed, extending my prescience to my limits, attempting to be aware of everything at the same time.

Following the directions I had received at the guildhall, I closed in on my final objective. The next village on my voyage was the large village of Phaedham. Again, the primary reason for its existence was its location. The Great Eastern Road crossed over the Phaed River on a large, arched stone bridge on its way to the distant south. The Great Southern Road ran from Phaedport on the north bank of the river, intersecting the Great Eastern Road just above the bridge. After crossing the bridge, it continued on to the west to the Western Sea. South of the bridge, the Great Eastern Road ran south to Goerskim, Bursk, Wendleford and Narwortland. The village of Phaedham existed on both sides of the bridge, controlling the roads and the portage that began just upstream. This combination made this an important location and a seat of power.

As always, I *faded* before entering the town. The half of the town on the northern side of the river had several professional guilds, but none that I could readily use. I was not a cooper, a smith, or a mason. On the south side of the river, I found the guilds of assassins, of thieves, of wizards, and of witches. I chose the Guild of Witches, Truth-Seekers and Wise Women.

The Wardress greeted me enthusiastically. "Welcome, High Mistress. Our guildhall in Tamvill alerted us to your arrival. All is in readiness. The Guild Mistress is awaiting you. Your room is ready. Would you like me to guide you to your room, then to the Mistress, or the other way around?"

I thought for a moment. "My room first, then the Mistress. Please, lead on."

Moments later, I entered a lovely, large room. A large window looked out over a pleasant, green courtyard.

The Wardress asked, "Do you have any clothing to be cleaned? I have fresh water, soap and fresh towels for you. The bed was remade this morning with freshly cleaned bedding. The tavern will open in one turn. Food will be ready in two turns. Is there any other way we can serve you, High Mistress?"

"Perhaps now, we should see the Guild Mistress?"

The Guild Mistress was as effusive as had been the Wardress. "Welcome, High Mistress, welcome to Phaedham. How may we be of service?"

Gilraën thought for a moment before replying. "I will use your mirror. I must communicate with the Grand High Mistress. If you will excuse me?"

Although she was somewhat taken aback, the Guild Mistress bowed her head and opened a small panel hiding the mirror. "Please, call me when you are done."

I waited for the Guild Mistress to depart before I gave the word of command and waited for the mirror to clear. A very female image of Talbot appeared. I was startled to see him appearing as a woman.

Talbot responded, "Oh, it's you!" His image wavered and returned to his more normal self. "Why have you contacted me?"

I told him about the situation in Higgleston, and what I had done. I explained my distribution of Gold and Silver, in Prince William's name. We discussed my mission, and his investigations into the Guild of Thieves in Goerskim.

"I am still unsure of Goerskim, Gilraën. Guild masters have been approached by outsiders, demanding their disbandment or their complicity in seceding from the guild and aligning with a new guild structure under Beckworth's Sorcerers. I believe we have discovered two examples. The Guild in Goerskim acceded to Beckworth's demands. The Guild in Higgleston refused.

"I advise you to be very careful. You are very near Beckworth's territory and far from my help. You have only your own resources, while he has legions of Sorcerers, and who knows what else."

I had to agree. "Yes, I know. I still must learn what is happening. If I do, then the Prince can respond knowledgeably. If I don't, he'll flail about as though blindfolded.

"And, I am not alone. I have made friends in Higgleston, and allies of the Guilds of Assassins, of Thieves, and of Witches. I've also endeared myself to the Guild of Barbers and of Hoteliers. They all know that Prince William has sent help and is seeking those who have committed the sacrileges to bring the miscreants to justice."

I Came

I concluded our communication and then summoned the Mistress. "I would like to meet with you, the guild staff, and everyone who is here. Tonight? In the tavern for dinner?"

"Indeed, Mistress. I have already made those arrangements. We will gather at supper."

When I entered the tavern, I saw eight women seated at four of the six tables. As was my wont, I scanned the room as I entered, as much to discover an enemy as to learn more about the people within. The Guild Mistress and the Warden had shielded minds. A woman sitting by herself was also shielded. The group of three was partially shielded, in that their immediate topic of conversation was observable, but they protected their inner selves. The other two women were completely open. Both smiled at me as I entered, as though aware of my mental probe.

I explained my mission, and, again, asked for the women's help. I perceived that all but one was eager to assist. That one was the woman sitting by herself. For several minutes, each of them volunteered what they knew. I learned that a group of about one hundred soldiers had arrived in Phaedham from the west about two weeks earlier. They had passed over the bridge heading north. Since then, three groups of twenty to thirty had returned and had marched down the southern road toward Goerskim.

I listened attentively. Much had been said, but they had withheld much more. I had many questions. "My sisters, I thank you. As you know, other guilds have been sacked and burned. Still others have been undermined and perverted from their purpose. I search as much to know this purpose as I do to find those who have murdered defenseless guildsmen, women, and townsfolk. Can any of you inform me?"

Most of the women's faces were blanks. The single woman remained silent and darkly ominous. I turned to her, saying, "Sister, you are strangely quiet, yet pregnant with thoughts. There is much you could tell me, if you so desire. Would you share your thoughts with me?"

Everyone turned to her. Each had a determined look, as though challenging her and demanding to know why she would not be of help in this time of mutual need.

She shifted in her seat.

A spear drove itself into my head. My mind was in great pain! Fighting back as best I could, I began to reinforce my helmet, but it took considerable energy. Gradually my helmet became ever stronger, brighter and more reflective until the probe turned back upon itself. Then, I sharpened my lance to the point of a pin and thrust toward the source of my pain. My pin became a nail… which became a spike. I drove it straight and true until it burst through a barrier of darkness, suddenly arriving in a world of light.

A voice spoke to me. *'Welcome, High One. I have awaited you and sought you out since King Melwasúl informed me of your presence. I shall come to your room. Await me there, and we shall talk at length. Let us part?'*

I could feel the woman struggling to maintain her outward calm. However, I could also feel a rising panic, as she realized that she had lost control and was helpless in my grasp.

'So be it!' I replied, releasing her.

I smiled, as though nothing untoward had taken place. Taking in the group, I asked "Please, sisters, if you have anything else to tell me, I will be in my room. However, I will be gone by sunrise for a day or two before I return. If needed during that time, await me here. Good night, sisters.

"Please, Wardress, would you serve a meal with a tankard in my room? Thank you."

I rose, and as I did so, I briefly scanned the group. Everyone was relieved and thankful, except the Mistress, who seemed anxious to speak with me.

Moments after I had entered my room, there was a quiet scratching on the door. The Mistress whispered, "High One, it is I, the Guild Mistress."

"Enter!"

I Came

"Thank you, I had to speak with you in a manner so as not to alarm the others. I come with a warning. Beckworth has contracted a Krell to kill you. A Sorcerer got drunk at the Guild of Thieves in Goerskim. He alluded to it, but then he suddenly became ill. He fell asleep, but kept mumbling on about a Krell hired to kill Prince William's Elf. There is no doubt that the Elf of whom he spoke is you."

"Yes, Mistress, I am aware of him. I have escaped him twice, but must face him eventually if I am to achieve my purpose and return to my home. So, I thank you for your warning, and ask you to inform me of anything you might yet learn.

"Now, what is it that I can do for you or the Guild?"

The Guild Mistress looked around nervously. "Tell King Richard that a new tribe of Orcs is being assembled in Eastport. They are preparing to sail. We are told they will attack in the west. Tell the King that there are many loyal to him, and we await his return."

I sat at the corner desk, digesting the news. I had to talk with Talbot. "I must converse with the Grand High Mistress later tonight, after I have eaten."

"Of course, High Mistress. At your command."

I considered the news. The Krell was old news. The Mistress had just confirmed what everyone suspected and for which I was prepared… I hoped. However, confirmation of an invasion of Orcs was news, indeed. Just what was 'west'? Perhaps Richard or William would know or Talbot could deduce what it meant.

Some time later I heard another scratch at the door. Rather than speak, I thought, 'Enter!'

The lone woman entered, and thought, '*Tapla!*'

I said, "I think better aloud. I'd rather not expose my thoughts at this time."

"Of course, Princess, I am honored to meet you, at last. I am Evërlÿnde Idril Silimæurë of the Elves of the Green Mountains. The Seeress informed King Melwasúl of your presence. He sent me to inform you, to guide you, and to assist you as I can.

"A Krell hunts you, as you know. Beckworth has attacked guildhalls, as you know. What you do not know is that Beckworth has received large numbers of off-worlders. He has changed them into monsters: Krells, Trolls, and new Orcs, which we call goblins. He is creating armies to attack King Richard's realm simultaneously from the east, south and west. Sorcerers will aid them. He is determined to conquer Richard in a single campaign.

"You are the only one that can stand in his way. Without you, he will succeed. With you, and with our aid, you will overcome him. Then, perhaps, we Elves can free ourselves.

"The Seeress will come to you. She will teach you what you must know. Then, you will lead us. Prepare yourself, Gilraën Gulámae."

"Help me? In what way?"

"We can do little directly. We have taken oaths of neutrality. The Adjudicars have great powers. It was they who destroyed the Elves of the Great Forest. Since then, all the Elvin tribes have maintained our neutrality. However, the Seeress may have found a way to circumvent our restrictions. If so, we might could act together to defeat them and drive them from this world. But, it all depends on you."

"Adjudicars? What are they?"

"We are not sure. They arrived on Trahe some time ago. They slowly achieved ascendancy, using combinations of extraordinary power and extortion. They have forced us and the Dwarves into neutrality, while disproportionately aiding Lord Beckworth far in excess of that afforded to King Richard."

"How can you help me?"

"I have. I have warned you. I have told you of our plan to defeat the Adjudicars and their pawn, Lord Beckworth. I have done what I can do without violating our neutrality and bringing down the wrath of the Adjudicars upon us all.

"I must leave you and return to the Elf Realm of the Green Mountains before I am discovered. Fare you well, Princess. Our hopes and our future are with you."

I Came

As Evërlŷnde left, the Wardress arrived, bearing a tray of food, a carafe, and a tall goblet. She nodded a curtsey and left, without saying a word.

The smell of the food was almost overwhelming. However, I remembered to test it for poisons and other deleterious ingredients. Caution was becoming my most important watchword. Discovering none, I dug in. It was only when I was finishing the last bit, sweeping the crust of bread over the plate to sop up the final drop of gravy, that I realized how hungry I had been.

I took the carafe and the goblet to the bed, where I sat back and rested on the backboard. 'What a day,' I thought. 'Everyone seemed to know about the Krell... the witches, the Elves... who else? And, what was all this Adjudicars stuff? They sounded like really bad guys. Were they trying to subjugate the entire planet? Where did they come from? And, how was I the 'last hope' not only of Richard and William, but of the Elves? I really have to talk with Prince William about this.'

Obviously, my immediate problem was the Krell. Nobody seemed to offer much hope concerning it. I spent many minutes trying to decide who knew of me that could hire a Krell to assassinate me?

'Assassinate! That's it!' I thought.

I left the tray outside her door and descended the stairs. "Wardress, I will be out for some time. I will return, so do not abandon your watch."

I left, *faded* and walked the streets, searching for the sigil I knew had to be there. Finally, I found it, deeply hidden... the Guild of Assassins. Entering what appeared to be an empty courtyard with no other exits, I gave the password as an assassin. A few moments passed before a portion of one of the walls dissolved away, and a doorway appeared. A man stood there, introducing himself as the Warden and bidding me to enter.

Once inside and the portal again closed, I saw four men walk past, each bearing a crossbow with bolts ready. Once they departed the room, I gave a single word of command, identifying myself as an Assassin Superior. "I will speak with the Guild Master."

"Of course, High One," the Warden replied.

Moments later, the Warden ushered me into the Guild Master's quarters.

"Welcome, High One. How may I be of service?"

'I am hunted by a Krell. I need to know who has commissioned this Krell?"

"Ah, High One, you, of all people, know that such a contract is private and not open to discussion. Even if I knew, I couldn't tell you."

Yet, he had revealed all. As he denied knowledge of the assassination, he revealed much. He didn't know directly of his own knowledge. However, other Masters had informed him of the contract. None of them knew who had contracted the 'hit,' but the general suspicion was Lord Beckworth.

"Master, do Krells perform Lord Beckworth's bidding?"

The Master gulped, stammered and hesitated, before answering, "It is said that he has command of large numbers of the... more 'difficult' races."

"But does he?"

Again, the Master dissembled. "Such things are hard to know for certain."

I persisted, "But such things are known, and you will tell me."

"I can not! This is Guild business, and I cannot divulge it."

However, he had. I perceived his deepest thoughts. He knew! Now I knew. The Adjudicars knew of my presence, and they were afraid of me!

"Thank you, Master. You have been of great help. I will so inform the High Master of your assistance and beneficence."

Leaving the astonished Master behind, I returned to my room with the sisters. Sleep was turmoil of thought: Adjudicars... Elves... Krells... Magic... Transformation... Savior. It was all too much. Somehow, some sort of sense needed to be made of it all.

I Came

I dreamed. I remembered, when I awoke, that there had been dreams, but I didn't remember their specific content.

When my eyes opened, the sun was shining, and the birds were singing. I was late! I had intended to contact Talbot before being off, long before dawn. *'At least one good thing would come of this. I could have a good breakfast before I leave.'*

I retrieved my clean clothes and repacked. Then I went downstairs to the tavern. They were still serving breakfast. Mine was excellent. I bid the Wardress and Mistress farewell and suggested that I'd return in a few days. I didn't say anything about the Krell.

I took the Great Eastern Road south of the river headed to Goerskim. I *faded* and proceeded at a 3-fold walk. It was a leisurely pace that would get me to my destination in less than an hour. Although I had eaten well, I still bled energy from my surroundings. There was no sense in dissipating my internal stores of energy, especially while I was still deep in enemy-held territory.

I was less than ten miles south of Phaedham, when I felt something strange. My suspicions were already aroused, so I took no chances and accelerated to a twelve-fold pace. I extended my prescience to its limits, hoping to perceive something… anything. For a moment, I felt weaker, as though something was draining my energy. But I persevered. I put on a huge burst of speed, greater than I had ever done before. The combination of the Krell's enervating power and my own exertions were almost too much for me. I sucked life energy from plants and animals in the area, hoping it was enough. Only when I could no longer feel the Krell's presence did I slow to a moderate four-fold pace.

'Damned Krell!' I groused to myself. *'Must I avoid him forever?'*

I felt a different being. It wasn't the ominous drain on my energies. Instead, it was the sensation of a Sorcerer, extending his surveillance over a wide area. It was faint, but characteristic of an active magical search.

I remained passive - sensing, but not seeking. It reminded me of radar. One could detect the use of radar at a far greater distance than the one using it. Thus it was, that I could detect whoever was doing the searching, but still would remain hidden.

I continued my passive search, detecting a group of common men. I slowed to a stop in a woodland. Leaping into a lower branch of a large tree, I climbed high where I hid within its leaves. I sat quietly, feeling… listening… accepting the information carried as the mental energies of those unguarded. There were many of them, perhaps fifty or more. There was also at least one… perhaps two Sorcerers. I didn't dare feel elated that my search had been successful. Instead, I used all my powers to hold my alignment with the fabric of the world, becoming as one with it. One Sorcerer spiked a search in my direction, possibly having detected a moment of misalignment as I settled myself.

Men conversed while sitting around campfires. It wasn't long before I could 'tune in' on a voice. Slowly, I separated the voices and catalogued the men, their positions, and their conversations. I found some fifty-three men, plus two Sorcerers, who sat by themselves just beyond the circle of men, tents, and campfires. Each of the men was pleased with the looting and pillaging they'd performed over the past few days.

One man mentioned Higgleston. The others laughed and rehashed their stories. Others related stories of individual atrocities they had committed. Still others spoke of the campaign, and the booty the Sorcerers had promised. But first, they'd return to Goerskim, rest up from a week of hiking across the countryside, and chase a few of the local women.

After that, their language turned ever more brutal. They spoke of the barmaids, the local women, and the girls at the local farms. And, they spoke of the Guildhall of Thieves as their headquarters, where they could take the local women, have their way with them, and no one could complain about them. Instead of complaining about Beckworth's soldiers, they'd complain about the Guild of Thieves.

I listened attentively, refusing to give in to my anger. To do so might reveal my presence. Instead, I concentrated on the Sorcerers.

Neither of them spoke aloud. Instead, they conversed mentally. Although their mental actions sufficed to protect their conversation from discovery by their troops, they revealed everything they were communicating to anyone with the ability to eavesdrop on them.

I Came

I quickly discovered that one of them was among the raiders that had annihilated Prince William's Company, which made him the one who had escaped me. The other had been responsible for the raid on Higgleston. They were awaiting 'justice' before they attacked Phaedham. I couldn't understand what they meant by 'justice.' Obviously, their idea of justice and mine were entirely different.

Slowly, I removed my backpack, jamming it into the crotch of the tree. Pulling the quiver with the unstrung bow from it, and sliding it over my back, I climbed carefully to the ground. Maintaining my serenity, I stepped through the bow and strung it, before removing two arrows to accompany the bow. I crept around the outskirts of the camp until I could clearly see the two Sorcerers. They were sitting silently at their campfire.

I laid the first arrow across the bow and nocked it to the string. Lifting the bow, I pulled the string to my lip in a single sweeping motion of draw and release. My hands now a blur, the second arrow was nocked, drawn and released at the second Sorcerer, even as the first arrow was but halfway to its target.

Before either arrow struck home, I gathered my energy, finally revealing myself to anyone with the slightest magical aptitude. I released it all in a single instant, and the fifty-three raiders fell dead. The two Sorcerers sat bolt upright at the revelation of nearby magic. That made them perfect statues to receive the arrows I had launched moments before. Fifty-three solders and two Sorcerers were small compensation for losing more than a hundred men and the sacking of the village of Higgleston. However, the total loss now of five Sorcerers would, hopefully, be a severe blow to Beckworth's military prowess and his ambitions.

I quickly retrieved my pack, before I went to the bodies of the Sorcerers and retrieved the two arrows. Such weapons were precious. Not only did I have only twenty-four in my quiver, but they were special in other ways. They were twice the diameter of normal arrows, tipped with conical iron, and reinforced with spells of power. Moreover, they were costly. Even at the castle, they still cost me a Silver a dozen. I thought the employment agreement covered them, but Talbot assured me that only the first dozen were included. Any beyond that had to be purchased out of my own funds.

226

It had the effect of making me more selective in choosing my targets, and the circumstances surrounding them, that I might try to retrieve my arrows for further use.

I raced to the road leading to Goerskim, my mind a whirl. I could picture my arrows speeding to the hearts of the Sorcerers. And I could see the faces of their corpses. I also felt the deaths of the troops. That was unexpected. I had assumed that dying was simply a loss of life. However, I'd felt their minds cease. At least there was no surge of energy. They'd just stopped.

Bang!

Suddenly, I was tumbling head over heels down the road, banging and crashing and careening off the road into the trees. I shook my head trying to clear it. Then, when I tried to stand, I felt puny, as though sapped of all my energy. '*Shit!*' I thought. '*Caught! What do I do now?*'

A huge, deep voice rumbled, "Gotcha! I've been chasing you for days. Damn, you're fast. I've never heard of anyone as fast as you."

I rolled over, trying to focus on a huge, man-like being. Like a man it had two arms, two legs, a body and a head. However, it was at least fifteen, maybe twenty feet tall, with muscles bulging on his muscles. His bare feet were covered with dark matted hair. His bare arms were equally hairy. His large head was disguised with a full beard, heavy eyebrows, and long, black hair. His eyes were large and black. His teeth were huge, yellow bricks, exposed only when he talked.

He wore what appeared to be leather jerkin and rough, leather, knee-length pants. A huge belt with a massive brass buckle girded his waist. A heavy hasp protruded from a huge black scabbard stuck beneath the belt. A heavy fingered hand, easily large enough to engulf me completely, rested on the hilt.

"I've been watching you. You were intent on them, so I could sneak up on you. Your magic doesn't work on me, you know. But, I wanted to see what you were doing.

"You know, you're fantastic. You disappeared as though you were a part of the tree or the air itself. Amazing!

I Came

"And, the way you killed those twisted bastards did my heart good. Of course, I just take the contracts. I don't give a damn; I just perform the contract and get paid for it.

"But, damn you're fast! Where did you learn that? I just gotta know!"

I was taken aback. What was all this? This was a Krell, no doubt. He should have killed me and been done with it. So, what was all this?

A dumb thought echoed through my woozy mind. I reasoned, *'What the hell? Why not?'*

"BEEP! BEEP!" I replied.

"Hah, Hah!" the Krell laughed. "I ain't heard that in years. So does that make me the coyote?"

"I didn't see the Acme rocket or the anvil. So, how did you trip me?"

"Acme, eh? How to you know anything about the coyote? What's his name?" he challenged.

"Wile E!"

"Damn! Who are you? Do I know you?"

"I don't know. Do I know you?"

"Who were you before you came here?

"Why? What would that mean to you?"

"Kiwl da Wabbit," he sang to the tune of the Ride of the Valkyries. "Who sang that?"

"Elmer Fudd, why?'

"You're from Earth... America to be exact. So, who were you?"

"Okay. On Earth I was Tony... Anthony Richardson."

"Oh, you've got to be kidding."

"I kid you not. Why do you ask?"

"Who did you game with? Anyone in particular?"

"Well, yeah. A couple of guys. Why?"

"Who?"

"Well, there was Reu and Greg. There was Linda..."

"What was Reu's name?"

"Reu? He hated me calling him that. His name was actually Rueben, Reuben Frederick Mayhugh... the third, if that means anything to you. He nearly killed me one time when he was testing an anti-burglar invention."

"Naw, I didn't even come close. You're as healthy as a horse."

"Even a horse can be electrocuted. I was lucky I didn't bounce all the way to the street. I would have been run over for... What the... How do you... Reu? What the hell? Reu, is that you?"

"In the flesh. Well, not exactly, but I think you know what I mean." The Krell stood back, giving me an appraising look, "You turned out pretty good there, Tony. So you decided to play the Sorceress shtick?"

"Nah, luck of the draw. I got turned into an Elf; a girl Elf. I was supposed to be a male archer. Let me tell you, being a girl... it's nothing like the games. Oh, and when I first arrived here, I nearly drowned. Something went wrong, and I got dropped in a culvert full of sewage and slop... cold, muddy, yucky filth."

"Damn, old buddy, you've put me in a hell of a position. I've got a contract to kill the Elf, but you're the Elf. Shit! So, what brings you here, anyway?"

"I'm on a quest."

"A quest? Really? Anything I might be interested in? Tell me about it."

I explained what had happened, what I'd found, and what I was doing. I concluded, saying, "So, there are these super-villains that are trying to take over the world. I'm the heroine. I have to overcome them to free this world. Along the way, I have to defeat the evil Beckworth, his Sorcerer henchmen, and the legions of soldiers amassed against the good guys. It's just another video game,

I Came

Reu, and we're the heroes. If you join my quest, we win, just like in the games. If not, we'll both lose.

"The only difference is we have to get this right the first time. There's no 'Save' function, and no 'Redo.' This is real, and there is no do-over."

"So, you're on a quest, a regular 'Dawn Quicks Oatey!'" he laughed. "And you're the good guy, which makes me the bad guy?"

"Reu…"

"Nah, it ain't Reu any more. I'm Justice."

"You're Justice? They were waiting for you. They are going to sack Phaedham. Do you really want that on your conscience, Reu… Justice? What kind of justice would that be?"

"So, they're playing me? Yah, could be. Hey, let's talk about this. I know a really good place…" He backed up another step, cocked his head and looked at me appraisingly before continuing, "Well, it's good for me. I don't know about a delicate flower like you. Then again, you might be a bit hardier than you look. It's a nice place; good food, good ale, a little pricey, but you get what you pay for. We might even bump into a friend."

"Sure, but first, we have to go to Goerskim. I have to clear up a problem. Wanna come? It should be interesting."

"Damn! Interesting, huh? I remember some of those 'interesting' little excursions you took us on in the games. We're lucky the team survived any of them. When someone else says 'interesting', they mean it in an academic sort of way. When you say 'interesting' it can mean anything. Sure, I'll tag along. After all, this is a quest, ain't it?"

Justice (*Crap! This will take some getting used to*) and I sped down the road toward Goerskim. As we raced at a 4-fold walk, I asked him, "So, how come you're a Krell?"

"Haven't the foggiest. I was sleeping in my chair in front of my computer. Then, ZAP! I was here, and huge beyond huge. It took me a while to figure it out, but I was big, fast, nearly invulnerable and strong beyond belief. Then, this guy, Lord Beckworth, says,

230

'Congratulations! You've been selected.' He told me a lot, and then introduced me to this guy, Caierne, the head Sorcerer. He tells me a story about how Beckworth is trying to overthrow the evil King Richard, and all I can think of is Richard III. You know, 'a horse…'

"So, anyway, he sends me out on a mission to hunt down a guy. I do. Then, he sends me out again, and again. Then, I'm told about an Elf. One of the Sorcerers in William's employ is a spy and knows where she is. So, I hunt her. I find her on a hilltop, but she goes invisible on me and races down a sheer cliff and escaped me."

"No way! That was you?"

"Who else? Anyway, now I know where she lives, so I haunt the area. I almost catch her a couple of times, but she's faster than anything I've ever seen. I do the Wile E. Coyote thing, but she's a real Road Runner.

"Then, we go out to kill a bunch of King Richard's troops. There's only about a hundred, but they've got four Sorcerers and me. So, I find them, and the Sorcerers kill them all. It doesn't settle well with me, but they tell me that we've got to defeat King Richard's troops, which sounds right to me.

"'*No Shit!*' I think to myself.

"Then I'm told she's killed some Sorcerers and their troops. I'm stunned, but I really don't believe it. Then, they sell me a contract. If I hunt down the Elf and kill it, I'll get twenty ingots of gold. I'm sure you know that's a shitload of money. And, I'll be able to take it home when this TOD is over.

"So, I agree. So, I hunt this Elf. I'm told she's near Prince William's castle really close to the border. I chase her half the length of the continent, and finally catch up to her, just in time to see her hunt down the Sorcerers and kill their troops.

"It's justified. I approve, but I have a contract. So, I lay a trap, and I catch the Road Runner! But then, she turns out to be you! Suddenly, everything is SNAFU. So, I listen, and find out I'm a bad guy. That's not the worst part. There are bad guys and good guys, but, I'm working for the bad guys' flunkies, and the real bad guys are real and rank up there with Hitler.

I Came

"So, here I am. What's our quest?"

"Evidently, the big bad guys are the Adjudicars, and I don't know if anyone has seen one of them. Perhaps the Elves or the Dwarves have, but I don't know. Anyway, they're supporting Beckworth. He's trying to take over the entire continent – Humans, Elves, Dwarves, Orcs, Krells and everyone. Then, they'll try to take the whole world. Nobody knows where they came from or what happens when they win. It's like Will Smith in the 4th of July, and the ultimate bad guys are going from planet to planet killing, murdering, looting and pillaging.

"I'm trying to stop them. I have a small troop of a dozen cavalry. Now, you and I are trying to stop the bad guys. Hopefully, we'll have some Elves to help us, but we're on the wrong end of the stick. We're outnumbered and in trouble. Unless we can do something, King Richard, Prince William, Princess Cassandra and I will be defeated, and the aliens will win.

"If that sounds encouraging, it isn't. But it's one hell of a game scenario, and just what we signed up for." I smiled at my old buddy. "Right?"

"Damn, Tony. You're a pain in the ass. I wish I'd never seen that ad, or that you encouraged us to enter." The tiny knob far atop the gigantic blob turned back and forth.

"As I seem to recall, it was you two who were trying to get me to join you in sending in our stats. I wasn't all that interested until you suckered in the whole team. How many others are here?"

"Hell if I know. You're the third one I've met."

"Oh? Who else?"

"Greg's here. He's off doing his thing, but we can sometimes meet him at this place I want to go to."

"Okay. We can go after I finish my business in Goerskim

"Okay. You win. 'The quest is the quest.'" Gilraën laughed at the Dr. Who reference. It was all too common for us to switch from show to show, genre to genre.

"OK, are you K9, or am I Romana?" he asked.

232

"I'd prefer Leila!"

They both chuckled. Then, he asked, "So what are we gonna do in Goerskim?"

"They took over the Guildhall of the Thieves. That's their center of operations in this area. Guilds are big in the kingdom. They're the centers of commerce and village life. And, they are my cover. I have access to most of them. I can go from town to town and disappear. So, the war against the Guilds is an attempt to limit my access to these lands and a punishment for those guilds that helped King Richard, Prince William and me.

"I intend to eliminate the threat of the Guild in Goerskim, restore the Guildhall to its proper functions, and then to return to Umbeqjaralii. Perhaps you would like to return with me. I know a martial arts master who would, no doubt, like to meet you."

"No, first you'll come with me and visit my friends. Then, we can head north. However, I'm not sure your martial arts master would have anything in common with me."

"Sure! Sounds great to me. Let me finish my business in Goerskim, and then we'll jaunt off to wherever this place is you want to go."

We weren't far from the village of Goerskim. I led Justice to the Guildhall of the Thieves. Justice joked, "Sure! I'm supposed to fit through that door? Hell, I'm bigger than the whole building. I'll stay here. You go do your thing. Then, we'll head out to a place where I can relax."

I nodded and gave him the thumbs up as I entered.

The Warden looked up and his mouth hung open for just a moment. "Womb! Lady!" he stammered, "I did not expect to see you... so soon, that is."

I laughed. "You did not expect to see me at all. Lead me to the Guild Master. Oh, not here? Never mind, you come with me." I grabbed the Warden by the arm and flung him towards the back office. I kicked the door, knocking it off its hinges.

I Came

"Sit!" I commanded, pointing to the chair in the corner. "Sleep!" I again commanded, and the warden did.

It took me only ten seconds to locate the hidden cupboard. A word of command, and Talbot's face appeared. I told Talbot what had happened over the past couple of days.

He was dumbfounded. "You've befriended a Krell? How! No, not now. What are your plans?"

"My cavalry should have arrived in Willicamp already. Dispatch them to Higgleston. Have them seek John the Barber and his wife, Maude the Wise Woman. Have them befriend the towns' folk. Tell them to scout the area and prepare to defend the village. Tell them I will return in a few days.

"Inform the Guild that they need a new Master in Goerskim. I will take the mirror with me so it is no longer in Beckworth's possession. I might leave it at the Guild Hall in Phaedham with the Guild Master or keep it myself."

Talbot shook his head both in admiration and amazement. "Please, Princess, protect yourself and return as quickly as you can."

Gilraën laughed. "Not right away. My friend and I have some business to attend to first."

* * * * *

Chapter 10 - Ozhemia's Shelf

Justice led the way due westward, following a small river into the Dwarf Mountains. At first, I was worried. I told Justice that Elves and Dwarves were adversaries, but he just shrugged his massive shoulders, saying, "Don't you worry. Krelli do what we please, and others step aside. It's sorta like the Hulk, you know, except I don't have to get mad."

Justice was loping along down the winding country lane. I raced at a three-fold Sorcerer's walk just to keep up.

"How many Krells are there?" I asked.

"Ah, yes. I am a Krell; we are Krelli, or, if you will, The Krelli. It's a minor point, but should you encounter another Krell, it would be better that you should know. Good manners and all that, you know.

"Anyway, not many. I've met only four Krelli, but I hear there may be seven or eight of us. Evidently, there used to be more, but somehow they got killed off. I've heard that we're originally from Earth, but I can't be sure.

"Now, how about you? I'd heard the Elves were out of it, on pain of death. How come you can oppose Beckworth?"

"I'm different!"

Justice stared at her with one eye closed, then laughed, "You can say that again; in just about every way that might matter."

"I'm different... so there!" We both laughed at our childish dialogue. "Sorry, Justice, it's that I'm not from here, so I'm not limited. And, I'm a princess, I'll have you know."

"Well, excuse me and lah dee dah, your majesty."

"Ah, my turn. It's not 'Your Majesty.' That's for kings and queens. I'm just 'Your Highness.' But, anyway, I supposedly have my own tribe somewhere back in Vermont. It's ridiculous, I know, but distinctions like this make everything possible on this world."

I Came

"Vermont, huh? I suppose your tribe has been hiding in that vast unclaimed wilderness?"

"Uh, something like that."

We both laughed again.

We headed sharply up a large hill where our pace slowed to a walk. Justice trudged up the slope, his size and weight working against him. I bounced from rock to rock, and slope to slope, like a mountain goat.

"This way," he puffed, pointing to a large hole in the mountainside.

"A hole? In the side of the mountain?"

"Looks can be deceiving. Come on, 'your highness'."

Entering, we found a huge cavern open to the south. Although the cave appeared to run back into the mountain for miles, we stopped a few dozen feet inside then sat at a ten-foot shelf nearest the entrance. Another shelf ran the length of the western wall. A pit ran behind it, and a Dwarf stood within that area. He spotted us, waved and then shouted, "Justice! Good to see you. The usual?"

"Sure!" my friend bellowed back. "And, my friend will have…" He looked at me.

"A tankard of your best," I replied.

Shortly, the Dwarf emerged from behind the stone bar, bearing a tankard and a 5-gallon pot. He laid them on a stone outcropping between us.

"Anything to eat?" the Dwarf rumbled.

"Sure," Justice replied, "but we'll wait a few. Oh, let me introduce you two. Theriozemphia, Master of the Hearth of Ozhemia's Shelf, this is Princess Gilraën, one of my oldest and dearest friends. Gilraën, meet Theriozemphia, Master of the Hearth of Ozhemia's Shelf, proprietor of my favorite hostelry. Here, you will find peace and shelter from any and all things that might assail you."

The Dwarf bowed deeply. "Greetings, Gilraën, Your Highness. I am honored by your presence. What brings you here?"

I rose, pressed my palms together before my face, and bowed deeply. "I am honored to be in the house of Ozhemia, and to be greeted by Theriozemphia, the Master of the Hearth of Ozhemia's Shelf. May our meeting presage honor and friendship between our houses."

I dropped my hands. "As for how I got here, I just followed my old friend, Justice. He told me of your Hearth and led me here. Besides, he couldn't fit into my Guildhall!"

The Dwarf barked from deep in his throat. "Yes, that could be a problem. I have many rooms, but they are all for Dwarves and Humans, although few Elves seek my hospitality. I have a special cavern for such as him or the occasional troll who might wish my accommodations. When you are hungry, just call out." He bowed and returned behind the bar.

"Cheers!" Justice toasted.

"Sliente!" I replied, testing for poisons before taking a hesitant sip. It was delicious! It was cool, but not cold; hearty but not heavy; hoppy but not bitter. "Now, I know why you've come this far. This is the finest local brew I've ever had. Thanks for introducing me to this place and this brew."

"I thought you'd like it, if I'd remembered your tastes correctly. Just... stay away from the off-color wines."

We sat for a while, watching Mummia move across the sky through the cave entrance. Chrybda rose to its zenith before I asked, "Is the food as good as the brew?"

"Oh, yes." He glanced up. "AHA! There he is."

A black creature scuttled around the corner, keeping close to the wall and well away from the sunlight. It raced up a fault line behind the bar, descending along a shadow beyond the bar, and across the floor following the discontinuities that formed the seat upon which we were resting. Then it popped up beside Justice. It jump-turned to view me with its six forward-facing eyes. Its long right front leg touched Justice on the arm. "She the one?" it hiss-squeaked.

"Yah, she's the one. For an Elf, she's all right. Mort, meet Gilraën. Gilraën, meet Mort."

I Came

He extended a front left leg, but I couldn't reach out to it. My entire psyche revolted, my breath came in gasps, and I panicked, wanting to flee for my life.

Mort was repulsive. His tri-lobed body was about the size of a Labrador retriever, but his eight legs had to be six feet long. His mouth was a pair of horizontal pincers six-inches long, surrounded by little feelers that were constantly in motion, as though pulling food into a hidden mouth. His movements were sudden, quick jumps. First, he was one place, and in the blink of an eye, he was somewhere else.

A Dwarf maid approached, delivering a goblet of teal blue liquid.

Justice guffawed, scaring the hell out of the few patrons in the cave. "You still drinking that piss?"

"Nectar of the gods," Mort hissed, grasping the stem with the small claw at the tip of a leg. He lifted it with remarkable delicacy to the slit between his pincers, the tiny feelers surrounding it wiggling madly.

Justice craned his neck to look down at me. "You just can't believe how horrible that stuff is. Turpentine tastes good by comparison. I can't believe you still drink this after the last time. Didn't you learn anything?"

The two fell into a friendly banter, which both seemed to enjoy. They seemed like an old married couple. However, it gave me time to look around to see more of the cave and its inhabitants. Three Dwarves sat near the eastern side at the entrance, laughing and drinking. A man and a woman sat at the same side of a table, looking longingly at each other while sipping goblets of red liquid. Just behind her, over her right shoulder six short, hairy beings with large pointed teeth were gorging on plates of raw, bloody meat and piles of tavor. Each drank heartily from their large tankards. Four Elves sat almost directly behind us. They were happily chatting in their lyrical voices. Each had a goblet with yellowish liquid, which they sipped delicately.

'*Eclectic sort of dive,*' I thought.

"Hello!" a huge voice boomed from above.

I looked up to see Justice leaning down to me. "Huh?" I answered. "Sorry, I was looking around. Everybody seems to be here. What are those?" I point to the group of hairy ones.

"Orcs. There's a tribe of Orcs just down the hill to the west. They've got a big farm, maybe four or five hundred of 'em. Good blokes, as long as you pretty much leave them alone. Most of the food here comes from them. The Dwarves brew the ale; the Elves supply the wine, and that blue piss Mort drinks."

"Don't knock it until you've tried it!" Mort quipped, holding up his empty goblet and waving it at the Dwarf maid. Getting the general idea, both Justice and I waved ours, as well.

The maid, rather than rushing off to the bar, approached us and asked, "Ready for food?"

Both Justice and Mort replied, "Usual."

I had no idea of what to order. "What do you have?"

The Dwarf maid replied, "Tonight, we have charder or porg. We also have a bhar pie, which is really good. Stuffed with tavor, jhig and foss in graz."

"Ooh," I exclaimed, "I'll have that. It sounds delicious."

The maid smiled and bounced down the slope to the bar. She returned in just moments lugging a huge pot, a tankard, and another goblet of that blue stuff for Mort. "It'll be ready in just a few."

She was right. Our meals arrived in just a few minutes. The pie was delicious. I dug in as though I was starved, which I really was. We'd walked a long way, and leaching tiny bits of energy from the local plant life may sustain life and energy but was hardly satisfying.

"Mort, old man, my advice to you is don't put your leg between her and her food. You'd lose it for sure!" Justice guffawed loudly again, which disturbed everyone.

I looked up. "What?"

Justice's laugh boomed; Mort hissed. "You were digging in like it was a matter of life and death."

I Came

I blushed. "Well, it sorta is. I really expend energy sometimes, depending on what I'm doing. Then, I gotta fill up, just in case I have to defend myself - or escape from a Krell," I laughed and poked at Justice.

Mort hissed, "Did she? Really?"

Justice put aside his side of Bhar and grinned. "Yea. Never saw anything like it. She's the fastest I've ever seen. Left me in the dust, but I caught her anyway."

Mort jump-shifted towards me. I almost fell backward off my seat, trying to avoid him. Ogling me with six of his eight eyes, he hissed, "He caught you? How?"

"He tripped me. He laid a trap, and I wasn't paying attention, like I should have. So, he caught me fair and square."

Mort went back to sucking on a plump glob, while Justice continued, "Yea, she's been telling me a lot of stuff that really makes sense. I could have been on the wrong side of all this. It might just be that Lord Beckworth is the bad guy in all this, and King Richard is the good guy. Whadda you think?"

Mort removed his pincers from the glob long enough to answer, "They're all the same to me. They hunt me and my family, so I trap 'em and eat 'em. It don't matter to me."

I asked, "Does everyone attack you? If so, how come you're welcome here?"

"Humans do. They have a pathological fear of us. Elves don't mind us; Dwarves drive us out of their caves. Orcs like us 'cause we hunt the creatures that eat their gardens, especially at night. Krells and Trolls don't care one way or the other."

Gilraën still didn't understand. "So, how come you and Justice are friends?"

"Oh, that. He got caught in a trap. Yessir, the great Justice found himself in a huge hole that even he couldn't get out. Men were all around throwing rocks down on him. They'd have killed him if I didn't happen to come along.

240

"I scared them off. I had to net a few that I brought back to my wife, but the rest ran away. Before they could come back, I made a net for him to climb out. So, after that Justice appreciated me. He buys me a drink and sometimes a meal. And, he helps my family, and even drove off a group of humans when they attacked us. So, it's been mutual.

"How about you? How come you aren't a light snack?"

"Oh!" Justice replied, "It's sorta like when you rescued me. When I was chasing her, I didn't realize who she was. When I caught her, she made me laugh. So, we talked a bit, and we discovered we're old friends from way back. You two knew each other, too. Just think back."

Mort jump-shifted again, and I backed right off my chair, falling on the stone floor with a squeal. "No, it can't be. Tony?"

"Greg?" I asked.

"Used to be," he replied, "but now I'm King of the Octopods. I got a great wife, whole bunches of offspring, and a wide, deep valley that's just perfect. So, how about you?"

For the next hour, I told Mort what I knew about the Adjudicars, the war between Beckworth and Richard, the threats against the Elves and the Dwarves, the transportation and modifications of off-worlders as Humans, Krells, Orcs and other beings. I told him about the annihilation of William's Company by Beckworth's Sorcerers, and how I had hunted down three of the four. I told about the arson and looting at Higgleston. And I told him about the infiltration of the Guilds.

When I ended my monologue, Mort just sat there, stunned. I wasn't sure whether it was the result of my story or the fact that Mort had finished his fourth goblet of that blue turpentine. Then, he raised his glass to the Dwarf maid, resolving that quandary. "That's a tale!" he replied in a long, drawn out hiss. "It explains much. I wondered why neither the Elves nor the Dwarves had intervened. And, these Adjudicars...what are they adjudicating? It sounds to me like an invasion by a few very powerful magicians. They don't have the numbers to invade, but they are strong enough and clever enough to divide and conquer."

I Came

He leapt and spun towards me, but lost his balance, as two legs collapsed, and he fell on his side.

I jumped up, squealing like a schoolgirl sighting a mouse.

Justice laughed so hard he fell over backward, spilling half a gallon of Dwarf ale all over himself.

Mort righted himself, and much more carefully sidled around to stare at us both – as much as six, multi-lens eyes can stare. He hissed, "It's not that funny! I just lost my footing. I've got eight of them to contend with, you know!"

Justice was rolling on the floor, howling in laughter. He gasped and held his stomach, trying desperately to catch his breath. And, of course, laughter is contagious. Within moments, I was lying beside him, giggling so hard I could barely breathe. The Elves, the Orcs, and the Dwarves were all caught up in it, laughing even though most of them had no idea why. Even Mort was caught up in it, falling face first on the floor as he began to whistle some sort of warble that I figured must be laughter.

Some time later, after several attempts to regain our composure, we all ordered a drink to make up for the ones that we spilled on the cave floor. The Elves had left, complimenting us on the best laugh they'd had in years. The Orcs bought us another round, as if that was what any if us needed. Even the Dwarves thought it was a grand time that would only enhance their business.

Finally, Mort asked the question he had meant to pose before he started this commotion. "So, what's your part in this, Gilraën? If the Elves and the Dwarves are constrained, and you're an Elf, how come you can do all the stuff you're doing?"

The question had been bothering me as well. I paused for a few moments considering the question then answered, "I don't know for sure. I've only been on this world a few weeks. I'm not really sure of who I am, or what I'm doing. I'm guessing that because I'm not from Trahe, the constraints on Jaralii Elves don't apply to me.

"I do know a few things. I've met Prince William and Princess Cassandra. Not only do I like them, very much, but I've found them to be honest and caring. I was there when Beckworth's Sorcerer,

William Norton, tried to assassinate them. Somehow, he blew himself up. I don't know how he did it, but it was huge, knocking down trees and buildings for miles around. It left behind a terrible and deadly dust. I deflected it, protecting the court, castle, and everyone I could. But, that settled it for me. Defeating an enemy in battle is one thing. Sending Sorcerers to destroy the land, the forests, the animals, and the innocent, along with their orchards, crops and herds, is unconscionable and beneath the contempt of all intelligent beings.

"As for me, I'm just trying to figure out what's going on. Reliable sources have informed me that Beckworth will attack King Richard's realm from the southwest, the south, and the southeast simultaneously. If so, where are his troops?

"I've traveled southeast and south from Prince William's castle in the south of the kingdom almost to the triple border. I have a troop in Higgleston protecting that town from attack. I've found fewer than one hundred of Beckworth's troops. I've killed five Sorcerers and some fifty troops. So, where are all those Battalions Beckworth has readied to invade Umbeqjaralii?"

"Who is your reliable source?"

"The Guild of Witches, Truth-Seekers and Wise Women."

"Ah," Mort sighed. "I have a history with that Guild. If they confirmed this is true, then it must be so." With that, he fell on his face, his legs curled beneath him, and he tumbled down the sloping floor toward the cave's mouth.

Justice leapt to his feet and raced after the tumbling ball of legs. He caught up with it just as it was about to fall over the edge and drop into the wood several hundred feet below. "Gilraën, come on. We've got to take care of him. Oh, pay the bill, will ya?"

I stood, but my head spun, and I quickly sat down. Okay, so I began to fall and successfully aimed, best I could, at the seat nearest me. Obviously, this Dwarf ale was potent stuff. I said a few words of healing, but they had little effect. Slowly, I gathered my strength and tried to find my balance.

I Came

The Dwarf maid intercepted me. Holding me by the elbow, she guided me to the bar, where Theriozemphia presented me with the tab. I studied it for a moment, but the squiggles wouldn't cooperate. They kept moving and then went out of focus before moving again. I covered one eye, which did help, but not much. The squiggles didn't move, but they didn't make any sense either.

I looked at the Dwarf and said, "I can't read this. How much?"

"Five Silvers, eight Coppers and three Zincs, and something for the server."

I dug deeply in my pack, finally locating my cache. I extracted seven Silvers, which I deposited on the bar. "Enough?" I asked.

He nodded and waved good-bye as I mastered my balance and teetered down to Justice's side. "Whew, that Dwarf stuff is strong!"

"I told you. Maybe the Wise Womban can help you, too."

I remember little of the journey down the hill and into the small town. There was a vague recollection of leaning against something very tall that was moving in the same direction. Justice led me as he carried Mort to a small house surrounded by a white picket fence on the outskirts of the town.

A woman opened the door. "Oh, it's you, again. What's wrong this time? He drunk again?"

"Yup!" Justice replied. "Her, too."

"Set them inside, will you? I'll look after them. Now, what do you need?"

"I'm OK, just had a little ale."

"Dwarves ale?"

"Of course! What else would I drink?"

"Fine, just set down beneath that big oak. I'll get to you after I've cared for them."

Justice handed Mort through the door, then sat down beneath the huge tree, leaned back against the trunk and promptly fell asleep. His snoring might have been enough to disturb the dead.

I followed the woman inside, half walking and half crawling. Finally, I sat at a large table in a dining room. I watched as the woman rolled Mort across the hallway into a separate room. She puttered and tsk-tsked several times. Then I heard a spoon stirring liquid in a glass. There was a gurgling sound, and then nothing.

The woman bustled into the dining room. "Now, how about you?" she asked. "Have you been drinking Dwarf ale, too?"

I looked up at her round, wrinkled and smiling face. "Yes, I was with Justice and Mort up in Master Theriozemphia cavern. Delicious!"

"Yes, Master Theriozemphia serves the finest food and beverages in all the kingdom. But, every Elf should know that."

I looked into the woman's eyes to see a look of disbelief and suspicion. "Well, I...," I started to explain, but then stopped. Instead, I said the password of a Guildswoman of Witches, Truth-Seekers and Wise Women.

"Oh!" the woman replied. "Welcome, Sister." She supplied the counter-password. "I am honored to meet a sister who is also an Elf. I did not know any Elves belonged to the guild."

"Only me," I replied. "I am Princess Gilraën Gulámae. I have come from the court of Prince William and Lady Cassandra seeking those who sacked the Guildhall of Thieves in Higgleston. They murdered all those inside and the many good townsfolk who tried to extinguish the blaze and save the inhabitants. I have hunted them down, killed the Sorcerers of Lord Beckworth, and killed the soldiers responsible. I then met Justice, and, while having a drink with him in Master Theriozemphia's cave, also met Mort, who scares the life out of me! How I got here," I looked around the room, "I'm not sure."

She handed me a tumbler of white stuff. "Drink it down. You'll feel better."

I tested it thoroughly, knowing that this woman understood poisons as well as mendicants. Finding nothing untoward, I gulped it down. It tasted chalky, but nothing else.

The woman smiled knowledgeably. "No, there's nothing harmful in it. Just a bit of chalk for an upset stomach, tree bark for the headache, and fruit juices as a restorative. I am Ethyl, Wise Womban, Healer, and Sister of the Guild of Witches, Truth-Seekers and Wise Womben.

"I know of you, Princess. All in our guild know of you. It is fortunate that you survived your encounter with the Krell. The fact that it was Justice is a most favorable circumstance. But, your meeting with Mort is suspicious. Some other hand is stirring this pot, and it is not that of an Adjudicar."

Surprised, Gilraën asked, "You know of them?"

"Oh, yes. Our guild is overlooked by all, since we are 'just womben.' Further, we hide our strengths, our knowledge and our abilities. There are many Sorcerers and magic users who would be unpleasantly surprised were they to discover our true nature." She spoke a word of command of guild sisterhood identifying herself as a High Mistress.

I recoiled, receiving the command and absorbing it much like a sponge absorbs water. In turn, I spoke a command of the guild, identifying myself as a Mistress Superior.

Mistress Ethyl bowed. "Welcome, High One. In what way may I serve?"

"Maintain and withhold your knowledge of me. I wish to pass from guildhall to guildhall in anonymity. However, circulate any information regarding the movements of Beckworth's troops and especially his Sorcerers throughout the Guild. I, and those I send, will ask for this information. King Richard and I will need this information."

"So it will be," Ethyl replied. She looked back over her shoulder. "And, it's time I should check on my other patient." She trundled off across the hall and into the next room.

I followed, somewhat unsteadily, but at least I was remaining upright. Mort was also upright, with his legs spread out like an eight-legged cocker spaniel. His multi-lens eyes couldn't close or defocus, but it was obvious he wasn't using them. A thin dribble of drool hung from his mouth onto the floor.

"Awaken!" Ethyl called to him. "Master Mort, it is time to awaken." She touched him on the peak of his head.

Mort trembled, and his legs twitched. His head moved, and his pincers clicked. He hissed, and his legs twitched again.

Ethyl turned to speak with me. "He'll recover. Let's go check on Justice." She walked out into her front yard. There, underneath the huge, old oak tree sat a giant, snoring mightily. "I'm not sure what I can do for him. I'd have to wake him up, which is never a good idea. Let's let him sleep, for now. Tea?"

As we sat, waiting for the guys to awaken, Ethyl told me how her world had changed since beginnings of the revolution. "You know that Beckworth is the child of old King George's second marriage, and half-brother of Richard, William and Cassandra?" I nodded. Ethyl continued, "It is said that it is he who brought the Adjudicars to this land.

"Rumors have it that old Caierne was messing about with transporting things to and from Earth. Then, he tried looking for other nearby worlds. The one he found was inhabited by Adjudicars. But then, the bird trapped the spider. It would have swallowed the spider, but the spider made a deal. In return for being spared, the spider would provide the Adjudicars with a world they could ravage.

"But, the Adjudicars are few… powerful, but few. They work through Beckworth. They work by dividing allies, then conquering them one at a time. That is how they conquered the Elves and neutralized the Dwarves.

"Since then, he has used Beckworth to work at conquering Richard. Soon, they will conquer this land entirely. Then, they will conquer the rest of this world, one land and one continent at a time. After that, they will be on to other lands in other worlds.

"You, Princess Gilraën, were chosen to save this world. You were brought to this world, because your world is next. So, by saving this world, you save your own."

"So I have heard, but never in such detail. So, it is up to me, my twelve archers, you, Justice and Mort to right the wrongs of this world, and to eject the evil from it. Is that what you are saying, Sister?"

"Indeed. However, you will create a new alliance. And, it will be from that confabulation of interests that you will accomplish this aspiration."

"I will need the help of the Guild."

"Of course, and you will receive it, else we too shall come to an end, once the Adjudicars learn of us. So, we also turn to you to protect us as we protect you."

At that point, Mort stumbled eight-fold into the kitchen. "Good lady," he hissed, "could I have a sweet water?"

"About time you stirred, Master Mort." She leaned to her cupboard to lift a larger bowl of water. Placing it on the floor in front of him, she said, "I think you'll find this meets your needs."

Mort reached for the bowl, grasping it delicately between his two, finger-like claws. He slurped it eagerly, his feelers wiggling madly. When he had finished, he gasped, "Better, much better. Ah, I'd better be getting along. Lyra is expecting me home any time now."

He turned to me, "Oh, dear Gilraën, when Justice awakens, be careful of him, He thrashes around and is a danger to himself and others. After a while, he'll be his old self. Then, our friend will return to you as good as ever.

"And, should you need me, go to the cavern of Theriozemphia, Hearth of Ozhemia's Shelf and whistle thusly." He emitted a sharp trilling sound. "I will hear it and come to you. Also, remember this whistle for it will protect you from others of my kind. They will recognize it as my call, and will protect and honor you. Live well, Lady. My regards to Justice." He scuttled out the door and disappeared through the backyard and into the woods beyond.

At that point, Justice rolled off his tree and fell to the ground. He snored, snorted and rubbed his nose with the back of his hand. One eye opened and peered around. He yawned widely. "Where am I?"

I answered hesitantly. "Mistress Ethyl's... the wise woman?"

"Crap! I had too much to drink, didn't I?"

"Yes, we all did... you, me and Mort."

"Mort? Oh, yes, he was there. And you, Road Runner. Beep-Beep, indeed." He rolled over and sat up. "Food!"

"Coming!" Mistress Ethyl raced into the yard, chasing a cheener, which was cheeping loudly.

Justice swiped at it, seized it, tore its head off and ate it whole. "Better," he burped. "Now what?"

"Now, I head to Higgleston. My troop is there, preparing to defend the town. I assume the enemy will attack, because that's the most direct way back to Beckworth's lands. If I hurry, I will get there in time to wipe out an entire contingent of Beckworth's forces."

"Great! A quest! Let's see, Higgleston. Higgleston... Where's that?"

"Sixty five miles north of Phaedham."

"Crap! That's like a hundred and fifty miles from here. When do we have to be there?"

"Tomorrow."

"Tomorrow? What the... When?

"Noon at the latest."

"Crap! Noon? We'll be up all night. Well, let's do it. I'll lead."

"OK, we're off."

* * *

It had been a long night. I had fed off the sleeping plants and animals, but Justice couldn't. Along the way, he seized a bhar that had come too near the road as we passed between Goerskim and Phaedham. He ate it whole. Then, part way to Tamvill, he purloined a porg from a farmer's yard, which again he ate whole. By the time we arrived in Higgleston, Justice's only topic of discussion was how much food he would eat.

I Came

Just outside of Higgleston, we happened on a herd of zhaks. He was about to leap on them when a lone archer leapt before him. "Stop! Thief! Or I shall shoot." Within seconds, three other archers had arrived, surrounding him.

Justice roared and was about to attack.

I jumped in front of him. "Stop!" I commanded, summoning all my power.

Justice slammed to a stop, as though he'd run into a rock. "What the….? Did you do that, Gilraën?"

"Yes! These are my men. I need them."

"Yah, but I need food."

"OK, come along." I led him to the home of John the Barber and his wife Maude, the Wise Woman. "John," I said, "I have a large friend in need of an equally large meal. Can you help?"

"I think so," he replied, "How much?" He followed me outside, where Justice was sitting under a tree waiting for us. "Oh, my! He's a Krell!"

"Of course, he's a Krell. That's why he has a big appetite. We need food. Where can we get a large meal?"

"Let me think. If the tavern were still here, we would have plenty, even for such as him. Hmm, let me think. The butcher… the baker…. Yes, I have it. It will take an hour or so, but we can do it." He turned, shouting, "Maude, we have guests!"

An hour later, Justice sat on the ground at a set of large tables. Maude, the village baker, the village butcher, and two other merchants were busily placing pots, tureens, dishes and implements on the table. My twelve Ghillies, John, Maude, and several important folk of the village were in attendance.

"So," Maude asked, "You have returned. In the meantime, you burden us with your troops and their animals. Now, you burden us with a Krell, perhaps the most rapacious, dangerous and untrustworthy of predators. What you have done to us is far worse than anything Lord Beckworth has done, but you ask for our friendship? Why should we? What would you have of us?"

I smiled like a patient mother. "Sister Maude," I laid special emphasis on the words, emphasizing our guild sisterhood. "I came here to assuage the tribulations Lord Beckworth caused to this community. I have done far more, in Prince William's name, to save this town and to help rebuild it.

"My troops have been here to protect you from further depredations. A body of Lord Beckworth's troops marched north from here to raid and pillage other villages. I could not protect those other villages, but I could protect you. I expect that the enemy will be on you this very day. My cavalry, with their zhaks, their chariots, and their arrows will defeat them utterly.

"And now, my friend and companion, Justice the Krell, will find a home here. He asks very little." I stopped long enough to look at Justice devouring food as though he were an entire army. I chuckled, "Well, perhaps not that little. Regardless, Justice has come here with me to ensure that you are protected.

"Justice will roam these lands, because that is what he does. However, he is no longer in the employ of Lord Beckworth. I might add that he is not in the employ of Prince William, King Richard or me. He does what he does, because he is an honorable being, my friend, and the friend of many who defy Lord Beckworth, none of whom you know or are likely to know.

"You are an island in a sea of Beckworth's depredations. I shall use this town as the beginning of the liberation of these lands. As such, you will become the center of conflict. The route between Higgleston and Willicamp will become a major highway for troops, supplies and materials. This town will never be the same.

"However, there will be many compensations for everyone. You are under my protection and the protection of your King. You will be rewarded for your loyalty and well compensated for your efforts.

"Now, prepare to be attacked. It will happen this day or tomorrow at the latest."

I turned to Harold. "Prepare for battle. Send scouts to the northwest through east. We need to know where they are, how many there are, how quickly they march, how they are armed, and such. Be sure to protect yourselves and your zhaks as best you can. This is the real thing. You are facing injury and death. Do all in your power to perform your duty, while protecting yourselves."

Justice looked up from the remains of a large leg. "Battle? Sounds like fun. Gilraën, your quests are really great. Where do you want me?"

"First, I want you to help prepare the town's defenses. The cavalry will inform us of the enemy's approach. When they do attack, you can have some fun. I will be trying to find their Sorcerer, so the bulk of the battle will be my Ghillies and you. Defend yourself, old friend, I wouldn't want to lose you, having just found you again."

Justice boomed a laugh that awoke babies all over town. "It'd take more than a few soldiers to do me in, and Sorcerers don't work on me, remember? I'll just pull a few things from my pack, and I'll be ready."

"And, I will help the people of this, the King's village, to prepare themselves for battle, should they be needed. In the meantime, I will help them fortify their town."

I turned to curious folk of the village who had gathered in the town's center. I stood as tall as I could, emanating power and majesty. "Today, you take back what is yours. Meet with me in the town square. Call every person near and far to that spot, where we will make our preparations. Go now and return quickly. Your lives and your property depend on your actions."

My words had a stimulating effect. Everyone seemed energized. They raced off to gather their friends and families. Just twenty minutes later, some one hundred folk – young, old, men, women and children – gathered at the four corners.

I studied them all as they approached, seeking to know who was prepared for battle and who was not; who would fight and who would flee. Many of the men and a few women were made of sturdy stuff – determined to protect themselves and their town. Others could barely move - fear coursed through their veins.

Those who exuded fear, I set to building structures, digging ditches and building palisades to defend the town against an enemy force. Their fear seemed to give them strength. They were doing something worthwhile to protect and defend them all. And through their toil they justified their position in the town and for all posterity.

The others armed themselves and protected their persons to the best of their ability. A few had swords. Most had pitchforks, or axes, or other sharp and bladed farm implements. With my help, the smith and several carpenters built long spears and sturdy shields for the thirty able-bodied and willing village warriors.

I divided them into five squads, assembled three along the barricades to the west, north and east. They assembled one in the open area just south of Barber's house. I stationed the fifth squad at the crossroad, ready to rush to whichever quadrant needed their reinforcement.

Several hours later, a chariot raced from the north, halting before the barricade. It was Schmidt. "Gilraën, they come. Some thirty soldiers heavily armed with spear, sword and shield. They are armored with helm, body armor, greaves and braces. They are marching rapidly and will arrive in less than an hour.

"Worse, they have a Troll. We also believe there is a Sorcerer, but we can't be sure."

"Excellent, Schmidt, well done. Return and tell the others to retreat before them. Keep me informed of their position."

I sent my thoughts to the rest of my troops, recalling them. Since each of them was already familiar with my thoughts, they understood and slowly retreated towards the town.

"Justice, they have a Troll with them. Anyone you might know?"

"Maybe, maybe not. I'll take care of it."

"OK, people!" I yelled. "Our information is they are coming down the North road. Get to your positions. And don't attack my cavalry!"

Moments later, three chariots came racing down the road. "Open the barricade," I yelled.

The three charioteers raced into the town, Faelnirv in the lead. "Gilraën, they are half a mile out. They'll be here in minutes."

I Came

I contacted my other three teams, learning they were already approaching. Surrounded by twelve charioteers and six stalwart townsfolk, I told Harold to engage his force as needed to prevent any of Beckworth's forces from breaking through.

"And, what will you be doing?" he asked,

"Finding their Sorcerer," I replied. "Now go!"

I retired into the butcher's shop, where I emptied my mind, and then extended my prescience as far as I could in all directions. I became as one with the universe, seeking any flaws or discontinuities resulting from the use of magic. Although I found none, I dared not relax. He was out there. I knew it. I had to find him and kill him before he could harm any of those under my protective wing.

I was aware of the approach of Beckworth's soldiers. At first, they were hesitant to attack the flimsy and hastily erected barrier. But then, they saw that the defenders were just the local town's folk. They quickly formed into a battle formation and attacked.

The fight was fierce. Their initial charge was deflected both right and left. They tried to turn the defender's flank, but other town's folk were defending. Several troops crossed over the east-west road and discovered the barriers ended. Charging ahead, they met half a dozen sturdy citizens who were immediately reinforced by another half dozen. A troop of ten raced around the right flank, only to be met by twelve archers, who mowed them down in a matter of seconds. The Ghillies raced back to the northern barriers, where they snuffed out a short-lived penetration of the defensive shell.

Just as the town's people had begun to celebrate their victory, a huge Troll crashed through the barriers and into the center of the town. As my Ghillies prepared to slay the monster, Justice raced into the center, shouting, "Stop! I know him."

The archers held their bows tautly, ready to release their fusillade of arrows.

Justice boomed, "Artestius, is that you?"

The Troll, intent on attacking the humans, stumbled to a stop. "Who's asking?" it croaked.

"Justice."

"Justice? What are you doing here?"

"I'm here with my friends. These are my friends, Artestius. Don't hurt them."

"I gotta, Justice. The Sorcerers have my contract, so I gotta."

"Then, we gotta fight." Justice replied, pulling a gigantic sword from behind his back.

"Crap!" the Troll replied, lifting an enormous spiked mace. "Do we hafta?"

"No, you could head along down the south road, back to your family."

"What about the Sorcerer? He'd know. He'd tell Beckworth, and then they'd come after me and my family. No, Justice, we gotta fight."

At that point, the Sorcerer betrayed himself. He, too, had listened in on the challenge between the Troll and the Krell. At first, he thought the Troll might betray Lord Beckworth, but then, the Troll figured out which side his bread was buttered. For just a second, he gloated, '*You're damn right we'd have hunted down you and your family.*' He quickly returned to monitoring the battlefield, searching for William's Sorcerers. Personally, he doubted that William had the guts or foresight to risk his precious magicians.

However, his momentary slip was all I needed to know that one that Beckworth's Sorcerers was nearby.

Justice wasn't eager to fight the Troll, though he knew he could win. He was better trained and had greater fighting skills. Regardless, he was worried that he might get hurt. Trolls are large, strong and tough. There was always uncertainty in any fight, and if one could be avoided it'd be to his advantage.

"You know, those archers are on my side, Artestius. I could just as easily step back and let them fill you with holes. I know an arrow or two won't hurt you, but thirty, forty, fifty will kill even you.

I Came

"Look, I don't want to hurt you, Artestius, and I'm sure, like you said, you want to get home to your family. Just go. I'll spread the word of a huge fight between us, and that we were evenly matched. Just go."

Three things happened almost simultaneously. Artestius realized that he was in a lose-lose position and decided to go home, while he still could.

Beckworth's Sorcerer sensed the Troll's surrender. Angry with the traitor, he suspended his prescient trance, concentrating his powers to kill the massive Troll.

I felt the Troll's surrender and the Sorcerers' preparation to assault the Troll. While maintaining my state of emotionless non-being, I analyzed the Sorcerer's attack. As he was about to utter his death command, I struck.

I pinned his mind inside a shell of my creation. Although he struggled like a fish caught in a net, I tightened my mental grip. He raised barrier after barrier to my penetration of his mind, but I lanced through them, and then tore them apart. I crushed his last resistance, finding his core of magical power. With one powerful thrust, I stabbed into its heart, utterly destroying it.

I felt his fear and his surprise, as he realized his death was at hand. He fought the great void for only the span of a single thought, and then he was no more.

Returning to the real world, I left the butcher's shop to stand in the street. I raised a barrier around the edge of the town, enclosing its citizens, my troops, the Krell, and the Troll. Then, I reached out to the soldiers still attacking the village and killed them, as one would crush ants underfoot.

As I walked toward Justice, I shouted, "It is over, Artestius the Troll. You are free to return to your home, as you and Justice have just negotiated. It is not my wish, for I perceive that you have killed King Richard's subjects wantonly. For that, I pass this judgment upon you. Leave this kingdom and do not return. If you do, I place the penalty of death upon you. Be gone, Artestius."

Artestius nodded and trundled south out of the village.

The raid was over. We had liberated Higgleston, ensuring the loyalty of the king's subjects. I had led my Cavalry in battle and had defeated the enemy. I had now killed six of Lord Beckworth's precious Sorcerers. I had met an old friend and had gained a powerful ally. And, I had infiltrated and been accepted by a powerful guild, whose true power was hidden, undiscoverable by the chauvinistic society in which it was embedded.

It was time to go home… and have a nice hot bath! And, William…. I smiled. *'Yes, William….'*

* * * * *

Chapter 11 – Congress of the Elves of Jaralii

"Why have you so urgently called for a Congress of the Tribes of Jaralii, Amarië? Your message was brief, offering little information," Fingolfin Sáralondë, King of the Elves of Blue Lake, inquired.

Amarië Ancalimë, Queen of the Elves of the Clouds, meticulously scrutinized each of the monarchs of the eight remaining Tribes of the Elves of Jaralii who had gathered at the great round table. Sadly, one chair, that of Queen Dominica of the Elves of the Great Forest, sat empty. Theirs had not been a large Tribe, but it had been a cornerstone for the Elves' rebellion against the Adjudicars. It had been annihilated, ending the Elves abortive attempt to defy the Adjudicars. Shaking off the memories of the young queen, Amarië folded her hands on the table before her, accepting that the loss would be something with which she would need to deal over centuries yet to pass.

"My apologies, Majesties. I would that we had the time for long contemplation and consideration of the issue I wish to bring before you. Unfortunately, we have little time for such. Little time and even less opportunity to take actions that will yield favor to the Elves."

"What then is this urgent issue, Amarië? We are here. Make this quest known that we might decide if it is something worth taking issue,' Fingolfin Sáralondë insisted.

Queen Amarië looked to the King of the Blue Lake, paused a moment, and then began, "Our Seeress called to me in a dream. The Dwarves had presented her with information garnered at great cost to them..."

"The Dwarves? Are we expected to believe anything the Nauglin have to say?" Tári Lossëhelin Nenhámra, Queen of the Elves of the Sea, spat venomously.

"They merely brought the matter to the attention of the Seeress," Amarië explained. "It was she who investigated to find the truth of their claims. The Dwarves do not always bespeak of things solely to the betterment of the Dwarves."

"Hummpf. What then, did the Seeress learn that was not already tainted?" King Aeradir Séregon of the White Cliffs replied, his words dripping with sarcasm.

"She saw the treachery of the Adjudicars... their perfidy seen at first hand. For this reason, she requested me to call an extraordinary Congress," Amarië continued. "She wishes to speak to us all concerning this treachery, which would envelop us, swallowing us whole."

Queen Órelindë Telemnar Anwarünya of the Elves of Gray Haven remarked, "There is little that could do that to the collective tribes of the Jaralii Elves. I vote we move on. The Elves have nothing to fear from this display of cowardice."

Queen Eilol of the Fire Elves of the Brown Hills replied hotly, "I would have you tell that to Dominica and the Elves of the Great Forest, if you dare."

"Indeed!" King Glorfindel of the Elves of the Brown Hills added, pounding his fist on the table. "It was our daughter's blood that was spilled."

The Queen of the Elves of the Sea slowly sat back into her chair, as her face paled, "Perhaps then, I shall listen. There might yet be words of import in this presentation."

"I thank you." Amarië continued. "The Seeress, as I said, wishes to address us all to present memories she has collected as evidence of her assertions. These and her recent observations might yet provide us a means by which we may intervene on behalf of the elder kingdom that has ever supported us and our rights in this land... a means by which we might proffer aid without incurring the wrath or the retribution of the Adjudicars.

"She wishes to bring a path to our attention that has been ... overlooked, and, by so doing, free us from the bonds we have so cunningly crafted, tying our hands in this matter. It is for this reason I called for this Congress to ask that we might hear her words and answer her faith."

I Came

King Arafinwë Lossëhelin of Green Glens warned, "We have all given oaths, Queen Amarië, not to interfere in this Human war."

"True,' Amarië agreed. "We have, but the Seeress has convinced me that we must hear her words, or face our own demise."

Each of the monarchs turned towards the others at the table, communing with them in their minds. None had the power to accept or reject. It required six of nine to assent or dissent.

Glorfindel, King of the Brown Hills, spoke first. "A vote. I call for a vote. All in favor of hearing of this plan raise your left hands... those opposed, your right... There remain two who have not offered their opinion in this matter. Neither path holds sway. You must vote, you cannot abstain."

Hesitantly, the two raised their left hands.

"Very well," Amarië concluded, "We have a vote of six; we shall listen."

The Seeress, Nèssa Narmölanya, appeared before the group of nine monarchs, smiled, and then immediately began speaking. No one opposed her evident lack of decorum in not recognizing their status as the leaders of their tribes.

"Thank you, Majesties. As little time remains to us all, I shall begin immediately. Unbeknownst to us, the Adjudicars have been importing an intelligent species to Jaralii. They also have inveigled themselves into the kingdom of those who have befriended us as well as the one that is against our principles. To both, they promised aid and support from the off-worlders. This is the first occurrence in direct violation of our own treaties with the Adjudicars, who stated that they would support neither side in favor of the other.

"Yet, in spite of their pledges both to us and to the Human realm which accepted our daughter into their courts, the Adjudicars have been supporting the rebellious realm to a far greater extent than that of our erstwhile friends. My investigations have shown me, as you see here, that more than half again the number of those brought to our world were assigned to the secessionist realm. Additionally, the quality of those assigned to that realm far exceeds that provided to those who would ever be our friends, including new species with the powers to overcome and kill even the mightiest of Elves."

"I have seen no such influx of other world troops, Seeress," Glorfindel Amder Melwasúl, King of the Green Mountains, argued. "I have many times invoked my right to view the recruits and have seen only large numbers of those who are native to our own world. It would seem to me that good fortune favors the rebellious realm, but I have seen no actions by the Adjudicars in that respect."

"You have. You simply have not recognized their work, oh King," the Seeress replied. "View this memory of things I have witnessed for myself, and then tell me if Krell, Troll, and Goblin are natives of our world. They are not, especially the Krell. It was they who murdered our Dominica, Queen of the Great Forest, who was the daughter of King Glorfindel Ancalímon and Queen Eilol Thösaendas."

For several moments, the monarchs sat absorbing the stream of consciousness the Seeress delivered to their minds.

Glorfindel, King of the Brown Hills gasped, "This... this is truth?"

"You have seen my mind. You have weighed my thoughts. You know it is the truth," the Seeress replied.

"There is more," she continued, "The Adjudicars plan to enslave all the Elves of Jaralii once they have subjugated the Humans of this continent. I could not contact my counterpart on the largest continent, but the others say unrest has begun on their continents. It would seem that the Adjudicars intend to enslave the entire world of Trahe.

"Moreover, one of the Sorcerers employed by the breakaway realm is, in actuality, an Adjudicar." She paused, letting the monarchs consider her worlds. "Yes, the Adjudicars are directly assisting those who we now know to be our enemies. His cunning disguise is that of a Trahean Sorcerer, but I have seen through his veil, as you have just seen in my memories. Our way of life is being threatened; all we need do for it to succeed is nothing.

"The Adjudicars have abrogated our treaties with them. They have violated the spirit and the essence of our agreements. They have decided that Elves are a weak, powerless and feckless race. To them, we are effete, and no longer have the will or the courage to defend ourselves."

Queen Nenhámra of the Elves of the Sea asked, "You would have us believe you have discerned this knowledge in a manner unbiased?"

The Seeress humbly replied, "I do. The Dwarves merely gave warning. They had no knowledge of when or where I would investigate. They could not have shaded the events for my benefit. To do so, they would necessarily have needed to warp all events pertaining to the Adjudicars and the realm of the Usurper. Further, I placed certain spells that the Dwarves could not shade, nor could the Adjudicars or any of their followers. We Elves are not a powerless race to be pitied and forgotten like the great beasts of memory from years past, or the world of Earth spoken of in our legends. This is especially true of your Seeress."

Amarië Ancalimë, Queen of the Clouds, affirmed, "I believe we all suspected such was the case, but we lacked proof. What, then, can we do? As you have said, the Adjudicars annihilated the Tribe of the Great Forest. None of us dare oppose them."

The Seeress replied, "Not as single tribes can we oppose them." She hesitated, taking them in one by one. "However, as a collective will, we yet have great power. It is through our combined strength that I propose to intercept off-world recruits. Our magics shall grant to them the appearance, strength, wisdom, and abilities of the Elves, such that those changed might provide support to that realm which has ever shown itself to be in alignment with our interests.

"For this to occur, I will need to draw upon the magic of each of our Tribes to generate the power that will accomplish those necessary changes. We will provide these Terran Elves with tribal markings unrelated to any of the tribes of Trahe. They shall be a powerful new tribe, not originally of this world as they, in actuality, are not."

The King Fingolfin Sáralondë of the Blue River asked, "How many shall we find necessary to affect the outcome of this war to our advantage?"

"One score and seven… given time and sufficient remaining collections."

He scoffed, "Is it possible for seven and twenty of Elves to make such a difference as to change the course of an entire war?"

The Seeress smiled benignly. "Twenty seven of the Elves I propose to bring to existence both can and will," she assured him.

"How is it possible you could know such? Have you had a vision?" the Eilol of the Fire Elves demanded.

"I know, dear King, because I have already brought the first of these Elves to our lands."

As the nine monarchs gasped almost in unison, the Seeress continued, as though she had only paused for breath. "Queen Gilraën Gulámae of the Elves of the Green Mountains-Maidstone Forest walks among us. She is being trained by the practitioners of Human magic of the court of the young prince who is disposed to our favor. Queen Gilraën has succeeded beyond all measure and has already recruited a band of Human archers to her service. At present, she is returning victorious from battle against the forces who threaten us all."

"By whose authority have you done this?" the King Arafinwë Glorfinél Lossëhelin of the Green Glens demanded.

The Seeress smiled, and, with a look of love and reason, replied, "I did so of my own authority, my child, as I have always done, and will continue to do, in preservation of all Elvin kind."

Although each of the monarchs wanted to object to the usurpation of their authority, none dared to confront the Seeress, for she was in her right.

After a long silence, King Amder Melwasúl of the Green Mountains asked, "What of later when the war is ended? What becomes of these Elves? Will we find ourselves fighting them to retain our lands and titles?"

"When the war has ended, these Elves will answer to their Queen, who I trust will become the new Queen of the Human lands, and thus our representative in their councils. Once again, Edhilin will a have voice on those Human councils.

"It is my desire that the Tribe shall settle in the lands of the Great Forest, repopulating that realm to remind us all of what once was, what might have been, and of the hope for what yet might be."

Several of the elders spoke simultaneously, but the King of the Blue Lake prevailed. "So, without our council, you have brought among us a High Elf. You have placed her under the tutelage of the Humans. You conspire to mate her to the Human prince, hoping to situate an Elf in the Human's councils. But, of us she knows nothing. How, then, can we believe she would be predisposed toward us?"

The Seeress smiled beneficently and spoke as a mother would to her child. "From the time she first arrived, she has been receiving training from the Humans. Soon, events shall conspire to bring her to me. At that time, I shall be of more direct influence. Soon also, she will walk among the Elves of your own Tribes that she might satisfy her curiosity concerning her heritage found only in the Elvin lines. When the time comes, she will be disposed to a favorable alliance with us all, for we are kindred.

"Unfortunately, time is ever short and fading. The numbers we might recruit grows smaller with each passing hour. For this reason, your decisions must be made in some haste. We do not have months, or even weeks to contemplate, to weigh these measures at our leisure then produce our decisions. There are but minutes before plans must begin to be set in stone, and our energies directed toward those who need to be changed and transported to our lands. Your decisions have but the duration of a rainbow before they must be voiced."

The nine sat quietly, each looking to the others for thoughts.

Queen Amarië Ancalimë broke the silence. "You ask for much with only your promises provided."

The Seeress reassured her, "I have already begun the process, and it has been successful. However, I alone do not have the power to bring about the changes in so many. Time is so very short. What I propose is to remove the guarantee of our servitude, which is absolute should we do nothing."

The monarchs of the Elvin tribes of Jaralii were not pleased, but they understood the need. A chance of obtaining their freedom was far better than the certainty of perpetual subservience beneath the boot of a hostile despot.

"Are we ready to vote?" asked Fingolfin Sáralondë.

"Who could be ready for this?" Lessien Calmcacil, Queen of the Hidden Lakes, asked rhetorically.

"I am ready," voiced King Arafinwë of the Green Glen.

"As am I," King Fingolfin added. "The Tribe of the Blue River is ready to vote."

Queen Órelindë demanded, "I call for a vote. Should we unite our energies with the Seeress to bring this new Tribe into existence? All those who would have it so, raise your left hands... those opposed, your right. Eight to... You wish to change your vote? So be it. The motion is unanimous."

She turned to face Nëssa Narmőlanya. "Seeress, begin your efforts. The Elves of Jaralii shall support you in this endeavor. We find ourselves in dire straits such as we have not faced in many thousand years. Your stratagem may be our last best hope."

The Seeress smiled ruefully. "Indeed, we must be in dire straits if our last best is nothing better than a forlorn hope."

* * * * *

Epilogue

Thus, the first prediction of the Seer, Cadrazhulea of Camazhule, has been fulfilled:

A High One among High Ones shall come from Beyond.
She shall wear an old face of the Verdant Hills

The epic saga of Jaralii Chronicles continues!
Coming soon:
Gilraën and the Prophecy
Book Two: I Saw.

Remember your Special Offer as a reader of Jaralii Chronicles:
Get your map of Jaralii
See where it's at!
Email your request to jaraliichronicles@gmail.com

www.ingramcontent.com/pod-product-compliance
Lightning Source LLC
Chambersburg PA
CBHW030157200626
46812CB00017B/2249